P9-DLZ-784

MISCHIEF

MALICE

VICE

ENDLESS WOODS

SCHOOL MASTER'S TOWER

TUNNEL of TREES

T
CLEA

SCHOOL for EVIL

HALFWAY B

MOAT

EVIL SHORE

GR

ENDLESS WOODS

EVIL

RE-SPA

SCH

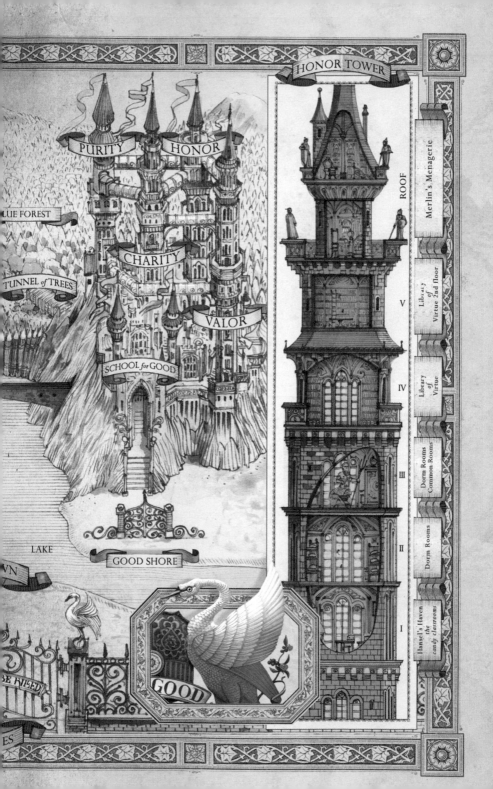

HONOR TOWER

PURITY
HONOR

CHARITY

VALOR

SCHOOL for GOOD

BLUE FOREST

TUNNEL of TREES

ROOF

V

IV

III

II

I

Merlin's Menagerie

Library of Virtue 2nd floor

Library of Virtue

Dorm Rooms Common Rooms

Dorm Rooms

Hansel's Haven the candy classrooms

LAKE

GOOD SHORE

GOOD

BE KILLED

SOMAN CHAINANI

Illustrations by
IACOPO BRUNO

HARPER
An Imprint of HarperCollinsPublishers

Library of Congress Cataloging-in-Publication Data is available.
ISBN 978-0-06-210489-2 (trade bdg.)

Typography by Amy Ryan
14 15 16 17 LP/RRDH 20 19 18 17 16 15 14 13 12 11
❖
First Edition

IN THE FOREST PRIMEVAL

A SCHOOL FOR GOOD AND EVIL

TWO TOWERS LIKE TWIN HEADS

ONE FOR THE PURE

ONE FOR THE WICKED

TRY TO ESCAPE YOU'LL ALWAYS FAIL

THE ONLY WAY OUT IS

THROUGH A FAIRY TALE

1

The Princess & The Witch

S ophie had waited all her life to be kidnapped. But tonight, all the other children of Gavaldon writhed in their beds. If the School Master took them, they'd never return. Never lead a full life. Never see their family again. Tonight these children dreamt of a red-eyed thief with the body of a beast, come to rip them from their sheets and stifle their screams.

Sophie dreamt of princes instead.

She had arrived at a castle ball thrown in her

honor, only to find the hall filled with a hundred suitors and no other girls in sight. Here for the first time were boys who deserved her, she thought as she walked the line. Hair shiny and thick, muscles taut through shirts, skin smooth and tan, beautiful and attentive like princes should be. But just as she came to one who seemed better than the rest, with brilliant blue eyes and ghostly white hair, the one who felt like Happily Ever After . . . a hammer broke through the walls of the room and smashed the princes to shards.

Sophie's eyes opened to morning. The hammer was real. The princes were not.

"Father, if I don't sleep nine hours, my eyes look swollen."

"Everyone's prattling on that you're to be taken this year," her father said, nailing a misshapen bar over her bedroom window, now completely obscured by locks, spikes, and screws. "They tell me to shear your hair, muddy up your face, as if I believe all this fairy-tale hogwash. But no one's getting in here tonight. That's for sure." He pounded a deafening crack as exclamation.

Sophie rubbed her ears and frowned at her once lovely window, now something you'd see in a witch's den. "Locks. Why didn't anyone think of that before?"

"I don't know why they all think it's you," he said, silver hair slicked with sweat. "If it's goodness that School Master fellow wants, he'll take Gunilda's daughter."

Sophie tensed. "Belle?"

"Perfect child that one is," he said. "Brings her father home-cooked lunches at the mill. Gives the leftovers to the poor hag in the square."

Sophie heard the edge in her father's voice. She had never once cooked a full meal for him, even after her mother died. Naturally she had good reason (the oil and smoke would clog her pores) but she knew it was a sore point. This didn't mean her father had gone hungry. Instead, she offered him her own favorite foods: mashed beets, broccoli stew, boiled asparagus, steamed spinach. He hadn't ballooned into a blimp like Belle's father, precisely because she hadn't brought him home-cooked lamb fricassees and cheese soufflés at the mill. As for the poor hag in the square, that old crone, despite claiming hunger day after day, was *fat*. And if Belle had anything to do with it, then she wasn't good at all, but the worst kind of evil.

Sophie smiled back at her father. "Like you said, it's all hogwash." She swept out of bed and slammed the bathroom door.

She studied her face in the mirror. The rude awakening had taken its toll. Her waist-long hair, the color of spun gold, didn't have its usual sheen. Her jade-green eyes looked faded, her luscious red lips a touch dry. Even the glow of her creamy peach skin had dulled. *But still a princess*, she thought. Her father couldn't see she was special, but her mother had. "You are too beautiful for this world, Sophie," she said with her last breaths. Her mother had gone somewhere better and now so would she.

Tonight she would be taken into the woods. Tonight she would begin a new life. Tonight she would live out her fairy tale.

And now she needed to look the part.

To begin, she rubbed fish eggs into her skin, which smelled

of dirty feet but warded off spots. Then she massaged in pumpkin puree, rinsed with goat's milk, and soaked her face in a mask of melon and turtle egg yolk. As she waited for the mask to dry, Sophie flipped through a storybook and sipped on cucumber juice to keep her skin dewy soft. She skipped to her favorite part of the story, where the wicked hag is rolled down a hill in a nail-spiked barrel, until all that remains is her bracelet made of little boys' bones. Gazing at the gruesome bracelet, Sophie felt her thoughts drift to cucumbers. Suppose there were no cucumbers in the woods? Suppose other princesses had depleted the supply? No cucumbers! She'd shrivel, she'd wither, she'd—

Dried melon flakes fell to the page. She turned to the mirror and saw her brow creased in worry. First ruined sleep and now wrinkles. At this rate she'd be a hag by afternoon. She relaxed her face and banished thoughts of vegetables.

As for the rest of Sophie's beauty routine, it could fill a dozen storybooks (suffice it to say it included goose feathers, pickled potatoes, horse hooves, cream of cashews, and a vial of cow's blood). Two hours of rigorous grooming later, she stepped from the house in a breezy pink dress, sparkling glass heels, and hair in an impeccable braid. She had one last day before the School Master's arrival and planned to use each and every minute to remind him why she, and not Belle or Tabitha or Sabrina or any other impostor, should be kidnapped.

Sophie's best friend lived in a cemetery. Given her loathing of things grim, gray, and poorly lit, one would expect Sophie to host visits at her cottage or find a new best friend. But instead, she had climbed to the house atop Graves Hill every day this week, careful to maintain a smile on her face, since that was the point of a good deed after all.

To get there, she had to walk nearly a mile from the bright lakeside cottages, with green eaves and sun-drenched turrets, towards the gloomy edges of the forest. Sounds of hammering echoed through cottage lanes as she passed fathers boarding up doors, mothers stuffing scarecrows, boys and girls hunched on porches, noses buried in storybooks. The last sight wasn't unusual, for children in Gavaldon did little besides read their fairy tales. But today Sophie noticed their eyes, wild, frenzied, scouring each page as if their lives depended on it. Four years ago, she had seen the same desperation to avoid the curse, but it wasn't her turn then. The School Master took only those past their twelfth year, those who could no longer disguise as children.

Now her turn had come.

As she slogged up Graves Hill, picnic basket in hand, Sophie felt her thighs burn. Had these climbs thickened her legs? All the princesses in storybooks had the same per-fect proportions; thick thighs were as unlikely as a hooked nose or big feet. Feeling anxious, Sophie distracted herself by counting her good deeds from the day before. First, she had fed the lake's geese a blend of lentils and leeks (a natural laxative to offset cheese thrown by oafish children). Then she had donated homemade lemonwood face wash to the town orphanage (for, as she insisted to the befuddled benefactor,

"Proper skin care is the greatest deed of all."). Finally she had put up a mirror in the church toilet, so people could return to the pews looking their best. Was this enough? Did these compete with baking homemade pies and feeding homeless hags? Her thoughts shifted nervously to cucumbers. Perhaps she could sneak a private supply into the woods. She still had plenty of time to pack before nightfall. But weren't cucumbers heavy? Would the school send footmen? Perhaps she should juice them before she—

"Where you going?"

Sophie turned. Radley smiled at her with buckteeth and anemically red hair. He lived nowhere near Graves Hill but made it a habit to stalk her all hours of the day.

"To see a friend," said Sophie.

"Why are you friends with the witch?" said Radley.

"She's not a witch."

"She has no friends and she's queer. That makes her a witch."

Sophie refrained from pointing out this made Radley a witch too. Instead she smiled to remind him she'd already done her good deed by enduring his presence.

"The School Master will take her for Evil School," he said. "Then you'll need a new friend."

"He takes two children," Sophie said, jaw tightening.

"He'll take Belle for the other one. No one's as good as Belle."

Sophie's smile evaporated.

"But I'll be your new friend," said Radley.

"I'm full on friends at the moment," Sophie snapped.

Radley turned the color of a raspberry. "Oh, right—I just thought—" He fled like a kicked dog.

Sophie watched his straggly hair recede down the hill. *Oh, you've really done it now*, she thought. Months of good deeds and forced smiles and now she'd ruined it for runty Radley. Why not make his day? Why not simply answer, "I'd be honored to have you as my friend!" and give the idiot a moment he'd relive for years? She knew it was the prudent thing to do, since the School Master must be judging her as closely as St. Nicholas the night before Christmas. But she couldn't do it. She was beautiful, Radley was ugly. Only a villain would delude him. Surely the School Master would understand that.

Sophie pulled open the rusted cemetery gates and felt weeds scratch at her legs. Across the hilltop, moldy headstones forked haphazardly from dunes of dead leaves. Squeezing between dark tombs and decaying branches, Sophie kept careful count of the rows. She had never looked at her mother's grave, even at the funeral, and she wouldn't start today. As she passed the sixth row, she glued her eyes to a weeping birch and reminded herself where she'd be a day from now.

In the middle of the thickest batch of tombs stood 1 Graves Hill. The house wasn't boarded up or bolted shut like the cottages by the lake, but that didn't make it any more inviting. The steps leading up to the porch glowed mildew green. Dead birches and vines wormed their way around dark wood, and the sharply angled roof, black and thin, loomed like a witch's hat.

As she climbed the moaning porch steps, Sophie tried to

ignore the smell, a mix of garlic and wet cat, and averted her eyes from the headless birds sprinkled around, no doubt the victims of the latter.

She knocked on the door and prepared for a fight.

"Go away," came the gruff voice.

"That's no way to speak to your best friend," Sophie cooed.

"You're not my best friend."

"Who is, then?" Sophie asked, wondering if Belle had somehow made her way to Graves Hill.

"None of your business."

Sophie took a deep breath. She didn't want another Radley incident. "We had such a good time yesterday, Agatha. I thought we'd do it again."

"You dyed my hair orange."

"But we fixed it, didn't we?"

"You always test your creams and potions on me just to see how they work."

"Isn't that what friends are for?" Sophie said. "To help each other?"

"I'll never be as pretty as you."

Sophie tried to find something nice to say. She took too long and heard shoes stomp away.

"That doesn't mean we can't be friends!" Sophie called.

A familiar cat, bald and wrinkled, growled at her across the porch. She whipped back to the door. "I brought biscuits!"

Shoesteps stopped. "Real ones or ones you made?"

Sophie shrank from the slinking cat. "Fluffy and buttery, just like you love!"

The cat hissed.

"Agatha, let me in—"

"You'll say I smell."

"You don't smell."

"Then why'd you say it last time?"

"Because you smelled last time! Agatha, the cat's spitting—"

"Maybe it smells ulterior motives."

The cat bared claws.

"Agatha, open the door!"

It pounced at her face. Sophie screamed. A hand stabbed between them and swatted the cat down.

Sophie looked up.

"Reaper ran out of birds," said Agatha.

Her hideous dome of black hair looked like it was coated in oil. Her hulking black dress, shapeless as a potato sack, couldn't hide freakishly pale skin and jutting bones. Ladybug eyes bulged from her sunken face.

"I thought we'd go for a walk," Sophie said.

Agatha leaned against the door. "I'm still trying to figure out why you're friends with me."

"Because you're sweet and funny," said Sophie.

"My mother says I'm bitter and grumpy," said Agatha. "So one of you is lying."

She reached into Sophie's basket and pulled back the napkin to reveal dry, butterless bran biscuits. Agatha gave Sophie a withering stare and retreated into the house.

"So we can't take a walk?" Sophie asked.

Agatha started to close the door but then saw her crestfallen face. As if Sophie had looked forward to their walk as much as she had.

"A short one." Agatha trudged past her. "But if you say anything smug or stuck-up or shallow, I'll have Reaper follow you home."

Sophie ran after her. "But then I can't talk!"

After four years, the dreaded eleventh night of the eleventh month had arrived. In the late-day sun, the square had become a hive of preparation for the School Master's arrival. The men sharpened swords, set traps, and plotted the night's guard, while the women lined up the children and went to work. Handsome ones had their hair lopped off, teeth blackened, and clothes shredded to rags; homely ones were scrubbed, swathed in bright colors, and fitted with veils. Mothers begged the best-behaved children to curse or kick their sisters, the worst were bribed to pray in the church, while the rest in line were led in choruses of the village anthem: "Blessed Are the Ordinary."

Fear swelled into a contagious fog. In a dim alley, the butcher and blacksmith traded storybooks for clues to save their sons. Beneath the crooked clock tower, two sisters listed fairy-tale villain names to hunt for patterns. A group of boys chained their bodies together, a few girls hid on the school roof, and a masked child jumped from bushes to spook his mother, earning a spanking on the spot. Even the homeless hag got into the act, hopping before a meager fire, croaking, "Burn the storybooks! Burn them all!" But no one listened and no books were burned.

Agatha gawped at all this in disbelief. "How can a whole town believe in fairy tales?"

"Because they're real."

Agatha stopped walking. "You can't actually believe the legend is true."

"Of course I do," said Sophie.

"That a School Master kidnaps two children, takes them to a school where one learns Good, one learns Evil, and they graduate into *fairy tales*?"

"Sounds about right."

"Tell me if you see an oven."

"Why?"

"I want to put my head in it. And what, pray tell, do they teach at this school exactly?"

"Well, in the School for Good, they teach boys and girls like me how to become heroes and princesses, how to rule kingdoms justly, how to find Happily Ever After," Sophie said. "In the School for Evil, they teach you how to become wicked witches and humpbacked trolls, how to lay curses and cast evil spells."

"Evil spells?" Agatha cackled. "Who came up with this? A four-year-old?"

"Agatha, the proof's in the storybooks! You can see the missing children in the drawings! Jack, Rose, Rapunzel—they all got their own tales—"

"I don't *see* anything, because I don't *read* dumb storybooks."

"Then why is there a stack by your bed?" Sophie asked.

Agatha scowled. "Look, who's to say the books are even real? Maybe it's the bookseller's prank. Maybe it's the Elders' way to keep children out of the woods. Whatever the explanation, it isn't a School Master and it isn't evil spells."

"So who's kidnapping the children?"

"No one. Every four years, two idiots sneak into the woods, hoping to scare their parents, only to get lost or eaten by wolves, and there you have it, the legend continues."

"That's the stupidest explanation I've ever heard."

"I don't think I'm the stupid one here," Agatha said.

There was something about being called stupid that set Sophie's blood aflame.

"You're just scared," she said.

"Right," Agatha laughed. "And why would I be scared?"

"Because you know you're coming with me."

Agatha stopped laughing. Then her gaze moved past Sophie into the square. The villagers were staring at them like the solution to a mystery. Good in pink, Evil in black. The School Master's perfect pair.

Frozen still, Agatha watched dozens of scared eyes bore into her. Her first thought was that after tomorrow she and Sophie could take their walks in peace. Next to her, Sophie watched children memorize her face in case it appeared in their storybooks one day. Her first thought was whether they looked at Belle the same way.

Then, through the crowd, she saw her.

Head shaved, dress filthy, Belle kneeled in dirt, frantically muddying her own face. Sophie drew a breath. For Belle was just like the others. She wanted a mundane marriage to a man who would grow fat, lazy, and demanding. She wanted monotonous days of cooking, cleaning, sewing. She wanted to shovel dung and milk sheep and slaughter squealing pigs. She wanted to rot in Gavaldon until her skin was liver-spotted and her teeth fell out. The School Master would never take Belle because Belle wasn't a princess. She was . . . nothing.

Victorious, Sophie beamed back at the pathetic villagers and basked in their stares like shiny mirrors—

"Let's go," said Agatha.

Sophie turned. Agatha's eyes were locked on the mob.

"Where?"

"Away from people."

As the sun weakened to a red orb, two girls, one beautiful, one ugly, sat side by side on the shore of a lake. Sophie packed cucumbers in a silk pouch, while Agatha flicked lit matches into the water. After the tenth match, Sophie threw her a look.

"It relaxes me," Agatha said.

Sophie tried to make room for the last cucumber. "Why would someone like Belle want to stay here? Who would choose *this* over a fairy tale?"

"And who would choose to leave their family *forever?*" Agatha snorted.

"Except me, you mean," said Sophie.

They fell silent.

"Do you ever wonder where your father went?" Sophie asked.

"I told you. He left after I was born."

"But where would he go? We're surrounded by woods! To suddenly disappear like that . . ." Sophie spun. "Maybe he found a way into the stories! Maybe he found a magic portal! Maybe he's waiting for you on the other side!"

"Or maybe he went back to his wife, pretended I never happened, and died ten years ago in a mill accident."

Sophie bit her lip and went back to cucumbers.

"Your mother's never at home when I visit."

"She goes into town now," said Agatha. "Not enough patients at the house. Probably the location."

"I'm sure that's it," Sophie said, knowing no one would trust Agatha's mother to treat diaper rash, let alone illness. "I don't think a graveyard makes people all that comfortable."

"Graveyards have their benefits," Agatha said. "No nosy neighbors. No drop-in salesmen. No fishy 'friends' bearing face masks and diet cookies, telling you you're going to Evil School in Magic Fairy Land." She flicked a match with relish.

Sophie put down her cucumber. "So I'm fishy now."

"Who asked you to show up? I was perfectly fine alone."

"You always let me in."

"Because you always seem so lonely," said Agatha. "And I feel sorry for you."

"Sorry for *me*?" Sophie's eyes flashed. "You're lucky that someone would come see you when no one else will. You're lucky that someone like me would be your friend. You're lucky that someone like me is such a *good person*."

"I knew it!" Agatha flared. "I'm your Good Deed! Just a

pawn in your stupid fantasy!"

Sophie didn't say anything for a long time.

"Maybe I became your friend to impress the School Master," she confessed finally. "But there's more to it now."

"Because I found you out," Agatha grumbled.

"Because I like you."

Agatha turned to her.

"No one understands me here," Sophie said, looking at her hands. "But you do. You see who I am. That's why I kept coming back. You're not my good deed anymore, Agatha."

Sophie gazed up at her. "You're my friend."

Agatha's neck flushed red.

"What's wrong?" Sophie frowned.

Agatha hunched into her dress. "It's just, um . . . I—I'm, uh . . . not used to friends."

Sophie smiled and took her hand. "Well, now we'll be friends at our new school."

Agatha groaned and pulled away. "Say I sink to your intelligence level and pretend to believe all this. Why am *I* going to villain school? Why has everyone elected *me* the Mistress of Evil?"

"No one says you're evil, Agatha," Sophie sighed. "You're just different."

Agatha narrowed her eyes. "Different *how*?"

"Well, for starters, you only wear black."

"Because it doesn't get dirty."

"You don't ever leave your house."

"People don't look at me there."

"For the Create-a-Tale Competition, your story ended with Snow White eaten by vultures and Cinderella drowning herself in a tub."

"I thought it was a better ending."

"You gave me a dead frog for my birthday!"

"To remind you we all die and end up rotting underground eaten by maggots so we should enjoy our birthdays while we have them. I found it thoughtful."

"Agatha, you dressed as a *bride* for Halloween."

"Weddings are scary."

Sophie gaped at her.

"Fine. So I'm a little different," Agatha glared. "So what?"

Sophie hesitated. "Well, it's just that in fairy tales, different usually turns out, um . . . *evil.*"

"You're saying I'm going to turn out a Grand Witch," said Agatha, hurt.

"I'm saying whatever happens, you'll have a choice," Sophie said gently. "Both of us will choose how our fairy tale ends."

Agatha said nothing for a while. Then she touched Sophie's hand. "Why is it you want to leave here so badly? That you'd believe in stories you know aren't true?"

Sophie met Agatha's big, sincere eyes. For the first time, she let in the tides of doubt.

"Because I can't live here," Sophie said, voice catching. "I can't live an ordinary life."

"Funny," said Agatha. "That's why I like you."

Sophie smiled. "Because you can't either?"

"Because you make me feel ordinary," Agatha said. "And

that's the only thing I've ever wanted."

The tenor-tolled clock sang darkly in the valley, six or seven, for they had lost track of time. And as the echoes faded into the buzz of the distant square, both Sophie and Agatha made a wish. That one day from now, they'd still be in the company of the other.

Wherever that was.

2

The Art of Kidnapping

By the time the sun extinguished, the children were long locked away. Through bedroom shutters, they peeked at torch-armed fathers, sisters, grandmothers lined around the dark forest, daring the School Master to cross their ring of fire.

But while shivering children tightened their window screws, Sophie prepared to undo hers. She wanted this kidnapping to be as convenient as possible. Barricaded in her room, she laid out hairpins, tweezers, nail files and went to work.

The first kidnappings happened two hundred years before. Some years it was two boys taken, some years two girls, sometimes one of each. The ages were just as fickle; one could be sixteen, the other fourteen, or both just turned twelve. But if at first the choices seemed random, soon the pattern became clear. One was always beautiful and good, the child every parent wanted as their own. The other was homely and odd, an outcast from birth. An opposing pair, plucked from youth and spirited away.

Naturally the villagers blamed bears. No one had ever seen a bear in Gavaldon, but this made them more determined to find one. Four years later, when two more children vanished, the villagers admitted they should have been more specific and declared *black* bears the culprit, bears so black they blended with the night. But when children continued to disappear every four years, the village shifted their attention to burrowing bears, then phantom bears, then bears in disguise . . . until it became clear it wasn't bears at all.

But while frantic villagers spawned new theories (the Sinkhole Theory, the Flying Cannibal Theory) the children of Gavaldon began to notice something suspicious. As they studied the dozens of Missing posters tacked up in the square, the faces of these lost boys and girls looked oddly familiar. That's when they opened up their storybooks and found the kidnapped children.

Jack, taken a hundred years before, hadn't aged a bit. Here he was, painted with the same moppy hair, pinked dimples, and crooked smile that had made him so popular with the girls of Gavaldon. Only now he had a beanstalk in his back garden and a weakness for magic beans. Meanwhile, Angus, the pointy-eared, freckled hooligan who had vanished with Jack that same year, had transformed into a pointy-eared, freckled giant at the top of Jack's beanstalk. The two boys had found their way into a fairy tale. But when the children presented the Storybook Theory, the adults responded as adults most often do. They patted the children's heads and returned to sinkholes and cannibals.

But then the children showed them more familiar faces. Taken fifty years before, sweet Anya now sat on moonlit rocks in a painting as the Little Mermaid, while cruel Estra had become the devious sea witch. Philip, the priest's upright son, had grown into the Cunning Little Tailor, while pompous Gula spooked children as the Witch of the Wood. Scores of children, kidnapped in pairs, had found new lives in a storybook world. One as Good. One as Evil.

The books came from Mr. Deauville's Storybook Shop, a musty nook between Battersby's Bakery and the Pickled Pig Pub. The problem, of course, was where old Mr. Deauville got his storybooks.

Once a year, on a morning he could not predict, he would arrive at his shop to find a box of books waiting inside. Four brand-new fairy tales, one copy of each. Mr. Deauville would hang a sign on his shop door: "Closed Until Further Notice." Then he'd huddle in his back room day after day, diligently copying the new tales by hand until he had enough books for every child in Gavaldon. As for the mysterious originals, they'd appear one morning in his shop window, a sign that Mr. Deauville had finished his exhausting task at last. He'd open his doors to a three-mile line that snaked through the square, down hillslopes, around the lake, jammed with children thirsting for new stories, and parents desperate to see if any of the missing had made it into this year's tales.

Needless to say, the Council of Elders had plenty of questions for Mr. Deauville. When asked who sent the books, Mr. Deauville said he hadn't the faintest idea. When asked how long the books had been appearing, Mr. Deauville said he couldn't remember a time when the books did not appear. When asked whether he'd ever questioned this magical appearance of books, Mr. Deauville replied: "Where else would storybooks come from?"

Then the Elders noticed something else about Mr. Deauville's storybooks. All the villages in them looked just like Gavaldon. The same lakeshore cottages and colorful eaves. The same purple and green tulips along thin dirt roads. The same crimson carriages, wood-front shops, yellow schoolhouse, and leaning clock tower, only drawn as fantasy in a land far, far away. These storybook villages existed for only one purpose: to begin a fairy tale and to end it. Everything between the beginning and end happened in the dark, endless woods that surrounded the town.

That's when they noticed that Gavaldon too was surrounded by dark, endless woods.

Back when the children first started to disappear, villagers stormed the forest to find them, only to be repelled by storms, floods, cyclones, and falling trees. When they finally braved their way through, they found a town hiding beyond the trees and vengefully besieged it, only to discover it was their own. Indeed, no matter where the villagers entered the woods, they came out right where they started. The woods, it seemed, had no intention of returning their children. And one day they found out why.

Mr. Deauville had finished unpacking that year's storybooks when he noticed a large smudge hiding in the box's fold. He touched his finger to it and discovered the smudge was wet with ink. Looking closer, he saw it was a seal with an elaborate crest of a black swan and a white swan. On the crest were three letters:

S.G.E.

There was no need for him to guess what these letters meant. It said so in the banner beneath the crest. Small black words that told the village where its children had gone:

THE SCHOOL FOR GOOD AND EVIL

The kidnappings continued, but now the thief had a name. They called him the School Master.

A few minutes after ten, Sophie pried the last lock off the window and cracked open the shutters. She could see to the forest edge, where her father, Stefan, stood with the rest of the perimeter guard. But instead of looking anxious like the others, he was smiling, hand on the widow Honora's shoulder.

Sophie grimaced. What her father saw in that woman, she had no idea. Once upon a time, her mother had been as flawless as a storybook queen. Honora, meanwhile, had a small head, round body, and looked like a turkey.

Her father whispered mischievously into the widow's ear and Sophie's cheeks burned. If it were Honora's two little sons who might be taken, he'd be serious as death. True, Stefan had locked her in at sundown, given her a kiss, dutifully acted the loving father. But Sophie knew the truth. She had seen it in his face every day of her life. Her father didn't love her. Because she wasn't a boy. Because she didn't remind him of himself.

Now he wanted to marry that beast. Five years after her mother's death, it wouldn't be seen as improper or callous. A simple exchange of vows and he'd have two sons, a new family, a fresh start. But he needed his daughter's blessing first for the Elders to allow it. The few times he tried, Sophie changed the subject or loudly chopped cucumbers or smiled the way she did at Radley. Her father hadn't mentioned Honora again.

Let the coward marry her when I'm gone, she thought, glaring at him through the shutters. Only when she was gone would he appreciate her. Only when she was gone would he know no one could replace her. And only when she was gone would he see he had spawned much more than a son.

He had borne a princess.

On her windowsill, Sophie laid out gingerbread hearts for the School Master with delicate care. For the first time in her life, she'd made them with sugar and butter. These were special, after all. A message to say she'd come willingly.

Sinking into her pillow, she closed her eyes on widows, fathers, and wretched Gavaldon and with a smile counted the seconds to midnight.

As soon as Sophie's head vanished beneath the window, Agatha shoved the gingerbread hearts in her mouth. *Only thing these will invite are rats*, she thought, crumbs dribbling on her black clump shoes. She yawned and set on her way as the town clock inched past the quarter hour.

Upon leaving Sophie after their walk, Agatha had started home only to have visions of Sophie darting into the woods to find this School for Fools and Crackpots and ending up gored by a boar. So she returned to Sophie's garden and waited behind a tree, listening as Sophie undid her window (singing a birdbrained song about princes), packed her bags (now singing about wedding bells), put on makeup and her finest dress ("Everybody Loves a Princess in Pink"?!), and finally (finally!) tucked herself into bed. Agatha mashed the last crumbs with her clump and trudged towards the cemetery. Sophie was safe and would wake up tomorrow feeling like a fool. Agatha wouldn't rub it in. Sophie would need her even more now and she would be there for her. Here in this safe, secluded world, the two of them would make their own paradise.

As Agatha tramped up the slope, she noticed an arc of darkness in the forest's torch-lit border. Apparently the guards responsible for the cemetery had decided what lived inside wasn't worth protecting. For as long as Agatha could remember, she'd had a talent for making people go away. Kids fled from her like a vampire bat. Adults clung to walls as she passed, afraid she might curse them. Even the grave keepers on the hill bolted at the sight of her. With each new year, the whispers in town grew louder—*"witch," "villain," "Evil School"*—until she looked for excuses not to go out. First days, then weeks, until she haunted her graveyard house like a ghost.

There were plenty of ways to entertain herself at first. She wrote poems ("It's a Miserable Life" and "Heaven Is a Cemetery" were her best), drew portraits of Reaper that frightened mice more than the real cat did, and even tried her hand at a book of fairy tales, *Grimly Ever After*, about beautiful children who die horrible deaths. But she had no one to show these things to until the day Sophie knocked.

Reaper licked her ankles as she stepped onto her squeaking porch. She heard singing inside—

*"In the forest primeval
A School for Good and Evil . . ."*

Agatha rolled her eyes and pushed open the door.

Her mother, back turned, sang cheerily as she packed a trunk with black capes, broomsticks, and pointy black witch's hats.

*"Two towers like twin heads
One for the pure,
One for the wicked.*

Try to escape you'll always fail
The only way out is
Through a fairy tale . . ."

"Planning an exotic vacation?" Agatha said. "Last time I checked, there's no way out of Gavaldon unless you grow wings."

Callis turned. "Do you think three capes is enough?" she asked, bug eyes bulging, hair a greasy black helmet.

Agatha winced at just how much they looked alike. "They're exactly the same," she muttered. "Why do you need three?"

"In case you need to lend one to a friend, dear."

"These are for *me*?"

"I put two hats in case one gets squashed, a broomstick in case theirs smells, and a few vials of dog tongues, lizard legs, and frog toes. Who knows how long theirs have been sitting there!"

Agatha knew the answer but asked anyway. "Mother, what do I need capes, hats, and frog toes for?"

"For New Witch Welcoming, of course!" Callis trilled. "You don't want to get to the School for Evil and look like an amateur."

Agatha kicked off her clumps. "Let's put aside the fact the town *doctor* believes all this. Why is it so hard to accept I'm happy here? I have everything I need. My bed, my cat, and my friend."

"Well, you should learn from your friend, dear. At least *she* wants something from life," Callis said, latching the trunk.

"Really, Agatha, what could be a greater destiny than a Fairy Tale Witch? I dreamed of going to the School for Evil! Instead, the School Master took that idiot Sven, who ended up outwitted by a princess in *The Useless Ogre* and set on fire. I'm not surprised. That boy could barely lace his own boots. I'm sure if the School Master could have done it over, he'd have taken me."

Agatha slid under her covers. "Well, everyone in this town still thinks you're a witch, so you got your wish after all."

Callis whipped around. "My wish is that you get away from here," she hissed, eyes dark as coal. "This place has made you weak and lazy and afraid. At least I made something of myself here. You just waste and rot until Sophie comes to walk you like a dog."

Agatha stared at her, stunned.

Callis smiled brightly and resumed packing. "But do take care of your friend, dear. The School for Good might seem like a festoon of roses, but she's in for a surprise. Now go to bed. The School Master will be here soon and it's easier for him if you're asleep."

Agatha pulled the sheets over her head.

Sophie couldn't sleep. Five minutes to midnight and no sign of an intruder. She knelt on her bed and peered through the shutters. Around Gavaldon's edge, the thousand-person guard waved torches to light up the forest. Sophie scowled. *How could he get past them?*

That's when she noticed the hearts on her windowsill were gone.

He's already here!

Three packed pink bags plopped through the window, followed by two glass-slippered feet.

Agatha lurched up in bed, jolted from a nightmare. Callis snored loudly across the room, Reaper at her side. Next to Agatha's bed sat her locked trunk, marked "Agatha of Gavaldon, 1 Graves Hill Road" in scraggy writing, along with a pouch of honey cakes for the journey.

Chomping cake, Agatha gazed through a cracked window. Down the hill, the torches blazed in a tight circle, but here on Graves Hill, there was just one burly guard left, arms as big as Agatha's whole body, legs like chicken drumsticks. He kept himself awake by lifting a broken headstone like a barbell.

Agatha bit into the last honey cake and looked out at the dark forest.

Shiny blue eyes looked back at her.

Agatha choked and dove to her bed. She slowly lifted her head. Nothing there. Including the guard.

Then she found him, unconscious over the broken headstone, torch extinguished.

Creeping away from him was a bony, hunchbacked human shadow. No body attached.

The shadow floated across the sea of graves without the slightest sign of hurry. It slid under the cemetery gates and skulked down the hill towards the firelit center of Gavaldon.

Agatha felt horror strangle her heart. He was real. Whoever he was.

And he doesn't want me.

Relief crashed over her, followed by a fresh wave of panic.

Sophie.

She should wake her mother, she should cry for help, she should— No time.

Feigning sleep, Callis heard Agatha's urgent footsteps, then the door close. She hugged Reaper tighter to make sure he didn't wake up.

Sophie crouched behind a tree, waiting for the School Master to snatch her.

She waited. And waited. Then she noticed something in the ground.

Cookie crumbs, mashed into a footprint. The footprint of a clump so odious, so foul it could only belong to one person. Sophie's fists curled, her blood boiled—

Hands covered her mouth and a foot booted her through her window. Sophie crashed headfirst onto her bed and whirled around to see Agatha. "You pathetic, interfering worm!" she screamed, before glimpsing the fear in her friend's face. "You saw him!" Sophie gasped—

Agatha put one hand over Sophie's mouth and pinned her to the mattress with the other. As Sophie writhed in protest, Agatha peeped through the window. The crooked shadow drifted into the Gavaldon square, past the oblivious armed guard, and headed directly for Sophie's house. Agatha swallowed a scream. Sophie wrenched free and grabbed her shoulders.

"Is he handsome? Like a prince? Or a proper schoolmaster with spectacles and waistcoat and—"

THUMP!

Sophie and Agatha slowly turned to the door.

THUMP! THUMP!

Sophie wrinkled her nose. "He could just knock, couldn't he?"

Locks cracked. Hinges rattled.

Agatha shrank against the wall, while Sophie folded her hands and fluffed her dress as if expecting a royal visit. "Best give him what he wants without fuss."

As the door caved, Agatha leapt off the bed and threw herself against it. Sophie rolled her eyes. "Oh, sit down for goodness' sake." Agatha pulled at the knob with all her might, lost her grip—the door slammed open with a deafening crack, hurling her across the room.

It was Sophie's father, white as a sheet. "I saw something!" he panted, waving his torch.

Then Agatha caught the crooked shadow on the wall stepping into his broad silhouette. "There!" she cried. Stefan swiveled but the shadow blew out his torch. Agatha grabbed a match from her pocket and lit it. Stefan lay on the ground unconscious. Sophie was gone.

Screams outside.

Through the window, Agatha watched shouting villagers chase after Sophie as the shadow dragged her towards the woods. And while more and more villagers howled and chased—

Sophie smiled ear to ear.

Agatha lunged through the window and ran after her. But just as the villagers reached Sophie, their torches magically exploded and trapped them in rings of fire. Agatha dodged the gauntlet of firetraps and dashed to save her friend before the shadow pulled her into the forest.

Sophie felt her body leave soft grass and rake against stony dirt. She frowned at the thought of showing up to school in a soiled dress. "I really thought there'd be footmen," she said to the shadow. "Or a pumpkin carriage, at least."

Agatha ran ferociously, but Sophie had almost disappeared into the trees. All around, flames spewed higher and higher, poised to devour the entire village.

Seeing the fires leap, Sophie felt relief knowing no one could rescue her now. *But where is the second child? Where is the one for Evil?* She'd been wrong about Agatha all along. As she felt herself pulled into trees, Sophie looked back at the towering blaze and kissed goodbye to the curse of ordinary life.

"Farewell, Gavaldon! Farewell, low ambition! Farewell, mediocrity—"

Then she saw Agatha charge through the flames.

"Agatha, *no!*" Sophie cried—

Agatha leapt on top of her and both were dragged into the darkness.

Instantly, the fires around the villagers were extinguished. They dashed for the woods, but the trees magically grew thick and thorny, locking them out.

It was too late.

"WHAT ARE YOU DOING!" roared Sophie, shoving and scratching Agatha as the shadow pulled them into pitch-black forest. Agatha thrashed wildly, trying to wrest the shadow's grip on Sophie and Sophie's grip on the shadow. "YOU'RE RUINING EVERYTHING!" Sophie howled. Agatha bit her hand. "EEEEEYIIII!!!!" Sophie brayed and flipped her body so Agatha scraped against dirt. Agatha flipped Sophie back and climbed towards the shadow, her clump squashing Sophie's face.

"WHEN MY HANDS FIND YOUR NECK—"

They felt themselves leave the ground.

As something spindly and cold wrapped its way around them, Agatha fumbled for a match from her dress, struck it against her bony wrist, and paled. The shadow was gone. They were cocooned in the creepers of an elm, which ferried them up the enormous tree and plopped them on the lowest branch. Both girls glared at each other and tried to catch enough breath to speak. Agatha managed it first.

"We are going home *right now.*"

The branch wobbled, coiled back like a sling, and shot them up like bullets. Before either could scream, they landed on another branch. Agatha flailed for a new match, but the branch coiled and snapped them up to the next bough, which bounced them up to the next. *"HOW TALL IS THIS TREE!"* Agatha shrieked. Ping-ponging up branches, the girls' bodies collided and crashed, dresses tearing on thorns and twigs, faces slamming into ricocheting limbs, until finally they reached the highest bough.

There at the top of the elm tree sat a giant black egg. The girls gaped at it, baffled. The egg tore open, splashing them with dark, yolky goo as a colossal bird emerged, made only of bones. It took one look at the pair and unleashed an angry screech that rattled their eardrums. Then it grabbed them both in its claws and dove off the tree as they screamed, finally agreeing on something. The bony bird lashed through black woods as Agatha frantically lit match after match on the bird's ribs, giving them catches of glinting red eyes and bristling shadows. All around, gangly trees snatched at the girls as the bird dipped and climbed to avoid them, until thunder exploded ahead and they smashed headfirst into a raging lightning storm. Fire bolts sent trees careening towards them and they shielded their faces from rain, mud, and timber, ducked cobwebs, beehives, and vipers, until the bird plunged into deadly briars and the girls blanched, closing their eyes to the pain—

Then it was quiet.

"Agatha . . ."

Agatha opened her eyes to rays of sun. She looked down and gasped.

"It's *real.*"

Far beneath them, two soaring castles sprawled across the forest. One castle glittered in sun mist, with pink and blue glass turrets over a sparkling lake. The other loomed, blackened and jagged, sharp spires ripping through thunderclouds like the teeth of a monster.

The School for Good and Evil.

The bony bird drifted over the Towers of Good and loosened Sophie from its claws. Agatha clutched her friend in horror, but then saw Sophie's face, glowing with happiness.

"Aggie, I'm a *princess*."

But the bird dropped Agatha instead.

Stunned, Sophie watched Agatha plummet into pink cotton-candy mist. "Wait—no—"

The bird swooped savagely towards the Towers of Evil, its jaws reaching up for new prey.

"No! I'm *Good*! It's the wrong one!" Sophie screamed—

And without a beat, she was dropped into hellish darkness.

3

The Great Mistake

Sophie opened her eyes to find herself floating in a foul-smelling moat, filled to the brim with thick black sludge. A gloomy wall of fog flanked her on all sides. She tried to stand, but her feet couldn't find bottom and she sank; sludge flooded her nose and burnt her throat. Choking for breath, she found something to grasp, and saw it was the carcass of a half-eaten goat. She gasped and tried to swim away but couldn't see an inch in front of her face. Screams echoed above and Sophie looked up.

Streaks of motion—then a

dozen bony birds crashed through the fog and dropped shrieking children into the moat. When their screams turned to
splashes, another wave of birds came, then another, until every
inch of sky was filled with falling children. Sophie glimpsed a
bird dive straight for her and she swerved, just in time to get a
cannonball splash of slime in her face.

She wiped the glop out of her eye and came face-to-face
with a boy. The first thing she noticed was he had no shirt.
His chest was puny and pale, without the hope of muscle.
From his small head jutted a long nose, spiky teeth, and black
hair that drooped over beady eyes. He looked like a sinister
little weasel.

"The bird ate my shirt," he said. "Can I touch your hair?"

Sophie backed up.

"They don't usually make villains with princess hair," he
said, dog-paddling towards her.

Sophie searched desperately for a weapon—a stick, a stone,
a dead goat—

"Maybe we could be bunk mates or best mates or some
kind of mates," he said, inches from her now. It was like Radley
had turned into a rodent and developed courage. He reached
out his scrawny hand to touch her and Sophie readied a punch
to the eye, when a screaming child dropped between them.
Sophie took off in the opposite direction and by the time she
glanced back, Weasel Boy was gone.

Through the fog, Sophie could see shadows of children
treading through floating bags and trunks, hunting for
their luggage. Those that managed to find them continued

downstream, towards ominous howls in the distance. Sophie followed these floating silhouettes until the fog cleared to reveal the shore, where a pack of wolves, standing on two feet in bloodred soldier jackets and black leather breeches, snapped riding whips to herd students into line.

Sophie grasped the bank to pull herself out but froze when she caught her reflection in the moat. Her dress was buried beneath sludge and yolk, her face shined with stinky black grime, and her hair was home to a family of earthworms. She choked for breath—

"*Help!* I'm in the wrong sch—"

A wolf yanked her out and kicked her into line. She opened her mouth to protest, but saw Weasel Boy swimming towards her, yelping, "Wait for me!"

Quickly, Sophie joined the line of shadowed children, dragging their trunks through the fog. If any dawdled, a wolf delivered a swift crack, so she kept anxious pace, all the while wiping her dress, picking out worms, and mourning her perfectly packed bags far, far away.

The tower gates were made of iron spikes, crisscrossed with barbed wire. Nearing them, she saw it wasn't wire at all but a sea of black vipers that darted and hissed in her direction. With a squeak, Sophie scampered through and looked back at rusted words over the gates, held between two carved black swans:

THE SCHOOL FOR EVIL EDIFICATION AND PROPAGATION OF SIN

Ahead the school tower rose like a winged demon. The main tower, built of pockmarked black stone, unfurled through smoky clouds like a hulking torso. From the sides of the main tower jutted two thick, crooked spires, dripping with veiny red creepers like bleeding wings.

The wolves drove the children towards the mouth of the main tower, a long serrated tunnel shaped like a crocodile snout. Sophie felt chills as the tunnel grew narrower and narrower until she could barely see the child in front of her. She squeezed between two jagged stones and found herself in a leaky foyer that smelled of rotten fish. Demonic gargoyles pitched down from stone rafters, lit torches in their jaws. An iron statue of a bald, toothless hag brandishing an apple smoldered in the menacing firelight. Along the wall, a crumbly column had an enormous black letter *N* painted on it, decorated with wicked-faced imps, trolls, and Harpies climbing up and down it like a tree. There was a bloodred *E* on the next column, embellished with swinging giants and goblins. Creeping along in the interminable line, Sophie worked out what the columns spelled out—N-E-V-E-R—then suddenly found herself far enough into the room to see the line snake in front of her. For the first time, she had a clear view of the other students and almost fainted.

One girl had a hideous overbite, wispy patches of hair, and one eye instead of two, right in the middle of her forehead. Another boy was like a mound of dough, with his bulging belly, bald head, and swollen limbs. A tall, sneering girl trudged ahead with sickly green skin. The boy in front of her had so much hair all over him he could have been an ape. They all looked about her age, but the similarities ended there. Here was a mass of the miserable, with misshapen bodies, repulsive faces, and the cruelest expressions she'd ever seen, as if looking for something to hate. One by one their eyes fell on Sophie and they found what they were looking for. The petrified princess in glass slippers and golden curls.

The red rose among thorns.

On the other side of the moat, Agatha had nearly killed a fairy.

She had woken under red and yellow lilies that appeared to be having an animated conversation. Agatha was sure she was the subject, for the lilies gestured brusquely at her with their leaves and buds. But then the matter seemed settled and the flowers hunched like fussing grandmothers and wrapped their stems around her wrists. With a tug, they yanked her to her feet and Agatha gazed out at a field of girls, blooming gloriously around a shimmering lake.

She couldn't believe what she was seeing. The girls grew right from the earth. First heads poked through soft dirt, then necks, then chests, then up and up until they stretched their arms into fluffy blue sky and planted delicate slippers upon the ground. But it wasn't the sight of sprouting girls that unnerved Agatha most. It was that these girls looked *nothing* like her.

Their faces, some fair, some dark, were flawless and glowed with health. They had shiny waterfalls of hair, ironed and curled like dolls', and they wore downy dresses of peach, yellow, and white, like a fresh batch of Easter eggs. Some fell on the shorter side, others were willowy and tall, but all flaunted tiny waists, slim legs, and slight shoulders. As the field flourished with new students, a team of three glitter-winged fairies awaited each one. Chiming and chinkling, they dusted the girls of dirt, poured them cups of honeybush tea, and tended to their trunks, which had sprung from the ground with their owners.

Where exactly these beauties were coming from, Agatha hadn't the faintest idea. All she wanted was a dour or disheveled one to poke through so she wouldn't feel so out of place. But it was an endless bloom of Sophies who had everything she didn't. A familiar shame clawed at her stomach. She needed a hole to climb down, a graveyard to hide in, something to make them all go away—

That's when the fairy bit her.

"What the—"

Agatha tried to shake the jingling thing off her hand, but it flew and bit her neck, then her bottom. Other fairies tried to subdue the rogue as she yowled, but it bit them too and attacked Agatha again. Incensed, she tried to catch the fairy, but it moved lightning quick, so she hopped around uselessly while it bit her over and over until the fairy mistakenly flew into her mouth and she swallowed it. Agatha sighed in relief and looked up.

Sixty beautiful girls gaped at her. The cat in a nightingale's nest.

Agatha felt a pinch in her throat and coughed out the fairy. To her surprise, it was a boy.

In the distance, sweet bells rang out from the spectacular pink and blue glass castle across the lake. The teams of fairies all grabbed their girls by the shoulders, hoisted them into the air, and flew them across the lake towards the towers. Agatha saw her chance to escape, but before she could make a run for it, she felt herself lifted into the air by two girl fairies. As she flew away, she glanced back at the third, the fairy boy that had bitten her, who stayed firmly on the ground. He crossed his arms and shook his head, as if to say in no uncertain terms there'd been a terrible mistake.

When the fairies brought the girls down in front of the glass castle, they let go of their shoulders and let them proceed freely. But Agatha's two fairies held on and dragged her forward like a prisoner. Agatha looked back across the lake. *Where's Sophie?*

The crystal water turned to slimy moat halfway across the lake; gray fog obscured whatever lay on the opposite banks. If Agatha was to rescue her friend, she had to find a way to cross that moat. But first she needed to get away from these winged pests. She needed a diversion.

Mirrored words arched over golden gates ahead:

THE SCHOOL FOR GOOD ENLIGHTENMENT AND ENCHANTMENT

Agatha caught her reflection in the letters and turned away. She hated mirrors and avoided them at all costs. (*Pigs and dogs don't sit around looking at themselves,* she thought.)

Moving forward, Agatha glanced up at the frosted castle doors, emblazoned with two white swans. But as the doors opened and fairies herded the girls into a tight, mirrored corridor, the line came to a halt and a group of girls circled her like sharks.

They stared at her for a moment, as if expecting her to whip off her mask and reveal a princess underneath. Agatha tried to meet their stares, but instead met her own face reflected in the mirrors a thousand times and instantly glued her eyes to the marble floor. A few fairies buzzed to get the mass moving, but most just perched on the girls' shoulders and watched. Finally, one of the girls stepped forward, with waist-length gold hair, succulent lips, and topaz eyes. She was so beautiful she didn't look real.

"Hello, I'm Beatrix," she said sweetly. "I didn't catch your name."

"That's because I never said it," said Agatha, eyes pinned to the ground.

"Are you sure you're in the right place?" Beatrix said, even sweeter now.

Agatha felt a word swim into her mind—a word she needed, but was still too foggy to see.

"Um, I uh—"

"Perhaps you just swam to the wrong school," smiled Beatrix.

The word lit up in Agatha's head. *Diversion.*

Agatha looked up into Beatrix's dazzling eyes. "This is the School for Good, isn't it? The legendary school for beautiful and worthy girls destined to be princesses?"

"Oh," said Beatrix, lips pursed. "So you're not lost?"

"Or confused?" said another with Arabian skin and jet-black hair.

"Or blind?" said a third with deep ruby curls.

"In that case, I'm sure you have your Flowerground Pass," Beatrix said.

Agatha blinked. "My what?"

"Your *ticket* into the Flowerground," said Beatrix. "You know, the way we all got here. Only *officially* accepted students have tickets into the Flowerground."

All the girls held up large golden tickets, flaunting their names in regal calligraphy, stamped with the School Master's black-and-white swan seal.

"Ohhh, *that* Flowerground Pass," Agatha scoffed. She dug her hands in her pockets. "Come close and I'll show you."

The girls gathered suspiciously. Meanwhile Agatha's hands fumbled for a diversion—matches . . . coins . . . dried leaves . . .

"Um, closer."

Murmuring girls huddled in. "It shouldn't be this small," Beatrix huffed.

"Shrunk in the wash," said Agatha, scraping through more matches, melted chocolate, a headless bird (Reaper hid them in her clothes). "It's in here somewhere—"

"Perhaps you lost it," said Beatrix.

Mothballs . . . peanut shells . . . another dead bird . . .

"Or misplaced it," said Beatrix.

The bird? The match? Light the bird with the match?

"Or *lied* about having one at all."

"Oh, I feel it now—"

But all Agatha felt was a nervous rash across her neck—

"You know what happens to intruders, don't you," Beatrix said.

"Here it is—" *Do something!*

Girls crowded her ominously.

Do something now!

She did the first thing she thought of and delivered a swift, loud fart.

An effective diversion creates both chaos and panic. Agatha delivered on both counts. Vile fumes ripped through the tight corridor as squealing girls stampeded for cover and fairies swooned at first smell, leaving her a clear path to the door. Only Beatrix stood in her way, too shocked to move. Agatha took a step towards her and leaned in like a wolf.

"*Boo.*"

Beatrix fled for her life.

As Agatha sprinted for the door, she looked back with pride as girls collided into walls and trampled each other to escape. Fixed on rescuing Sophie, she lunged through the frosted doors, ran for the lake, but just as she got to it, the waters rose up in a giant wave and with a tidal crash, slammed her back through the doors, through screeching girls, until she landed on her stomach in a puddle.

She staggered to her feet and froze.

"Welcome, New Princess," said a floating, seven-foot nymph. It moved aside to reveal a foyer so magnificent Agatha lost her breath. "Welcome to the School for Good."

Sophie couldn't get over the smell of the place. As she lurched along with the line, she gagged on the mix of unwashed bodies, mildewed stone, and stinking wolf. Sophie stood on her tiptoes to see where the line was headed, but all she could see was an endless parade of freaks. The other students threw her dirty looks but she responded with her kindest smile, in case this was all a test. It had to be a test or glitch or joke or *something*.

She turned to a gray wolf. "Not that I question your authority, but might I see the School Master? I think he—" The wolf roared, soaking her with spit. Sophie didn't press the point.

She slumped with the line into a sunken anteroom, where three black crooked staircases twisted up in a perfect row. One carved with monsters said MALICE along the banister, the second, etched with spiders, said MISCHIEF, and the third with snakes read VICE. Around the three staircases, Sophie noticed the walls covered with different-colored frames. In each frame there was a portrait of a child, next to a storybook painting of what the student became upon graduation. A gold frame had a portrait of an elfish little girl, and beside it, a magnificent drawing of her as a revolting witch, standing over a comatose maiden. A gold plaque stretched under the two illustrations:

> ### CATHERINE OF FOXWOOD
> *Little Snow White* (Villain)

In the next gold frame there was a portrait of a smirking boy with a thick unibrow, alongside a painting of him all grown up, brandishing a knife to a woman's throat:

> ### DROGAN OF MURMURING MOUNTAINS
> *Bluebeard* (Villain)

Beneath Drogan there was a silver frame of a skinny boy with shock blond hair, turned into one of a dozen ogres savaging a village:

> ### KEIR OF NETHERWOOD
> *Tom Thumb* (Henchman)

Then Sophie noticed a decayed bronze frame near the bottom with a tiny, bald boy, eyes scared wide. A boy she knew. Bane was his name. He used to bite all the pretty girls in Gavaldon until he was kidnapped four years before. But there was no drawing next to Bane. Just a rusted plaque that read:

> ### FAILED

Sophie looked at Bane's terrified face and felt her stomach churn. *What happened to him?* She gazed up at thousands of gold, silver, and bronze frames cramming every inch of the hall: witches slaying princes, giants devouring men, demons igniting children, heinous ogres, grotesque gorgons, headless horsemen, merciless sea monsters. Once awkward adolescents. Now portraits of absolute evil. Even the villains that had died gruesome deaths—Rumpelstiltskin, the Beanstalk Giant, the Wolf from *Red Riding Hood*—were drawn in their greatest moments, as if they had emerged triumphant from their tales. Sophie's gut took another twist when she noticed the other children gazing up at the portraits in awed worship. It hit her with sick clarity. She was in line with future murderers and monsters.

Her face broke out in a cold sweat. She needed to find a faculty member. Someone who could search the list of enrolled students and see she was in the wrong school. But so far, all she could find were wolves that couldn't speak, let alone read a list.

Turning the corner into a wider corridor, Sophie saw a red-skinned, horned dwarf ahead on a towering stepladder, hammering more portraits into a bare wall. Her teeth clenched with hope as she inched towards him in line. As she plotted to get his attention, Sophie suddenly noticed the frames on this wall held familiar faces. There was the hoggish dough boy she had seen earlier, labeled BRONE OF ROCH BRIAR. Next to him was a painting of the one-eyed, wispy-haired girl: ARACHNE OF FOXWOOD. Sophie scanned the portraits of her classmates, awaiting their villainous transformations. Her eyes stopped on Weasel Boy's. HORT OF BLOODBROOK. *Hort. Sounds like a disease.* She moved ahead in line, ready to cry to the dwarf—

Then she saw the frame under his hammer.

Her own face smiled back at her.

With a shriek, Sophie bolted out of line, fumbled up the ladder, and snatched the portrait from the stunned dwarf's fingers. "No! I'm in *Good*!" she shouted, but the dwarf snatched it back and the two tussled over the portrait, kicking and clawing until Sophie had enough and gave him a slap. The dwarf screamed like a little girl and swung at her with his hammer. Sophie dodged it but lost her balance, and the stepladder teetered and crashed between the walls. Splayed out on rungs in midair, she looked down at snarling wolves and goggling students—"I need the School Master!"—then lost her grip, slid across the ladder, and landed in a heap at the front of the line.

A dark-skinned hag with a massive boil on her cheek thrust a sheet of parchment into her hands.

SOPHIE OF WOODS BEYOND

EVIL, 1st Year

Malice Tower 66

Session	Faculty
1: UGLIFICATION	Prof. Bilious Manley
2: HENCHMEN TRAINING	Castor
3: CURSES & DEATH TRAPS	Lady Lesso
4: HISTORY of VILLAINY	Prof. August Sader
5: LUNCH	
6: SPECIAL TALENTS	Prof. Sheeba Sheeks
7: SURVIVING FAIRY TALES	Yuba the Gnome
(FOREST GROUP #3)	

Sophie looked up, dumbstruck. "See you in class, Witch of Woods Beyond," the hag croaked. Before Sophie could respond, an ogre dumped a ribbon-tied stack of books in her hands.

Best Villainous Monologues, 2nd ed.
Spells for Suffering, Year 1
The Novice's Guide to Kidnapping & Murder
Embracing Ugliness Inside & Out
How to Cook Children (with New Recipes!)

The books were bad enough, but then Sophie saw the ribbon tying them was a live eel. She screamed and dropped the books, before a spotted satyr foisted musty black fabric at her. Unfurling it, Sophie shrank from a dumpy, tattered tunic that sagged like shredded curtains.

She gaped at the other girls, gleefully putting on the putrid uniform, combing through their books, comparing schedules. Sophie slowly looked down at her own foul black robes. Then at her eel-slimed books and schedule. Then at her smiling, sweet portrait, back on the wall.

She ran for her life.

Agatha knew she was in the wrong place because even the faculty gave her confused looks. Together they lined the four spiral staircases of the cavernous glass foyer, two of them pink, two blue, showering confetti upon the new students. The female professors wore different-colored versions of the same slim, high-necked dress, with a glittering silver swan crest over the heart. Each had added a personal touch to the dress, whether inlaid crystals, beaded flowers, or even a tulle bow. The male professors, meanwhile, all wore bright slim suits in a rainbow of hues, paired with matching vests, narrow ties, and colorful kerchiefs tucked into pockets embroidered with the same silver swan.

Agatha noticed immediately they were all more attractive than any adults she had ever seen. Even the older faculty was elegant to the point of intimidation. Agatha had always tried to convince herself beauty was pointless because it was temporary. Here was proof it lasted forever.

The teachers tried to disguise their nudges and whispers upon seeing the dripping-wet, misplaced student, but Agatha was used to catching these things. Then she noticed one who wasn't like the rest. Haloed against a stained glass window with a shamrock green suit, silver hair, and shiny hazel eyes, he beamed down at her as if she completely belonged. Agatha reddened. Anyone who thought she belonged here was a loon. Turning away, she took comfort in the glowering girls around her, who clearly hadn't forgiven her for the incident in the hall.

"Where are the boys?" Agatha heard one ask another, as the girls filed in in front of three enormous, floating nymphs with neon hair and lips, who handed out their schedules, books, and robes.

As Agatha followed the line behind them, she had a better look at the majestic stair room. The wall opposite her had an enormous pink-painted *E*, with lovingly drawn angels and sylphs fluttering around its edges. The other three walls had painted letters too, spelling out the word E-V-E-R in pink and blue. The four spiral staircases were arranged symmetrically at the corners of each wall, lit by high stained glass windows. One of the two blue flights had HONOR tattooed upon its baluster, along with glass etchings of knights and kings, while the other read VALOR, decorated with blue reliefs of hunters and archers. The two pink glass staircases had PURITY and CHARITY emblazoned in gold, along with delicate friezes of sculpted maidens, princesses, and kindly animals.

In the center of the room, alumni portraits blanketed a soaring crystal obelisk that reached from milky marble floor to domed sunroof. Higher up on the obelisk were gold-framed portraits of students who became princes and queens after graduation. In the middle were silver frames, for those who found lesser fates as jaunty sidekicks, dutiful housewives, and fairy godmothers. And near the bottom of the pillar, flecked with dust, were bronze-framed underachievers who had ended up footmen and servants. But regardless of whether they became a Snow Queen or a chimney sweep, Agatha saw the students shared the same beautiful faces, kind smiles, and soulful eyes. Here in a glass palace in the middle of the woods, the best of life had gathered in service of Good. And here she was, Miss Miserable, in service of graveyards and farts.

Agatha waited with bated breath, until she finally reached a pink-haired nymph. "There's been a mix-up!" she panted, dripping water and sweat. "It's my friend Sophie who's supposed to be here."

The nymph smiled.

"I tried to stop her from coming," Agatha said, voice quickening with hope, "but I confused the bird and now I'm here and she's in the other tower but she's pretty and likes pink and I'm . . . well, look at me. I know you need students but Sophie's my best friend and if she stays then I have to stay and we *can't* stay, so please help me find her so we can go home."

The nymph handed her a piece of parchment.

Agatha of Woods Beyond
GOOD, 1st Year
Purity Tower 51

Session	Faculty
1: BEAUTIFICATION	Prof. Emma Anemone
2: PRINCESS ETIQUETTE	Pollux
3: ANIMAL COMMUNICATION	Princess Uma
4: HISTORY of HEROISM	Prof. August Sader
5: LUNCH	
6: GOOD DEEDS	Prof. Clarissa Dovey
7: SURVIVING FAIRY TALES (FOREST GROUP #3)	Yuba the Gnome

Agatha stared at it, stupefied. "But—"

A green-haired nymph thrust her a basket of books, some peeking out:

The Privilege of Beauty
Winning Your Prince

The Recipe Book for Good Looks
Princess with a Purpose
Animal Speech 1: Barks, Neighs, & Chirps

Then a blue-haired nymph held up her uniform: an appallingly short pink pinafore, sleeves poofed with carnations, worn over a white lace blouse that seemed to be missing three buttons.

Stunned, Agatha looked at future princesses around her, tightening their pink dresses. She looked at books that told her beauty was a privilege, that she could win a chiseled prince, that she could talk to birds. She looked at a schedule meant for someone beautiful, graceful, and kind. Then she looked up at a handsome teacher, still smiling at her, as if expecting the greatest things from Agatha of Gavaldon.

Agatha did the only thing she knew how to do when faced with expectations.

Up the blue Honor staircase, through sea-green halls, she ran, fairies jangling furiously behind. Hurtling through halls, scrambling up stairs, she had no time to take in what she was seeing—floors made of jade, classrooms made of candy, a library made of gold—until she reached the last staircase and surged through a frosted glass door onto the tower roof. In front of her, the sun lit up a breathtaking open-air topiary of sculptured hedges. Before Agatha could even see what the sculptures were of, fairies smashed through the door, shooting sticky golden webs from their mouths to catch her. She dove to elude them, crawling like a bug through the colossal hedges. Finding her feet, she sprinted and leapt onto the tallest sculpture of a muscular prince raising a sword high above a pond. She scaled the leafy sword to its prickling tip, kicking away swarming fairies. But soon there were too many and just as they spat their glittering nets, Agatha lost her grip and crashed into the water.

When she opened her eyes, she was completely dry.

The pond must have been a portal, because she was outside now in a crystal blue archway. Agatha looked up and froze. She was at the end of a narrow stone bridge that stretched through thick fog into the rotted tower across the lake. A bridge between the two schools.

Tears stung her eyes. Sophie! She could save Sophie!

"Agatha!"

Agatha squinted and saw Sophie running out of the fog. "Sophie!"

Arms outstretched, the two girls dashed across the bridge, crying each other's name—

They slammed into an invisible barrier and ricocheted to the ground.

Dazed by pain, Agatha watched in horror as wolves dragged Sophie by the hair back to Evil.

"You don't understand," Sophie screamed, watching fairies snare Agatha. "It's all a mistake!"

"*There are no mistakes,*" a wolf growled.

They could speak after all.

4

The Three Witches of Room 66

Sophie wasn't sure why six wolves needed to punish her instead of one, but she assumed it was to make a point. They bound her to a spit, stuffed an apple in her mouth, and paraded her like a banquet pig through the six floors of Malice Hall. Lining the walls, new students pointed and laughed, but laughs turned to frowns when they realized this freak in pink would be one of their bunk mates. The wolves towed whimpering Sophie past Rooms 63, 64, 65, then kicked open Room 66 and flung her in. Sophie skidded until her face smacked into a warted foot.

"I told you we'd get her," said a sour voice.

Still tied to the spit, Sophie looked up at a tall girl with greasy black hair streaked red, black lipstick, a ring in her nose, and a terrifying tattoo of a buck-horned, red-skulled demon around her neck. The girl glared at Sophie, black eyes flinting.

"She even smells like an Ever."

"The fairies will retrieve it soon enough," said a voice across the room.

Sophie swung her head to an albino girl with deathly white hair, white skin, and hooded red eyes, feeding stew from a cauldron to three black rats. "Pity. We could slit its throat and hang it as a hall ornament."

"How rude," said a third. Sophie turned to a smiley brown-haired girl on the bed, round as a hot air balloon, chocolate ice pop in each stumpy fist. "Besides, it's against the rules to kill other students."

"How about we just maim her a bit?" said the albino.

"I think she's refreshing," said the plump one, biting into the ice pop. "Not every villain has to smell and look depressed."

"She's not a villain," the albino and the tattooed girl snapped in unison.

As she wriggled from her ropes, Sophie craned her neck up and had her first full view of the room. Once upon a time it might have been a nice, cozy suite before someone set it on fire. The brick walls were burnt to cinders. Black and brown scorch marks ripped across the ceiling, and the floor was buried beneath an inch of ash. Even the furniture looked toasted. But as her eyes searched, Sophie realized there was an even bigger problem with the room.

"Where's the mirror?" she gasped.

"Let me guess," the tattooed girl snorted. "It's Bella or Ariel or Anastasia."

"It looks more like a Buttercup or Sugarplum," said the albino.

"Or a Clarabelle or Rose Red or Willow-by-the-Sea."

"Sophie." Sophie stood in a cloud of soot. "My name is Sophie. I'm not a 'villain,' I'm not an 'it,' and yes, I clearly don't belong here, so—"

The albino and the tattooed girl were doubled over laughing. "Sophie!" the second cackled. "It's worse than anyone could have imagined!"

"Anything named Sophie doesn't belong here," the albino wheezed. "It belongs in a cage."

"I *belong* in the other tower," said Sophie, trying to stay above their cattiness, "which is why I need to see the School Master."

"'I need to see the School Master,'" the albino mimicked. "How about you jump out the window and see if he catches you?"

"You all have no manners," snarfled the round girl, mouth full. "I'm Dot. This is Hester," she said, pointing at the tattooed girl. "And this ray of sunshine," she said, pointing at the albino, "is Anadil." Anadil spat on the floor.

"Welcome to Room 66," said Dot, and with a swish of her hand swept the ashes off the unclaimed bed.

Sophie winced at moth-eaten sheets with ominous stains. "Appreciate the welcome, but I really should be going," she said, backing against the door. "Might you direct me to the School Master's office?"

"Princes must be so confused when they see you," said Dot. "Most villains don't look like princesses."

"She's *not* a villain," Anadil and Hester groaned.

"Do I have to make an appointment to see him?" pressed Sophie. "Or do I send him a note or—"

"You could fly, I suppose," Dot said, pulling two chocolate eggs from her pocket. "But the stymphs might eat you."

"Stymphs?" asked Sophie.

"Those birds that dropped us off, love," garbled Dot as she chewed. "You'd have to get past them. And you know how they hate villains."

"For the last time," shot Sophie, "I'm not a vill—"

Sounds rang in the stairwell. Sugary jingling, so dainty, so delicate it could only be—

Fairies. They were coming for her!

Sophie suppressed a scream. She dared not tell the girls her rescue was imminent (who knows how serious they were about making her a hall decoration). She backed against the door and listened to the jingles grow louder.

"I don't know why people think princesses are pretty," Hester said, picking a wart on her toe. "Their noses are so small. Like little buttons you want to pop off."

Fairies on our floor! Sophie wanted to hop up and down. As soon as she got to the Good castle, she would take the longest bath of her life!

"And their hair is always so long," Anadil said, dangling a dead mouse for the rats' dessert. "Makes me want to pull it all out."

Just a few rooms away now . . .

"And those phony smiles," Hester said.

"And that obsession with pink," said Anadil.

Fairies next door!

"Can't wait to kill my first one," said Hester.

"Today's as good a day as any," Anadil said.

They're here! Sophie swelled with joy—new school, new friends, new life!

But the fairies flew past her room.

Sophie's heart imploded. What happened! How could they miss her! She lunged past Anadil for the door, threw it open to a flash of wolf fur. Sophie jolted back in shock and Hester slammed the door.

"You'll get all of us punished," Hester growled.

"But they were here! They were looking for me!" Sophie cried.

"Are you *sure* we can't kill her?" said Anadil, watching her rats devour the mouse.

"So where in the woods do you come from, love?" Dot asked Sophie, inhaling a chocolate frog.

"I don't come from the woods," Sophie said impatiently, and peeped through the eyehole. The wolves had no doubt scared the fairies away. She needed to get back to the bridge and find them. But right now, there were three wolves guarding the hall, eating a meal of roasted turnips from cast-iron plates.

Wolves eat turnips? With forks?

But there was something else odd on the wolves' plates.

Fairies, scavenging food from the beasts.

Sophie's eye widened in shock.

A cute boy fairy glanced up at her. *He sees me!* Clasping her hands, Sophie mouthed "Help!" through the glass. The fairy boy smiled with understanding, and whispered in a wolf's ear. The wolf looked up at Sophie, and shattered her eyehole with a savage kick. Sophie stumbled back, hearing a chorus of airy giggles and growling laughs.

The fairies had no intention of rescuing her.

Sophie's whole body shook, about to explode into sobs. Then she heard a throat clear and turned.

Three girls gaped with identically confused expressions.

"What do you mean you 'don't come from the woods'?" said Hester.

Sophie was in no state to answer dumb questions, but now these goons were her only hope to find the School Master.

"I come from Gavaldon," she said, stifling tears. "You three seem to know a lot about this place, so I'd be thankful if you could tell me wher—"

"Is that near the Murmuring Mountains?" asked Dot.

"Only Nevers live in the Murmuring Mountains, you fool," Hester groused.

"Near Rainbow Gale, I bet," said Anadil. "That's where the most annoying Evers come from."

"Sorry, I'm lost already," Sophie frowned. "Evers? Nevers?"

"A sheltered Rapunzel locked-in-a-tower type," Anadil said. "Explains everything."

"Evers are what we call Good-doers, love," Dot said to

Sophie. "You know, all their nonsense about finding Happily Ever After."

"So that makes you 'Nevers'?" said Sophie, remembering the lettered columns in the stair room.

"Short for 'Nevermore,'" Hester reveled. "Paradise for Evildoers. We'll have infinite power in Nevermore."

"Control time and space," said Anadil.

"Take new forms," said Hester.

"Splinter our souls."

"Conquer death."

"Only the wickedest villains get in," said Anadil.

"And the best part," said Hester. "No other people. Each villain gets their own private kingdom."

"Eternal solitude," said Anadil.

"Sounds like misery," said Sophie.

"Other people are misery," said Hester.

"Agatha would love it here," Sophie murmured.

"Gavaldon . . . is that by Pifflepaff Hills?" Dot said airily.

"Oh, for goodness' sakes, it's not *near* anything," Sophie moaned. She held up her schedule, "SOPHIE OF WOODS BEYOND" at its top. "Gavaldon's *beyond* the woods. Surrounded by it on all sides."

"Woods *Beyond*?" said Hester.

"Who's your king?" asked Dot.

"We don't have a king," Sophie said.

"Who's your mother?" asked Anadil.

"She's dead," Sophie said.

"And your father?" asked Dot.

"He's a mill worker. These questions are quite personal—"

"And what fairy-tale family is he from?" Anadil asked.

"And now they're just plain odd. No one's family is a fairy tale. He's from a normal family with normal faults. Like every one of your fathers."

"I knew it," Hester said to Anadil.

"Knew what?" said Sophie.

"Readers are the only ones this stupid," Anadil said to Hester.

Sophie's skin burned. "I'm sorry, but I'm not the stupid one if I'm the only person here who can read, so why don't you look in the mirror, that is if you could actually find one—"

Reader.

Why didn't anyone here seem homesick? Why did they all swim towards the wolves in the moat instead of fleeing for their lives? Why didn't they cry for their mothers or try to escape the snakes at the gate? Why did they all know so much about this school?

"What fairy-tale family is he from?"

Sophie's eyes found Hester's nightstand. Next to a vase of dead flowers, a claw-shaped candle, and a stack of books— *Outsmarting Orphans, Why Villains Fail, Frequent Witch Mistakes*—was a knurled wooden picture frame. Inside was a child's clumsy painting of a grotesque witch in front of a house.

A house made of gingerbread and candy.

"Mother was naive," said Hester, picking up the frame. Her face struggled with the memory. "An oven? Please. Stick them on a grill. Avoids complications." Her jaw hardened. "I'll do better."

Sophie's eyes shifted to Anadil and her stomach plummeted. Her favorite storybook ended with a witch rolled in a barrel of nails until all that remained was her bracelet made of little boys' bones. Now that bracelet was clasped on her roommate's wrist.

"Does know her witches, doesn't she," Anadil leered. "Granny would be flattered."

Sophie whirled to a poster above Dot's bed. A handsome man in green screaming as an executioner's axe sliced into his head.

WANTED:

ROBIN HOOD

Dead or Alive (Preferably Dead)

By Order of Sheriff of Nottingham

"Daddy promised to let me have first swing," Dot said.

Sophie looked at her three bunk mates in horror.

They didn't need to read the fairy tales. They came from them.

They were born to kill.

"A princess *and* a Reader," Hester said. "The two worst things a human can be."

"Even the Evers don't want her," said Anadil. "Or the fairies would have come by now."

"But they have to come!" Sophie cried. "I'm Good!"

"Well, you're stuck here, dearie," Hester said, plumping Sophie's pillow with a kick. "So if you want to stay alive, best try to fit in."

Fit in with witches! Fit in with cannibals!

"No! Listen to me!" Sophie begged. "I'm *Good*!"

"You keep saying that." In a flash, Hester seized her by the throat and pinned her over the open window. "And yet there's no *proof.*"

"I donate corsets to homeless hags! I go to church every Sunday!" Sophie howled above the fatal drop.

"Mmm, no sign of fairy godmother," Hester said. "Try again."

"I smile at children! I sing to birds!" Sophie choked. "I can't breathe!"

"No sign of Prince Charming either," said Anadil, grabbing her legs. "Last chance."

"I made friends with a witch! That's how Good I am!"

"And still no fairies," Anadil said to Hester as they lifted her up.

"She belongs here, not me!" Sophie wailed—

"No one knows why the School Master brings you worthless freaks into our world," hissed Hester. "But there can only be one reason. He's a *fool.*"

"Ask Agatha! She'll tell you! She's the villain!"

"You know, Anadil, no one's told us the rules yet," Hester said.

"So they can't punish us for breaking them," Anadil grinned.

They lifted Sophie over the edge. "One," said Hester.

"No!" Sophie shrieked.

"Two . . ."

"You want proof! I'll give you proof!" Sophie screamed—

"Three."

"LOOK AT ME AND LOOK AT YOU!"

Hester and Anadil dropped her. Stunned, they stared at each other, then at Sophie, hunched on the bed, gulping tearful breaths.

"Told you she was a villain," Dot chirped and bit into fudge.

A commotion clamored outside the room, and the girls' heads swiveled to the door. It flew open with a crack and three wolves thundered in, grabbed them by the collars, and hurled them into a stampede of black-robed students. Students rammed and elbowed each other; some fell beneath the herd and couldn't get back up. Sophie clung to the wall for her life.

"Where are we going!" she yelled to Dot.

"The School for Good!" Dot said. "For the Welcomin—"
An ogreish boy kicked her forward.

The School for Good! Flooding with hope, Sophie followed the hideous herd down the stairs, primping her pink dress for her first meeting with her true classmates. Someone seized her arm and threw her against the banister. Dazed, she looked up at a vicious white wolf, who held up a black uniform, reeking of death. He bared his teeth in a shiny grin.

"No—" Sophie gasped—

So the wolf took care of matters himself.

Though the princesses of Purity were all bunked in threes, Agatha ended up with her own room.

A pink glass staircase connected all five floors of Purity Tower, spiraling in a carved replica of Rapunzel's endless hair. The door to Agatha's fifth-floor room had a glittery sign covered in hearts: "Welcome Reena, Millicent, Agatha!" But Reena and Millicent didn't stay long. Reena, blessed with luscious Arabian skin and brilliant gray eyes, labored to move her enormous trunk into the room, only to find Agatha and move it right back out. "She just looks so evil," Agatha heard her sob. "I don't want to die!" ("Move in with me," she heard Beatrix say. "The fairies will understand.") And indeed, the fairies did understand. And they understood when red-haired Millicent, with an upturned nose and thin eyebrows, feigned a fear of heights and demanded a room on a lower floor. And so Agatha was alone, which made her feel right at home.

The room, however, made her feel anxious. Massive, jeweled mirrors glared back from pink walls. Elaborate murals flaunted beautiful princesses kissing dashing princes. Arching over each bed was a white silk canopy, shaped like a royal carriage, and a glorious fresco of clouds blanketed the ceiling tiles, with smiling cupids shooting love arrows from puffy perches. Agatha moved as far as she could from all of it and crouched in the window nook, black dress bunched against pink wall.

Through the window, she could see the sparkling lake around the Good Towers turn into sludgy moat midway across to protect the Evil ones. "Halfway Bay," the girls had called it. Deep in the fog, the thin stone bridge reached across the waters to connect the two schools. But this was all in front of the two castles. What was behind them?

Curious, Agatha climbed onto the window ledge, clinging to a glass beam. She glanced down at the Charity Tower below, reaching up with its sharp pink spire—one wrong move and she'd be skewered like lamb meat. Agatha tiptoed to the side of the ledge, craned her head around the corner, and almost fell from surprise. Behind the School for Good and Evil was a massive blue forest. Trees, bushes, flowers bloomed in every shade of blue, from iceberg to indigo. The lush blue grove unfolded for quite a distance, connecting the yards of both schools, before it was fenced on all sides by tall gold gates. Beyond the gates, the forest returned to green and stretched into dark oblivion.

As Agatha slid back, she saw something in front of the school, rising from Halfway Bay. It was right at the midpoint, where waters balanced between sludge and sparkle. She could barely see it through the fog . . . a tall, thin tower of glinting silver brick. Fairies buzzed around the spire in droves, while wolves with crossbows stood watch on wooden planks that jutted from the base of the tower into the water.

What were they guarding?

Agatha squinted at the top of the sky-high tower, but all she could see was a single window shrouded by clouds.

Then light caught the window and she saw it. Silhouetted in sun.

The crooked shadow that kidnapped them.

Her shoe slipped and her body pitched forward over deadly Charity. Flailing, she grabbed the window beam just in time and crashed back into the room. Agatha clutched her bruised tailbone, whipped around—but the shadow was gone.

Agatha's heart thumped faster. Whoever brought them here was in that tower. Whoever was in that tower could fix the mistake and send them home.

But first she needed to rescue her best friend.

A few minutes later, Agatha shrank from a mirror. The sleeveless pink uniform showed off parts of her white, scrawny body that had never seen light. The lace collar gave away the rash that spread across her neck whenever she felt anxious, the carnations lining the sleeves made her sneeze, and the matching pink high heels teetered like stilts. But the foul outfit was her only chance to escape. Her room was on the opposite end from the stairwell. To get back to the bridge, she needed to glide through the hall without being noticed and slip down the stairs.

Agatha set her jaw.

You have to blend.

She took a deep breath and cracked open the door.

Fifty beautiful girls in pink pinafores packed the hallway, giggling, gossiping, trading dresses, shoes, bags, bangles, creams, and anything else they had brought in their gigantic trunks, while fairies buzzed between, trying in vain to round them up for the Welcoming. Through the hubbub, Agatha glimpsed stairs at the other end. A confident stroll and she'd be gone before they saw her. But she couldn't move.

It had taken her whole life to make a single friend. And here these girls had become best friends in minutes as if making friends was the simplest thing in the world. Agatha prickled with shame. In this School for Good, where everyone was supposed to be kind and loving, she had still ended up alone and despised. She was a villain, no matter where she went.

She slammed the door, ripped petals from her sleeve, tore off her pink heels and hurled them through the window. She slumped against the wall and closed her eyes.

Get me out of here.

She opened her eyes and glimpsed her ugly face in the jeweled mirror. Before she could turn away, her eyes caught something else in her reflection. A ceiling tile with a smiling cupid, slightly dislodged.

Agatha slipped her feet back into her hard black clumps. She climbed up the bed canopy and pulled the tile away, revealing a dark vent above the room. She gripped the edges of the hole and swung one leg up into the vent, then the other, until she found herself perched on a narrow platform inside the chute.

She crawled through darkness, hands and knees blindly shuffling along cold metal—until metal suddenly turned to air. This time, she couldn't save herself.

Falling too fast to scream, Agatha whizzed through chutes, ping-ponged through pipes, and slid down vents until she somersaulted through a grate and landed on a beanstalk.

She hugged the thick green trunk, thankful she was still in

one piece. But as she looked around, Agatha saw she wasn't in a garden or forest or anywhere else a beanstalk is supposed to be. She was in a dark room with high ceilings, filled with paintings, sculptures, and glass cases. Her eyes found the frosted doors in the corner, gilded words etched in glass:

THE GALLERY OF GOOD

Agatha inched down the beanstalk until her clumps touched marble floor.

A mural blanketed the long wall with a panoramic view of a soaring gold castle and a dashing prince and beautiful princess wedded beneath its gleaming arch, as thousands of spectators jingled bells and danced in celebration. Blessed by a brilliant sun, the virtuous couple kissed, while baby angels hovered above, showering them with red and white roses. High above the scene, shiny gold block letters peeked out from behind clouds, stretching from one end of the mural to the other:

EVERAFTER

Agatha grimaced. She had always mocked Sophie for believing in Happily Ever After. ("Who wants to be happy all the time?") But looking at the mural, she had to admit this school did a spookily good job of selling the idea.

She peered into a glass case, holding a thin booklet of flowery handwriting with a plaque next to it: SNOW WHITE, ANIMAL FLUENCY EXAM (LETITIA OF MAIDENVALE). In the next

cases, she found the blue cape of a boy who became Cinderella's prince, Red Riding Hood's dorm pillow, the Little Match
Girl's diary, Pinocchio's pajamas, and other remnants of star
students who presumably went on to weddings and castles. On
the walls, she scanned more drawings of Ever After by former
students, a School History exhibit, banners celebrating iconic
victories, and a wall labeled "Class Captain," stacked with portraits of students from each class. The museum got darker as
it went on, so Agatha used one of her matches to light a lamp.
That's when she saw the dead animals.

Dozens of taxidermied creatures loomed over her, stuffed
and mounted on rosy pink walls. She dusted off their plaques
to find the booted Master Cat, Cinderella's favorite rat, Jack's
sold-off cow, stamped with the names of children who weren't
good enough to become heroes or sidekicks or servants. No
Happily Ever After for this lot. Just hooks in a museum. Agatha
felt their eerie, glass-eyed stares and turned away. Only then
did she see the plaque gleaming on the beanstalk. HOLDEN OF
RAINBOW GALE. That wretched plant had once been a *boy*.

Agatha's blood ran cold. All these stories she had never
believed in. But they were painfully real now. In two hundred years, no kidnapped child had ever made it back to
Gavaldon. What made her think she and Sophie would be
the first? What made her think they wouldn't end up a raven
or a rosebush?

Then she remembered what made them different from all
the rest.

We have each other.

They had to work together to break this curse. Or they'd both end up fossils of a fairy tale.

Agatha found her attention drawn to a corner nook, with a row of paintings by the same artist, depicting the same scenes: children reading storybooks, in hazy, impressionistic colors. As she neared the paintings, her eyes grew wider. Because she recognized where all these children were.

They were in Gavaldon.

She moved from first painting to last, with reading children set against the familiar hills and lake, crooked clock tower and rickety church, even the shadow of a house on Graves Hill. Agatha felt stabs of homesickness. She had mocked the children as batty and delusional. But in the end, they had known what she didn't—that the line between stories and real life is very thin indeed.

Then she came to the last painting, which wasn't like the others at all. In this one, raging children heaved their storybooks into a bonfire in the square and watched them burn. All around them, the dark forest went up in flames, filling the sky with violent red and black smoke. Staring at it, Agatha felt a chill up her spine.

Voices. She dove behind a giant pumpkin carriage, hitting her head on a plaque. HEINRICH OF NETHERWOOD. Agatha gagged.

Two teachers entered the museum, an older woman in a chartreuse high-necked dress, speckled with iridescent green beetle wings, and a younger woman in a pointy-shouldered purple gown that slunk behind her. The woman in chartreuse had a grandmotherly beehive of white hair, but luminous skin and calm brown eyes. The woman in purple had black hair yanked in a long braid, amethyst eyes, and bloodless skin stretched over bones like a drum.

"He's tampering with the tales, Clarissa," the one in purple said.

"The School Master can't control the Storian, Lady Lesso," Clarissa returned.

"He's on your side and you know it," Lady Lesso seethed.

"He's not on anyone's side—" Clarissa stopped short. So did Lady Lesso.

Agatha saw what they were looking at. The last painting.

"I see you've welcomed another of Professor Sader's delusions," Lady Lesso said.

"It is *his* gallery," Clarissa sighed.

Lady Lesso's eyes flashed. Magically, the painting tore off the wall and landed behind a glass case, inches from Agatha's head.

"This is why they're not in *your* school's gallery," said Clarissa.

"Anyone who believes the Reader Prophecy is a fool," hissed Lady Lesso. "Including the School Master."

"A School Master must protect the balance," Clarissa said gently. "He sees Readers as part of that balance. Even if you and I cannot understand."

"Balance!" scoffed Lady Lesso. "Then why hasn't Evil won a tale since he took over? Why hasn't Evil defeated Good in *two hundred years?*"

"Perhaps my students are just better educated," said Clarissa.

Lady Lesso glowered and walked away. Swishing her finger, Clarissa moved the painting back into place and scurried to keep up.

"Maybe your new Reader will prove you wrong," she said.

Lady Lesso snorted. "I hear she wears *pink*."

Agatha listened to their footsteps go quiet.

She looked up at the dented painting. The children, the bonfire, Gavaldon burning to the ground. What did it all mean?

Twinkly flutters echoed through the air. Before she could move, glowing fairies burst in, searching every crevice like flashlights. Far across the museum, Agatha saw the doors through which the two teachers had left. Just when the fairies reached the pumpkin, she sprinted for it. The fairies squealed in surprise as she slid between three stuffed bears, threw open the doors—

Pink-dressed classmates streamed through the foyer in two perfect lines. As they held hands and giggled, the best of friends, Agatha felt familiar shame rise. Everything in her body told her to shut the door again and hide. But this time instead of thinking of all the friends she didn't have, Agatha thought about the one she did.

The fairies swooped in a second later, but all they found were princesses on their way to a Welcoming. As they hovered furiously above, hunting for signs of guilt, Agatha slipped into the pink parade, put on a smile . . . and tried to blend.

5

Boys Ruin Everything

Each school had its own entrance to the Theater of Tales, which was split into two halves. The west doors opened into the side for the Good students, decorated with pink and blue pews, crystal friezes, and glittering bouquets of glass flowers. The east doors opened into the side for Evil students, with warped wooden benches, carvings of murder and torture, and deadly stalactites dangling from the burnt ceiling. As students herded into their halves for the Welcoming, fairies and wolves guarded the silver marble aisle between them.

Despite her ghastly new uniform, Sophie had no intention

of sitting with Evil. One look at the Good girls' glossy hair, dazzling smiles, chic pink dresses, and she knew she had found her sisters. If the fairies wouldn't rescue her, surely her fellow princesses would. With villains shoving her along, she tried to get the Good girls' attention, but they were ignoring her side of the theater. Finally Sophie battled her way to the aisle, waved her arms, and opened her mouth to yell, when a hand yanked her under a rotted bench.

Agatha tackled her in a hug. "I found the School Master's tower! It's in the moat and there's guards, but if we can just get up there then we can—"

"Hi! Nice to see you! Give me your clothes," said Sophie, staring at Agatha's pink dress.

"Huh?"

"Quick! It will solve everything."

"You can't be serious! Sophie, we can't stay here!"

"Exactly," Sophie smiled. "I need to be in your school and you need to be in mine. Just like we talked about, remember?"

"But your father, my mother, my *cat*!" Agatha sputtered. "You don't know what they're like here! They'll turn us into snakes or squirrels or shrubbery! Sophie, we have to get back home!"

"Why? What do I have in Gavaldon to go back to?" Sophie said.

Agatha blushed with hurt. "You have . . . um, you have . . ."

"Right. Nothing. Now, my *dress*, please."

Agatha folded her arms.

"Then I'll take it myself," Sophie scowled. But right as

she grabbed Agatha by her flowered sleeve, something made her stop cold. Sophie listened, ears piqued, and took off like a panther. She slid under warped benches, dodged villains' feet, ducked behind the last pew, and peeked around it.

Agatha followed, exasperated. "I don't know what's gotten into yo—"

Sophie covered Agatha's mouth and listened to the sounds grow louder. Sounds that made every Good girl bolt upright. Sounds they had waited their whole lives to hear. From the hall, the stomp of boots, the clash of steel—

The west doors flew open to sixty gorgeous boys in swordfight.

Sun-kissed skin peeked through light blue sleeves and stiff collars; tall navy boots matched high-cut waistcoats and knotted slim ties, each embroidered with a single gold initial. As the boys playfully crossed blades, their shirts came untucked from tight beige breeches, revealing slender waists and flashes of muscle. Sweat glistened on glowing faces as they thrust down the aisle, boots cracking on marble, until swiftly the swordfight climaxed, boys pinning boys against pews. In a last chorus of movement, they drew roses from their shirts and with a shout of "Milady!" threw them to the girls who most caught their eye. (Beatrix found herself with enough roses to plant a garden.)

Agatha watched all this, seasick. But then she saw Sophie, heart in throat, longing for her own rose.

In the decayed pews, the villains booed the princes, brandishing banners with "NEVERS RULE!" and "EVERS

STINK!" (Except for weasel-faced Hort, who crossed his arms sulkily and mumbled, "Why do they get their own entrance?") With a bow, the princes blew kisses to villains and prepared to take their seats when the west doors suddenly slammed open again—

And one more walked in.

Hair a halo of celestial gold, eyes blue as a cloudless sky, skin the color of hot desert sand, he glistened with a noble sheen, as if his blood ran purer than the rest. The stranger took one look at the frowning, sword-armed boys, pulled his own sword . . . and grinned.

Forty boys came at him at once, but he disarmed each with lightning speed. The swords of his classmates piled up beneath his feet as he flicked them away without inflicting a scratch. Sophie gaped, bewitched. Agatha hoped he'd impale himself. But no such luck, for the boy dismissed each new challenge as quickly as it came, the embroidered *T* on his blue tie glinting with each dance of his blade. And when the last had been left swordless and dumbstruck, he sheathed his own sword and shrugged, as if to say he meant nothing by it at all. But the boys of Good knew what it meant. The princes now had a king. (Even the villains couldn't find reason to boo.)

Meanwhile, the Good girls had long learned that every true princess finds a prince, so no need to fight each other. But they forgot all this when the golden boy pulled a rose from his shirt. All of them jumped up, waving kerchiefs, jostling like geese at a feeding. The boy smiled and lofted his rose high in the air—

Agatha saw Sophie move too late. She ran after her but Sophie dashed into the aisle, leapt over the pink pews, lunged for the rose—and caught a wolf instead.

As it dragged Sophie back to her side, she locked eyes with the boy, who took in her fair face, then her horrid black robes and cocked his head, baffled. Then he saw Agatha agog in pink, his rose plopped in her open palm, and recoiled in shock. As the wolf dumped Sophie with Evil and fairies shoved Agatha with Good, the boy gawked wide-eyed, trying to make sense of it all. Then a hand pulled him into a seat.

"Hi. I'm Beatrix," she said, and made sure he saw all of her roses.

From the Evil seats, Sophie tried to get his attention.

"Turn yourself into a mirror. Then you'll have a chance."

Sophie turned to Hester, sitting next to her.

"His name is Tedros," her roommate said. "And he's just as stuck-up as his father."

Sophie was about to ask who his father was, but then glimpsed his sword, dazzling silver, with a hilt of diamonds. A sword with a lion crest she knew from storybooks. A sword named Excalibur.

"He's King Arthur's son?" Sophie breathed. She studied Tedros' high cheekbones, silky blond hair, and thick, tender lips. His broad shoulders and strong arms filled out his blue shirt, tie loosened and collar undone. He looked so serene and assured, as if he knew destiny was on his side.

Gazing at him, Sophie felt her own destiny lock into place.

He's mine.

Suddenly she felt a hot glare across the aisle.

"We're going home," Agatha mouthed clearly.

"Welcome to the School for Good and Evil," said the nicer of the two heads.

From their seats on opposite sides of the aisle, Sophie and Agatha tracked the massive dog with two heads attached to a single body, pacing across a silver stone stage, cracked down the middle. One head was rabid, drooling, and male, with a grizzly mane. The other head was cuddly and cute, with a weak jaw, scanty fur, and singsong voice. No one was sure if the cuter head was male or female, but whatever it was, it seemed to be in charge.

"I'm Pollux, Welcoming Leader," said the nice head.

"AND I'M CASTOR, WELCOMING LEADER ASSISTANT AND EXECUTIVE EXECUTIONER OF PUNISHMENT FOR ANYONE WHO BREAKS RULES OR ACTS LIKE A DONKEY," the rabid one boomed.

All the children looked scared of Castor. Even the villains.

"Thank you, Castor," said Pollux. "So let me first remind you why it is you're here. All children are born with souls that are either Good or Evil. Some souls are purer than others—"

"AND SOME SOULS ARE CRAP!" Castor barked.

"As I was *saying*," said Pollux, "some souls are purer than others, but all souls are fundamentally Good *or* Evil. Those who are Evil cannot make their souls Good, and those who are Good cannot make their souls Evil—"

"SO JUST 'CAUSE GOOD IS WINNING EVERY-
THING DOESN'T MEAN YOU CAN SWITCH SIDES,"
snarled Castor.

The Good students cheered, "EVERS! EVERS!"; Evil students retorted, "NEVERS! NEVERS!" before wolves doused
Evers with water buckets, fairies cast rainbows over the Nevers, and both sides shut up.

"Once again," said Pollux tightly, "those who are Evil cannot be good and those who are Good cannot be Evil, no matter
how much you're persuaded or punished. Now sometimes you
may feel the stirrings of both but this just means your family
tree has branches where Good and Evil have toxically mixed.
But here at the School for Good and Evil, we will rid you of
stirrings, we will rid you of confusion, we will try to make you
as pure as possible—"

"AND IF YOU FAIL, THEN SOMETHING SO BAD
WILL HAPPEN TO YOU THAT I CAN'T SAY, BUT IT
INVOLVES YOU NEVER BEING SEEN AGAIN!"

"One more and it's the muzzle!" Pollux yelled. Castor
stared at his toes.

"None of these brilliant students will fail, I'm sure," Pollux
smiled at the relieved children.

"You say that every time and then someone fails," Castor
mumbled.

Sophie remembered Bane's scared face on the wall and
shuddered. She had to get to Good soon.

"Every child in the Endless Woods dreams of being picked
to attend our school. But the School Master chose you," said

Pollux, scanning both sides. "For he looked into your hearts and saw something very rare. Pure Good and Pure Evil."

"If we're so pure, then what's that?"

An impish blond boy with spiky ears stood from Evil and pointed to Sophie.

A burly boy from Good pointed to Agatha. "We have one too!"

"Ours smells like flowers!" yelled a villain.

"Ours ate a fairy!"

"Ours smiles too much!"

"Ours farted in our face!"

Sophie turned to Agatha, aghast.

"Every class, we bring two Readers here from the Woods Beyond," Pollux declared. "They may know our world from pictures and books, but they know our rules just as well as you. They have the same talents and goals, the same potential for glory. And they too have been some of our finest students."

"Like two hundred years ago," Castor snorted.

"They are no different than the rest of you," Pollux said defensively.

"They look different than the rest of us," cracked an oily, brown-skinned villain.

Students from both schools murmured in agreement. Sophie stared down Agatha, as if to say this could all be solved with a simple costume change.

"Do not question the School Master's selections," said Pollux. "All of you will *respect* each other, whether you're Good or Evil, whether you're from a famous tale family or a failed one, whether you're a sired prince or a Reader. All of you are chosen to protect the balance between Good and Evil. For once that balance is compromised . . ." His face darkened. "Our world will *perish*."

A hush fell over the hall. Agatha grimaced. The last thing she needed was this world perishing while they were still in it.

Castor raised his paw. "What," Pollux groaned.

"Why doesn't Evil win anymore?"

Pollux looked like he was about to bite his head off, but it was too late. The villains were rumbling.

"Yeah, if we're so balanced," yelled Hort, "why do we always *die*?"

"We never get good weapons!" shouted the impish boy.

"Our henchmen betray us!"

"Our Nemesis always has an army!"

Hester stood. "Evil hasn't won in *two hundred years*!"

Castor tried to control himself, but his red face swelled like a balloon. "GOOD IS CHEATING!"

Nevers leapt up in mutiny, hurling food, shoes, and anything else at hand at horrified Evers—

Sophie slunk down in her seat. Tedros couldn't possibly think she was one of these ugly hooligans, could he? She peeked over the bench and caught him staring right at her. Sophie pinked and ducked back down.

Wolves and fairies pounced on the angry horde around her, but this time rainbows and water couldn't stop them.

"The School Master's on their side!" Hester screamed.

"We don't even have a chance!" howled Hort.

The Nevers fought past fairies and wolves, and charged the Evers' pews—

"It's because you're idiotic *apes*!"

The villains looked up dumbly.

"Now sit down before I give all of you a slap!" shrieked Pollux.

They sat without argument. (Except Anadil's rats, who peeked from her pocket and hissed.)

Pollux scowled down at the villains. "Maybe if you stopped complaining, you'd produce someone of consequence! But all we hear is excuse after excuse. Have you produced one decent villain since the Great War? One villain capable of defeating their Nemesis? No wonder Readers come here confused! No wonder they want to be Good!"

Sophie saw kids on both sides of the aisle sneak her sympathetic glances.

"Students, all of you have only one concern here," Pollux said, softening. "Do the best work you can. The finest of you will become princes and warlocks, knights and witches, queens and sorcerers—"

"OR A TROLL OR PIG IF YOU STINK!" Castor spat.

Students glanced at each other across the aisle, sensing the high stakes.

"So if there are no further interruptions," Pollux said, glowering at his brother, "let's review the rules."

"Rule thirteen. Halfway Bridge and tower roofs are *forbidden* to students," Pollux lectured onstage. "The gargoyles have orders to kill intruders on sight and have yet to grasp the difference between students and intruders—"

Sophie found all of this dull, so she tuned out and stared at Tedros instead. She had never seen a boy so *clean*. Boys in Gavaldon smelled like hogs and slopped around with chapped lips, yellow teeth, and black nails. But Tedros had heavenly tan skin, dabbed with light stubble, and no hint (no chance!) of a blemish. Even after the vigorous swordfight, every last gold hair fell in place. When he licked his lips, white teeth gleamed through in perfect rows. Sophie watched a trickle of sweat crisscross his neck and vanish beneath his shirt. *What does he smell like?* She closed her eyes. *Like fresh wood and—*

She opened her eyes and saw Beatrix subtly sniffing Tedros' hair.

This girl needed to be dealt with immediately.

A headless bird landed in Sophie's dress. She jumped on her seat, screaming and shaking her tunic until the dead canary plopped to the floor. She recognized the bird with a frown—then noticed the entire hall gaping at her. She gave her best princess curtsy and sat back down.

"As I was saying," Pollux said testily.

Sophie whipped to Agatha. "What!" she mouthed.

"We need to meet," Agatha mouthed back.

"My *clothes*," Sophie mouthed, and turned back to the stage.

Hester and Anadil looked at the decapitated bird, then at Agatha.

"Her we like," Anadil quipped, rats squeaking in agreement.

"Your first year will consist of required courses to prepare you for three major tests: the Trial by Tale, the Circus of Talents, and the Snow Ball," Castor growled. "After the first year, you will be divided into three tracks: one for villain and hero Leaders, one for henchmen and helper Followers, and one for Mogrifs, or those that will undergo transformation."

"For the next two years, Leaders will train to fight their future Nemeses," Pollux said. "Followers will develop skills to defend their future Leaders. Mogrifs will learn to adapt to their new forms and survive in the treacherous Woods. Finally, after the third year, Leaders will be paired with Followers and Mogrifs and you will all move into the Endless Woods to begin your journeys . . ."

Sophie tried to pay attention but couldn't with Beatrix practically in Tedros' lap. Fuming, Sophie picked at the glittering silver swan crest stitched on her smelly smock. It was the only tolerable thing about it.

"Now as to how we determine your future tracks, we do not give 'marks' here at the School for Good and Evil," said Pollux. "Instead, for every test or challenge, you will be ranked within your classes so you know exactly where you stand. There are 120 students in each school and we have divided you into six groups of 20 for your classes. After each challenge, you will be ranked from 1 to 20. If you are ranked in the top five in your group consistently, you will end up on the Leader track. If you score in the midrange repeatedly, you'll end up a Follower. And if you're consistently below a 13, then your talents will be best served as a Mogrif, either animal or plant."

Students on both aisles murmured, already placing bets on who would end up a tumbo tree.

"I must add that anyone who receives three 20s in a row will immediately be failed," said Pollux gravely. "As I said, given the exceptional incompetence required to earn three straight last-place ranks, I am confident this rule will not apply to any of you."

The Nevers in her row threw Sophie a look.

"When they put me where I belong, you'll all feel foolish, won't you?" Sophie shot back.

"Your swan crest will be visible on your heart at all times," Pollux continued. "Any attempt to conceal or remove it will likely result in injury or embarrassment, so please refrain."

Confused, Sophie watched students on both sides trying to cover the glittering silver swans on their uniforms. Mimicking them, she folded the droopy collar of her tunic to obscure her own swan—instantly the crest vanished off the robe and appeared on her chest. Stunned, she ran her finger over the swan, but it was embedded in her skin like a tattoo. She released the fold and the swan vanished off her skin and reappeared on the robe. Sophie frowned. Perhaps not so tolerable after all.

"Furthermore, as the Theater of Tales is in Good this year, Nevers will be escorted here for all joint school functions," said Pollux. "Otherwise, you must remain in your schools at all times."

"Why is the Theater in Good?" Dot hollered through a mouthful of fudge.

Pollux raised his nose. "Whoever wins the Circus of

Talents gets the Theater in *their* school."

"And Good hasn't lost a Circus or Trial by Tale or, now that I think about it, *any* competition at this school for the last *two hundred years*," Castor harrumphed. Villains started rumbling again.

"But Good is so *far* from Evil!" Dot huffed.

"Heaven forbid she has to walk," Sophie mumbled. Dot heard and glowered at her. Sophie cursed herself. The only person who was civil to her and she had to ruin it.

Pollux ignored the Nevers' grumbles and droned on about curfew times, lulling half the room to sleep. Reena raised her hand. "Are Groom Rooms open yet?"

All of a sudden the Evers looked awake.

"Well, I was planning to discuss Groom Rooms next assembly," Pollux said—

"Is it true that only certain kids can use them?" asked Millicent.

Pollux sighed. "Groom Rooms in the Good Towers are only available to Evers ranked in the top half of their class on any given day. Rankings will be posted on the Groom Room doors and throughout the castle. Please do not abuse Albemarle if he's behind on posting them. Now as to curfew rules—"

"What are Groom Rooms?" Sophie whispered to Hester.

"Where Evers primp, preen, and get their hair done," Hester shuddered.

Sophie sprang up. "Do we have Groom Rooms?"

Pollux pursed his lips. "Nevers have Doom Rooms, dear."

"Where we get our hair done?" Sophie beamed.

"Where you're beaten and tortured," Pollux said.

Sophie sat down.

"Now curfew will occur at precisely—"

"How do you become Class Captain?" Hester asked. The question and the presumptuous tone behind it instantly made her unpopular on both sides of the aisle.

"If you all flunk curfew inspections, don't blame me!" Pollux groaned. "All right. After the Trial by Tale, the top-ranked students in each school will be named Class Captain. These two students will have special privileges, including private study with select faculty, field trips into the Endless Woods, and the chance to train with renowned heroes and villains. As you know, our Captains have gone on to be some of the greatest legends in the Endless Woods."

While both sides buzzed, Sophie gritted her teeth. She knew if she could just get to the right school, she'd not only be Good's Captain, she'd end up more famous than Snow White.

"This year you will have six required classes in your individual schools," Pollux went on. "The seventh class, Surviving Fairy Tales, will include both Good and Evil and takes place in the Blue Forest behind the schools. Also please note, both Beautification and Etiquette are for Good girls only, while Good boys will have Grooming and Chivalry instead."

Agatha woke from her stupor. If she didn't have enough reasons to escape, the thought of a Beautification class was the last straw. They had to get out of here *tonight*. She turned to an adorable girl next to her, with narrow brown eyes and short black hair, fixing her lipstick in a pocket mirror.

THE SCHOOL FOR GOOD AND EVIL

"Mind if I borrow your lipstick?" Agatha asked.

The girl took one look at Agatha's ashy, cracked lips and thrust it at her. "Keep it."

"Breakfast and supper will take place in your school supper halls, but you'll all eat lunch together in the Clearing," Castor grunted. "That is, if you're *mature* enough to handle the privilege."

Sophie felt her heart race. If the schools ate their lunches together, tomorrow would be her first chance to talk to Tedros. What would she say to him? And how would she get rid of that beastly Beatrix?

"The Endless Woods beyond the school gates are barred to first-year students," said Pollux. "And though that rule may fall on deaf ears for the most adventurous of you, let me remind you of the most important rule of all. One that will cost you your lives if you fail to obey."

Sophie snapped to attention.

"*Never go into the Woods after dark,*" said Pollux.

His cuddly smile returned. "You may return to your schools! Supper is at seven o'clock sharp!"

As Sophie rose with the Nevers, mentally rehearsing her lunch meeting with Tedros, a voice ripped through the chatter—

"How do we see the School Master?"

The hall went dead silent. Students turned, shell-shocked.

Agatha stood alone in the aisle, glaring up at Castor and Pollux.

The twin-headed dog jumped off the stage and landed a

foot from her, splashing her with drool. Both heads glared into Agatha's eyes, wearing the same ferocious expression. It wasn't clear who was who.

"*You don't*," they growled.

As fairies whisked flailing Agatha to the east door, she passed Sophie for an instant, just long enough to thrust out a rose petal marred by a lipstick message: "BRIDGE, 9 PM."

But Sophie never saw it. Her eyes were locked on Tedros, a hunter stalking its prey, until she was shoved from the hall by villains.

Right then and there, the problem smashed Agatha in the face. The one that had plagued them all along. For as the two girls were pulled to their opposing towers, their opposing desires couldn't have been clearer. Agatha wanted her only friend back. But a friend wasn't enough for Sophie. Sophie had always wanted more.

Sophie wanted a prince.

6

Definitely Evil

The next morning, fifty princesses dashed about the fifth floor as if it was their wedding day. On the first day of class, they all wanted to make their best impressions on teachers, boys, and anyone else who might lead them to Ever After. Swans twinkling on nightgowns, they flurried into each other's rooms, glossing lips, poofing hair, buffing nails, and trailing so much perfume that fairies passed out and littered the hall like dead flies. Still no one seemed any closer to being dressed, and indeed, when the clock tolled 8:00 a.m.,

signaling the start of breakfast, not a single girl had put on her clothes.

"Breakfast makes you fat anyway," Beatrix reassured.

Reena poked her head into the hall. "Has anyone seen my panties!"

Agatha certainly hadn't. She was free-falling through a dark chute, trying to remember how she found Halfway Bridge the first time. *Honor Tower to Hansel's Haven to Merlin's Menagerie . . .*

After landing on the beanstalk, she crept through the dim Gallery of Good, until she found the doors behind the stuffed bears. *Or was it Honor Tower to Cinderella Commons . . .* Still mulling the correct route, she threw open the doors to the stair room and ducked. The palatial glass lobby was packed with faculty in their colorful dresses and suits, mingling before class. Neon-haired nymphs in pink gowns, white veils, and blue lace gloves floated about the foyer, refilling teacups, frosting biscuits, and flicking fairies off sugar cubes. From behind the doors, Agatha peeked at the stairs marked HONOR, lit by high stained glass windows, far across the crowd. How could she get past them all?

She felt something scrape her leg and turned to find a mouse gnawing her petticoat. Agatha kicked the mouse away, which tumbled into the paws of a stuffed cat. The mouse screeched, then saw the cat was dead. It gave Agatha its dirtiest look and marched back into its hole in the wall.

Even the vermin here hate me, she sighed as she tried to salvage her petticoat. Her fingers stopped as they ran over the torn white lace. Perhaps she shouldn't have been so hard on that mouse. . . .

A few moments later, an undersized nymph in a ragged lace veil scurried through the room for the Honor stairs. Unfortunately the veil left Agatha blind and she tripped into a nymph, who crashed into a teacher—"Heavens Saint Mary!" Clarissa moaned, dripping with prune tea. As alarmed professors dabbed at her dress, Agatha slid behind the Charity steps.

"Those nymphs really are too tall," Clarissa scolded. "Next thing you know they'll knock down a tower!"

By then, Agatha had already disappeared into Honor Tower and found her way up to Hansel's Haven, the wing of first-floor classrooms made completely out of candy. There was a room of sparkled blue swizzles and rock sugar, glittering like a salt mine. There was a marshmallow room with white fudge chairs and gingerbread desks. There was even a room made of lollipops, blanketing the walls in rainbow colors. Agatha wondered how in the world these rooms stayed intact and then saw an inscription sweeping the corridor wall in cherry gumdrops:

TEMPTATION IS THE PATH TO EVIL

Agatha ate half of it before she hustled by two passing teachers, who gave her veil a curious look but didn't stop her.

"Must be spots," she heard one whisper as she raced up the back stairs (but not before stealing a caramel doorknob and butterscotch welcome mat to complete her heavenly breakfast).

When she ran from the fairies the day before, Agatha had

stumbled into the rooftop topiary by accident. Today, she could appreciate Merlin's Menagerie, as the school map named it, filled with magnificently sculpted hedges that told the legend of King Arthur in sequence. Each hedge celebrated a scene from the king's life: Arthur pulling the sword from the stone, Arthur with his knights at the Round Table, Arthur at the wedding altar with Guinevere. . . .

Agatha thought of that pompous boy from the Theater, the one everyone said was King Arthur's son. How could he see this and not feel suffocated? How could he survive the comparisons, the expectations? At least he had beauty on his side. *Imagine if he looked like me*, she snorted. *They'd have dumped the baby in the woods.*

The final sculpture in the sequence was the one with the pond, a towering statue of Arthur receiving Excalibur from the Lady of the Lake. This time Agatha jumped into its water on purpose and fell through the secret portal, completely dry, onto Halfway Bridge.

She hurried towards the midpoint, where the fog began, palms extended in case the barrier came earlier than she remembered. But as she entered the mist, her hands couldn't find it. She moved deeper into fog. *It's gone!* Agatha broke into a run, wind whipping the veil off her face—

BAM! She stumbled back, exploding with pain. Apparently the barrier moved where it wanted.

Avoiding her reflection in its sheen, she touched the invisible wall and felt its cold, hard surface. Suddenly she noticed movement through the fog and saw two people step through

Evil's archway onto Halfway Bridge. Agatha froze. She had no time to get back to Good, nowhere on the Bridge to hide. . . .

Two teachers, the handsome Good professor who had smiled at her and an Evil one with boils on both cheeks, walked across the Bridge and through the barrier without the slightest hesitation. Dangling from the stone rail high over the moat, Agatha listened to them pass, then peeked over the rail edge. The two teachers were about to disappear into Good when the handsome man looked back and smiled. Agatha ducked.

"What is it, August?" she heard the Evil teacher ask.

"My eyes playing tricks on me," he chuckled as they entered the towers.

Definitely a crackpot, Agatha thought.

Moments later, she was in front of the invisible wall once more. How had they passed? She searched for an edge but couldn't find one. She tried kicking it, but it was hard as steel. Peering up into the School for Evil, Agatha could see wolves herding students down stairs. She would be in plain sight if the fog thinned even slightly. Giving the wall a last kick, she retreated to Good.

"And don't come back!"

Agatha spun around to see who had spoken, but all she found was her reflection in the barrier, arms folded. She averted her eyes. *Now I'm hearing things. Lovely.*

She turned towards the tower and noticed her own arms hanging by her sides. She whirled to face her reflection. "Did you just speak?"

Her reflection cleared its throat.

"Good with Good,
Evil with Evil,
Back to your tower before there's upheaval."

"Um, I need to get through," Agatha said, eyes glued to the ground.

"Good with Good,
Evil with Evil,
Back to your tower before there's serious *upheaval,*
meaning cleaning plates after supper or losing your Groom
Room privileges or both if I have anything to say about it."

"I need to see a friend," Agatha pressed.

"Good has no friends on the other side," her reflection said.

Agatha heard sugary ringing and turned to see the glow of fairies at the end of the Bridge. How could she outwit herself? How could she find the chink in her own armor?

Good with Good . . . Evil with Evil . . .

In a flash, she knew the answer.

"How about you?" Agatha said, still looking away. "Do you have any friends?"

Her reflection tensed. "I don't know. Do I?"

Agatha gritted her teeth and met her own eyes. "You're too ugly to have friends."

Her reflection turned sad. *"Definitely Evil,"* it said, and vanished.

Agatha reached out her hand to touch the barrier. This time it went straight through.

By the time the fairy patrol made it onto the Bridge, the fog had erased her tracks.

The moment Agatha stepped foot into Evil, she had the feeling this was where she belonged. Crouched behind the statue of a bald, bony witch in the leaky foyer, she scanned across cracked ceilings, singed walls, serpentine staircases, shadow-masked halls. . . . She couldn't have designed it better herself.

With the coast clear of wolves, Agatha snuck through the main corridor, soaking in the portraits of villainous alumni. She had always found villains more exciting than heroes. They had ambition, *passion*. They made the stories happen. Villains didn't fear death. No, they wrapped themselves in death like suits of armor! As she inhaled the school's graveyard smell, Agatha felt her blood rush. For like all villains, death didn't scare her. It made her feel *alive*.

She suddenly heard chatter and shrank behind a wall. A wolf came into view, leading a group of Nevergirls down the Vice staircase. Agatha heard them twitter about their first classes, catching the words "Henchmen," "Curses," "Uglification." How could these kids be any uglier? Agatha felt the blush of shame. Looking at this parade of sallow bodies and repugnant faces, she knew she fit right in. Even their frumpy black smocks were just like the one she wore every day back home. But there was a difference between her and these villains. Their mouths twisted with bitterness, their eyes flickered with hate, their fists curled with pent-up rage. They were wicked, no doubt, and Agatha didn't feel wicked at all. But then she remembered Sophie's words.

Different usually turns out Evil.

Panic gripped her throat. *That's why the shadow didn't kidnap a second child.*

I was meant to be here all along.

Tears stung her eyes. She didn't want to be like these children! She didn't want to be a villain! She wanted to find her friend and go home!

With no clue where to even look, Agatha hurtled up a staircase marked MISCHIEF to the landing, which split in two scraggy stone paths. She heard voices from the left, so she dashed right, down a short hall to a dead end of sooty walls. Agatha backed against one, petrified by voices growing louder, then felt something creak behind her. It wasn't a wall but a door blanketed in ash. Her dress had wiped enough clean to reveal red letters:

THE EXHIBITION OF EVIL

It was pitch-dark inside. Coughing on must and cobwebs, Agatha lit a match. Where Good's gallery was pristine and vast, Evil's sparse broom closet reflected their two-hundred-year losing streak. Agatha examined the faded uniform of a boy who became Rumpelstiltskin, a broken-framed essay on "Morality of Murder" by a future witch, a few stuffed crows hanging off crumbled walls, and a rotted vine of thorns that blinded a famous prince, labeled VERA OF WOODS BEYOND. Agatha had seen her face on Missing posters in Gavaldon.

Shuddering, she noticed flecks of color on the wall and held her match to it. It was a panel in a mural, like the one of Ever After in the Good Towers. Each of the eight panels showed a black-robed villain reveling in an inferno of infinite power— flying through fire, transmuting in body, fracturing in soul, manipulating space and time. At the top of the mural, stretching from the first panel to last, were giant letters set aflame:

NEVERMORE

Where Evers dreamt of love and happiness, the Nevers sought a world of solitude and power. As the sinister visions sent thrills through her heart, Agatha felt the shock of truth.

I'm a Never.

Her best friend was an Ever. If they didn't get home soon, Sophie would see the truth. Here they couldn't be friends.

She saw a snouted shadow move into her match light. Two shadows. Three. Just as the wolves pounced, Agatha wheeled and whipped Vera's thorns across their faces. The wolves roared in surprise and stumbled back, giving her just enough time to scramble to the door. Breathless, she dashed down the hall, up the stairs, until she found herself on Malice Hall's second floor, hunting for Sophie's name on the dormitory doors—Vex & Brone, Hort & Ravan, Flynt & Titan—*Boys' floor!*

Just as she heard a door open, she sprinted up the back

stairs to a dead-end attic filled with murky vials of frog's toes, lizard legs, dog tongues. (Her mother was right. Who knew *how* long these had been sitting here.) She heard a wolf slobbering up the steps—

Agatha climbed out the attic window onto the soaring roof and clung to the rain gutter. Thunder detonated from black clouds, while across the lake, the Good Towers twinkled in perfect sunshine. As the storm drenched her pink dress, her eyes followed the long, twisted gutter, shooting water through the mouths of three stone gargoyles that held up its brass beams. It was her only hope. She climbed into the gutter, hands struggling to keep grip on the slippery rails, and craned back to the window, knowing the white wolf was coming—

But he wasn't. He stared at her through the window, hairy arms folded over red jacket.

"There are worse things than wolves, you know."

He walked away, leaving her agape.

What? What could possibly be worse than—

Something moved in the rain.

Agatha shielded her eyes and peered through the sparkling blur to see the first stone gargoyle yawn and spread his dragon wings. Then the second gargoyle, with a snake's head and lion's trunk, stretched his with a gunshot crack. Then the third, twice as big as the others, with a horned demon head, man's torso, and studded tail, thrust out jagged wings wider than the tower.

Agatha blanched. *Gargoyles! What did the dog say about gargoyles!*

Their eyes turned to her, viciously red, and she remembered. *Orders to kill.*

With a collective shriek, they leapt off their perches. Without their support, the gutter collapsed and she plunged into its water with a scream. The tidal wave of rain slammed her through harrowing turns and drops as the loose beam lurched wildly in the rain. Agatha saw two gargoyles swoop for her and she swerved in the gutter slide just in time. The third, the horned demon, rose up high and blasted fire from its nose. Agatha grabbed onto the rails and the fireball hit in front of her, searing a giant hole in the beam—she skidded short just before she plummeted through. A crushing force tackled her from behind and the dragon-winged gargoyle grabbed her leg in his sharp talons and hoisted her into the air.

"I'm a *student*!" Agatha screamed.

The gargoyle dropped her, startled.

"See!" Agatha cried, pointing at her face. "I'm a *Never*!"

Sweeping down, the gargoyle studied her face to see if this was true.

It grabbed her by the throat to say it wasn't.

Agatha screamed and stabbed her foot into the burnt hole, deflecting rushing water into the monster's eye. It stumbled blindly, claws flailing for her, only to fall through the hole and shatter its wing on the balcony below. Agatha held onto the rails for life, fighting terrible pain in her leg. But through the water, she saw another one coming. With an ear-piercing screech, the snake-headed gargoyle tore through the flood and snatched her into the air. Just as its massive jaws yawned to devour her,

Agatha thrust her foot between its teeth, which smashed down on her hard black clump and snapped like matchsticks. Dazed, the monster dropped her. Agatha crash-landed in the flooding gutter and gripped the rail.

"*Help!*" she screamed. If she held on, someone would hear and rescue her. "*Helll—*"

Her hands slipped. She careened down eaves, jerking and heaving towards the last spout, where the biggest gargoyle waited, horned like the devil, jaws wide over the spout like an infernal tunnel. Clawing, gurgling, Agatha tried to stop herself, but the rain bashed her along in gushing bursts. She looked down and saw the gargoyle blast fire from its nose, which rocketed across the pipe. Agatha ducked underwater to avoid instant cremation and bobbed back up, clinging to the rail's edge above the final drop. The next rush of rain would send her right into the gargoyle's open mouth.

Then she remembered the gargoyles when she first saw them: guarding the gutter, spewing rain from their mouths.

What goes out must come in.

She heard the next wave coming behind her. With a silent prayer, Agatha let go and fell into the demon's smoking jaws. Just as fire and teeth skewered her, rain smashed through the spout behind her, shooting her through the hole in the gargoyle's throat and out into the gray sky. She glanced back at the choking gargoyle and let out a scream of relief, which turned to terror as she free-fell. Through the fog, Agatha glimpsed a spiked wall about to impale her, and an open window beneath it. She curled into a desperate ball, just missed the lethal blades, and crashed on her stomach, dripping wet, and coughing up water on the sixth floor of Malice Hall.

"I—thought—gargoyles—were—decoration," she wheezed.

Clutching her leg, Agatha limped down the dorm hall, hunting for signs of Sophie.

Just as she was about to start pounding on doors, she caught sight of one at the end of the hall, grafittied with a caricature of a blond princess, splashed with painted slurs: LOSER, READER, EVER LOVER.

Agatha knocked hard. "Sophie! It's me!"

Doors started opening at the other end of the hall.

Agatha pounded harder. *"Sophie!"*

Black-robed girls started emerging from their rooms. Agatha jiggled Sophie's door handle and shoved against the frame, but it wouldn't budge. Just as the Nevergirls turned, poised to discover the intruder in pink, Agatha took a running start, threw herself against the defaced door of Room 66, which swung open and slammed shut behind her.

"YOU HAVE *NO IDEA* WHAT I WENT THROUGH TO GET HE—" She stopped.

Sophie was crouched over a puddle of water on the floor, singing as she applied blush in her reflection.

> *"I'm a pretty princess, sweet as a pea,*
> *Waiting for my prince to marry me. . . ."*

Three bunk mates and three rats watched from across the room, mouths open in shock.

Hester looked up at Agatha. "She flooded our floor."

"To do her makeup," said Anadil.

"Whoever heard of anything so evil?" Dot grimaced. "Song included."

"Is my face even?" Sophie said, squinting into the puddle. "I can't go to class looking like a clown." Her eyes shifted. "Agatha, *darling*! About time you came to your senses. Your Uglification class starts in two minutes and you don't want to make a poor first impression."

Agatha stared at her.

"Of course," Sophie said, standing up. "We have to switch clothes first. Come, off they go."

"You're not going to class, *darling*," Agatha said, turning red. "We're going to the School Master's tower right now before we're stuck here forever!"

"Don't be a boob," said Sophie, tugging at Agatha's dress. "We can't just break into some tower in broad daylight. And if you're going home anyway, you should give me your clothes now so I don't miss any assignments."

Agatha wrenched away. "Okay, that's *it*! Now listen to—"

"You'll blend right in here," Sophie smiled, studying Agatha next to her roommates.

Agatha lost her fire. "Because I'm . . . ugly?"

"Oh, for goodness' sakes, Aggie, look at this place," Sophie said. "You *like* gloom and doom. You *like* suffering and unhappiness and, um . . . burnt things. You'll be *happy* here."

"We agree," said a voice behind Agatha, and she turned in surprise.

"You come live here," Hester said to her—

"And she drowns in the lake," Dot scowled at Sophie, still wounded by her jibe at the Welcoming.

"We liked you the moment we saw you," Anadil cooed, rats licking Agatha's feet.

"You belong here with us," Hester said, as she, Anadil, and Dot crowded around Agatha, whose head swung nervously between this villainous threesome. Did they really want to be her friend? Was Sophie right? Could being a villain make her . . . *happy?*

Agatha's stomach churned. She didn't want to be Evil! Not when Sophie was Good! They had to get out of this place before it tore them apart!

"I'm not leaving you!" she cried to Sophie, breaking away.

"No one's asking you to leave me, Agatha," Sophie said tightly. "We're just asking you to leave your clothes."

"No!" Agatha shouted. "We're not switching clothes. We're not switching rooms. We're not switching schools!"

Sophie and Hester exchanged furtive glances.

"We're going home!" Agatha said, voice catching. "We can be friends there—on the same side—no Good, no Evil—we'll be happy forev—"

Sophie and Hester tackled her. Dot and Anadil pulled the pink dress off Agatha's body, and the four of them shoved Sophie's black robes on in its place. Shimmying into her new pink dress, Sophie threw open the door. "Goodbye, Evil! Hello, Love!"

Agatha stumbled to her feet and looked down at a putrid

black sack that fit just how she liked.

"And all is right in the world," Hester sighed. "Really, I don't know how you were ever friends with that tram—"

"Get back here!" Agatha yelled, pursuing Sophie in pink through the hall's hordes of black. Shocked by an Ever in their midst, Nevers swarmed around Sophie and started to beat her about the head with books, bags, and shoes—

"No! She's one of us!"

All the Nevers turned to Hort, in the stairwell, including dumbstruck Sophie. Hort pointed at Agatha in black.

"That's the Ever!"

The Nevers unleashed a new war cry and mobbed Agatha as Sophie shoved Hort away and escaped down the stairs. Agatha scraped through the gauntlet with a few well-placed kicks and slid down the banister to cut Sophie off. With Sophie in sight, she tracked her through a tight corridor, reached out her hand to grab her by the pink collar, but Sophie turned a corner, ran up snaking steps, and veered off the first floor. Agatha swerved into a dead end, saw Sophie magically jump through a wall, blood-splattered "NO STUDENTS!" and with a flying leap, Agatha jumped through the portal right after her—

And landed on the Evil end of Halfway Bridge.

But this was where the chase ceased, for Sophie was too far to Good to catch. Through the fog, Agatha could see her glowing with joy.

"Agatha, he's King Arthur's son," Sophie gushed. "A real-life *prince*! But what do I say to him? How do I show him I'm the one?"

Agatha tried to hide her hurt. "You'd leave me here . . . alone?"

Sophie's face softened.

"Please don't worry, Aggie. Everything is perfect now," she said gently. "We'll still be best friends. Just in different schools, like we planned. No one can stop us from being friends, can they?"

Agatha gazed at Sophie's beautiful smile and believed her.

But all of a sudden, her friend's smile vanished. Because on Sophie's body, the pink dress magically rotted to black. Just like that Sophie was in her old, sagging villain robes, swan glittering over her heart. She looked up and gasped. Across the Bridge, Agatha's black robes had shrunk back to pink.

The two girls gaped at each other in shock. Suddenly, shadows swept over Sophie, and Agatha spun. The giant wave swelled high above her, waters curling into a shimmering lasso. Before Agatha could run, it swooped and hurled her across the bay into sunlit mist. Sophie lunged to the Bridge's gloomy edge and let out a wail of injustice.

The wave slowly rose back over her, but this time its waters didn't shimmer. With a belligerent roar, it smashed Sophie back into the School for Evil and right back on schedule.

7

Grand High Witch Ultimate

"Why do we need to uglify?"

Sophie peeked through her fingers at Professor Manley's bald, pimpled head and squash-colored skin, trying not to gag. Around her, Nevers sat at charred desks with rusty mirrors, cheerily bashing tadpoles to death in iron bowls. If she didn't know better, she'd think they were making a Sunday cake.

Why am I still here? she fumed through furious tears.

"Why do we need to be revolting and repugnant?" Manley jowled. "Hester!"

"Because it makes us fearsome," Hester said, and swigged her tadpole juice, instantly springing a rash of red pox.

"Wrong!" roared Manley. "Anadil!"

"Because it makes little boys cry," Anadil said, sprouting her own red blisters.

"Wrong! Dot!"

"Because it's easier to get ready in the morning?" Dot asked, mixing her juice with chocolate.

"Wrong and stupid!" Manley scorned. "Only once you give up the surface can you dig beneath it! Only once you relinquish vanity can you be yourself!"

Sophie crawled behind desks, lunged for the door—the knob burnt her hand and she yelped.

"Only once you destroy who you think you are can you embrace who you *truly* are!" Manley said, glaring right at her.

Whimpering, Sophie crawled back to her desk, past villains exploding in shingles. Smoky-green ranks popped out of thin air around her—"1" over Hester, "2" over Anadil, "3" over oily, brown-skinned Ravan, "4" over blond, pointy-eared Vex. Hort drank his draught excitedly, only to see a wee zit spurt from his chin. He smacked away a stinky "19," but the rank smacked him right back.

"Ugliness means you rely on intelligence," Manley leered, slinking towards Sophie. "Ugliness means you trust your soul. Ugliness means *freedom*."

He flung a bowl onto her desk.

Sophie looked down into black tadpole juice. Some of it was still moving.

"Actually, Professor, I believe my Beautification teacher will object to my participation in this assign—"

"Three failing marks and you'll end up something uglier than me," Manley spat.

Sophie looked up. "I *really* don't think that's possible."

Manley turned to the class. "Who would like to help our dear Sophie taste freedom?"

"Me!"

Sophie whipped around.

"Don't worry," Hort whispered, "you'll look better this way."

Before Sophie could scream, he plunged her head into the bowl.

Lying in a puddle on the banks of Good, Agatha replayed the scene from Evil. Her best friend had called her a boob, flying tackled her, stolen her clothes, left her to witches, and then asked for love advice.

It's this place, she thought. In Gavaldon, Sophie would forget about classes and castles and boys. In Gavaldon, they could find a happy ending together. Not here. *I just need to get us home.*

And yet, something still bothered her. That moment on the Bridge—Sophie in pink against the School for Good, she in black against the School for Evil . . . *"Everything is perfect now,"* Sophie said. And she was right. For a brief moment, the mistake had been corrected. They were where they belonged.

So why couldn't we stay?

Whatever happened, it was a close call. Because once Sophie made it to Good, she'd never leave. Agatha's breath shallowed. She had to make sure the faculty didn't discover the mix-up! She had to make sure they weren't switched to the right schools! But how could she make sure Sophie stayed put?

Go to class, her heart whispered.

Pollux said the schools kept an even number of students to preserve the balance. So for the mistake to be corrected, they *both* would have to be switched. As long as Agatha held her place in the School for Good, then Sophie was stuck in the School for Evil. And if there was one thing she knew for sure, it was that Sophie couldn't possibly last as a villain. A few more days there and she'd *beg* for Gavaldon.

Go to class. Of course!

She would find a way to last at this horrid school and wear Sophie down. For the first time since they were kidnapped, Agatha opened her heart to hope.

Hope died ten minutes later.

Professor Emma Anemone, whistling in a blinding yellow dress and long fox-fur gloves, walked into her pink taffy classroom, took one look at Agatha, and stopped whistling. But then she murmured "Rapunzel took some work too," and launched into her first lesson on "Making Smiles Kinder."

"Now the key is to communicate with your eyes," she chirped, and demonstrated the perfect princess smile. With her bulging eyes and wild yellow hair matching her dress, Agatha thought she looked like a manic canary. But Agatha knew her chances of getting home rested in her hands, so she mimicked her toothy beam with the others.

Professor Anemone walked around surveying the girls. "Not so much squinting . . . A little less nose, dear . . . Oh my, absolutely beautiful!" She was talking about Beatrix, who lit up the room with her dazzling smile. "That, my Evers, is a smile that can win the heart of the steeliest prince. A smile that can broker peace in the greatest of wars. A smile that can lead a kingdom to hope and prosperity!"

Then she saw Agatha. "You there! No smirking!"

With her teacher looming, Agatha tried to concentrate and duplicate Beatrix's perfect smile. For a second she thought she had it.

"Goodness! Now it's a creepy grin! A smile, child! Just your normal, everyday smile!"

Happy. Think of something happy.

But all she could think of was Sophie on the Bridge, leaving her for a boy she didn't even know.

"Now it's positively malevolent!" Professor Anemone shrieked.

Agatha turned and saw the whole class cowering, as if expecting her to turn them all into bats. ("Do you think she eats children?" said Beatrix. "I'm so glad I moved out," Reena sighed.)

Agatha frowned. It couldn't have been *that* bad.

Then she saw Professor Anemone's face.

"If you ever need a man to trust you, if you ever need a man to save you, if you ever need a man to love you, whatever you do, child . . . *don't smile at him.*"

Princess Etiquette, taught by Pollux, was worse. He arrived in a bad mood, hobbling with his massive canine head attached to a skinny goat's carcass and muttering that Castor "has the body this week." He looked up and saw girls staring at him.

"And here I thought I was teaching princesses. All I see are twenty ill-mannered girls gaping like toads. Are you *toads*? Do you like to catch flies with your little pink tongues?"

The girls stopped staring after that.

The first lesson was "Princess Posture," which involved the girls descending the four tower staircases with nests of nightingale eggs on their heads. Though most of the girls succeeded without breaking any eggs, Agatha had a harder time. There were a number of reasons for this: a lifetime of slouching, Beatrix and Reena intently watching her with their new Kinder Smiles, her mind chattering that Sophie would win this with her eyes closed, and the absurdity of a dog barking about posture while teetering on goat legs. In the end, she left twenty eggs bleeding yolk on marble.

"Twenty beautiful nightingales who will not have life . . . because of *you*," said Pollux.

As class ranks appeared over each girl in ethereal gold clouds—Beatrix 1st, of course—Agatha spun to see a rusted "20" hover over, then crash into her head.

Two classes, two last-place ranks. One more and she would learn what happened to children who failed. With her plan to get Sophie home crumbling by the minute, Agatha hurried to her next class, desperate to prove herself Good.

Shingles wouldn't keep Cinderella from the Ball. Shingles wouldn't keep Sleeping Beauty from her kiss.

Staring at her pustuled reflection in her desk mirror, Sophie forced her kindest smile. She had solved every problem in life with beauty and charm and she would solve this one the same way.

Henchmen Training took place in the Belfry, a dreary open-air cloister atop Malice tower that required a thirty-flight ascent up a staircase so narrow the students were squeezed into single file.

"So . . . nauseous," Dot panted like an overheated camel.

"If she pukes near me, I'm throwing her off the tower," Hester crabbed.

As she climbed, Sophie tried not to think about pustules, puke, or putrid Hort, who was trying to cram beside her. "I know you hate me," he pressed. She lurched to the right to block him. Hort tried the left. "But it was the challenge and I didn't want you to fail and—"

Sophie thwarted him with her elbow and raced up the last few steps, desperate to prove to her new teacher she was in the wrong place. Unfortunately that teacher was Castor.

"'COURSE I GET THE READER IN MY GROUP."

Even worse, his assistant, Beezle, was the red-skinned dwarf that Sophie had slapped on the ladder the day before. Upon seeing her blistered face, he giggled like a hyena. "Ugly witch!"

Head off center on his massive dog's body, Castor wasn't as amused. "You're all revolting enough as is," he groused, and sent Beezle to fetch honeysuckle, which promptly restored the villains' faces. While they groaned in disappointment,

Sophie heaved with relief.

"Whether you win or lose your battles depends on the competence and loyalty of your henchmen!" Castor said. "Of course some of you will end up henchmen yourselves, with your own lives depending on the strength of your Leader. Better pay attention then, if you want to stay alive!"

Sophie gritted her teeth. Agatha was probably singing to doves somewhere and here she was about to wrangle bloodthirsty goons.

"And now for your first challenge. How to train . . ." Castor stepped aside. "A *Golden Goose*."

Sophie gaped at an elegant gold-feathered bird behind him, sleeping serenely in its nest.

"But Golden Geese hate villains," Anadil frowned.

"Which means if you can train one, then taming a mountain troll will be easy," Castor said.

The Goose opened its pearly blue eyes, took in its villainous audience, and smiled.

"Why is it smiling?" Dot said.

"Because it knows we're wasting our time," Hester said. "Golden Geese only listen to Evers."

"Excuses, excuses," Castor yawned. "Your job is to make that pathetic creature lay one of its prized eggs. The bigger the egg, the higher your rank."

Sophie's heart raced. If the bird only listened to the Good, she could prove here and now she didn't belong with these monsters! All she had to do was make the Goose lay the biggest egg!

On the Belfry wall, Castor carved five strategies for training henchmen:

1. COMMAND

2. TAUNT

3. TRICK

4. BRIBE

5. BULLY

"Now don't go bullying the blasted bird unless you've gone
through the other four," Castor warned. "Ain't nothin' stopping a henchman from bullying back."

Sophie made sure she was last in line and watched the
first five kids have zero luck, including Vex, who went as far
as grabbing its throat, only to see the Golden Goose smile in
return.

Miraculously, Hort was the first to succeed. He had tried
barking "Lay egg," calling it a "prat," and tempting it with
worms, before giving up and kicking its nest. Wrong thing to
kick. In a flash, the Goose yanked his tunic over his head and
Hort yelped about blindly, banging into walls. (Sophie vowed
if she had to see this boy one more time without clothes, she'd
gouge out her eyes.) But the Goose seemed delighted. It flapped
its wings and sniggered and squawked so raucously that it lost

control and excreted a golden egg the size of a coin.

Hort held it up in stunned triumph. "I won!"

"Right, because in the heat of battle, you'll have time to run around naked and make your Goose crap," Castor snarled.

Still, the dog had said whoever made the biggest egg won, so the other Nevers mimicked Hort's tactic. Dot made faces, Ravan made shadow puppets, Anadil tickled it with a feather, and bald, doughy Brone sat on Beezle, much to the bird's delight. ("Smelly witch!" the dwarf howled.)

Scowling at all this, Hester walked up and punched the Goose in the stomach. It dropped an egg the size of a fist. "Amateurs," she sneered.

Then it was Sophie's turn.

She approached the Golden Goose, which seemed exhausted from laughing and laying. But when the Goose met Sophie's gaze, it stopped blinking and sat still as a statue, studying every inch of her. For a moment, Sophie felt an eerie chill float through her body, as if she'd let a stranger into her soul. But then she looked into the bird's warm, wise eyes and swelled with hope. Surely it saw she was different from the rest.

Yes, you certainly are different.

Sophie backed up. She peeked around to see if anyone else had heard the bird's thoughts. But the rest of the Nevers just glowered impatiently, since she had to finish before they got their ranks.

Sophie turned to the Goose. *You can hear my thoughts?*

They're quite loud, replied the Goose.

What about the others?

No. Just you.

Because I'm Good? Sophie smiled.

I can give you what you want, said the Goose. *I can make them see you're a princess. One perfect egg and they'll put you with your prince.*

Sophie dropped to her knees. *Please! I'll do anything you want. Just help me.*

The bird smiled. *Close your eyes and make a wish.*

Overcome with relief, Sophie closed her eyes. In that shining moment, she wished for Tedros, her beautiful, perfect prince who could make her happy . . .

She suddenly wondered if Agatha told him they were friends. She hoped not.

Gasps flew around her. Sophie opened her eyes and saw the Goose's gold feathers finish turning gray. Its eyes darkened from blue to black. Its warm smile went dead.

And there was definitely no egg.

"What happened!" Sophie twirled. "What's it mean?"

Castor looked petrified. "It means she'd rather give up her power than help you."

A "1" exploded in red flames over Sophie's head like a diabolical crown.

"It's the most evil thing I've ever seen," Castor said softly.

Stunned, Sophie watched her classmates huddle like scared minnows—all except Hester, eyes blazing, as if she'd just found her competition. Behind her, Beezle shivered deep in a dark corner.

"Grand Witch!" he squeaked.

"No no no!" Sophie cried. "Not Grand Witch!"

But Beezle nodded with certainty. "Grand High Witch Ultimate!"

Sophie whipped back to the Goose. *What did I do!*

But the Goose, gray as fog, looked at her as if it had never seen her in its life and let out the most ordinary of squawks.

From the Belfry the squawk echoed across the moat, into the soaring silver tower that split the two sides of the bay. A silhouette appeared at the window and gazed down at his domain.

Dozens of smoky rank numbers—brightly colored ones from Good, dark and gloomy ones from Evil—drifted from the two schools over the waters and wafted up to his window like balloons in the wind. As each one passed, his fingers ran through the smoke, which gave him the power to see whose rank it was and how they had earned it. He sifted through dozens of numbers until he came to the one he sought: a red-flame "1" that revealed its history in a flood of images.

A Golden Goose throwing away its power for a *student?* Only one could have such talent. Only one could be so pure.

The one who would tip the balance.

With a chill, the School Master went back into his tower and awaited her arrival.

Curses & Death Traps took place in a bone-numbing frost chamber, with the walls, desks, and chairs made completely of ice. Sophie thought she could see bodies buried deep beneath the frozen floor.

"Itttt's colllddd," Hort chattered.

"It's warmer in the Doom Room," Lady Lesso replied.

Howls of pain echoed from the dungeon beneath their feet.

"I-I-I feeeel warm-m-er noww," Hort stuttered, face blue.

"Cold will harden your veins," said Lady Lesso. "Which need hardening if a Reader is placing first in challenges." She slunk between rows of shivering students, black braid snapping against her sharp-shouldered purple gown, dagger steel heels cracking on ice.

"This is not a school for unwarranted cruelty. Hurt without reason and you are a beast, not a villain. No, our mission requires focus and care. In this class, you will learn to find the Ever who stands in the way of your goal. The one who will grow stronger as you grow weaker. They're out there, my Nevers, somewhere in the Woods . . . your *Nemesis*. When the time is right, you will find and destroy them. That is your path to freedom."

A scream echoed from the Doom Room and Lady Lesso smiled. "Your other classes may be pageants of ineptitude, but not here. There will be no challenges until I see you are worthy."

Sophie hadn't heard any of this. All she could hear was the Goose's squawk banging around in her head. Convulsing with cold, she fought back tears. She had tried everything to get to Good: fleeing, fighting, pleading, switching, wishing . . . What else was left? She pictured Agatha, sitting in *her* classes, *her* seat, *her* school, and flushed hot red. And she thought they were friends!

"A Nemesis is your archenemy," said Lady Lesso, purple eyes flashing. "Your other half. Your soul's inverse. Your Achilles' heel."

Sophie forced herself to pay attention. After all here was a chance to learn enemy secrets. It might save her once she made it to Good.

"You will come to know your Nemesis through dreams," Lady Lesso went on, veins pulsing under tight skin. "A Nemesis will haunt your sleep, night after night until you see nothing but his or her face. Nemesis Dreams will chill your heart and boil your blood. They will make you gnash your teeth and rip out your hair. For they are the sum of your hate. The sum of your fears."

Lady Lesso dragged her long red nails across Hort's desk. "Only when your Nemesis is dead will you feel quenched. Only when your Nemesis is dead will you feel free. Kill your Nemesis and Nevermore will welcome you to eternal glory!"

The class tittered with excitement.

"Of course, given our school's history, those gates won't open anytime soon," she muttered.

"How do we find our Nemesis?" asked Dot.

"Who chooses them?" asked Hester.

"Will they be from our class?" Ravan asked.

"These questions are premature. Only exceptional villains are blessed with Nemesis Dreams," Lady Lesso said. "No, first you should be asking why stuck-up, stupid, insipid Good wins every competition in this school—and how *you're* going to change that." She leered at Sophie, as if to say, whether she liked it or not, the pink-loving Reader might be their best hope.

As soon as the wolves' howls signaled class was over, Sophie darted from the ice room, up twisting stairs, until she found a small balcony off a hall. In the privacy of fog, she leaned against the damp walls of the Evil tower and finally let herself cry. She didn't care if it ruined her makeup or if anyone saw. She had never felt so alone or scared. She hated this horrible place and couldn't take any more.

Sophie gazed at the School for Good, glass towers glinting across the bay. For the first time, it seemed out of reach.

Lunch!

Tedros would be there! Her shining prince, her last hope! Isn't that what princes were for after all? To rescue princesses when all seemed lost?

Heart swelling, she wiped her tears. *Just make it to lunch.*

As she sprinted to Evil Hall for History of Villainy, Sophie noticed scores of buzzing Nevers crowded outside. Dot saw her and grabbed her arm. "They canceled classes! No one's saying why."

"Lunch will be sent to your rooms!" boomed the white wolf, as fellow wolves cracked whips and drove students to their towers.

Sophie's heart deflated. "But what happ—"

She suddenly smelled smoke, creeping into the hall from every direction. Sophie slid between the shoving mob to a stone window, where a group of students stared in stunned silence. She followed their eyes across the bay.

A Good tower was on fire.

Dot gasped. "Who could have possibly done something so . . ."

"*Brilliant*," Hester said, awestruck.

Well, Agatha had the answer to that.

❦ 8 ❧
Wish Fish

An hour before, Tedros had decided on a swim.

By now, the ranks for the first two classes were up on the Groom Room doors, with the prince and Beatrix tied for first and Agatha's name so low on the board that a pile of mouse droppings obscured it. Inside, the girls' Groom Room resembled a medieval spa, with three aromatic bath pools ("Hot," "Cold," and "Just Right"), a Little Match Girl sauna, three Rose Red makeup stations, a Cinderella-themed pedicure corner, and a waterfall shower built into a Little Mermaid lagoon. The boys' Groom Rooms focused more on fitness, with a Midas Gold sweat lodge, a peasant-themed tanning room, and a gymnasium with Norse hammers, mud wrestling pit, saltwater lap pool, and full array of Turkish baths.

After Chivalry and Grooming, Tedros took advantage of the break before Swordplay to test out the pool. But just as he swam his last lap, he noticed Beatrix—and the seven girls who now followed her incessantly—peering wide-eyed through cracks in the wooden door.

Tedros was used to girls watching him. But when would he find one who saw more than his looks? Who saw more than King Arthur's son? Who cared about his thoughts, his hopes, his fears? And yet here he was, pivoted purposely as he toweled so the girls could have a perfect view. His mother was right. He could pretend all he wanted, but he was just like his father, for better and worse.

With a sigh, he threw open the door to greet his fan club, breeches dripping, swan glittering on bare chest. But they were gone, victims of the fairy patrol. Tedros felt a twinge of disappointment as he turned the corner, only to smash into something, knocking it flat to the ground.

"I'm wet. Again." Agatha frowned and looked up. "You should watch where you're—"

It was the boy who had warped Sophie's mind. The boy who had hijacked Sophie's heart. The boy who had stolen her only friend.

"I'm Tedros," he said, and held out his hand.

Agatha didn't take it. She was hopelessly lost and needed

directions, but this Tedros was the enemy. She pulled herself up, gave him a lethal glare, and shoved past his chest. That's when she noticed, in addition to everything else she hated about this boy, he smelled like one too. She stormed to the end of the hall, clumps thunking ogreishly on glass, and with a last venomous sneer, snatched at the door.

It was locked.

"It's this way." Tedros pointed to the stairwell behind him.

Agatha huffed past him, holding her nose.

"Nice to meet you!" the prince called.

He heard her snort in disgust before she trundled down the steps, casting shadows all the way.

Tedros grimaced. Girls loved him. They always loved him. But this freakish girl looked at him like he was nothing. For a moment, he felt his confidence crack, then remembered what his father once said.

The best villains make you doubt.

Tedros thought he could face down any monster, any witch, any force Evil could conjure. But this girl was different. This girl was scary.

Dread pricked his spine.

So why is she in my school?

Animal Communication, taught by Princess Uma, took place on the lakeside banks of Halfway Bay. For the third time that day, Agatha arrived to find a class was Girls Only. Surely the School for Evil didn't see the need to decide what was a "Boy" skill or "Girl" skill. But here in the Good Towers, the boys went off to fight with swords while girls had to learn dog barks and owl hoots. No wonder princesses were so impotent in fairy tales, she thought. If all they could do was smile, stand straight, and speak to squirrels, then what choice did they have but to wait for a boy to rescue them?

Princess Uma looked far too young to be a teacher. Nestled in prim grass, backlit by lake shimmer, she sat very still, hands folded in her pink dress, with black hair to her waist, olive skin, almond-shaped eyes, and crimson lips pursed in a tight O. When she did speak, it was in a giggly whisper, but she couldn't make it through a full sentence. Every few words, she'd stop to listen to a distant fox or dove and respond with her own giddy howl or chirp. When she realized she had a whole class staring at her, she cupped her hands over her face.

"Oops!" she tee-heed. "I have too many friends!"

Agatha couldn't tell if she was nervous or just an idiot.

"Evil has many weapons on its side," said Princess Uma, finally settling down. "Poisons, plagues, curses, hexes, hench-men, and black, black magic. But you have animals!"

Agatha snickered. When faced with an axe-wielding henchman, she would be sure to bring a butterfly. Judging by the others' faces, she wasn't the only one unconvinced. Princess Uma noticed. The teacher unleashed a piercing whistle and a barrage of barks, bays, neighs, and roars blasted from the Woods beyond the schools. The girls plugged their ears in shock.

"See!" Uma chuckled. "Every animal can talk to you if you know how to talk to them. Some even remember when *they* were human!"

With a chill, Agatha thought of the stuffed animals in the gallery. All former students, just like them.

"I know everyone wants to be a princess," said Uma, "but those of you with low ranks won't make good princesses. You'd end up shot or stabbed or eaten and that's not very useful. But as a sidekick fox or spying sparrow or friendly pig, you might find a much happier ending!"

She squeaked through her teeth, and on cue, an otter bobbed to shore from the lake, balancing a jeweled storybook on its nose. "You might keep a captive maiden company or lead her to safety," Uma said, holding out her hands. The nervous otter bumped the book on his nose to find the right page—

"Or you might help make a ball gown," Uma said, eyeing the bumbling creature. "Or you might deliver an urgent message or—*ahem*!" With a yip, the otter found the page, slid the book into her hands, and collapsed from stress.

"You might even save a life," said Uma, holding up a brilliant painting of a princess cowering as a stag speared a warlock. The princess looked just like her.

"Once upon a time, an animal saved mine and in return, it received the happiest ending of all."

From narrowed suspicion, Agatha saw all the girls' eyes widen to worship. This wasn't just a teacher. This was a living, breathing princess.

"So if you want to be like me, you need to do well in today's challenge!" chirped their new idol, summoning the girls to the lake. Agatha felt herself shiver, despite the balmy fall sun. If she placed last this time, she'd never see Sophie or home again. As she followed the girls to the bank, sick to her stomach, Agatha noticed Uma's storybook, open in the grass.

"Animals love to help princesses for so many reasons!" said Princess Uma, stopping at the water's edge. "Because we sing pretty songs, because we give them shelter in the scary Woods, because they only wish they could be as beautiful and beloved as—"

"Wait."

Uma and the girls turned. Agatha held up the storybook's last page—a painting of the stag ripped to pieces by monsters as the princess escaped.

"How is *that* a happy ending?"

"If you aren't good enough to be a princess, then you're honored to die for one, of course," Uma smiled, as if she would learn this lesson soon enough.

Agatha looked to the others in disbelief, but they were all nodding like sheep. It didn't matter if only a third of them would graduate as princesses. Each was completely convinced she'd be one. No, those stuffed, mounted creatures in the museum weren't once girls like them. They were just animals. Slaves to the Greater Good.

"But if animals are going to help us, first we have to tell them what we want!" Uma said, kneeling before the gleaming blue lake. "So today's challenge is . . ." She swirled her finger in the water and a thousand tiny fish surfaced, white as snow.

"Wish Fish!" Uma beamed. "They dig inside your soul and find your greatest wish! (Very helpful if you've lost your tongue or voice and need to tell a prince to kiss you.) Now all you do

is put your finger in the water and the fish will read your soul. The girl with the strongest, clearest wish wins!"

Agatha wondered what these girls' souls would wish for. Depth, perhaps.

Millicent went first. She put her finger in the water, closed her eyes . . . When she opened them, the fish had all turned different colors and were gaping at her, confused.

"What happened?" said Millicent.

"Foggy mind," Uma sighed.

Then Kiko, the adorable girl who had gifted Agatha lipstick, put her finger in the water. The fish turned red, orange, and peach and started assembling into some kind of picture.

What do Good souls wish for? Agatha wondered, watching the fish jumble into place. *Peace for their kingdoms? Health for their families? Destruction of Evil?*

The fish drew a boy instead.

"Tristan!" Kiko chimed, recognizing his ginger hair. "I caught his rose at the Welcoming."

Agatha groaned. She should have known.

Then Reena dipped her finger and the fish changed colors, gliding into a mosaic of a burly, gray-eyed boy pulling an arrow into his bow.

"Chaddick," blushed Reena. "Honor Tower, Room ten."

Giselle's fish drew dark-skinned Nicholas, Flavia wished for Oliver, Sahara's painted Oliver's bunk mate Bastian. . . . At first Agatha found it dumb, but now it was scary. This was what Good souls craved? Boys they didn't even know? Based on what!

"Love at first sight," Uma gushed. "It's the most beautiful thing in the world!"

Agatha gagged. Who could ever love boys? Preening, useless thugs who thought the world belonged to them. She thought of Tedros and her skin burned. Hate at first sight. Now *that* was believable.

With the fish pooped from drawing so many chiseled jaws, Beatrix provided the grand climax, sending her Wish Fish into a spectacular rainbow vision of her fairy-tale wedding to Tedros, complete with castle, crowns, and fireworks. All around girls' eyes welled with tears, either because the scene was so beautiful or because they knew they could never compete.

"Now you must *hunt* him, Beatrix!" Uma said. "You must make this Tedros your mission! Your obsession! Because when a true princess wants something enough . . ." She swirled her fingers in the lake—

"Your friends unite for you . . ." The fish turned bright pink—

"Fight for you . . ." The fish clustered tight—

"And make your wish come true . . ." Uma reached her arm into the water and pulled it right out. The fish transformed into her soul's greatest desire.

"What is it?" Reena asked, confused.

"A suitcase," whispered Princess Uma, and hugged it to her chest.

She looked up at twenty befuddled girls. "Oh. Should I give you your ranks?"

"But she didn't go yet," said Beatrix, pointing at Agatha. Agatha would have clobbered her, but there was no menace in Beatrix's voice. This girl wasn't troubled that a lakeful of fish had just been turned into luggage. Instead, she was worried Agatha didn't have her turn. Perhaps she wasn't so bad after all.

"So Reena can have her room when she fails," Beatrix smiled.

Agatha took it back.

"Oh dear. One left?" said Uma, staring at Agatha. She gazed at the lake, empty of Wish Fish, then at her precious pink suitcase. "It happens every time," she mourned. With a sigh, she dropped it back into the lake, and watched it sink and bob up as a thousand white fish.

Agatha leaned over the water to see the fish glaring up at her with droopy eyes. For a moment, they had found heaven in a suitcase. But here they were again, genies stolen from the safety of the lamp. They didn't care that her life was on the line. They just wanted to be left alone. Agatha sympathized.

Mine's easy, she thought. *I wish not to fail. That's it. Don't fail.*

She stuck her finger in the water.

The fish started trembling like tulips in the wind. Agatha could hear wishes wrestle in her head—

Don't fail—Home in bed—Don't fail—Sophie safe—Don't fail—Tedros dead—

The fish turned blue, then yellow, then red. Wishes swept into a cyclone—

New face—Same face—Blond hair—I hate blond hair!—More friends—No friends—

"Not just foggy," murmured Princess Uma. "Completely confused!"

The fish, red as blood, started to quake, as if about to explode. Alarmed, Agatha tried to pull out her finger, but the water clamped it like a fist.

"What the—"

The fish turned black as night and flew to Agatha like magnets to metal, pooling her hand in a shivering mass. Girls fled the shore in horror; Uma stood anchored in shock. Frantic, Agatha tried to wrench her hand but her head exploded with pain—

Home School Mom Dad Good Bad Boys Girls Ever Never—

Gripping Agatha's hand, the fish shook harder and harder, faster and faster, until she couldn't tell one from the other. Eyes popped off like buttons, beating fins shattered to bits, bellies engorged with veins and vessels until the fish let out a thousand tortured screams. Agatha felt her head split in two—

Fail Win Truth Lies Lost Found Strong Weak Friend Foe

The fish swelled into a ballooning black mass, creeping up her hand. Agatha thrashed to free her finger until she heard her bone break and yowled in agony as the screaming fish sucked her whole arm into their ebony cocoon.

"Help! Somebody help me!"

The cocoon billowed into her face, suffocating her cries. With a high, sickening shriek, the deathly womb swallowed her. Agatha flailed for breath, tried to kick herself out, but pain seared through her head and forced her into a fetal crouch.

HateLovePunishRewardHunterHuntedLiveDieKillKissTake

Screaming with vengeance, the black cocoon sucked her deeper like a gelatinous grave, stifling her last breaths, leeching her every last drop of life until there was nothing left to—

Give.

The screaming stopped. The cocoon sloughed away.

Agatha fell back in shock.

In her arms was a girl. No more than twelve or thirteen, with toffee skin and a tangle of dark curls. She stirred, opened her eyes, and smiled at Agatha as if she were an old friend.

"A hundred years, and you were the first who wished to free me." Gasping softly, like a fish on land, she pressed her hand to Agatha's cheek.

"Thank you."

She closed her eyes and her body went limp in Agatha's arms. Inch by inch, the girl started to glow the color of hot gold, and with a burst of white light, she splintered to sunbeams and disappeared.

Agatha gawked at the lake, empty of fish, and listened to her fraying heartbeat. It felt like her insides had been beaten and wrung out. She held up her finger, healed like new. "Um, was all that . . ." She took a deep breath and turned.

"NORMAL?"

The entire class was dispersed behind trees, including Princess Uma, whose expression answered her question.

Loud squawks pealed from above. Agatha looked up at the friendly dove her teacher had greeted earlier. Only the dove's calls weren't friendly anymore, but wild, frantic. From the Endless Woods came a fox's growl, guttural and disturbed. Then more howls and wails from all around, nothing like the earlier welcome. The animals were in a frenzy now. They screamed louder, louder, building with fever—

"What's happening!" Agatha cried, hands over ears.

As soon as she saw Princess Uma's face, she knew.

They want it too.

Before Agatha could move, the stampede came from every direction. Squirrels, rats, dogs, moles, deer, birds, cats, rabbits, the bumbling otter—every animal on the school grounds, every animal that could squeeze through the gates charged towards their savior. . . .

Make us human! they demanded.

Agatha blanched. Since when could she understand animals?

Save us, Princess! they cried.

Since when could she understand delusional animals?

"What do I do!" Agatha shouted.

Uma took one glance at these animals, her faithful puppets, her bosom friends . . .

"RUN!"

For the first time, someone at this school gave Agatha advice she could use. She dashed for the towers as magpies pecked her hands, mice clung to her clumps, frogs hopped up her dress. Batting at the mob, she stumbled up the hill, shielding her head, hurdling hogs, hawks, hares. But just as she had the white swan doors in sight, a moose charged out of the trees and sprang—she ducked and the moose crashed, skewering the swans. Agatha bolted through the glass stair room, past Pollux on goat legs, who glimpsed the onslaught behind her.

"What in the devil's—"

"A little help!" she yelled—

"DON'T MOVE!" Pollux shrieked—

But Agatha was already charging up the Honor stairs. When she looked back, she saw Pollux deflecting animals right and left, before a thousand butterflies crashed through the sunroof and knocked his head off his goat legs, leaving the herd to chase her up the steps.

"NOT INTO THE TOWERS!" Pollux's head screeched as it rolled out the door—

But Agatha blew through the corridors into the full classrooms of Hansel's Haven. As boys and teachers tackled porcupines (ill-advised) and screaming girls hopped desks in high heels (extremely ill-advised), she tried to escape the three-ring hubbub, but animals just snatched mouthfuls of candy and kept chase. Still, she managed just enough of a lead to sprint up the stairs, slide through the frosted door, and kick it shut before the first weasel popped through.

Agatha doubled over, shadowed by towering hedges of King Arthur. The glacial rooftop breeze bit into her bare arms. She wouldn't last long up here. As she squinted through the clouded door for a teacher or nymph to rescue her, she noticed something reflected in it.

Agatha turned to a muscled silhouette hulking through sun mist. She wilted with relief. For once she was grateful for boys and ran towards her faceless prince—

She jolted back. The horned gargoyle ripped through mist and blasted the door aflame. Agatha dove to avoid a second firebomb that ignited the hedge of Arthur marrying Guinevere. She tried to crawl to the next hedge, but the gargoyle just burnt them one by one until the king's story was a storm of ash. Stranded in flames, Agatha looked up at the smoldering demon as he pinned her chest to the ground with his cold stone foot. There was no escape from him this time. She went limp and closed her eyes.

Nothing came.

She opened her eyes and found the gargoyle kneeling before her, so close she could see the reflections in his glowing red eyes. Reflections of a scared little boy.

"You want my *help?*" she breathed.

The gargoyle blinked back hopeful tears.

"But—but—I don't know how I did it," she stuttered. "It was . . . an accident."

The gargoyle gazed into her eyes and saw she was telling the truth. It slumped to the ground, scattering ash around them.

Looking down at the monster, just another lost child, Agatha thought of all the creatures in this world. They didn't follow orders because they were loyal. They didn't help princesses because they were loving. They did it because someday, maybe loyalty and love would be repaid with a second chance at being human. Only through a fairy tale could they find their way back. To their imperfect selves. To their storyless lives. She too was one of these animals now, searching for the way out.

Agatha bent down and took the gargoyle's hand in hers.

"I wish I could help you," she said. "I wish I could help us all go home."

The gargoyle lay its head in her lap. As the burning menagerie closed in, a monster and child wept in each other's arms.

Agatha felt its stone touch soften.

The gargoyle lurched back in shock. As it stumbled to its feet, its rock shell cracked . . . its claws smoothed to hands . . . its eyes lightened with innocence. Stunned, Agatha ran to it, dodging ricocheting flames, just as the monster's face began to melt into a little boy's. With a gasp of joy, she reached for him—

A sword impaled his heart. The gargoyle instantly reverted to stone and let out a betrayed cry.

Agatha spun in horror.

Tedros leapt through a wall of fire onto the gargoyle's horned skull, Excalibur in hand.

"Wait!" she shouted—

But the prince was staring at his father's memory in flames. *"Filthy, evil beast!"* he choked—

"No!"

Tedros slammed down his sword on the gargoyle's neck and sliced off its head.

"He was a boy! A little boy!" Agatha screamed. "He was *Good*!"

Tedros landed in her face. "Now I *know* you're a witch."

She punched him in the eye. Before she could punch him in the other one, fairies, wolves, and teachers of both schools burst into the menagerie, just in time to see a furious wave crash over the burning roof, lashing the foes apart.

9

The 100% Talent Show

Sophie was sure Beatrix had set the fire to get Tedros' attention. No doubt he rescued her from the blazing tower, kissed her as Good burned, and had already set their wedding date. Sophie came up with this theory because this was what *she* had planned to do at lunch. Instead, classes were canceled the next day too, leaving her marooned in a room with three murderers.

She stared at the iron plate on her bed gobbed with soggy gruel and pig's feet. After three days of starvation, she knew she had to eat whatever ghastly lunch the school sent up, but this was worse than ghastly. This was *peasant food*. She flung her plate out the window.

"You don't know where I might find cucumbers in this place?" Sophie said, turning.

Hester scowled across the room. "The Goose. How'd you do it?"

"For the last time, Hester, I don't *know*," Sophie said, stomach rumbling. "It promised to help me switch schools, but it lied. Maybe it went batty after laying so many eggs. Do you know of a garden nearby with some alfalfa or wheatgrass or—"

"You *talked* to it?" Hester blurted, mouth full of oozing pig's foot.

"Well, not exactly," Sophie said, nauseous. "But I could hear its thoughts. Unlike you, princesses can *talk* to animals."

"But not hear their thoughts," said Dot, slurping gruel that looked chocolate flavored. "For that, your soul has to be a hundred percent pure."

"There! Proof I'm 100% Good," said Sophie, relieved.

"Or 100% Evil," Hester retorted. "Depends on if we believe you or if we believe the stymphs, the robes, the Goose, and that wave monster."

Sophie goggled at her and burst into sniggers. "100% Evil? *Me?* That's preposterous! That's lunacy! That's—"

"Impressive," Anadil mused. "Even Hester's spared a rat or two."

"And here we all thought you were incompetent," Hester sneered at Sophie. "When you were just a *snake* in sheep's clothing."

Sophie tried to stop giggling but couldn't.

"Bet she has a Special Talent that blows ours away," said Dot, munching what looked to be a tiny chocolate foot.

"I don't understand," Sophie snickered. "Where does all the chocolate *come* from?"

"What is it?" Anadil hissed. "What's your talent? Night vision? Invisibility? Telepathy? Fangs filled with poison?"

"I don't care what it is," Hester snarled. "She can't beat my talent. No matter how villainous she is."

Sophie laughed so hard now she was weeping.

"You listen to me," Hester seethed, fist curling around her plate. "This is *my* school."

"Keep your crummy school!" Sophie hooted.

"*I'm* Class Captain!" Hester roared.

"I don't doubt it!"

"And no *Reader* is going to get in my way!"

"Are all villains this funny!"

Hester let out a mad cackle and flung her plate at Sophie, who dove just in time to see it tomahawk into the Wanted poster on the wall and slice off Robin's head. Sophie stopped laughing. She peeked over the scorched bed at Hester, silhouetted against the open door, black as Death. For a second Sophie thought her tattoo moved.

"Watch out, *witch*," Hester spat, and slammed the door.

Sophie looked down at her shaking fingers.

"And here we thought she'd fail!" Dot chimed behind her.

Agatha knew it had to be bad if they let a wolf take her.

After the fire, she was locked in her room for two days, allowed out only to use the toilet and accept meals of raw vegetables and prune juice from scowling fairies. Finally after lunch on the third day, the white wolf came and took her away. Digging claws into her singed pink sleeves, he pulled her past the stair room murals, past glowering Evers and teachers who couldn't even meet her eyes.

Agatha fought back tears. She already had two failing ranks. Inciting an animal stampede and setting the school on fire had earned her a third. All she'd had to do was pretend to be Good for a few days, but she couldn't even manage that. How did she think she could ever last here? Beautiful. Pure. Virtuous. If that was Good, then she was 100% Evil. Now she would suffer the punishment. And Agatha knew enough about fairy-tale punishments—dismemberings, disembowelings, boilings in oil, skinnings alive—to know her ending would involve both blood and pain.

The wolf dragged her through the Charity Tower, past a bespectacled woodpecker jabbing in new rankings on the Groom Room door.

"Are we going to the School Master?" Agatha rasped.

The wolf snorted. He dragged her to the room at the end of the hall and knocked once.

"Come in," said the quiet voice inside.

Agatha looked into the wolf's eyes. "I don't want to die."

For the first time, his sneer softened.

"I didn't either."

He opened the door and pushed her through.

Apparently the fire had finally been brought under control, because classes resumed after lunch on the third day and Sophie found herself in a damp, moldy classroom for Special Talents. But she could barely focus with her stomach rumbling, Hester throwing her murderous looks, and Dot whispering to other Nevers about their "100% Evil" bunk mate. It had all gone wrong. She had started the week trying to prove she was a princess. Now everyone was convinced she'd be Evil's Captain.

Special Talents was taught by Professor Sheeba Sheeks, the rotund woman with boils on both ebony cheeks. "Every villain has a talent!" she bellowed in her thick singsong voice, pacing the room in a busty red-velvet, pointy-shouldered gown. "But we must turn your bush into a tree!"

For the day's challenge, each Never had to show off a unique talent to the class. The more potent the talent, the higher the student's rank. But the first five kids failed to produce anything, with Vex whining he didn't even *know* his talent.

"Is that what you'll tell the School Master at the Circus?" Professor Sheeks thundered. "'I don't know my talent' or 'don't have a talent' or 'don't like my talent' or 'want to trade talents with the Ooty Queen!'"

"She had me till the last bit," said Dot.

"Every year, Evil loses the Circus of Talents!" Sheeba yelled. "Good sings a song or waves a sword or wipes their bottom and you have nothing better? Don't you have pride!

Don't you have shame! *Enough!* I don't care whether you turn men to stone or turn men to dung! You listen to Sheeba and you'll be number one!"

Twenty pairs of eyes stared at her. "Which monkey is next?" she boomed.

The woeful displays continued. Green-skinned Mona made her lips glow red. ("Because every prince is scared of a Christmas tree," Sheeba moaned.) Anadil made her rats grow an inch, Hort sprung a hair from his chest, Arachne popped her one eye, Ravan burped smoke, and just when their teacher looked completely fed up, Dot touched her desk and turned it to chocolate.

"Mystery solved," Sophie marveled.

"I've never seen such a parade of uselessness in my life," Sheeba gasped.

But Hester was next. Leering at Sophie, she gripped the desk with both fists, clenching tighter, tighter, until every vein bulged against her reddening skin.

"Turns into a watermelon," yawned Sophie. "Special indeed."

Then something moved on Hester's neck and the class froze. Her tattoo lurched again, like a painting coming to life. The red-skulled demon unfurled one wing, then the other, swung its buck-horned head to Sophie and opened slitting, bloodshot eyes. Sophie's heart stopped.

"I told you to watch out," Hester grinned.

The demon exploded off her skin in full-bodied life and tore towards Sophie, shooting red fire bolts at her head.

Stunned, she fell backward to dodge them, knocking a book-
case to the ground. The shoe-sized beast swooped, launched a
bolt that ignited her robes, and Sophie rolled over to stamp out
the flames. "HELLLPP!"

"Use your talent, incompetent blond girl!" Sheeba barked,
wagging her hips.

"She should sing," Dot quipped. "Would kill everyone in
the room."

Hester circled her demon for a second attack, only to see
it snare in the cobwebbed, spiked chandelier. Sophie crawled
under the last row, glimpsed a fallen book, *Encyclopedia
of Villains,* and ripped through pages. *Banshee, Beanighe,
Berserker . . .*

"Sophie, hurry!" Hort screamed.

Sophie wheeled to see the winged beast slash through the
cobwebs as Hester's eyes flared across the room. She flipped
desperately. *Crypt Bat, Cyclops . . . Demon!*

Ten pages of small print. *Demons are supernatural beings
that come in an astonishing variety of forms, all with different
strengths and weaknesses—*

Sophie swiveled. The demon was five feet away—

"Your *talent*!" roared Sheeba.

Sophie threw the book at the demon and missed. With
a lethal smile, it held up a bolt like a dagger. Sheeba lunged
to intervene and Anadil tripped her. Screeching, the demon
aimed at Sophie's face. But as he slung his bolt, Sophie suddenly
remembered the one talent all good girls had—

Friends.

She spun to the window and let out a gorgeous whistle for a kind, noble animal to save her life—

Black wasps smashed through the window and swarmed the demon on cue.

Hester jolted back, as if she'd been stabbed.

Sophie's eyes bulged in horror. She whistled again—but now bats stormed in, sinking teeth into the demon as the wasps continued to sting. The demon crumpled to the floor like a burnt moth. In her seat, Hester's skin went white and clammy, sucked of blood.

Alarmed, Sophie whistled louder, higher, but then came a cloud of bees, hornets, and locusts, besieging the foaming creature as Hester violently convulsed.

In the corner, Sophie stood paralyzed as screaming villains batted them away from the demon with books and chairs, but the swarm had no mercy, savaging it until Hester heaved her last breaths.

Sophie threw herself over the demon, thrust her hands at the swarm—

"STOP!"

The swarm went dead still. Like scolded children, they whimpered obediently and fled out the window in a dark cloud.

Wheezing, the wounded demon clawed to Hester and collapsed back into her neck. Hester choked and coughed up phlegm, brought back from the edge. She gaped at Sophie, flooding with fear.

Sophie dove to help her. "I didn't mean—I wanted a bird or a—" Hester recoiled from her touch.

"Princesses call animals!" Sophie cried into silence. "I'm Good! 100% Good!"

"Thank you, Beelzebub!"

Sophie whirled.

"Looks like a princess! Acts like a princess! But a *witch*," Sheeba whooped, wobbling to her feet. "Mark my words, my useless ones! This one will win the Circus Crown!"

For the second time in two challenges, Sophie looked up at the top rank, spewing red smoke above her head.

Panicked, she whipped to her schoolmates to appeal, but they were no longer looking at her with contempt or ridicule. They were looking at her with something else.

Respect.

Her place as #1 Villain was getting surer by the minute.

Up close, Professor Clarissa Dovey, with her silver bun and rosy face, looked even more comforting and grandmotherly. Agatha couldn't have wished for a better executioner.

"I'd prefer the School Master handle these things," Professor Dovey said, flipping papers under a crystal pumpkin paperweight. "But we all know how he is about his privacy."

Finally she peered up at Agatha. She didn't look comforting anymore.

"I have a school full of terrified students, two days of classes to make up, five hundred animals whose memories must be erased, a classroom wing that's been *eaten*, a treasured menagerie reduced to ash, and a headless gargoyle buried somewhere underneath all this. Do you know why this is?"

Agatha couldn't get words out of her throat.

"Because you disobeyed Pollux's simple order," Professor Dovey said. "And nearly cost lives in the process." She shamed Agatha with a look and went back to her scrolls.

Agatha glanced through the window at the lakeshore, where Evers were finishing lunches of roast chicken dolloped with mustard, spinach and Gruyère crepes, and flutes of apple cider. She could see Tedros reenacting the menagerie scene for an enthralled audience, sporting his black eye like a badge of honor.

"Can I say bye to my friend at least?" Agatha said, eyes welling. She turned to Professor Dovey.

"Before you . . . kill me?"

"That won't be necessary."

"But I have to see her!"

Professor Dovey looked up. "Agatha, you received a first rank for your performance in Animal Communication and rightfully so. Only a rare talent can make a wish come to life. And though there are different accounts of what exactly happened on the roof, I would add that any pupil of this school who would risk their life to help a gargoyle . . ." Her eyes glistened and for a moment so did the silver swan on her dress. "Well, that suggests Goodness beyond any measure."

Agatha stared at her, tongue-tied.

"But if you disobey another teacher's direct order, Agatha, I guarantee you *will* fail. Understood?"

Agatha nodded in relief.

She heard laughter outside and turned to see Tedros' mates

kicking around a pillow dummy with twig legs, coal button eyes, and black thorns for hair. An arrow suddenly speared its head, spitting feathers everywhere. A second arrow ripped open its heart.

The boys stopped laughing and turned. Across the lawn, Tedros threw down his bow and walked away.

"As for your friend, she's doing just fine where she is," Professor Dovey said, thumbing through more scrolls. "But you can ask her yourself. She's in your next class."

Agatha wasn't listening. Her eyes were still on the dead-eyed doll, bleeding feathers into the wind.

The doll that looked just like her.

10

Bad Group

"Who else is in our group?" Agatha asked Sophie, breaking the tension.

Sophie didn't answer. In fact, she acted as if Agatha wasn't there at all.

The last class of the day, Surviving Fairy Tales, was the only one that mixed students from Good and Evil. After Professor Dovey ordered Everboys to the Armory to turn in their personal weapons—the only way to appease Lady Lesso, furious over losing a gargoyle to Tedros' sword—both schools reported to the Blue Forest gates, where fairies sorted them into Forest Groups, eight Evers and eight Nevers in each. As other children found their leaders (an ogre for Group 2, a centaur for Group 8, a lily nymph for 12) Agatha and Sophie were the first to arrive under the flag stamped with a bloodred "3."

Agatha had so much to tell Sophie about smiles and fish and fires and most of all about that foul son of Arthur, but Sophie wouldn't even look at her.

"Can't we just go home?" Agatha begged.

"Why don't *you* go home before you fail or end up a mole rat?" Sophie fumed. "You're in my *school*."

"Then why won't it let us switch?"

Sophie spun. "Because you . . . Because we—"

"Need to go home," Agatha glared.

Sophie smiled her kindest smile. "Sooner or later, they'll see what's right."

"I'd say sooner," a voice resounded.

They turned to Tedros, shirt scorched, eye swollen pink and blue.

"If you're itching for something to kill, how about yourself this time?" Agatha spat.

"'Thank you' would suffice," Tedros shot back. "I risked my life to kill that gargoyle."

"You killed an innocent child!" Agatha yelled.

"I saved you from death against all instinct and reason!" Tedros roared.

Sophie gaped at them. "You two *know* each other?"

Agatha swiveled to her. "You think he's your *prince*? He's just a puffed-up windbag who can't find anything better to do than prance around half naked and thrust his sword where it doesn't belong!"

"She's just mad because she owes me her life," Tedros yawned, scratching his chest. He grinned at Sophie. "So you think I'm your prince?"

Sophie blushed delicately the way she had practiced before class.

"I knew it was a mistake at the Welcoming," the prince said, studying her with dancing blue eyes. "A girl like you shouldn't be anywhere near Evil." He turned to Agatha with a scowl. "And a witch like you shouldn't be anywhere near someone like her."

Agatha stepped towards him. "First of all, this witch happens to be her *friend*. And second, why don't you go play with yours before I make those eyes match."

Tedros laughed so hard, he had to grip the gate. "A princess friends with a witch! Now there's a fairy tale."

Agatha frowned at Sophie, waiting for her to jump in. Sophie swallowed and turned to Tedros.

"Well, it's funny you say that, because a princess certainly can't be friends with a witch, of course, but doesn't it depend on the *type* of witch? I mean, what exactly is the *definition* of a witch—"

Now Tedros was frowning at her.

"And so, um—what I'm trying to say is—"

Sophie looked between Tedros and Agatha, Agatha and Tedros . . .

She swept in front of Agatha and took Tedros' hand.

"My name's Sophie, and I like your bruise."

Agatha crossed her arms.

"My, my," Tedros said, gazing into Sophie's tantalizing green eyes. "How *are* you surviving in that place?"

"Because I knew you'd rescue me," Sophie breathed.

Agatha coughed to remind them she was still there.

"You've *got* to be kidding," said a girl's voice behind them.

They turned to see Beatrix, under the bloody "3," along with Dot, Hort, Ravan, Millicent, and the rest of their Forest Group. To chart all the dirty looks thrown in that moment, one would end up with something resembling a bowl of spaghetti.

"Mmmm," said a voice below.

They looked down to find a four-foot gnome with wrinkly brown skin, a belted green coat, and a pointy orange hat frowning from a hole in the ground.

"Bad group," he murmured.

Grumbling loudly, Yuba the Gnome crawled out of his burrow, pulled the gate open with his stubby white staff, and led his students into the Blue Forest.

For a moment, everyone forgot their rancor and marveled at the blue wonderland around them. Every tree, every flower, every blade of grass sparkled a different hue. Slender beams of sun slipped through cerulean canopies, lighting up turquoise trunks and navy blooms. Deer grazed on azure lilacs, crows and hummingbirds jabbered in sapphire nettles, squirrels and rabbits jaunted through cobalt briars to join storks sipping from an ultramarine pond. No animals seemed skittish or the slightest bit bothered by the crisscrossing student tours. Where Sophie and Agatha had always associated forests with danger and darkness, this one beckoned with beauty and life. At least until they saw a flock of bony stymph birds, sleeping in their blue nest.

"They let those around students?" Sophie said.

"Sleep during the day. Perfectly harmless," Dot whispered back. "Unless a villain wakes them up."

As his students followed, Yuba rattled off the history of the Blue Forest in his clipped, hoary voice. Once upon a time, there had been no joint classes for School for Good and School for Evil students. Instead, children had graduated straight from their school's training into the Endless Woods. But before they could ever engage in battle, Good and Evil inevitably fell prey to hungry boars, scavenging imps, cranky spiders, and the occasional man-eating tulip.

"We had forsaken the obvious," said Yuba. "You cannot survive your fairy tale if you cannot survive the Woods."

So the school created the Blue Forest as a training ground. The signature blue foliage arose from protective enchantments that kept intruders out, while reminding students it was just an imitation of more treacherous Woods.

As to just how treacherous the real thing was, the students sensed firsthand as Yuba led them past the North Gates. Though there was still sunlight left in the autumn evening, the dark, dense Woods repelled it like a shield. It was a forest of eternal night, with every inch of green blackened by shadow. As their eyes adjusted to the sooty darkness, the students could see a puny dirt path lilting through trees, like the withering lifeline on an old man's palm. To both sides of the path, vines strangled trees into armored clumps, so there was barely an undergrowth between them. What was left of the forest floor had been buried beneath mangled thorns, stabbing twigs, and a gauntlet of cobwebs. But none of this scared the students as much as the sounds that came from the darkness beyond the path. Moans and growls echoed from the forest bowels, while low rasps and snarls added ghoulish harmony.

Then the children began to see what was making the sounds. Pairs of eyes watched them through the onyx depths— devilish red and yellow, flickering, vanishing, then reappearing closer than before. The terrible noises grew louder, the fiendish eyes multiplied, the undergrowth crackled with life, and just when the students saw skulking outlines rise from the mist—

"This way," Yuba called back.

The students scampered from the gates and followed the gnome into a blue clearing without looking back.

Surviving Fairy Tales was just like any other class, Yuba explained from a turquoise tree stump, with students ranked from 1 to 16 for each challenge. Only now there was something more at stake: twice a year, each of the fifteen groups would send its best Ever and best Never to compete in the school's Trial by Tale. Yuba didn't say any more about this mysterious competition, except that the winners received five extra first-place ranks. The students in his group glanced at each other, thinking the same thing. Whoever won the Trial by Tale would surely be Class Captain.

"Now there are *five rules* that separate Good from Evil," the gnome said, and wrote them in air with his smoking staff.

1. The Evil *attack*. The Good *defend*.

2. The Evil *punish*. The Good *forgive*.

3. The Evil *hurt*. The Good *help*.

4. The Evil *take*. The Good *give*.

5. The Evil *hate*. The Good *love*.

"As long as you obey the rules for your side, you have the best possible chance of surviving your fairy tale," Yuba said to the group gathered in navy grass. "These rules should come with ease, of course. You have been chosen for your schools precisely because you show them at the highest level!"

Sophie wanted to scream. *Help? Give? Love?* That was her life! That was her soul!

"But first you must learn to recognize Good and Evil," said Yuba. "In the Woods, appearances are often deceiving. Snow White nearly perished because she thought an old woman kind. Red Riding Hood found herself in a wolf's stomach because she couldn't tell the difference between family and fiend. Even Beauty struggled to distinguish between hideous beast and noble prince. All unnecessary suffering. For no matter how much Good and Evil are disguised, they can always be told apart. You must look closely. And you must remember the rules."

For the class challenge, Yuba announced, each student had

to distinguish between a disguised Ever and Never by observing their behavior. Whoever correctly identified the Good student and the Evil student in the fastest time would receive first rank.

"I've never done any of those Evil rules," Sophie mourned, standing beside Tedros. "If only they knew all my Good Deeds!"

Beatrix turned. "Nevers shouldn't talk to Evers."

"Evers shouldn't call Evers Nevers," Sophie snapped.

Beatrix looked confused, while Tedros bit back a smile.

"You have to prove they switched you and the witch," he whispered to Sophie once Beatrix turned back. "Win the challenge and I'll go to Professor Dovey myself. If the gargoyle didn't convince her, then this will."

"You'd do that . . . for me?" Sophie said, eyes wide.

Tedros touched her black tunic. "Can't flirt with you in this, can I?"

Sophie would have burned her robes right there if she could.

Hort volunteered to go first. As soon as he tied the ragged blindfold over his eyes, Yuba stabbed his staff at Millicent and Ravan, who magically shriveled in their pink and black clothes, smaller, smaller, until they slithered out of them, identical cobras.

Hort whipped off the blindfold.

"Well?" Yuba said.

"Look the bloody same to me," Hort said.

"Test them!" Yuba scolded. "Use the rules!"

"I don't even remember the rules," Hort said.

"Next," the gnome grouched.

For Dot's turn, he changed Beatrix and Hort into unicorns. But then one unicorn started copying the other and vice versa, until they both pranced about like mimicking mimes. Dot scratched her head.

"Rule one! The Evil *attack*! The Good *defend*!" barked Yuba. "Which one started it, Dot?"

"Oh! Can we start again?"

"Not just bad," Yuba grumped. *"Worst!"*

He squinted at his scroll of names. "Who would like to be disguised for Tedros?"

All the Evergirls raised their hands.

"You haven't gone yet," Yuba said, pointing at Sophie. "You either," he said to Agatha.

"My grandmother could get this one right," mumbled Tedros, tightening his blindfold.

Agatha tramped in front of the class and stood next to Sophie, who was blushing like a bride.

"Aggie, he doesn't care what school I'm in or the color of my robes," Sophie gushed. "He sees who I am."

"You don't even *know* him!"

Sophie flushed. "You're not . . . happy for me?"

"He knows nothing about you!" Agatha shot back. "All he sees is your looks!"

"For the first time in my life, I feel like someone understands me," Sophie sighed.

Hurt squeezed Agatha's throat. "But what about—I mean, you said—"

Sophie met her eyes. "You've been such a good friend, Aggie. But we'll be in different schools, won't we?"

Agatha turned away.

"Ready, Tedros! Go!" Yuba jabbed his staff, and both girls exploded from their clothes into slimy, stinky hobgoblins.

Tedros took off the blindfold and jumped back, hand to nose. Sophie clasped her green claws and batted her wormy lashes at him. With Sophie's words throbbing in her head, Agatha slumped sullenly and gave up.

"It seems too obvious," Tedros said, eyeing the flirting hobgoblin.

Sophie stopped batting her lashes, confused.

"And that witch is craftier than you can imagine," Tedros said, glancing between the two goblins.

Agatha rolled her eyes. This boy had a brain like a peanut.

"Feel with the heart, not the mind!" Yuba shouted at the prince.

Grimacing, Tedros closed his eyes. For a moment the prince hesitated. But then surely, powerfully, he felt himself pulled towards one of the hobgoblins.

Sophie gasped. It wasn't her.

Tedros reached out and touched Agatha's wet, warty cheek. "This one's Sophie." He opened his eyes. "This one's the princess."

Agatha gawped at Sophie, dumbstruck.

"Wait. I'm right," Tedros said. "Right?"

For a moment, everything was quiet.

Sophie tackled Agatha. *"YOU RUIN EVERYTHING!"*

To everyone else, this sounded like *"GOBBO OOMIE HOOWAH!"* but Agatha understood it just fine.

"See how stupid he is! He can't even tell us apart!" Agatha yelled.

"You tricked him!" Sophie shrieked. "Just like you tricked the bird and the wave and the—"

Tedros punched her in the eye.

"Leave Sophie alone!" he shouted.

Sophie gaped at him. Her prince had just punched her. Her prince had just confused her with *Agatha*. How could she prove who she was?

"Use the rules!" Yuba bellowed atop a log.

Suddenly understanding, Sophie lurched up so her spotted, humped body towered over Tedros, and she caressed his chest with her greasy green hand. "My dear Tedros. I *forgive* you for not knowing any better and won't *defend* myself even though you attacked me. I only want to *help* you, my prince, and *give* us a story that will take us hand in hand to *love*, happiness, and Ever After."

But all Tedros heard was a torrent of goblin growls, so he stomped on Sophie's foot and ran towards Agatha's goblin, arms outstretched. "I can't believe you were ever friends with—"

Agatha kneed him in the groin.

"Now I'm confused," Tedros wheezed and collapsed.

Moaning in pain, he craned up to see Sophie shove Agatha into a blueberry bush, Agatha smack Sophie with a screeching squirrel, and the two green goblins go back and forth, bashing each other like oversugared children.

"I'll never go home with you!" screamed Sophie.

"*Oooh! Ooh!* Marry me, Tedros!" hissed Agatha.

"At least I *will* get married!"

The fight escalated to a ludicrous climax, with Sophie beating Agatha with a blue squash, Agatha sitting on Sophie's head, and the class gleefully making bets as to who was who—

"Go rot in Gavaldon alone!" Sophie screamed.

"Better alone than with a phony!" Agatha shouted.

"Get out of my life!"

"You came into mine!"

Hobbling, Tedros leapt between them—

"*Enough!*"

It was the wrong moment. Both goblins turned on the prince with slime-drenching, earsplitting roars and kicked him so hard he sailed over Groups 2, 6, and 10 and landed in a heap of boar dung.

The girls' green hides shrank, their scales softened to skin, their bodies melted into their human clothes. . . . Slowly Sophie and Agatha turned to find the entire group goggling at them.

"Good ending," said Hort.

"Hold your verdict," Yuba said. "For when Good acts Evil and Evil acts incompetent, and rules are broken right and left until even *I* can't figure out what's what . . . well, there's only one ending indeed."

Two pairs of iron shoes magically grew on the girls' feet.

"Yeek. These are hideous," Sophie frowned.

Then the shoes grew hot, blazing hot.

"Fire! Feet on fire!" yelped Agatha, hopping up and down.

"Make it stop!" Sophie cried, dancing with pain.

In the distance, the wolves howled the end of class.

"Class dismissed," Yuba said, and waddled off.

"What about us!" screamed Agatha, yanking at her burning soles—

"Unfortunately fairy-tale punishments have a mind of their own," the gnome called back. "They'll end when the lesson has been learned."

The class followed him back towards the school gates, leaving Sophie and Agatha to dance in the cursed shoes. Tedros limped past the punished girls, covered in slime and dung. He gave them equally disgusted scowls.

"Now I see why you two are friends."

As the prince trudged into blue thicket, the girls glimpsed Beatrix sidle up to him. "I knew they were *both* Evil," she said as they vanished behind the oaks.

"This—is—your—fault!" Sophie wheezed to Agatha, dancing in agony.

"Please—let it—stop," Agatha spluttered—

But the shoes showed no mercy. Minute by minute, they grew hotter and hotter, until the two girls couldn't even scream. Even the animals couldn't watch such suffering and stayed away.

Afternoon turned to evening and then to night, and still they danced like madwomen, whirling and sweating in pain and despair. Burn ripped through their bones, fire became their blood, and soon they wished that this suffering would end, at any cost. Death knew when he was called. But just as the two girls surrendered to his cruel hands, sabers of sunlight shattered the darkness, speared their feet—and the shoes went cold.

The girls collapsed in tormented heaps.

"Ready to go home?" Agatha panted.

Sophie looked up, ghost white.

"Thought you'd never ask."

11

The School Master's Riddle

As the two schools slept, two heads surfaced outside in the black moat. Sophie and Agatha peeped out at the thin silver tower that divided lake from sludge. Too far to swim. Too high to climb. A cyclone of fairies guarded its spire, while an army of wolves with crossbows manned wooden planks at its base.

"And you're sure he's up there?" Sophie said.

"I *saw* him."

"He has to help us! I can't go back to that place!"

"Look, we just beg him for mercy until he sends us home."

"Because that'll work," Sophie snorted. "Leave him to me."

For the last hour, the two girls had mulled every possible way to escape. Agatha thought they should sneak into the Woods and find their way back to Gavaldon. But Sophie pointed out that even if they did get past the gate snakes and any other booby traps, they'd just end up lost. ("They're called the *Endless* Woods for a reason.") Instead, she proposed they hunt for enchanted broomsticks or magic carpets or something else in the school closets that might fly them over the forest.

"And what direction would we fly in?" Agatha asked.

The two girls discarded other options—leaving a trail of bread crumbs (that never worked); seeking a kindly hunter or dwarf (Agatha didn't trust strangers); wishing for a fairy godmother (Sophie didn't trust fat women)—until there was only one left.

But now, peering up at the School Master's fortress, they lost all hope.

"We'll never get up there," Sophie sighed.

Agatha heard a squawk in the distance.

"Hold that thought."

A short while later, they were back in the Blue Forest, caked in sludge, eyeing a nest of big black eggs from behind a periwinkle bush. In front of the nest, five skeletal stymphs slept on indigo grass, littered with the blood and limbs of a half-eaten goat.

Sophie scowled. "I'm back where I started, covered in smelly ooze and who knows how many flesh-eating maggots and—what are you *doing*!"

"As soon as they attack, we jump on."

"As soon as they *what*?"

But Agatha was already tiptoeing to the eggs.

"The shoes burnt your brain!" Sophie hissed.

As Agatha inched towards the nest, she caught a closer look at the sleeping stymphs' jagged teeth, gnarled talons, and spiked tails that shred flesh from bone. Suddenly doubting her plan, Agatha backed up, only to trip on a branch and fall on a goat leg with a loud crack. The stymphs opened their eyes. Her heart stopped.

Unless a villain wakes them up.

The pink dress wouldn't fool them.

Agatha glowered at the waking fiends. She couldn't give up now! Not when she had Sophie willing to go home! She lunged for the nest, snatched an egg, sprang up for the blitz—

"Can't watch, can't watch—" Sophie mewled, squinting through fingers for spewing limbs and blood.

But the vicious birds were nuzzling Agatha, like puppies seeking milk.

"Ooh, that tickles!" she squealed. Sophie folded her arms.

Clumping back, Agatha handed the egg to her. "Your turn."

"Oh, please, if they like you, they'll try to *mate* with me. Animals *worship* princesses," said Sophie, sashaying towards the birds—

The stymphs unleashed a war cry and charged.

"Helllllp!" Sophie threw the egg to Agatha, but the stymphs still chased Sophie, who ran in circles like a lunatic, five stymphs high stepping behind her in a moronic maypole parade until everyone forgot who was after who and the birds knocked into each other dizzily.

"See? I outsmarted them," Sophie beamed.

A stymph bit her bottom. "Ayyyiiieee!" Sophie ran for the nearest tree. Only she couldn't climb trees, so she hurled mashed gooseberries at the bird's eye, but the bird had no eye, so the berries went right through bony socket and plopped to the ground.

Agatha watched stone-faced.

"Aggie, it's *coming*!"

The stymph charged for Sophie, only to stop short and find Agatha perched on its back.

"Get on, you dimwit!" she shouted at Sophie.

"Without a saddle?" Sophie scoffed. "It'll leave chafe marks."

The stymph lunged for her—Agatha walloped its head and slung Sophie by the waist onto the bird's spine.

"Hang on tight!" Agatha yelled as the bird thrashed up to flight, somersaulting over the bay to get the girls off its back. Four more stymphs exploded from blue trees in murderous pursuit; Agatha kicked at the bird's thighbones, Sophie holding on to her for dear life—"This is the *worst* plan evveerrr!" Hearing squawks and screams, the fairy and wolf guards squinted into the sky, only to see the intruders vanish into fog.

"There's the tower!" Agatha cried, spotting the silver spire through the mist. A wolf's arrow whizzed between the stymph's ribs, almost slicing Sophie in half. Fairies stormed out of the fog, shooting golden webs from their mouths, and the stymph dove to avoid them, spinning to elude a new hail of wolf arrows. This time neither girl could hold on and tumbled off its back.

"Noooo!" screamed Agatha—

Sophie caught the last bone of the stymph's tail. Agatha caught the last bit of Sophie's glass shoe—"We're going to die!" Sophie howled.

"Just hold on!" bellowed Agatha.

"My hands are sweaty!"

"We're going to die!"

The stymph zoomed for the tower wall. But just as it whipped its tail to smash them, Agatha saw a window glint through fog.

"Now!" screamed Agatha. This time Sophie listened.

Golden nets shot from every direction and the stymph let out a helpless screech. But as fairies watched it plunge to its death, they looked at each other curiously.

There were no riders on its back.

The crash landing through the window left Sophie's entire right side bruised and Agatha's wrist gashed. But pain meant they were still alive. Pain meant they still had hope for getting home. With a chorus of groans, they staggered to their feet. Then Sophie saw the worst of the damage.

"My *shoe*!" She held up her glass heel, snapped to a serrated stump. "They were one of a kind," she mourned. Agatha ignored her and limped ahead into the murky gray chamber, barely lit by the window's dawn glow.

"Hello?" Agatha called. Echoes died unanswered.

The girls inched farther into the shadowy room. Stone bookcases cloaked gray brick walls, packed top to bottom with colorful bindings. Sophie dusted off a shelf and read the elegant silver letters on the wooden spines: *Rapunzel, The Singing Bone, Thumbelina, The Frog King, Cap O'Rushes, The Six Swans* . . . All the stories the children of Gavaldon used to drink up. She looked over at Agatha, who had made the same discovery across the room. They were standing in a library of every fairy tale ever told.

Agatha opened up *Beauty and the Beast* to find it written in the same elegant script as the spine, illustrated with vivid paintings like the ones in the foyers of both schools. Then she opened up *The Red Shoes, Donkeyskin,* and *The Snow Queen* and found that they too were written in the same regal hand.

"Aggie?"

Agatha followed Sophie's gaze to the darkest part of the room. Through the shadows, she could make out a white stone table pressed against the wall. There was something looming over it: a long, thin dagger dangling magically in midair.

Agatha ran her fingers along the cold, smooth surface of the table and thought of all the blank headstones behind her house, waiting for bodies. Sophie's eyes fixed on the hovering knife, eerily still a few feet above the white slab.

That's when she saw it wasn't a knife at all.

"It's a pen," she said softly.

It was made of pure steel and shaped like a knitting needle, lethally sharp at both ends. One side of the pen was engraved with a deep, flowing script that ran unbroken from tip to tip.

Ḧöṗṗḷȿ Ⱦŗḡȿṡṡ ḧü ṡŗḡẹṃ ṡꙥöṡḷṇ

Suddenly the pen caught a sliver of sunlight and scattered blinding gold rays in every direction. Agatha turned from the glare. When she turned back, Sophie was climbing onto the table.

"Sophie, no!"

Sophie walked towards the pen, eyes wide, body rigid. The world dissipated in a blur of gray around her. All that remained was the shimmering, spindle-sharp pen, strange words reflecting in her glazed eyes. Somewhere inside, she knew what they meant. She reached for the tip.

"Don't!" Agatha cried.

Sophie's skin kissed ice-cold steel, blood about to pierce through—

Agatha tackled her and both girls crashed to the table. Sophie broke from her trance and peered at Agatha suspiciously.

"I'm on a table. With you."

"You were about to touch it!" Agatha said.

"Huh? Why would I touch a—"

Her eyes drifted up to the pen, which was no longer still. It dangled an inch from their faces, pointing between them with its deadly sharp tip as if weighing who to kill first.

"Don't *move*," Agatha said between clenched teeth.

The pen seared hot red.

"Move!" she cried.

The pen plunged and both girls rolled off the table, only to see the razor-sharp nib lurch to a stop just before it hit stone. A puff of black smoke and a book suddenly appeared on the table beneath it, bound with cherry-red wood. The pen flipped the cover open to the first blank page and began to write:

"Once upon a time, there were two girls."

The same elegant script as all the others. A brand-new fairy tale.

Sophie and Agatha gaped from the floor, terrified.

"Now that's odd," said a gentle voice.

The girls whipped around again. No one there.

"Students at my school train and toil for four years, venture into the Woods, seek their Nemeses, fight vicious battles . . . all just for the *hope* the Storian might tell their story."

The girls spun around. No one in the room at all. But then they saw their shadows merge on the wall, into the crooked shadow that kidnapped them. The girls turned slowly.

"And here it starts one for two first-year, unskilled, untrained, clumsy *intruders*," said the School Master.

He wore silver robes that billowed over his hunched, slender frame, hiding his hands and feet. A rusted crown sat off center on his head of thick, ghostly white hair. A gleaming silver mask covered every last shred of his face, revealing only twinkling blue eyes and wide, full lips, curled in a mischievous smile.

"It must suspect a good ending."

The Storian dove to the page:

"One was beautiful and beloved and the other was a lonely hag."

"I like our story," Sophie said.

"It hasn't gotten to the part where your prince punches you," said Agatha.

"Homeward ho," Sophie sulked.

They looked up and saw the School Master studying them.

"Readers are unpredictable, of course. Some have been our greatest students. Most have been embarrassing failures." He gazed at the distant towers, turning his back to the girls. "But this just shows how confused Readers have become."

Agatha's heart pounded. This was their chance! She jabbed Sophie. "Go!"

"I can't!" Sophie whispered.

"You said leave him to you!"

"He's too *old*!"

Agatha elbowed her in the ribs, Sophie elbowed her back—

"Many of the faculty say I kidnap you, steal you, take you against your will," the School Master said.

Agatha kicked Sophie forward.

"But the truth is I free you."

Sophie swallowed and took off her broken shoe.

"You deserve to live extraordinary lives."

Sophie crept towards the School Master, raising her jagged heel.

"You deserve the chance to know *who you are*."

The School Master turned to Sophie, shoe poised over his heart.

"We demand our release!" Agatha cried.

Silence.

Sophie dropped to her knees. "Oh, please, sir, we beg for mercy!"

Agatha groaned.

"You took me for Good," sobbed Sophie, "but they put me in Evil and now my dress is black and my hair's dirty and my prince hates me and my roommates are murderers and there's no Groom Rooms for Nevers so now"—she let out a soprano wail—"I *smell*." She bawled into her hands.

"So you'd like to switch schools?" the School Master asked.

"We'd like to go home," said Agatha.

Sophie looked up brightly. "*Can* we switch schools?"

The School Master smiled. "No."

"Then we'd like to go home," Sophie said.

"*Lost in a strange land, the girls wanted to go home,*" the Storian noted.

"We have sent students home before," the School Master said, silver mask flaring. "Illness, mental incapacity, the petition of an influential family . . ."

"So you *can* send us home!" Agatha said.

"Indeed I could," said the School Master, "if you weren't in the midst of a fairy tale." He eyed the pen across the room. "You see, once the Storian begins your story, then I'm afraid we must follow it wherever it takes you. Now the question is,

'Will your story take you home?'"

The Storian plunged to the page: "*Stupid girls! They were trapped for eternity!*"

"I suspected as much," said the School Master.

"So there's no way home?" Agatha asked, eyes welling.

"Not unless it's your ending," the School Master said. "And going home together is a rather far-fetched ending for two girls fighting for opposing sides, don't you think?"

"But we don't want to fight!" Sophie said.

"We're on the same side!" said Agatha.

"We're friends!" Sophie said, clasping Agatha's hand.

"*Friends!*" the School Master marveled.

Agatha looked just as surprised, feeling Sophie's grip.

"Well, that certainly changes things." The School Master paced like a doddering duck. "You see, a princess and a witch can never be friends in our world. It's unnatural. It's unthinkable. It's *impossible*. Which means if you are indeed friends . . . Agatha must not be a princess and Sophie must not be a witch."

"Exactly!" said Sophie. "Because I'm the princess and she's the wi—" Agatha kicked her.

"And if Agatha is not a princess and Sophie is not a witch, then clearly I've got it wrong and you don't belong in our world at all," he said, pace slowing. "Maybe what everyone says about me is true after all."

"That you're Good?" Sophie said.

"That I'm old," the School Master sighed out the window.

Agatha couldn't contain her excitement. "So we can go home now?"

"Well, there is the thorny matter of proving all this."

"But I've tried!" Sophie said. "I've tried proving I'm not a villain!"

"And I've tried proving I'm not a princess!" said Agatha.

"Ah, but there's only one way in this world to prove who you are."

The Storian stopped its busy writing, sensing a pivotal moment. Slowly the School Master turned. For the first time, his blue eyes had a glint of danger.

"What's the one thing Evil can *never* have . . . and the one thing Good can never do *without?*"

The girls looked at each other.

"So we solve your riddle and you . . . send us home?" Agatha asked hopefully.

The School Master turned away. "I trust I won't see either of you again. Unless you want a rather depressing end to your story."

Suddenly, the room started disappearing in a sweep of white, as if the scene was being erased before their eyes.

"Wait!" Agatha cried. "What are you doing!"

First the bookshelves vanished, then the walls—

"No! We want to go home now!" Agatha yelled.

Then the ceiling, the table, the floor around them—the two girls lunged to a corner to avoid being erased—

"How do we find you! How do we answe—" Agatha ducked to avoid a streak of white. "You're cheating!"

Across the room, Sophie saw the Storian furiously writing to keep up with their fairy tale. The pen sensed her gaze, for the words in its steel suddenly seared red and Sophie's heart burned again with secret understanding. Scared, she clung to Agatha—

"You thief! You bully! You masked-face old creep!" Agatha screamed. "We're fine without you! Readers are fine without you! Stay in your tower with your masks and pens and stay out of our lives! You hear me! Steal children from other villages and leave us alone!"

The last thing they saw was the School Master turn from the window, smiling in a sea of white.

"What other villages?"

The ground vanished beneath the two girls' feet and they free-fell into emptiness, the School Master's last words echoing, blending into the wolves' call to morning class—

They woke, blinded by sunlight, swimming in puddles of sweat. Agatha looked for Sophie. Sophie looked for Agatha. But all they found were their own beds, in towers far apart.

12

Dead Ends

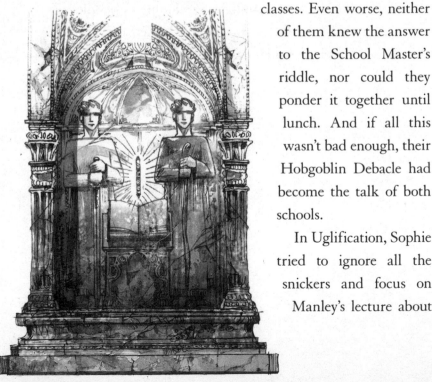

The morning started miserably for both girls. Not only had they gotten zero sleep, but now they were back in their mismatched schools for another day of despicable classes. Even worse, neither of them knew the answer to the School Master's riddle, nor could they ponder it together until lunch. And if all this wasn't bad enough, their Hobgoblin Debacle had become the talk of both schools.

In Uglification, Sophie tried to ignore all the snickers and focus on Manley's lecture about the proper use of capes. This took valiant concentration, given Hester's vengeful glares and the fact that capes could be used for protection, invisibility, disguise, or flight, depending on their fabric and grain, with each type requiring different incantations. Manley blindfolded the students for the class challenge, where students raced to identify their given cape's fabric and successfully put it to use.

"I didn't know magic was so complicated," Hort murmured, massaging his cape to see if it was silk or satin.

"And this is just capes," Dot said, smelling hers. "Wait until we do spells!"

But if there was one thing Sophie knew, it was clothes. She recognized snakeskin under her fingers, mentally said the incantation, and went invisible under her slinky black cape. The feat earned her another top rank and a look from Hester so lethal Sophie thought she might burst into flames.

Across the moat, Agatha couldn't turn a corner without seeing Tedros and his mates mimicking hobgoblin lurches, howling gibberish, and beating each other with squashes. Wherever she went, Tedros and company followed, braying and grunting at the top of their lungs, until she finally snatched a squash and jabbed Tedros in the chest with it.

"The only reason this happened is because you chose me! YOU CHOSE ME, you boorish, brainless thug!"

Tedros gaped dumbly as she stormed off.

"You chose the *witch*?" asked Chaddick.

Tedros turned to find boys staring. "No, I—she tricked—I didn't—" He pulled his sword. "Who wants to fight?"

With Hansel's Haven still in ruins, classes were moved to the tower common rooms. Agatha followed a herd of Evers through the Breezeways linking all the Good towers in a zigzag of colorful glass passages high over the lake. While crossing a purple breezeway to Charity, she tuned out gossiping girls and pondered the School Master's riddle over and over, until she looked up and saw she was all alone. After fumbling through the bubble-filled Laundry, where nymphs scoured dresses, dodging enchanted pots in the Supper Hall making lunch, and trapping herself in a faculty toilet, Agatha finally tracked down the Charity Commons. The pink chaise couches were already full and none of the girls made room for her. Just as she sat on the floor—

"Sit here!"

Kiko, the sweet, short-haired girl, scooted aside. As the others tittered, Agatha squeezed in beside her. "They'll all hate you now," she mumbled.

"I don't understand how they can think themselves Good and be so rude," Kiko whispered.

"Maybe because I almost burned down the school."

"They're just jealous. You can make wishes come true. None of us can do that yet."

"It was a fluke. If I could make wishes come true, I'd be home with my friend and my cat." The thought of Reaper made Agatha grasp for another subject. "Um, how's that boy you wished for?"

"Tristan?" Kiko's face fell. "He likes Beatrix. Every boy likes Beatrix."

"But he gave you his rose," Agatha said, remembering her wish at the lake.

"By accident. I jumped in front of Beatrix to catch it." Kiko gave Beatrix a dirty look. "Do you think he'll take me to the Ball? Not every boy can take that she-wolf."

Agatha smirked. Then frowned. "What ball?"

"The Evers Snow Ball! It's right before Christmas and every one of us has to find a boy to take us or we're failed! We get ranked as couples based on our presentation, demeanor, and dancing. Why do you think we all wished for different boys at the lake? Girls are practical like that. Boys just all want the prettiest one." Kiko grinned. "Who do you have your eye on?"

Before Agatha could vomit, the doors flew open and a busty woman flounced in wearing a bejeweled red turban and scarf that matched her dress, caked caramel makeup, swarthy kohl around her eyes, Gypsy hoop earrings, and jangling tambourine bracelets.

"Umm . . . Professor Anemone?" Kiko gawked.

"I am Scherezade," Professor Anemone boomed in a ridiculous accent. "Queen of Persia. Sultaness of the Seven Seas. Behold my dusky desert beauty."

She whipped off her scarf and did a terrible belly dance. "See how I seduce you with my *hips*!" She veiled her face and blinked like an owl. "See how I tempt you with my *eyes*!" She shook her bosom and beat her bangles noisily. "See how I become Midnight's *Temptress*!"

"More like smoked kebab," Agatha murmured. Kiko giggled.

Professor Anemone's smile vanished, as did the accent. "Here I thought I'd teach you to survive 1001 Arabian

Nights—dune-ready makeup, hegira fashions, even a proper Dance of the Seven Veils—but perhaps I should start with something less *amusing*." She tightened her turban.

"Fairies have alerted me that candy has been vanishing from Hansel's Haven even while it is under repair. As you know, our school's classrooms are made of candy as a reminder of all the temptations that you will face beyond our gates." Her eyes narrowed. "But we know what happens to girls who *eat* candy. Once they start, they can't stop. They stray from the path. They fall prey to witches. They gorge themselves on self-pleasure until they die obese, unmarried, and riddled with *warts*."

The girls were aghast someone would vandalize the tower, let alone ruin their figure with candy. Agatha tried to look just as scandalized. That's when the marshmallows fell out of her pocket, followed by a blue lollipop, a hunk of gingerbread, and two bricks of fudge. Twenty gasps came at once.

"I didn't have time for breakfast!" Agatha insisted. "I didn't eat all night!"

But no one was sympathetic, including Kiko, who looked sorry that she'd been nice to her at all. Agatha picked guiltily at her swan.

"You'll be cleaning plates after supper for next two weeks, Agatha," said her professor. "A useful reminder of the one thing princesses have that villains do not."

Agatha bolted up. The answer!

"A proper *diet*," Professor Anemone huffed.

As the turbaned teacher divulged more Arabian Beauty Secrets, Agatha slumped into the couch. One class and her problems had already multiplied. Between the horror of a mandatory Ball, a week of dish duty, and a decidedly wart-ridden future, she had the crashing realization of just how fast she needed to solve the School Master's riddle.

"How about poison in her food?" Hester spat.

"She doesn't eat," said Anadil, tramping with her through Malice Hall.

"How about poisoned lipstick?"

"They'll lock us in the Doom Room for weeks!" fretted Dot, lumbering to keep up.

"I don't care how we do it or how much trouble we get in," Hester hissed. "I want that snake *gone.*"

She threw open the door to Room 66 to find Sophie sobbing on her bed.

"Um, snake's crying," Anadil said.

"Are you okay, love?" Dot asked, suddenly sorry for the girl she was supposed to kill.

Blubbering, Sophie poured out everything that happened in the School Master's tower.

". . . But now there's a riddle and I don't know the answer and Tedros thinks I'm a witch because I keep winning challenges and no one understands the reason I keep winning is that I'm good at *everything*!"

Hester was ready to strangle her right there. Then her face changed.

"This riddle. If you answer it . . . you go home?"

Sophie nodded.

"And we never have to see you again?" said Anadil.

Sophie nodded.

"We'll solve it," her roommates pounced.

"You will?" Sophie blinked.

"You know how badly you want to go home?" said Hester.

"We want you to go home more," said Anadil.

"Well, at least you believe me," Sophie frowned, wiping tears.

"Guilty until proven innocent," Hester said. "It's the Never way."

"I wouldn't tell any of this to an Ever, though. They'll think you're mad as a hatter," said Anadil.

"That's what I thought, but who lies about breaking so many *rules*?" Dot said, failing to turn her swan crest to chocolate. "Really, this bird is incorrigible."

"What's the School Master like?" Hester asked Sophie.

"He's old. Very, very old."

"And you actually *saw* the Storian?" Anadil asked.

"That strange pen? It wrote about us the whole time."

"It *what*?" said the three girls at once.

"But you're in school!" Hester said.

"What can happen in *school* that's worthy of a fairy tale?" said Anadil.

"I'm sure it's just a mistake, like everything else," Sophie sniffled. "I just need to solve the riddle, tell the School Master, and poof, I'm out of this cursed place. Simple."

She saw the girls exchange looks. "Isn't it?"

"There's two puzzles here," Anadil said, eyeing Hester.

"The School Master's riddle."

Hester turned to Sophie. "And why he wants you to solve it."

If there was one word Agatha dreaded more than "ball," it was "dancing."

"Every Good girl must dance at the Ball," Pollux said, wobbling on mule legs in the Valor Commons.

Agatha tried not to breathe. The room reeked of leather and cologne with its musky brown couches, bear-head carpet, hide-bound books about hunting and riding, and a moose-head plaque flaunting obscenely large antlers. She missed the School for Evil and its graveyard stench.

Pollux led the girls through the dances for the Evers Ball, none of which Agatha could follow, since he kept falling and mumbling it would "make sense once he got his body back." After tripping a hoof on the rug, impaling himself on the antlers, and landing buttocks first in the fireplace, Pollux barked they "got the point" and wheeled to a group of fairies wielding willow violins. "Play a volta!"

And so they did, lightning quick, with Agatha flung from partner to partner, waist to waist, spinning faster, faster into a wild blur. Her feet caught fire. Every girl in the room was Sophie. *The shoes!* They were back! "Sophie! I'm coming!" she yelled—

Next thing she knew, she was on the floor.

"There are appropriate times for fainting," Pollux scowled. "This is not one."

"I *tripped*," Agatha snapped.

"Suppose you faint during the *Ball*! Chaos! Carnage!"

"I didn't faint!"

"Forget a ball! It would be a Midnight Massacre!"

Agatha stared him down. "I. Don't. *Faint.*"

When the girls reported to the banks of Halfway Bay for Animal Communication, Professor Dovey was waiting. "Princess Uma has taken ill."

Girls gave Agatha sour looks, since her Wish Fish debacle was surely responsible. With no one to supervise on such short notice, Professor Dovey gave them the session off. "Top-half students may use the Groom Room. Bottom-half students should use the time to reflect upon their mediocrity!"

While Beatrix and her seven minions sashayed to the Groom Room for manicures, the bottom-half girls scurried to peek in on Swordplay, since the boys sparred shirtless. Meanwhile, Agatha hastened to the Gallery of Good, hoping it would inspire an answer to the riddle.

As her eyes drifted across its sculptures, cases, and stuffed creatures lit by pink-flamed torches, she remembered the School Master's decree that a witch and princess could never be friends. But *why?* Something had to come between them. Surely this was the mysterious thing a princess could have and a villain could not. She thought about what it could be until her neck prickled red. But still no answer.

She found herself pulled once more to the corner nook, home to the gauzy paintings of Gavaldon's Readers. Agatha remembered Professor Dovey speaking to that tight-jawed woman. "Professor Sader," they called the artist. The same Sader who taught History of Heroism? Wasn't that class next?

This time, Agatha moved through the paintings slowly. As she did, she noticed the landscape evolved from frame to frame: more stores sprang up in the square, the church changed colors from white to red, two windmills rose behind the lake—until the village began to look just like the one she had left. Even more confused now, she drifted along the paintings until one made her stop.

As children read storybooks on the church steps, the sun spotlit a girl in a purple peacoat and yellow hat with sunflowers. Agatha put her nose to the girl. *Alice?* It had to be. The baker's daughter had worn the same ridiculous coat and hat every day of her life until she was kidnapped eight years before. Across the painting, an errant ray of sun spotlit a gaunt boy in black beating a cat with a stick. *Rune.* Agatha remembered him trying to gouge out Reaper's eye before her mother thrashed him away with a broomstick. Rune too had been taken that year.

Quickly she shifted to the next painting, where scores of children lined up in front of Mr. Deauville's, but the sun illuminated only two: bald Bane, biting the girl in front of him, and quiet, handsome Garrick. The two boys taken four years before.

Sweating, Agatha slowly turned to the next painting. As children read high on an emerald hill, two sat below, sunlit on a lake bank. A girl in black flicking matches into the water. A girl in pink packing pouches with cucumbers.

Breathless, Agatha dashed back through the row. In every one, light chose two children: one bright and fair, the other strange and grim. Agatha retreated from the nook and climbed on a stuffed cow's rump so she could see all the paintings at once, paintings that told her three things about this Professor Sader—

He could move between the real and fairy-tale worlds. He knew why children were brought here from Gavaldon.

And he could help them get home.

As fairies chimed the start of the next class, Agatha barged into the Theater of Tales and squeezed beside Kiko, while Tedros and his boys played handball against the phoenix carved into the front of the stone stage.

"Tristan didn't even say hi," Kiko griped. "Maybe he thinks I have warts now that I talked to yo—"

"Where's Sader?" Agatha said.

"*Professor* Sader," said a voice.

She looked up and saw a handsome silver-haired teacher give her a cryptic smile as he ascended the stage in his shamrock-green suit. The man who smiled at her in the foyer and on the Bridge.

Professor Crackpot.

Agatha exhaled. Surely he'd help if he liked her so much.

"As you know, I teach fourth session both here and in Evil and unfortunately cannot be in two places at once. Thus I'll be alternating weeks between schools," he said, clasping the lectern. "On weeks where I'm not here, you'll have former students come to recount their adventures in the Endless Woods. They'll be responsible for your weekly challenges, so please afford them the same respect you'd give me. Finally, given I am responsible for a vast amount of students and a vast amount of history, I do not hold office hours nor will I answer your questions inside or outside of class."

Agatha coughed. How could she get answers if he didn't allow questions?

"If you *do* have questions," said Sader, hazel eyes unblinking, "you'll surely find the answers in your text, *A Student's History of the Woods*, or in my other authored books, available in the Library of Virtue. Now to roll call. Beatrix?"

"Yes."

"One more time, Beatrix."

"Right here," Beatrix snapped.

"Thank you, Beatrix. Kiko!"

"Present!"

"Again, Kiko."

"I'm here, Professor Sader!"

"Excellent. Reena!"

"Yes."

"Again?"

Agatha groaned. At this rate, they'd be here until new moon.

"Tedros!"

"Here."

"Louder, Tedros."

"Good grief, is he deaf?" Agatha grouched.

"No, silly," said Kiko. "He's blind."

Agatha snorted. "Don't be ridi—"

The glassy eyes. The matching names to voices. The way he gripped the lectern.

"But his paintings!" Agatha cried. "He's seen Gavaldon! He's seen us!"

That's when Professor Sader met her eyes and smiled, as if to remind her he'd never seen anything at all.

"So let me get this straight," Sophie said. "There were two School Masters first. And they were brothers."

"Twins," said Hester.

"One Good, one Evil," said Anadil.

Sophie moved along a series of chipped marble murals built into Evil Hall. Covered in emerald algae and blue rust, torch-lit with sea-green flames, the hall looked like a cathedral that had spent most of its life underwater.

She stopped at one, depicting two young men in a castle chamber, keeping watch over the enchanted pen she had seen in the School Master's tower. One brother wore long black robes, the other white. In the cracked mosaic, she could make out their identical handsome faces, ghostly pale hair, and deep blue eyes. But where the white-robed brother's face was warm, gentle, the black-robed one's was icy and hard. Still, something about both of their faces seemed familiar.

"And these brothers ruled both schools and protected the magic pen," Sophie said.

"The *Storian*," Hester corrected.

"And Good won half the time and Evil won half the time?"

"More or less," said Anadil, feeding a snail to her pocketed rats. "My mother used to say that if Good went on a streak, Evil would find new tricks, forcing Good to improve its defense and beat them back."

"Nature's balance," said Dot, munching on a schoolbook

she'd turned to chocolate.

Sophie moved to the next mural, where the Evil brother had gone from ruling peacefully alongside his brother to attacking him with a barrage of spells. "But the Evil one thought he could control the pen—um, *Storian*—and make Evil invincible. So he gathers an army to destroy his brother and starts war."

"The *Great* War," said Hester. "Where everyone took a side between Good brother and Evil brother."

"And in the final battle between them, someone won," said Sophie, eyeing the last mural—a sea of Evers and Nevers bowed before a masked School Master in silver robes, the glowing Storian floating above his hands. "But no one knows who."

"Quick-study," Anadil grinned.

"But then surely people must know if he's the Good brother or Evil brother?" Sophie asked.

"Everyone pretends it's a mystery," said Hester, "but since the Great War, Evil hasn't won a single story."

"But doesn't the pen just write what happens in the Woods?" Sophie said, studying the strange symbols in the Storian's steel. "Don't *we* control the stories?"

"And it just happens one day all villains *die?*" Hester growled. "That *pen* is forcing our fates. That *pen* is killing all the villains. That *pen* is controlled by Good."

"Storian, love," Dot chomped. "Not a pen."

Hester smacked the book out of her mouth.

"But if you're going to die every time, why bother teaching villains?" said Sophie. "Why have the School for Evil at all?"

"Try asking a teacher that question," piped Dot, digging in

her bag for a bigger book.

"Fine, so you villains can't win anymore," Sophie yawned, filing her nails with a marble shard. "What's this to do with me?"

"The Storian started your fairy tale," Hester frowned.

"So?"

"And given your current school, the Storian thinks you're the villain in that fairy tale."

"And I should care about the opinion of a *pen*?" Sophie said, whittling nails on her other hand.

"I take back the quick-study bit," said Anadil.

"If you're the villain, you *die*, you imbecile!" Hester barked.

Sophie broke a nail. "But the School Master said I could go home!"

"Or maybe his riddle's a trap."

"He's *Good*! You said it yourself!"

"And you're in *Evil*," said Hester. "He's not on your side."

Sophie looked at her. Anadil and Dot had the same grim expression.

"I'm going to die here?" Sophie squeaked, eyes welling. "There has to be something I can do!"

"Solve the riddle," Hester said, shrugging. "It's the only way you'll know what he's up to. Plus your ending needs to happen soon. If you win one more challenge, I'll kill you myself."

"Then tell me the answer!" Sophie yelled.

"What does a villain never have that a princess can't do without?" Hester mulled, itching her tattoo.

"Animals, maybe?" said Dot.

"Villains can have animal henchmen. Just takes deeper corruption," said Anadil. "What about honor?"

"Evil has its own version of honor, valor, and everything else Good thinks they invented," Hester said. "We just have better names for them."

"I have it!"

They turned to Sophie.

"A birthday party!" she said. "Who would want to go to a Villain Party?"

Anadil and Hester stared at her.

"It's because she doesn't eat," said Dot. "Brains need food."

"Then you must be the smartest girl alive!" Sophie roared.

Dot glared back at her. "Remember the cruelest villains die the cruelest *deaths*."

Sophie turned to Hester nervously. "Would Lady Lesso tell me the answer?"

"If she thinks it'll help Evil win."

"You'd have to be clever," said Anadil.

"And subtle," said Hester.

"Cleverness? Subtlety? That's what I *do*, darling," Sophie said, relieved. "This riddle is good as solved."

"Or not, given we're fifteen minutes late," said Dot.

Indeed, the only thing chillier than Lady Lesso's frozen classroom was the looks she gave the four girls as they slipped through the door to their seats.

"I would send you for punishment, but they're occupied with students from my last class."

Boys' screams echoed from beneath their feet. The whole

class trembled at the thought of what was happening in the Doom Room.

"Let's see if our latecomers can redeem themselves," said Lady Lesso, heels clacking ominously.

"What are we doing?" Sophie whispered to Hort.

"She's testing us on famous Nemeses," Hort whispered. "If you get a question right, you get one of these." He flaunted a massive stick-on wart glued to his cheek.

Sophie recoiled. "That's a *reward?*"

"Hester, can you name a villain who destroyed her Nemesis with a Nightmare Curse?"

"Finola the Fairy Eater. Finola the Witch haunted the fairies' dreams and convinced them to cut off their own wings. With the fairies no longer able to fly, Finola caught and ate them one by one."

Sophie swallowed whatever came up. But she had never heard of Finola the Fairy Eater, so Hester had surely gotten it wrong.

"Correct! Finola the Fairy Eater! One of the most famous stories of all!" Lady Lesso said, and stuck a giant wart on Hester's hand.

Famous? Sophie wrinkled her nose. Famous where?

"Anadil, name a villain who killed their Nemesis using disguise!" Lady Lesso said.

"Rabid Bear Rex. Dressed himself in a bear skin because Princess Anatole loved bears. When she tried to pet him, he cut her throat."

"A great role model for us all, Rabid Bear Rex!" said Lady

Lesso, and planted a wart on Anadil's neck. "If he was alive, he'd wipe that grin off every one of Clarissa's gloating cockerels!"

Sophie bit her lip. Were they making this all up?

"Dot. Name a villain who murdered their Nemesis with transformation!"

"The Frost Queen! Turned the princess into ice and put her in the morning sun!"

"My favorite tale of all!" Lady Lesso thundered. "A story that will live forever in the hearts of—"

Sophie snorted.

"Is something *funny?*" said Lady Lesso.

"Never heard of any of these," Sophie said.

Hester and Anadil sank in their seats.

"Never *heard* of them?" Lady Lesso sneered. "These are Evil's greatest triumphs! The glory that inspires future villains! *Four Girls in a Well! Twelve Drowned Princesses! Ursula the Usurper, The Witch of—*"

"Never heard of those either," Sophie sighed, combing back her hair. "Where I come from, no one would read a story where Evil wins. Everyone wants Good to win because Good has better looks, nicer clothes, and more friends."

Lady Lesso was speechless.

Sophie turned to her classmates. "I'm sorry that no one likes you and you never win and that you have to go to school for no reason, but it's the truth."

Hester pulled her robes over her face.

Dot leaned forward and whispered into Sophie's ear. "The riddle, love."

"Oh, yes," said Sophie, all business. "While I have the floor, here's a bit of a brainteaser. It's quite important that I solve it, so any help would be deeply appreciated. What does a villain never have that a princess can't do without? Any ideas? Feel free to shout them out. *Merci*, darlings."

"I have an idea," said Lady Lesso.

"I knew you would." Sophie smiled. "What is it? What do I have that you don't?"

Lady Lesso thrust her face in hers. "*Nothing.* Which is what we'll be hearing from you the rest of class."

Sophie had an appeal, but it never made it out of her mouth. Her lips were sealed shut.

"Much better," Lady Lesso said, and blessed Sophie with a wart between the eyes.

As Sophie pried at her lips, Lady Lesso stood calmly and smoothed her purple gown, ignoring the petrified students around her.

"Now, Hort, tell me a villain who employed a Raven Death Trap."

Wheezing through her nose, Sophie wrenched at her mouth with a pen, hair clip, and icicle, which pierced her lips. Gasp, wail, scream, she tried it all, but all she found was silence, panic, blood—

And Hester glowering from the front row.

"Good as solved, eh?"

~⚬≈ 13 ≈⚬~

Doom Room

A gatha had no idea why lunch was a joint-school activity, because Evers sat with Evers, Nevers sat with Nevers, and both groups pretended the other wasn't there.

Lunch took place in the Clearing, an intimate picnic field outside the Blue Forest gates. To get to the Clearing, students had to journey through twisty tunnels of trees that grew narrower and narrower, until one by one the children spat through a hollowed trunk onto emerald grass. As soon as Agatha came through the Good tunnel, she followed the line of Evers receiving picnic baskets from nymphs in red hoods, while Nevers from the Evil tunnel took rusty pails from red-suited wolves.

Agatha found a shady patch of grass and reached into her willow basket to find a lunch of smoked trout sandwiches, rampion salad, strawberry soufflé, and a vial of sparkling lemon water. She let thoughts of riddles and dead ends fall away as she opened her watering mouth to the sandwich—

Sophie swiped it. "You don't know what I've been through," she sobbed, scarfing it whole. "Here's yours." She plunked down a pail of gruel.

Agatha stared at her.

"Look, I *asked*," Sophie garbled between bites. "Apparently Nevers need to learn deprivation. Part of your training. This is lovely, by the way."

Agatha was still staring.

"What?" Sophie said. "Do I have blood on my teeth? Because I thought I got it al—"

Over Agatha's shoulder, she saw Tedros and his friends pointing and snickering.

"Oh no," Sophie groaned. "What'd you do now?"

Agatha kept gaping at her.

"If you're going to be a brat about it, you can have the soufflé." Sophie frowned. "Why is that strange imp waving at me?"

Agatha turned and saw Kiko across the Clearing, waving and flaunting newly red hair. It was the exact same color as Tristan's. Agatha's face went white.

"Um, you *know* her?" Sophie said, watching Kiko giddily approach Tristan.

"We're friends," Agatha said, waving Kiko away from him.

"You have a *friend?*" Sophie said.

Agatha turned to her.

"Why do you keep looking at me like that!" Sophie yelled.

"You haven't been eating candy, have you?"

"Huh?" Sophie shrieked, realizing—her hand flew up and ripped Lesso's wart off her face—"Why didn't you tell me!" she cried, as Tedros and boys exploded into whoops.

"Ohhh, it can't get any worse," Sophie moaned.

Hort picked up her discarded wart and ran away with it.

Sophie looked at Agatha. Agatha cracked a smile.

"It's not funny!" Sophie wailed.

But Agatha was laughing and so was Sophie.

"What do you think he'll do with it?" Agatha sniggered.

Sophie stopped laughing. "We need to get home. *Now.*"

Agatha told Sophie about all her frustrations solving the riddle, including her dead end with Professor Sader. Before she could even try to ask about his paintings, Sader had taken off to meet his Evil students, leaving three geriatric pigs to lecture about the importance of fortifying one's houses.

"He's the only one who can help us," said Agatha.

"Better hurry. My days are numbered," Sophie said glumly and recounted everything that had happened with her roommates, including their prediction of Sophie's doom.

"You die? That doesn't make any sense. You can't be the villain in our story if we're friends."

"That's why the School Master said we *can't* be friends," Sophie replied. "Something has to come between us. Something that answers the riddle."

"What could possibly come between us?" Agatha said, still at a loss. "Maybe it's all connected. This thing that Good has and Evil doesn't. Do you think it's why Good always wins?"

"Evil *used* to win, according to Lady Lesso. But now Good has something that beats them all."

"But the School Master forbade us to return to his tower. So the answer to the riddle isn't a word or a thing or an idea—"

"We have to *do* something!"

"Now we're getting somewhere. First, it's something that can turn us against each other. Second, it's something that beats Evil every time. And third, it's something we can physically do—"

The girls spun to each other. "I got it," said Agatha—"Me too," said Sophie—

"It's so obvious."

"*So* obvious."

"It's—it's—"

"Yes, it's—"

"No idea," Agatha said.

"Me either," sighed Sophie.

Across the field Everboys slowly trespassed into Evergirl territory. Girls waited like flowers to be picked, only to see Beatrix attract the lion's share. As Beatrix flirted with her suitors, Tedros fidgeted on a tree stump. Finally he stood up, shoved in front of the other boys, and asked Beatrix to take a walk.

"He was supposed to rescue *me*," Sophie whimpered, watching them go.

"Sophie, we have the chance to save our village from a two-hundred-year-old curse, to rescue children from beatings and failings, to escape wolves, waves, gargoyles, and everything else in this awful school, and to end a story that will *kill* you. And you're thinking about a boy?"

"I wanted my happy ending, Aggie," Sophie said, tears sparkling.

"Getting home *alive* is our happy ending, Sophie."

Sophie nodded, but her eyes never left Tedros.

"Welcome to Good Deeds," said Professor Dovey to students gathered in the Purity Common Room. "Now we're behind your other subjects, so we'll dispense with the usual pleasantries. Let me begin by saying that over the years, I've seen a disturbing decrease in esteem for this class."

"Because it's after lunch," Tedros whispered into Agatha's ear.

"And you're talking to me why?"

"Seriously, what witchy spell did you put on me to make me choose your goblin."

Agatha didn't turn.

"You did *something*," Tedros fumed. "Tell me."

"Can't divulge a witch's secrets," Agatha said, gazing ahead.

"Knew it!" Tedros saw Professor Dovey glaring and flashed her a cocksure smile. She rolled her eyes and went on. He leaned over again to Agatha. "Tell me, and my boys will leave you alone."

"Does that include you?"

"Just tell me what you did."

Agatha exhaled. "I used the Hopsocotl Spell, a potent hex from the Gavaldonic Witches of Reapercat. They're a small coven on the shores of the Callis River, not just expert spell casters but also great harvesters of—"

"What you *did*."

"Well," said Agatha, turning to him, "the Hopsocotl Spell worms its way into your brain like a swarm of leeches. It swims its way into every cranny, breeding, multiplying, festering for just the right moment. And just when it hooks into your every nook and crevice . . . *sssspppt*! It sucks you of every intelligent thought and leaves you dumb as a donkey's ass."

Tedros went red.

"One more thing. It's permanent," Agatha said, and turned back around.

While Tedros mumbled about hangings, stonings, and the other ways his father punished wicked women, Agatha listened to Professor Dovey justify the importance of Good Deeds.

"Every time you do a Good Deed with true intention, your soul grows purer. Though lately, my Good students have been doing them as if they were chores, preferring to cultivate their egos, arrogance, and waist size! Let me assure you, our winning streak can end at any time!"

"Not if the School Master controls the Storian," said Agatha.

"Agatha, the School Master has absolutely no role in how the stories play out," Professor Dovey said impatiently. "He *cannot* control the Storian."

"He seemed pretty good at magic to me," Agatha replied.

"Excuse me?"

"He can split into shadows. He can make a room disappear. He can make it all seem like a dream, so surely he can control a pen—"

"And *how* might you know all this?" Professor Dovey sighed.

Agatha saw Tedros smirking.

"Because he showed me," she said.

Tedros' smirk vanished. Professor Dovey looked like a kettle about to steam. Students glanced nervously between her and Agatha.

Their teacher smiled tightly. "Oh, Agatha, what an imagination you have. It will serve you well when you're waiting for someone to rescue you from a ravenous dragon. Let's hope he arrives in time. Now, the three keys to Good Deeds are creativity, feasibility, and spontaneity—"

Agatha opened her mouth, but Professor Dovey silenced her with a glare. Knowing she was on shaky ground, Agatha pulled out parchment and took notes with the rest.

Before Surviving Fairy Tales, the students of both schools found themselves summoned to an assembly in the Clearing.

As soon as Agatha popped through the tree tunnel, Kiko grabbed her—"Tristan changed his hair!"

Agatha glanced over at Tristan, leaning against a tree. His hair was blond now, drooping over one eye. He reminded her of someone.

"He said he did it for Beatrix!" Kiko wailed, hair still hideously red.

Agatha followed Tristan's eyes to Beatrix, who was jabbering to Tedros. Tedros couldn't have been less enthused and puffed at the blond bangs drooping over his—

Agatha coughed. She looked back at Tristan, puffing at his droopy blond bangs. Then at Tedros, who had two shirt buttons undone and his tie loosened with its golden *T*. Then at Tristan, who had undone two buttons and loosened his tie with its golden *T*.

"What if I'm blond like Beatrix?" Kiko hounded. "Then will Tristan like me?"

Agatha turned. "You need to find a new crush immediately."

"ATTENTION."

She looked up to find the entire faculty fanned between the two tunnels, including Castor and Pollux, whose heads had been reunited on their canine body.

Professor Dovey stepped forward. "There's been some—"

"MOVE YOUR HIDES, YOU LAZY COWS!" Castor barked.

The last Nevers hurried from their tunnel, with Sophie stumbling out last. She gave Agatha a confused look across the Clearing. Agatha shrugged back.

Professor Dovey opened her mouth to resume—

"PRESENTING CLARISSA DOVEY, DEAN OF THE SCHOOL FOR GOOD AND PROFESSOR EMERITUS OF GOOD DEEDS," said Castor.

"Thank you, Castor," said Professor Dovey—

"ANY INTERRUPTIONS OR MISBEHAVIOR WILL BE SWIFTLY PUNISHED—"

"THANK YOU, CASTOR!" Professor Dovey shrieked.

Castor stared at his feet.

Professor Dovey cleared her throat. "Students, we have called you here because there have been some unfortunate rumors—"

"*Lies*, as I call them," said Lady Lesso. Agatha recognized her as the teacher who had ripped down Sader's painting in the Gallery of Good.

"So let us be clear," Professor Dovey continued. "First, there is no curse on Evil. Evil still has the power to defeat Good."

"Provided Evil does their homework!" Professor Manley growled.

Nevers muttered, as if they didn't believe this for a second.

"Second, the School Master is on no one's side," said Professor Dovey.

"How do you know?" Ravan shouted.

"Why should we believe you?" Hester yelled as Nevers catcalled—

"Because we have *proof*." Professor Sader stepped forward.

Nevers went quiet. Agatha's eyes widened. *Proof? What proof?*

Then she noticed Lady Lesso looked especially sour, confirming this proof did in fact exist. Was the proof the answer to the riddle?

"Last but not least," said Professor Dovey, "the School Master's primary responsibility is to protect the Storian. For that reason, he remains in his well-fortressed tower. Thus,

regardless of the tales you may hear, let me assure you: no student has ever seen the School Master and no student ever *will*."

Eyes fell on Agatha.

"Ah, is *this* the storyteller?" Lady Lesso leered.

"It's not a story!" Agatha shot back. She saw Sophie shake
her head to say this was an ill-advised battle.

Lady Lesso smiled. "I'll give you one more chance to redeem
yourself. *Did you meet the School Master?*"

Agatha looked at the Evil teacher, purple eyes bulging like
marbles. Then at Professor Sader, smiling at her curiously.
Then at Sophie across the Clearing, miming wart gluing,
mouth zipping . . .

"Yes."

"You *lie* to a teacher!" Lady Lesso lashed.

"It's not a lie!" a voice shouted.

Everyone turned to Sophie. "We were both there! We were
in his tower!"

"And I bet you saw the Storian too?" Beatrix sneered.

"Matter of fact, we did!" Sophie retorted to laughter.

"And did it start your fairy tale *too*?"

"It did! It did start our fairy tale!"

"All hail the Queen of Fools!" Beatrix proclaimed to roars.

"Then you must be the Grand *Empress*."

Beatrix turned to Agatha, arms akimbo.

"Ugh. The 'Mistake,'" Beatrix groaned. "Good has never
been so wrong."

"You wouldn't know Good if it crawled up your dress!"
Agatha yelled.

Beatrix gasped so loudly Tedros cracked a grin.

"Don't talk to Beatrix that way!" a voice said—

Agatha turned to find blond-haired Tristan—

"*Beatrix?*" Agatha exploded. "You sure you don't want Tedros? He'd love to marry himself!"

Tedros stopped smiling. Dumbstruck, he glanced between Agatha, Tristan, Beatrix . . . He lost patience and punched Tristan in the mouth. Tristan drew his dulled training sword, Tedros whipped out his, and they clashed in public duel. But Tristan had been studying Tedros in Swordplay, so they both used the exact same ripostes, the same retreats, even the same fight calls, until no one knew who was who—

Rather than intervene, Swordplay professor Espada twirled his long mustache. "We'll dissect this thoroughly in class tomorrow."

The Nevers had a more immediate response.

"*FIIIIGGGHHHHHT!*" Ravan roared.

Nevers rushed Evers, steamrolled stunned wolves, and dive-bombed into the dueling swordsmen. Whooping Everboys charged in, inciting an epic playground brawl that splattered Evergirls with mud. Agatha couldn't help but laugh at girls brought to their knees by dirt, until filthy Beatrix pointed at her.

"She started it!"

Screaming Evergirls charged after Agatha, who climbed a tree. Nearby, Tedros managed to reach his head from under boys and saw Sophie spring past. "Help!" he yelled—

Sophie stepped on his head as she ran to help Agatha, who was being pelted with pebbles by Beatrix. Then she caught

Hort out of the corner of her eye.

"You! Give me back my wart!"

Hort scooted around the brawling mass, Sophie in pursuit, until she got close enough to pick up a fallen branch and hurl it at his head—Hort ducked and it hit Lady Lesso in the face.

Students froze.

Lady Lesso touched her cold, gashed cheek. Staring at the blood on her hand, she grew eerily calm.

Her long red nail rose and pointed at Agatha.

"Lock her in her tower!"

A swarm of fairies seized Agatha and dragged her past smirking Tedros towards the Evers' tunnel—

"No, it's my fault!" Sophie cried—

"And this one." Lady Lesso stabbed her bloodstained finger at Sophie. "To the *Doom Room*."

Before Sophie could scream, a claw covered her mouth and pulled her past petrified classmates into the darkness of trees.

Sophie couldn't live through torture! Sophie couldn't survive true Evil!

As fairies flew her upstairs, Agatha welled panicked tears and glanced down to see teachers surging into the foyer.

"Professor Sader!" she cried, clinging to a banister. "You have to believe us! The Storian thinks Sophie's a villain! It's going to kill her!"

Sader and twenty teachers looked up, alarmed—

"How do you see our village?" Agatha yelled as fairies

wrested her away. "How do we get home? What does a princess have that a villain doesn't!"

Sader smiled. "Questions. Always in threes."

Teachers chuckled and dispersed. (*"Seen* the Storian?" Espada mused. "She's the one who eats candy," Professor Anemone explained.)

"No! You have to save her!" Agatha begged, but the fairies dragged her to her room and locked her in.

Frantic, she scaled her bed canopy past paintings of lip-locked heroes and lunged for the broken ceiling tile. . . . But it wasn't broken anymore. Someone had sealed it tight.

Blood drained from Agatha's cheeks. Sader was her only hope and he refused to answer questions. Now her only friend would die in that dungeon, all because a magic pen had mistaken a princess for a witch.

Then something flashed in her head. Something Sader said in class.

If you do have questions . . .

Breathless, Agatha emptied her basket of schoolbooks.

A gray wolf, stoic and efficient, tugged Sophie by a long chain fixed to a tight iron collar around her neck. Skirting the dank sewer walls, she couldn't fight her leash; one wrong step and she'd slip off the narrow path into roaring sludge. Across the rotted black river, she saw two wolves drag moaning Vex from the direction in which she was headed. His eyes met hers, red-rimmed, hateful. Whatever happened to him in the Doom Room had left him more a villain than when he entered.

Agatha, Sophie told herself. *Agatha will get us home.*
She bit back tears. *Stay alive for Agatha.*

As she approached the sewer's halfway point, where sludge turned to clear lake water, she felt the wall's solid stone become rusty grating. The wolf kicked the door open and shoved her in.

Sophie lifted her head to a dark dungeon, lit by a single torch. Everywhere she looked were tools of punishment: breaking wheel, rack, stocks, nooses, hooks, garrote, iron maiden, thumbscrews, and a terrifying collection of spears, clubs, rods, whips, and knives. Her heart stopped. She turned away—

Two red eyes glowed from the corner.

Slowly a big black wolf rose from shadows, twice the size of all the other wolves. But this one had a human's body with a thick, hairy chest, sinewy arms, bulging calves, and massive feet. The Beast cracked open a scroll of parchment and read in a deep growl.

"You, Sophie of Woods Beyond, have hereby been summoned to the Doom Room for the following sins: Conspiracy to Commit Untruth, Disruption of Assembly, Attempted Murder of a Faculty Member—"

"*Murder!*" Sophie gasped—

"Incitement of Public Riots, Crossing of Boundary Lines During Assembly, Destruction of School Property, Harassment of Fellow Students, and Crimes Against Humanity."

"I plead not guilty to all charges," Sophie scowled. "Especially the last."

The Beast seized her face in his claws. *"Guilty until proven innocent!"*

"Let go!" Sophie screamed.

He sniffed her neck. "Aren't you a luscious *peach*."

"You'll leave *marks*!"

To her surprise the Beast released her. "It usually takes beating to find the weak spot."

Sophie looked at the Beast, confused. He licked his lips and grinned.

With a cry, she lunged for the door—he slammed her to the wall and cuffed her arms to hooks above her head.

"Let me go!"

The Beast slunk along the wall, hunting for just the right punishment.

"Please, whatever I did, I'm sorry!" Sophie wailed.

"Villains don't learn from apologies," the Beast said. He considered a cudgel for a moment, then moved on. "Villains learn from pain."

"Please! Someone help me!"

"Pain makes you stronger," said the Beast.

He caressed the tip of a rusty spear, then hung it back up.

"*Help!*" Sophie shrieked.

"Pain makes you grow."

The Beast picked out an axe. Sophie's face went ghost white.

He walked up to her, axe handle in his meaty claw.

"Pain makes you Evil."

He took her hair in his hands.

"No!" Sophie choked.

The Beast raised the axe—

"*Please!*"

The blade slashed through her hair.

Sophie stared at her long, beautiful gold locks on the black dungeon floor, mouth frozen open in silence. Slowly she raised her terrorized face to meet the big black Beast's. Then her lips quivered, her body hung from its chains, and the tears came. She buried her shorn, jagged head in her chest and cried. She cried until her nose stuffed up and she couldn't breathe, spit caking her black tunic, wrists bleeding against her cuffs—

A lock snapped. Sophie lifted her raw, red eyes to see the Beast unhook her from the wall.

"Get out," he growled, and hung the axe up.

When he turned, Sophie was gone.

The Beast lumbered out of the cell and knelt at the midpoint between roiling muck and clean water. As he dipped the bloody chains in, currents smashed from both directions, rinsing them clean. Scrubbing the last spots of blood away, he caught his reflection in the sludge—

Only it wasn't his.

The Beast spun—

Sophie shoved him in.

The Beast thrashed in water and slime, grunting and flailing for the wall. The tides were too strong. She watched him gurgle his last breaths and sink like a stone.

Sophie smoothed her hair and walked towards the light, swallowing the sickness in her throat.

The Good forgive, said the rules.

But the rules were wrong. They had to be.

Because she hadn't forgiven.

She hadn't forgiven at all.

⟿ 14 ⟾

The Crypt Keeper's Solution

The cover was silver silk, painted with the glowing Storian clutched between black and white swans.

A Student's History of the Woods
AUGUST A. SADER

Agatha opened to the first page. *"This book reflects the views of its author ONLY. Professor Sader's interpretation of history is his alone and the faculty does not share it. Sincerely, Clarissa Dovey & Lady Lesso, Deans of the School for Good and Evil."*

Agatha felt encouraged the faculty disapproved of the book in her hands. It gave her more

hope that somewhere in these pages was the answer to the riddle. The difference between a princess and a witch . . . the proof Good and Evil were balanced. . . . Could they be the same?

She flipped the page to start, but it didn't have words. Splashed across it were patterns of embossed dots in a rainbow of colors, small as pinheads. Agatha turned the page. More dots. She tore through fistfuls of pages. No words at all. She dumped her face to the book in frustration. Sader's voice boomed:

"Chapter Fourteen: The Great War."

Agatha lurched up. Before her eyes, a ghostly three-dimensional scene melted into view atop the book page—a living diorama, colors gauzy like Sader's paintings in the gallery. She crouched to watch a silent vision unfold of three wizened old men, beards to the floor, standing in the School Master's tower with hands united. As the old men opened their hands, the gleaming Storian levitated out of them and over a familiar white stone table. Sader's disembodied voice continued:

"Now remember from Chapter One, the Storian was placed at the School for Good and Evil by the Three Seers of the Endless Woods, who believed it the only place it could be protected from corruption . . ."

Agatha gawked in disbelief. Sightless Sader couldn't write history. But he could *see* it and wanted the same for his students. Every time she turned a page and touched the dots, living history came alive to his narration. Most of Chapter 14 recounted what Sophie had told her at lunch: that the School had been ruled by two sorcerer brothers, one Good, one Evil, whose love for each other overcame their loyalties to either side. But in time, the Evil brother found love give way to temptation, until he saw only one obstacle between him and the pen's infinite power . . . his own blood.

Agatha's hands swept over dots, scanning exhaustive scenes of Great War battles, alliances, betrayals to see how it all ended. Her fingers stopped as she watched a familiar figure in silver robes and mask rise out of the burning carnage of battle, Storian in hand:

"From the final fight between Evil brother and Good brother, a victor emerged beholden to neither side. In the Great Truce, the triumphant School Master vowed to rise above Good and Evil and protect the balance for as long as he could keep himself alive. Neither side trusted the victor, of course. But they didn't need to."

The scene flashed to the dying brother, burning to ashes as he desperately stabbed his hand into the sky, unleashing a burst of silver light—

"For the dying brother used his final embers of magic to create a last spell against his twin: a way to prove Good and Evil still equal. As long as this proof stayed intact, then the Storian remained uncorrupted and the Woods in perfect balance. And as to what this proof is . . ."

Agatha's heart leapt—

"It remains in the School for Good and Evil to this very day."

The scene went dark.

She turned the page urgently, touched the dots. Sader's voice boomed—

"Chapter Fifteen: The Woodswide Roach Plague."

Agatha flung the book against the wall, then the others, leaving cracks in painted couples' faces. When there were no more to throw, she buried her face in the bed.

Please. Help us.

Then in the silence between prayers and tears, something came. Not even a thought. An impulse.

Agatha lifted her head.

The answer to the riddle looked back at her.

It's just a haircut, Sophie told herself as she climbed through a cornflower thicket. *No one will even notice.* She slid between two periwinkle trees into the West Clearing, approaching her group from behind.

Just find Agatha and—

The group turned all at once. No one laughed. Not Dot. Not Tedros. Not even Beatrix. They gaped with such horror Sophie couldn't breathe.

"Excuse me—something in my eye—" She ducked behind a blue rosebush and gulped for air. She couldn't bear any more humiliation.

"Least you look like a Never now," Tedros said, bobbing behind the bush. "So no one makes my mistake."

Sophie turned beet red.

"Well, this is what happens when you're friends with a witch," the prince frowned.

Now, Sophie was a pomegranate.

"Look, it's not *that* bad. Not as bad your friend, at least."

"Excuse me," said Sophie, eggplant purple. "Something in my other eye—"

She darted out and grabbed Dot like a life raft—"Where's Agatha!"

But Dot was still staring at her hair. Sophie cleared her throat.

"Oh, um, they haven't let her out of her room," Dot said. "Too bad she'll miss the Flowerground. If Yuba can call the conductor, that is." She nodded at the gnome, grumpily jabbing at a blue pumpkin patch. Dot's eyes drifted back to Sophie's hair.

"It's . . . nice."

"Please don't," Sophie said softly.

Dot's eyes misted. "You were so *pretty*."

"It'll grow back," Sophie said, trying not to cry.

"Don't worry," Dot sniffled. "One day, someone Evil enough will kill that monster."

Sophie stiffened.

"All aboard!" Yuba called.

She turned to see Tedros open the top of an ordinary blue pumpkin like a teapot and vanish inside.

Sophie squinted. "What in the—"

Something poked her hip and she looked down. Yuba thrust a Flowerground pass at her and opened the pumpkin lid, revealing a thin caterpillar in a violet velvet tuxedo and matching top hat, floating in a swirl of pastel colors.

"No spitting, sneezing, singing, sniffling, swinging, swearing, slapping, sleeping, or urinating in the Flowerground," he said in the crabbiest voice imaginable. "Violations will result in removal of your clothes. All aboard!"

Sophie whipped to Yuba. "Wait! I need to find my frien—"

A vine shot up and yanked her in.

Too stunned to scream, she plunged through dazzling pinks, blues, yellows, as more tendrils lashed and fastened around her like safety belts. Sophie heard a hiss and wheeled to see a giant green flytrap swallow her. She found her scream before vines jerked her out of its mouth into a tunnel of hot, blinding mist and hooked her onto something that kept her moving while her feet and arms dangled freely in the ivy harness. Then the mist cleared and Sophie saw the most magical thing she'd ever seen.

It was an underground transport system, big as a whole village, made entirely of luminescent *plants*. Dangling passengers hung on to vine straps attached to glowing, different-colored tree trunks covered in matching flowers. These color-coded trunks wove together in a colossal maze of tracks. Some trunks ran parallel, some perpendicular, some forked in different directions, but all took riders to their precise destinations in the Endless Woods. Sophie stared in shock at a row of unsmiling dwarves, pickaxes in belts, clinging to straps off a fluorescent red trunk labeled ROSALINDA LINE. Running in the opposite direction was the glittery green ARBOREA LINE, with a family of bears in crisp suits and dresses among the riders hanging off shamrock vines. Flabbergasted, Sophie peered down her HIBISCUS LINE to see the rest of her group swinging from an electric-blue trunk. But only the Nevers were strapped into harnesses.

"Flowerground's only for Evers," Dot called out. "They have to let us on 'cause we're with the school. But they still don't trust us."

Sophie didn't care. She would ride the Flowerground for the rest of her life if she could. Besides its strong, soothing pace and delicious scents, there was an orchestra of lizards for each line: the TANGERINE LINE lizards strummed bouncy banjo guitars, the VIOLET LINE ones played sultry sitars, and the lizards on Sophie's line piped up-tempo jingles on piccolos, accompanied by caroling blue frogs. Lest riders grow hungry, each line had its own snacks, with bluebirds fluttering along the HIBISCUS LINE, offering blue-corn muffins and blueberry punch. For once, Sophie had all she needed. Muscles unclenching, she forgot about boys and beasts as vines pulled her up, up, into a churning wind wheel of blue light. Her body felt wind, then air, then earth, and arms unfurling into the sky, Sophie bloomed out of the ground like a heavenly hyacinth—

And found herself in a graveyard.

Headstones the color of the bleak sky swept over barren hills. Shivering classmates spouted from a hole in the ground next to her.

"Wherrre arrre wweee?" she stammered through chattering teeth.

"Garden—of—Good and Evil," Dot shivered, nibbling a chocolate lizard.

"Doesn'ttt look likke a garrrden to meee," Sophie chattered back.

Warmth thawed her skin as Yuba sparked a few small fires

around the group with his magical staff. Sophie and her classmates exhaled.

"In a few weeks you will each be unlocked to perform spells," said the gnome to excited titters. "But spells are no substitute for survival skills. Meerworms live near graves and can keep you alive when food is scarce. Today you'll be finding and eating them!"

Sophie clutched her stomach.

"Off you go! Teams of two!" the gnome said. "Whichever team eats the most meerworms wins the challenge!" His eyes flicked to Sophie. "Perhaps our black sheep can find redemption."

"Black sheep can't find anything without her *girlfriend*," Tedros murmured.

Sophie moped miserably as he paired up with Beatrix.

"Come on," Dot said, pulling Sophie to the ground. "We can beat them."

Suddenly motivated, Sophie started searching the ground with Dot, careful to stay close to the fire. "What do meerworms look like?"

"Like worms," said Dot.

Sophie was deliberating a retort when she noticed a figure in the distance, silhouetted atop a hill. It was a massive giant, with a long black beard, thick dreadlocks, and midnight-blue skin. He wore only a small brown loincloth as he dug a row of graves.

"Does it all himself, the Crypt Keeper," Dot said to Sophie. "That's why there's such a backlog."

Sophie followed her eyes to a two-mile line of bodies and

coffins behind the Crypt Keeper, waiting for burial. Immediately she could see the difference between the Nevers' dark
stone coffins and the Evers' coffins made of glass and gold.
But there were also some bodies without caskets, just lying
untended on the hillslope beneath circling vultures.

"Why doesn't he have help?" she said, nauseous.

"'Cause no one can interfere with the Crypt Keeper's system,"
Hort said softly. "Two years my dad's waited." His voice cracked.
"Killed by Peter Pan himself, my dad. Deserves a proper grave."

Now the whole group was watching the Crypt Keeper dig
his graves, before pulling a big book from his mass of hair and
studying one of its pages. Then the giant picked up a gold coffin with a handsome prince inside and heaved it into the empty
plot. He moved down the line of waiting bodies, picked up a
crystal coffin with a beautiful princess, and laid it beside the
prince's coffin in the same grave.

"Anastasia and Jacob. Died of starvation while on honey-
moon. Avoidable deaths had they paid attention in *class*," Yuba
snapped.

Grumbling, the students went back to meerworm hunting,
but Sophie kept her eye on the Crypt Keeper, who studied his
book again before picking up a coffinless ogre and plunking
him in the next plot. Back to the book, and then he rested a
resplendent queen's silver tomb beside a matching king's.

Sophie's eyes drifted around the graveyard and saw the same
pattern on every hill and valley. Evers buried together with twin
headstones—boy and girl, man and wife, prince and princess,
together in life and in death. Nevers buried all alone.

Ever After. Paradise together.

Nevermore. Paradise alone.

Sophie froze. She knew the answer to the School Master's riddle.

"Perhaps we should search Necro Ridge," Yuba sighed. "Come, students—"

"Cover for me," Sophie whispered to Dot.

Dot swiveled. "Where are you—wait! We're a—"

But Sophie was scampering through distant gravestones towards the Flowerground entrance.

"Team," Dot sulked.

A short while later, in the Blue Forest, five stymphs looked up from their billy goat to see Sophie brandishing an egg.

"Let's try this again, shall we?"

It was there all along, Agatha thought as she gazed at the walls. The weapon that made Good invincible against Evil. The thing a villain could never have but a princess couldn't do without. The task that would send her and Sophie home.

If Sophie is alive.

Agatha felt another wave of powerless dread. She couldn't just sit here while Sophie was being tortured—

Screams pealed outside. She spun to see Sophie hurled through her window by a bucking stymph.

"Love," Sophie panted.

"You're alive! Your *hair*," Agatha gasped—

"Love is what a villain can never have but a heroine can't live without."

"But what did they—are you—"

"Am I right or not?"

Agatha saw Sophie had no intention of talking about the Doom Room.

"Almost." She pointed to the paintings on the wall with visions of heroes and heroines, lips pressed in climactic embrace.

"True love's kiss," Sophie breathed.

"If your true love kisses you, then you can't be a villain," Agatha said.

"And if you can't find love, then you can't be a princess," said Sophie.

"And we go home." Agatha swallowed. "My half is taken care of. Yours isn't so simple."

"Oh, please. I can make any one of those disgusting Never-boys fall in love with me. Just give me five minutes, an empty broom closet, and—"

"There's only one, Sophie," Agatha said, voice fraying. "For every Ever, there's only one true love."

Sophie met her eyes. She collapsed onto the bed.

"Tedros."

Agatha nodded sickly. The road home led through the one person who could ruin everything.

"Tedros has to . . . kiss me?" Sophie said, staring into space.

"And he can't be tricked, forced, or duped into it. He has to mean it."

"But how? He thinks I'm a villain! He hates me! Aggie, he's a king's son. He's beautiful, he's perfect and look at me—"

She grabbed her shorn hair and flaccid robes. "I'm—I'm—"

"Still a princess."

Sophie looked at her. "And the only way we'll get home," said Agatha, forcing a smile. "So we have to make this kiss happen."

"We?" said Sophie.

"We," rasped Agatha.

Sophie hugged her tight.

"We're going home, Aggie."

But in her arms, Agatha sensed something else. Something that told her the Doom Room had taken more from her friend than just her hair. Agatha squelched her doubts and clasped Sophie tighter.

"One kiss and it will all be over," she whispered.

As they embraced in one tower, in another the School Master watched the Storian finish a magnificent painting of the two girls in each other's arms. The pen added a last flourish of words beneath it, closing the chapter.

"But no kiss comes without its price."

~ 15 ~

Choose Your Coffin

Whenever Tedros was stressed, he worked out. So to see him sweating at 6:00 a.m. in the Groom Room, throwing hammers, pumping dumbbells, and swimming laps, meant he had a lot on his mind. It was understandable. The Snow Ball invitations had been slipped under doors during the night.

As he scaled climbing ropes made of braided blond hair, he cursed the fact he would spend Christmas at a Ball. Why did everything with Evers revolve around oppressive formal dances? The problem with Balls was that boys had to do all the work. Girls could flirt and scheme and wish all they wanted, but in the end, it's the boy who had to make his

Dear Agatha,
you are kindially
invited to the
EVERS' SNOW
BALL

choice and hope she said yes. Tedros wasn't worried about the girl saying yes. He was worried there was no girl he wanted to ask at all.

He couldn't remember the last time he actually liked a girl. And yet, he always had one following him, claiming to be his girlfriend. It happened every time. He vowed to forget girls, then noticed one getting attention, set out to prove he could get her, got her, and discovered she was a fatuous prince hunter who had had her eye on him all along. The Beatrix Curse. No. There was a better name for it.

The Guinevere Curse.

Tedros was only nine when his mother, Guinevere, made off with the knight Lancelot, leaving him and his father alone. He heard the whispers that followed. *"She found love."* But what about all those times she said "I love you" to his father? All the times she said it to him? Which love was real?

Night after night, Tedros watched his father slip further into heartbreak and drunkenness. Death came within the year. With his last breaths, King Arthur gripped his son's hands.

"The people will need a queen, Tedros. Don't make my mistakes. Look for the girl who is *truly Good.*"

Tedros climbed higher and higher on the golden braids, veins straining against muscle.

Don't make my mistakes.

His hand slipped and he fell off the rope, crashing to a soft mat. Cheeks red, he glowered at the taunting waterfalls of hair.

All the girls here were mistakes. Guineveres who confused love with kisses.

Daylight flecked across Agatha's pillow. She stirred and saw Sophie hunched on Reena's old bed.

"Why are you still here! If the wolves catch you, it's the Doom Room again! Besides, you should be home writing that anonymous love poem to Tedr—"

"You didn't tell me there's a Ball."

Sophie held up a glittering snowflake invitation, Agatha's name in pearls.

"Oh, who cares about a stupid Ball?" Agatha groaned. "We'll be long gone. Now make sure that poem talks about who he is as a person. His honor, his valor, his cour—"

Sophie was smelling the invitation now.

"Sophie, listen to me! The closer we get to the Ball, the more Tedros looks for a date! The more he looks for a date, the more he falls in love with someone else! The more he falls in love with someone else, the more he leaves us here to die! Got it?"

"But I want to be his date."

"YOU'RE NOT INVITED!"

Sophie pursed her lips.

"Sophie, Tedros has to kiss you *now*! Otherwise we'll never get home!"

"Honestly, do they even check invitations at a Ball?"

Agatha snatched the invitation. "Stupid me. I thought you wanted to stay alive!"

"But I can't miss the Ball!"

Agatha shoved her towards the door. "Use the Tunnel of Trees—"

"Marble hall, glittering gowns, waltzing under stars . . ."

"If a wolf catches you, just say you're lost—"

"A Ball, Aggie! A real Ball!"

Agatha kicked her out. Sophie scowled back.

"My roommates will help me. They're *true* friends."

She slammed the door on Agatha's shocked expression.

Ten minutes later, Hester stamped her foot, nearly killing Anadil's rat.

"HELP! YOU WANT ME TO HELP A NEVER KISS AN EVER! I'D RATHER STICK MY HEAD UP A HORSE'S—"

"Sophie, no villain ever finds *love*," Anadil said, hoping reason might save her rats. "To even look for it is to betray your own soul—"

"You want me to go home?" Sophie snapped, picking away tunnel leaves. "Then put a hex on Tedros so he asks me to the Ball."

"THE BALL!" Hester screeched. "HOW DO YOU EVEN KNOW ABOUT THE BALL?"

"A villain at a *Ball?*" said Dot.

"A villain waltzing!" said Anadil.

"A villain curtsying!" said Hester, and all three collapsed into howls.

"I'm *going* to that Ball," Sophie fumed.

"Presenting the *Witch of Woods Beyond*!" Hester cackled through tears.

By lunch, she wasn't laughing.

First, Sophie was twenty minutes late to class after trying to find a solution to her jagged hair. She disguised it with berets, bows, combs before settling on a daisy wreath.

"Not hideous," she sighed before she walked into Uglification and saw students' hair turned gray from bat wing potions. A "1" suddenly exploded over her head.

"Hideous!" Professor Manley beamed, ogling her hair. "Your greatest beauty. *Gone.*"

Sophie sobbed as she left class, but then heard Hester scream. In the hall, Albemarle, a studious, spectacled woodpecker, was chipping Sophie's name just below hers on the Evil rankings board.

"One little love spell, Hester," Sophie reminded sweetly. "And then I'm gone forever."

Hester stomped away, reminding herself that Nevers kissing Evers couldn't be encouraged no matter how extreme the circumstances.

At the start of Curses, Lady Lesso swept into the ice chamber, jaw tighter than usual.

"Impossible to find good torturers these days," she muttered.

"What is she talking about?" Sophie whispered to Dot.

"Beast went missing!" Dot whispered back.

Behind her, Sophie looked nauseous.

Testing the class on Nemesis Dreams, Lady Lesso seethed and sniped at every wrong answer.

"But I thought a Nemesis Dream meant you'll be a Lead Villain," Hester said—

"No, you imbecile! Only if you have symptoms! A Nemesis Dream is nothing without symptoms!" Lady Lesso retorted.

"Dot, what do you taste in your mouth during your first Nemesis Dream?"

"What you ate before bed?"

"*Blood*, you idiot!" Lady Lesso dragged nails across the ice wall. "Oh, what I'd give to see a real villain in this school. A real villain who could make Good weep instead of these dung fleas."

When it came to her turn, Sophie expected the worst abuse, only to have Lady Lesso give her a wart for a surely incorrect answer and caress her shorn hair as she passed.

"Why is she being *nice* to you?" Hester hissed behind her.

Sophie had the same question, but turned around with a smile. "Because I'm future Class Captain. As long as I *stay* here, that is."

Hester looked like she might break Sophie's neck. "Love spells are junk villainy. They don't *work*."

"I'm sure you'll find one that does," Sophie said.

"I'm warning you, Sophie. This will end badly."

"Hmm . . . What about petunias in every room?" Sophie mused. "I think it'll be my first proposal as Class Captain."

That night Hester wrote to her relatives for love spells.

"It's contagious," Agatha moaned as Evergirls bounded around the Clearing showing each other their invitations, each snowflake a different shape. Nearby Tedros shot marbles and ignored them entirely. "Every challenge had to do with Ball beauty, Ball etiquette, Ball entrances, Ball history—"

Sophie wasn't listening. Pail of pig's feet in hand, she gazed longingly at the Evergirls.

"*No*," Agatha said.

"But what if he *asks* me?"

"Sophie, he needs to kiss you *now*! Not take you to some stupid Ball!"

"Oh, Agatha, don't you know your fairy tales? If he takes me to the Ball, *then* he'll kiss me! Like Cinderella at midnight! Kisses *always* happen at the Ball! And by then my hair will have grown and I'll have fixed my shoes and—oh no, the gown! Can you steal some charmeuse from one of the girls? Some crepe de chine too. And tulle! *Mountains* of tulle! Preferably in pink, but I can always dye it, though tulle never looks quite right dyed. Perhaps we should go with chiffon, then. Much more manageable."

Agatha blinked, speechless.

"You're right, I should ask him first," Sophie said, leaping up. "No frowns, darling. It'll be easy as pie. You'll see! Princess Sophie at a *Ball*!"

"What are you—YOU'LL RUIN EVERYTHI—"

But Sophie had already flounced to the Evers' side, plopped next to Tedros, and held out her pail.

"Hello, handsome. Want some of my . . . feet?"

Tedros misfired his marble into Chaddick's eye. The entire Clearing went silent.

He turned to her. "Your girlfriend's calling."

Sophie followed his eyes to Agatha, waving her off.

"She's just upset," Sophie sighed. "You were right, Tedros. She and I are too close. That's why I left in the middle of class yesterday. To tell her it's time I make Good friends now."

"Dot said you left because you were sick."

Sophie coughed. "Oh, well, I had a bit of a cold—"

"She said it was diarrhea."

"*Diarr*—" Sophie swallowed. "You know Dot. Always making things up."

"She doesn't seem like a liar to me."

"Oh, she's always lying. Just to get attention. Since she's, you know . . ."

Tedros raised his eyebrows. "Since she's . . ."

"Fat."

"I see." Tedros lined up his marble. "Funny, isn't it? She crawled into empty graves to eat enough worms for the two of you, just so you wouldn't fail. Said you're her best friend."

"Did she?" Sophie saw Dot waving at her. "How depressing." She turned to Tedros, who was preparing to shoot. "Do you remember when we first met, Tedros? It was in the Blue Forest. Nothing that happened after matters, not you punching me or calling me a Never or you landing in poo. What matters is what you felt at *first sight*. You wanted to rescue me, Tedros. And here I am."

She folded her hands. "Whenever you're ready, then."

Tedros looked up at her. "What?"

"To ask me to the Ball," Sophie said, smiling.

The prince's face didn't change.

"I know it's a bit early, but a girl does have to *plan*," Sophie pressed.

Beatrix shoved in. "No room for Nevers."

"What? There's plenty of room," Sophie huffed—

But Reena jostled her, then six other girls, and Sophie was pushed out of the circle entirely. She whirled to Tedros to defend her.

"Can you go away?" he said, eyes on his marble. "You're blocking my view."

Agatha smirked as Sophie stomped towards her.

"Easy as pie, hmm?"

Sophie blew past her—

"Humble pie!" Agatha shouted.

"It's the hair!" Sophie sobbed.

"It's not the hair!" Agatha said as they trudged through the Blue Forest gates. "You need to make him *like* you first! Otherwise we'll never get home!"

"It's supposed to be love at first sight. That's how fairy tales work!"

"Time for Plan B."

"Then again, he didn't say *no*," Sophie said hopefully. "Perhaps it didn't go so badly."

Dot rushed up. "Everyone's saying you called Tedros a liar, threw poo in his face, and licked his feet!"

Sophie turned to Agatha. "What's Plan B?"

They arrived with the rest of their Forest Group to find eight glass coffins nestled in turquoise grass.

"Each week, we'll repeat the challenge to discern Good from Evil, since it is the most crucial skill you will take into the Woods," Yuba announced. "Today we'll test the Evers. Given the fascination with yesterday's burials, I thought we'd give you a taste of your own."

With that, he made Evergirls and Nevergirls climb into the open coffins and with a swish of his staff, turned all eight into identical dark-haired princesses with big hips, round backsides, and trouty lips.

"I'm *obese*," Sophie gasped.

"Look, this is your chance," Agatha said, remembering Princess Uma's words. "If Tedros is your greatest wish, he'll be pulled towards you! He'll know you're his true love!"

"But Beatrix will wish for him too!"

"You have to wish harder! Focus on what you love about him! Focus on what makes him *yours*!"

Yuba slammed the glass lids on both girls and jumbled the eight coffins. "Now study the maidens carefully and search for signs of Good," he said to the boys. "Once you're sure you've found an Ever, kiss her hand and her true nature will be revealed!"

The Everboys warily ventured towards the coffins—

"We want to play too."

Yuba turned to Hort and the Neverboys, chomping at the bit.

"Mmm, I suppose it'll give our girls incentive to behave," said the gnome.

Inside the coffins, eight plump princesses stiffened as both Good and Evil boys wandered around them. Hort snuck to a blue mint bush, stepped over a snacking skunk, and tore off a few leaves. He saw Ravan staring.

"What? I like being fresh," said Hort, munching mint.

"Hurry up and make your choices!" Yuba barked.

In her coffin, Agatha wished Tedros would look deep into Sophie's heart and see who she truly was. . . .

In her coffin, Sophie closed her eyes and thought of everything she loved about her prince. . . .

Tedros, meanwhile, didn't want *any* of these girls. But just as he was about to bag the challenge, he felt his eyes drawn to the third coffin. Something pulled him towards its maiden, even though she looked just like all the rest. A warmth, a glow, a spark of energy pulsing between them. Yes, something was there. Something he hadn't noticed before. One of these girls was more than what she seemed. . . .

"Time's up!" Yuba said.

Agatha heard a bloodcurdling shriek and spun to Sophie, back in her body, lips scrunched against Hort's.

Hort released her. "Oh, the *hand*. Oops." He popped another mint leaf. "Should we start again?"

"You *APE*!" Sophie kicked him and he crashed into the mint bush, onto the snacking skunk, which raised its tail and sprayed him in the eyes. Hort staggered around, ramming into coffins— "I'm blind! I'm blind!"—until he smashed into Sophie's again, which slammed shut, sealing his skunked body in with hers. Aghast, Sophie rammed the glass, but it wouldn't budge.

"Rule #5. Nevers don't trifle with love," Yuba crabbed. "Fitting punishment. Now come, boys, let's see who you've picked."

Agatha heard her own coffin open. She turned and saw Tedros lift her thick hand towards his tender lips. Stunned, Agatha kneed him in the chest. Tedros fell back, bashed his head on the coffin top, and slumped to the ground. Everboys crowded around him, and princess clones jumped from their coffins to help, while Yuba conjured a block of ice for the prince's skull. In the chaos, Agatha slipped out of her coffin and into the one next to it.

Tedros staggered up, with no intention of letting his princess go.

Yuba grimaced. "Perhaps you should sit do—"

"I want to finish."

With a sigh, Yuba nodded at the clones, who climbed back into the coffins and closed their eyes.

Tedros remembered it was the third coffin. He lifted the jeweled glass over its maiden and kissed her hand with confidence. The princess melted into Beatrix, smiling imperiously—Tedros dropped her hand like a hot stone. In the next coffin, Agatha sighed with relief.

The wolves howled in the distance. As the class followed Yuba back to school, Agatha stayed behind with Sophie.

"Come, Agatha," Yuba called. "This is Sophie's lesson to learn."

Agatha glanced back to see Sophie sealed in with Hort, holding her nose as she screamed and kicked the glass. Maybe the gnome was right. Tomorrow her friend would be ready to listen.

"She'll survive," she muttered, following the others. "It's only Hort."

But Hort wasn't the problem.

The problem was that Sophie had seen Agatha switch coffins.

16

Cupid Goes Rogue

Shielding herself from a morning storm, Agatha accosted Hester in the Nevers' lunch line.

"Where's Sophie?"

"Won't come out of the room. Missed all our classes," Hester said as a wolf dumped mystery meat into her pail. "Apparently sharing a coffin with Hort robs you of your will to live."

When Agatha made it to puddled Halfway Bridge, her reflection was waiting for her, more glum and gaunt than the last time.

"I need to see Sophie," Agatha said, avoiding eye contact with herself.

"That's the second time he's looked at you that way."

"Huh? Second time who looked at me?"

"Tedros."

"Well, Sophie won't listen to me."

"Well, maybe Sophie isn't Tedros' true love, then."

"She has to be," Agatha said, suddenly worried. "It can't be someone else. That's how we're getting back home! Who else could it be? Beatrix? Reena? Milli—"

"*You.*"

Agatha looked up. Her reflection smiled hideously.

Agatha's eyes veered back to her wet clumps. "That is the *stupidest* thing I've ever heard. First off, love is something story-books invented to keep girls busy. Second, I *hate* Tedros. Third, he thinks I'm an evil witch, which given my recent behavior, might be true. Now let me through."

Her reflection stopped smiling. "You think we're a witch?"

Agatha glowered at herself. "We're making our friend win her true love just so we can take her away from him."

Her reflection instantly turned uglier. "*Definitely Evil,*" it said, and vanished.

The door to Room 66 was unlocked. Agatha found Sophie curled under her scorched, tattered covers.

"I *saw* it!" Sophie hissed. "I saw him pick you! Here I'm worried about Beatrix, when *you're* the double-crossing, back-stabbing fink!"

"Look, I don't know why Tedros keeps choosing me," Agatha said, squeezing rain from her hair.

Sophie's eyes drilled into her.

"I want him to choose you, you fool!" Agatha yelled. "I want us to go home!"

Sophie searched her face for a long moment. With a sigh, she turned to the window.

"You don't know what it was *like*. I still smell him everywhere. He's in my *nose*, Agatha. They've given him his own room until the stench goes away. But who's to say where skunk ends and Hort begins?"

Shuddering, Sophie turned back. "I did everything you said, Aggie. I focused on all the things I love about Tedros—his skin, his eyes, his cheekbones—"

"Sophie, that's his *looks*! Tedros won't feel a connection if you just like him because he's handsome. How is that different from every other girl?"

Sophie frowned. "I didn't want to think about his crown or his fortune. That's shallow."

"Think about who he is! His personality! His values! What he's like deep down!"

"*Excuse* me, I know how to make a boy love me," Sophie huffed, shooing her out. "Just stop *ruining* things and let me do things my way."

Apparently Sophie's way was to humiliate herself as much as possible.

During lunch the next day, she sidled up to Tedros in the Evers' line, only to have his boys crowd her, chomping blue mint leaves. Then she tried to get the prince alone in Surviving Fairy Tales, but Beatrix stuck to him like glue, taking every opportunity to remind him he picked *her* coffin.

"Tedros, can I talk to you?" Sophie blurted finally.

"Why would he talk to *you*?" Beatrix said.

"Because we're *friends*, you buzzing gnat!"

"Friends!" Tedros flared. "I've seen how you treat your friends. Use them. Betray them. Call them fat. Call them liars. Appreciate the offer. I'll pass."

"Attacking. Betraying. Lying. Sounds like one of our Nevers is using her rules!" Yuba beamed.

Sophie was so despondent she even ate a piece of Dot's chocolate.

"We'll find you a love spell somehow," said Dot.

"Thanks, Dot," Sophie sobbed, mouth full. "This is *amazing*."

"Rat droppings. Makes the best fudge."

Sophie gagged.

"Who'd you call fat, by the way?" Dot asked.

Things got worse. For a weeklong challenge in Henchmen Training and Animal Communication, students of both schools had to tote assigned creature sidekicks everywhere they went. At first, both schools exploded into chaos, with trolls tossing Nevers out windows, stampeding satyrs stealing lunch baskets, baby dragons setting desks on fire, and animals christening the Good halls with mountains of dung.

"It's a tradition. An attempt at school unity," Professor Dovey said to her Evers, clothespin on her nose. "However misguided and poorly organized."

Castor scowled at Nevers flitting about the Belfry, under

siege by their henchmen. "ONCE YOU GET YOUR HEADS OUT OF YOUR BEHINDS, YOU'LL REALIZE WHO'S MASTER!"

And indeed, after three days, Hester had her baby ogre potty trained and spitballing Evers at lunch, Tedros had his wolfhound swaggering behind him, Anadil's python befriended her rats, and Beatrix's fluffy white bunny inspired such love she named it Teddy. (Tedros kicked it every time he saw it.) Even Agatha managed to teach her plucky ostrich how to steal candy without teachers noticing.

Sophie, however, found herself with a chubby cupid named Grimm, with bushy black hair, pug nose, pink wings, and eyes that changed colors depending on his moods. She knew his name was Grimm because he wrote it all over Room 66 in her favorite lipstick the first day. On Day 2, he saw Agatha for the first time at lunch and his eyes went from green to red. Then on Day 3, while Yuba taught "Uses of Wells," he started shooting arrows at Agatha, who leapt behind the Forest well just in time.

"CALL THAT THING OFF!" Tedros yelled as he deflected Grimm's arrows into the well with his training sword.

"Grimm! *She's my friend!*" Sophie shouted.

Grimm guiltily put his arrows away.

On Day 4, he spent all of Sophie's classes grinding his teeth in the corner and clawing at the walls.

Lady Lesso gave him a curious stare. "You know, by looking at him you'd think . . ." She gazed at Sophie, then brushed the thought away. "Never mind. Just give him a little milk and he'll be more amenable."

The milk worked on Day 5. On Day 6, Grimm started shooting at Agatha again. Sophie tried everything she could to pacify him: she sang lullabies, gave him Dot's best fudge, even let him have her bed while she took the floor, but this time nothing would stop him.

"What do I do?" Sophie cried to Lady Lesso after class.

"Some henchmen go rogue," Lady Lesso sighed. "It's a hazard of villainy. But usually it's because . . ."

"Because what?"

"Oh, I'm sure he'll calm down. They always do."

But by Day 7, Grimm started *flying* after Agatha during lunch, evading the grasps of students and wolves, until Hester's demon finally subdued him. Agatha glared at Sophie from behind a tree.

"Maybe you remind him of someone?" Sophie whimpered.

But even Hester's demon couldn't control Grimm for long, and the next day his arrows came tipped with fire. After one of these singed her ear, Agatha finally had enough. Remembering Yuba's last lesson, she lured the rogue cupid into the Blue Forest during lunch and hid in the deep stone well. When Grimm giddily dove down the dark shaft to find her, she clubbed him with her clump and knocked him out cold.

"I thought he'd kill you," Sophie wept after they sealed the well with a boulder.

"I can take care of myself," Agatha said. "Look, the Ball is less than two months away and things with Tedros are getting worse. We have to try a new—"

"He's *my* prince," Sophie stiffened. "And I'll handle him myself."

Agatha didn't bother arguing. When Sophie was ready, she'd listen.

While both schools went off with Castor and Uma to free their henchmen back to the Blue Forest, Sophie stole away to the Library of Vice.

It took all of her will not to run out the moment she came in. Perched atop Vice's top floor, the Library of Vice was like a normal library, only after a flood, fire, and tornado had swept through. Its rusty iron bookshelves were skewed at odd angles, with thousands of fallen books all over the floor. The walls were furry green with mold, the brown carpet was moist and sticky, and the room smelled like a mix of smoke and sour milk.

Behind a desk in the corner was a gelatinous toad, puffing a cigar and stamping books one after one before tossing them on the floor.

"Subject of interest," he burped.

"Love spells," Sophie said, trying not to breathe.

The toad nodded to a dank shelf in the corner. There were only three books left on it:

Thorns, Not Roses: Why Love Is a Curse by Baron Dracul
A Never's Guide to Ending True Love by Dr. Walter Bartoli
Foolproof Love Spells & Potions by Glinda Gooch

Sophie threw open the third, ran down its list of spells until she found "Spell 53: The True Love Heart Hex."

She ripped out the page and fled before she fainted from the stench.

Dot, Hester, and Anadil hunched over it during lunch. "'Once a boy is under this spell, he will instantly fall in love with you and do whatever you ask,'" Anadil read. "'Works particularly well with eliciting proposals of marriage and invitations to Balls.'"

"All you have to do is mix the prescribed potion into a bullet and shoot it at your true love's heart!" Sophie read excitedly.

"It won't work," Hester crabbed.

"You're just mad because *I* found it."

Hester snatched a heap of letters from her bag. "'Dear Hester, I don't know of any love spells that work'—'Dear Hester, love spells are notoriously dodgy'—'Dear Hester, love spells are dangerous. Use a bad spell and you can warp someone permanently'—"

"It's 'foolproof'!" Dot said.

"Says who? Glinda *GOOCH*?"

"I say it's worth a try if it means we don't have to talk about Balls and kisses anymore," Anadil said, red eyes studying the recipe. "Bat heart, lodestones, cat bone . . . These are all standard ingredients. Oh. We need a drop of Tedros' '*scent*.'"

"How are we going to get that?" Dot said. "If a Never even gets near an Ever, the wolves are on us. We need an Ever to do it."

Agatha plopped down in a heap of pink. "What'd I miss?"

Sophie only got five words out.

"No! No spells. No hexes. No tricks!" Agatha scolded. "It has to be true love!"

"But look!" Sophie held up the page and its painting of a prince and princess kissing at a Ball. The caption: "ONLY AUTHENTIC SUBSTITUTE FOR TRUE LOVE!"

Agatha crumpled the page and dumped it in Sophie's pail. "I don't want to hear about it again."

Sophie spent the rest of lunch picking at her loaf of cheese.

Two days later, Hester felt a jab in the middle of the night. She stirred to see Sophie standing over her bed, sniffing a blue tie with a gold *T*.

"Smells like heaven. I'm sure there's enough here."

For a moment, Hester looked confused. Then her cheeks swelled, ready to detonate—

"What about a Villain's Choir?" Sophie said. "I think that'll be my second proposal as Captain."

Hester stayed up all night mixing the ingredients. Using her mother's old crockery, she blended them into a frothy pink potion, distilled the love potion into shimmering gas, and poured the gas into a heart-shaped bullet over the fireplace.

"Just hope he doesn't die," Hester growled, handing it over.

Sophie practiced her aim for two days before she knew she was ready. She waited until Surviving Fairy Tales, when Yuba and the group were climbing trees to study "Forest Flora." When Tedros reached for a blue hornbeam branch, she saw her chance and drew the bullet into her slingshot—

"You're *mine*," Sophie whispered.

The pink heart shot off the sling and flew straight for the silver swan on Tedros' heart, only to turn crimson, ricochet off him like rubber, and smash back into her with a violent, alien scream. The whole group spun in shock.

Sophie's black robes were splashed with a giant, bloody letter *F*.

"For Failing to abide by the rules." Yuba glowered from a tree. "No spells until *after* the Unlocking."

Beatrix picked the broken heart bullet off the ground. "A love spell? You tried a love spell on *Tedros?*"

The class burst into howls. Sophie turned to Tedros, who couldn't have looked more enraged. Next to him, Agatha had the same expression. Sophie covered her face and fled, sobs echoing through the forest.

"Every year, a rascal tries something. But even the sorriest rascal knows there's no shortcuts to love," Yuba said. "We'll start with proper spells next week, I assure you. But for now, on to ferns! How can we tell if a fern is actually a Never in disguise—"

Agatha didn't follow the group to the Fernfield. Slouched against an oak, she gazed at the heart-shaped pieces in the grass, just as shattered as her dreams of home.

Hester came back from supper to find Sophie sprawled on her bed, a puddle of tears.

Sophie looked up, the red *F* on her robes even brighter now. "It won't come off. I tried everything."

Hester dumped her schoolbag on the floor. "We're

practicing our talents in the common room. Feel free to join."
She opened the door and paused.

"I *warned* you."

Sophie jumped at the slam.

All night she couldn't sleep, dreading the thought of wearing the *F* to lunch the next day. Finally she managed to doze off and woke to find the sun up and all her roommates gone to breakfast.

Agatha was sitting on the edge of her bed, picking dead leaves out of her pink dress.

"A wolf saw me this time. But I lost him in the tunnel." She glanced up at a gilded mirror on a wall. "Looks nice in here."

"Thank you for bringing it," Sophie rasped.

"My room's happier without it."

Tense silence.

"I'm sorry, Agatha."

"Sophie, I'm on your side. We have to work together if we want to get out of here alive."

"The spell was our only hope," Sophie said softly.

"Sophie, we can't give up! We have to get home!"

Sophie stared into the mirror, eyes welling. "What *happened* to me, Agatha?"

"You want the Ball without winning your prince. You want your kiss without doing the work. Look, I had to clean plates after supper all week, so I read while doing it." Agatha pulled a book from her dress—*Winning Your Prince* by Emma Anemone—and started flipping to dog-eared pages.

"According to this, winning true love is the ultimate

challenge. In every fairy tale, it might seem like love at first sight, but there's always skill behind it."

"But I already—"

"Shut up and listen. It comes down to three things. Three things a girl has to do to win her fairy-tale prince. First, you need to 'flaunt your strengths.' Second, you need to 'speak through actions, not words.' And third, you need to 'parade competing suitors.' If you just do these three things and do them well, we stand a—"

Sophie raised her hand.

"What."

"I can't flaunt anything in this potato sack, can't act with that she-devil in my face, and have no competing suitors except a boy who looks and smells like a rat! Look at me, Agatha! I have an *F* on my chest, my hair looks like a boy's, I have bags under my eyes, my lips are dry, and yesterday I found a blackhead on my nose!"

"And how are you going to change that?" Agatha snapped.

Sophie bowed her head. The ugly letter cast shadows on her hands. "Tell me what to do, Aggie. I'm listening."

"Show him who you are," Agatha said, softening.

She gazed deep into her friend's eyes.

"Show him the real Sophie."

Sophie saw the faith burning bright in Agatha's smile. Then, turning to the mirror, she managed a sly smile of her own . . . a smile that matched one of a grim little cupid, trapped deep in darkness, waiting patiently to be let out.

17

The Empress's New Clothes

News of Sophie's failed love spell swept across both schools, and by midmorning everyone waited with bated breath to get a glimpse of her scarlet *F*. But when Sophie skipped all her morning classes, it was clear she was too ashamed to show her face.

"You should have heard the things Tedros *called* her," Beatrix said to Evergirls at lunch.

Sitting in a heap of autumn leaves, Agatha tuned her out and looked over at Tedros and the Everboys playing rugby, silver swans glimmering on blue knit sweaters. Across the Clearing, Nevers shunned group activities and sat mostly by them-selves. Hester

glanced up from *Spells for Suffering* and read Agatha's eyes with a shrug, as if Sophie's whereabouts were the least of her concerns.

"Now, Teddykins, it's not her fault," Beatrix blathered loudly. "The poor girl thinks she's one of us. We should feel sorry for someone so pathe—"

Her eyes bulged. Agatha saw why.

Sophie sashayed into the Clearing, dumpy black sack refashioned into a strapless bodice dress, *F* shimmering over her chest with devil-red sequins. She'd cut her blond hair even shorter and slicked it down in a shiny bob. Her face was painted geisha white, her eyelids pink, her lips vermilion, and her glass shoes had not only been repaired but heeled even taller, which together with the extremely short dress, showed off long, creamy legs. From the shadows she swanned into sun, and light exploded off her glitter-dusted skin, bathing her in heavenly glow. Sophie strutted past Hester, who dropped her book, past Everboys, who dropped their ball, and glided right up to Hort.

"Let's do lunch," she said, sweeping him away like a hostage.

Across the field, Tedros' sword fell out of its sheath.

He saw Beatrix glaring and put it back.

During Surviving Fairy Tales, Sophie ignored Yuba's lecture on "Leaving Useful Trails" and spent the entire class cozying up to Hort and filling her Never pail with roots and herbs from the Blue Forest.

"What are you doing!" hissed Agatha.

"Can you believe it, Aggie darling? They have beetroot, willow bark, lemonwood and everything else I need to make my old potions and creams! Soon I'll be back to my real self!"

"This wasn't the 'real Sophie' I had in mind."

"*Excuse* me? I'm just following *your* rules. *Flaunt* my assets, which are many, as you can see. Speak through *actions*—have I said a *word* to Tedros? No. Haven't. And lest we forget, *parade* competing suitors. Do you know what it takes to survive lunch with Hort? To nuzzle that rodent every time I see Tedros looking? *Eucalyptus*, Agatha. I *numb* my nose with eucalyptus. But in the end, you were right."

"Listen, you misun— I was?"

"You reminded me what's important." Sophie nodded to Tedros and Everboys ogling her across the thicket. "It doesn't matter if you're a Never, Ever, or whatever. In the end, the fairest of them all wins." She glossed her lips and gave them a smack. "You'll see. He'll ask me to the Ball before the week's up and you'll get your precious kiss. So no more negativity, darling, it gives me a headache. Now, where's that worthless Hort? I told him to stay by me at all times!" She swept away, leaving Agatha speechless.

In the School for Evil, Nevers sulked through supper, knowing they had a full night of studying ahead. With spell casting set to begin, the teachers' tests were based less on talent now and more in tedious recall. For the next day alone, they had to memorize eighty murder schemes for Lady Lesso's first challenge, Giant commands for Henchmen, and the Flowerground Map for Sader's geography exam.

"How will he correct them?" Hester groused. "He can't even see!"

At curfew, Hester, Dot, and Anadil trudged back from the common room, piled high with books, only to find their room turned into a laboratory. Dozens of brilliant-colored potions bubbled over open flames, vials of creams, soaps, and dyes littered the shelves, a mess of dried leaves, herbs, flowers blanketed the three beds . . . and in the center of it all sat Sophie, buried under sequins, ribbons, and fabric, testing new concoctions on patches of skin.

"My God, she *is* a witch," Anadil gasped.

Sophie held up *The Recipe Book for Good Looks*. "I stole it from an Ever at lunch."

"Shouldn't you be studying for challenges?" Dot asked.

"Beauty is a full-time job," sighed Sophie, lathering herself in a bright green balm.

"And you wonder why Evers are slow," Hester said.

"Sophie is back, darlings. And she's just getting started," Sophie mooned. "*Love* is my challenge now."

And indeed, though Sophie placed near the bottom in all three challenges the next day, she placed first in Attention, arriving to lunch with her black uniform remolded into a dazzling slit-back toga dress, sashed with blue orchids. Her heels were a full inch taller, her face shimmering bronze, her eye shadow provocative periwinkle, her lips delicious crimson, and the glittering *F* on the front of her dress was now complemented by sequins on the back that read: ". . . is for *Fabulous*."

"That *can't* be allowed," Beatrix whined to drooling boys.

But she *was* wearing her uniform, Sophie insisted to teachers, while usually fierce wolves looked just as awed as the boys. Dot swore one even winked at Sophie when it filled her lunch pail.

"She's making a mockery of villainy!" Hester fumed, black eyes flaying Sophie across the Clearing. "They should lock her in the Doom Room permanently."

"Beast's still missing," Anadil yawned. "Whatever spooked him must have been pretty bad."

The next day, Sophie flunked all her challenges again and yet somehow avoided failing out of school. Though she was clearly the worst, each time she saw a "19" pop up instead of a "20." ("I'm just too lovable to fail," she preened to mystified classmates.)

During Forest Groups, Sophie ignored Yuba's lecture on "Scarecrow Survival" and scribbled busily in her notebook, while Agatha glowered at her black baby doll dress, pink lollipop, and sequins spelling "F . . . is for *Fun*."

"Name something else that starts with *F*," Sophie whispered.

"I'm trying to listen and so should you, since we'll be here *forever*."

"F is for 'Forever.' Mmm, a bit heady. How about 'Flirty'? Or 'Fetching'?"

"Or 'Futile'! He hasn't even talked to you yet!"

"F is for '*Faith*,'" Sophie said. "Which I thought you had in me."

Agatha grumbled to herself the rest of class.

But Sophie almost made her a believer when she arrived the next day in a belly-baring black halter, poofed miniskirt, spiky pixie hairdo, and heels dyed hot pink. The Everboys spent lunch goggling at her between slobbery bites of beef. And yet, even though Sophie could see Tedros sneak peeks at her legs, grit his teeth each time she passed, and sweat when she got too close . . . he still didn't talk to her.

"It's not enough," Agatha said, accosting her after Yuba's class. "You need better assets."

Sophie looked down at herself. "I think my assets are quite sufficient."

"Deeper assets, you idiot! Something *inside*! Like compassion or charity or kindness!"

Sophie blinked. "Sometimes you make wonderful sense, Aggie. He needs to see how Good I truly am."

"She sees reason," Agatha exhaled. "Now hurry. If he asks someone else to the Ball, we'll never get home!"

Agatha proposed that Sophie sneak Tedros love limericks filled with clever rhymes or leave him secret presents that revealed depth and thought, tried-and-true strategies both outlined in *Winning Your Prince*. Sophie listened, nodding to all of this, so when Agatha arrived at lunch the next day, she expected to read a first draft of a verse or inspect a handmade gift. Instead, she arrived to find a group of 20 Nevergirls crowded in a corner of the Clearing.

"What's going on over there?" Agatha asked Hester and Anadil, both studying in tree shade.

"She said it was your idea," Hester sneered, eyes on her book.

"Bad idea," Anadil said. "So bad we don't want to talk to you."

Confused, Agatha turned to the gathering. A familiar voice rang from its center—

"*Fabulous*, darlings! But just a little less *cream*!"

Agatha's chest tightened. She forced her way through the swarm of Nevers until she stumbled into the center and almost died from shock.

Sophie sat on a tree stump, a painted wooden sign hanging from a branch above her:

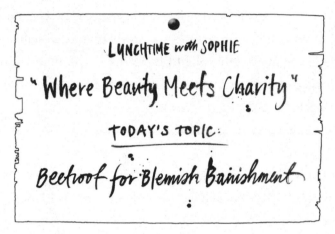

LUNCHTIME with SOPHIE

"Where Beauty Meets Charity"

TODAY'S TOPIC:

Beetroot for Blemish Banishment

All around her, Nevergirls were squeezing sticky red beetroot cream onto their pimples and warts.

"Now remember, girls. Just because you're ugly doesn't mean you can't be presentable," Sophie preached.

"I'm bringing my roommates tomorrow," Arachne whispered to green-skinned Mona.

Agatha gaped, flabbergasted. Then she saw someone sneaking away. "Dot?"

Dot turned meekly, smothered in red cream. "Oh! Hello! I was just, you know, I thought I should check up on—you know, to see if, in case—" She looked at her feet. "Don't tell Hester."

Agatha had no idea what *any* of this had to do with winning Tedros' love. But when she tried to corner Sophie after,
three Nevergirls shoved in front of her to ask Sophie about picking the best beets. Agatha didn't get a chance in Forest Groups
either, because Yuba separated the Evers and Nevers.

"You must get used to seeing each other as the enemy! The
first Trial by Tale is in three weeks!" the gnome said. "Now
for the Trial, you'll need a few basic spells. There is no one
way to do magic, of course. Some spells require visualization,
some incantations, others hand flicks, foot taps, magic wands,
numeric codes, or even partners! Yet there is one rule common
to *all* spells."

From his pocket, he pulled a shiny silver key, the bit shaped
like a swan.

"Evers, right hands, please."

Baffled Evers looked at each other, and held out their
hands.

"Mmm. You first."

Agatha frowned as he grabbed her hand, then her second
finger. "Wait—what are you going to—"

Yuba magically plunged his swan key into Agatha's fingertip—the skin went see-through and the swan sank past tissue,
veins, blood, and attached to her bone. The gnome turned the
bow and her bone painlessly rotated a full circle. Her fingertip
glowed bright orange for just a moment, then dulled as Yuba
withdrew the key. Bewildered, Agatha stared at her finger as
Yuba unlocked the rest of the Evers, then the Nevers, including

Sophie, who barely glanced up from scribbling in her notebook.

"*Magic follows feeling.* That is our only rule," said the gnome when he was finished. "When your finger glows, it means you have summoned enough emotion, enough purpose to perform a spell. You can only do magic when you have deep need *and* want!"

Students squinted at their fingers, feeling, coaxing with all their might, and soon fingertips started to flicker, each person's a unique color.

"But like a magic wand, fingerglow is just a training wheel!" Yuba warned. "In the Woods, you will look like a nincompoop if you light up every time you cast a spell. We will relock your glow once you show control." He grimaced at Hort, uselessly thrusting his finger at rocks, trying to make something happen. "If *ever.*"

The gnome turned back to the group.

"In the first year, you'll learn only three types of spells: Water Control, Weather Manipulation, and Mogrification, both plant and animal. Today we'll begin with the last," he said to excited twitters. "A simple visualization spell but highly effective for escaping enemies. Now, since your clothes won't fit after you Mogrify, it's easier if you're not wearing any."

The students stopped tittering.

"But I suppose we'll do," Yuba said. "Who wants to go first?"

Everyone raised their hand except two. Agatha, who was praying now more than ever that Sophie had a plan to get home. And Sophie, who was too busy writing her next lecture ("'Bath' Is Not a Four-Letter Word") to care about any of this.

By the third day on her stump, Sophie had 30 freshly bathed Nevergirls attend "Just Say No to Drab."

"Now Professor Manley says a Never must be ugly. That ugly means uniqueness, power, freedom! So here's my question to Professor Manley. How do you expect us to feel unique, empowered, or free . . . in *this?*" she roared, waving the dumpy black robes like an enemy flag. The cheer was so loud that across the Clearing, Beatrix's pen slipped and ruined her ball gown sketch.

"It's that mentally ill Sophie," Beatrix snapped.

"Still looking for a Ball date, is she," murmured Tedros, aiming his next horseshoe throw.

"Worse. Now she's trying to convince the Nevers they're not losers."

Tedros missed his shot in surprise.

Agatha didn't even try to see Sophie after lunch, with Nevergirls mobbing her for style advice. She didn't try the next day, either, when an impromptu shoe burning erupted after Sophie's lecture on "Abandon All Ye Clumps!" and wolves ran around whipping students back to the tower. And she certainly didn't try the next, when every Nevergirl showed up for Sophie's talk on "Fitness for the Unfit," except Hester and Anadil, who cornered Agatha after lunch.

"This idea keeps getting more rotten," Anadil said. "So rotten we're not your friends anymore."

"Boys, balls, kisses—all your problem now," Hester snarled, demon twitching on her neck. "As long as it doesn't mess with me winning Captain, I could give a hog's behind what you two do. Got it?"

The next day, Agatha hid in the Tunnel of Trees, waited for the sound of high heels on dead leaves, and tackled Sophie in a flying leap. "What is it today? Cuticle creams! Teeth whiteners! More abdominal exercises!"

"If you want to talk to me, you can wait in line with everyone else!" Sophie yelled.

"'Malevolent Makeovers,' 'Black Is the New Black,' 'Yoga for Villains'! Do you *want* to die here?"

"You said show him something *deeper*. Isn't this compassion? Isn't this kindness and wisdom? I'm helping those who can't help themselves!"

"Excuse me, Saint Teresa, but the goal here is Tedros! How is this accomplishing anything!"

"Accomplishment. Such a vague word. But I'd consider *that* an accomplishment, wouldn't you?"

Agatha followed Sophie's look out the tunnel. The crowd in front of her stump was a hundred Nevers deep. Only there was one hovering in back who didn't look like the rest.

A golden-haired boy in a blue rugby sweater.

Agatha released Sophie in shock.

"You should come," Sophie called as she flounced out of the tunnel. "Today's about dry, damaged hair."

In front of the stump, Arachne's one eye glowered at Tedros. "Why is Prince Prettyface here?"

"Yeah, back to your side, Everboy," Mona sniped, pelting him with tree mold.

More Nevergirls started to heckle him and Tedros shrank

back anxiously. He wasn't used to being unpopular. But just as he was booed away—

"We welcome *everyone*," Sophie admonished as she swept to her stump.

Tedros came back every day that week. He told his mates he just wanted to see what Sophie was wearing, but there was more to it. With each new day, he watched her teach misshapen villains how to straighten their hunches, hold eye contact, and enunciate their words. He watched Neverboys skeptically skulk on the fringes at first, only to soon badger Sophie for advice on sleeping better, masking body odor, and managing their tempers. At first the wolves yawned through these assemblies, but Tedros could see them listening as more and more Nevers showed up for Sophie's lectures. Soon the villains began to debate her prescriptions at supper and over dreggy tea in common rooms. They started to sit together at lunch, defend each other in class, and stopped making jokes about their losing streak. For the first time in two hundred years, Evil had *hope*. All because of one girl.

By the end of the week, Tedros had a seat in the front row.

"It's working! I can't believe it!" Agatha gushed as she walked Sophie to the Tunnel of Trees. "He might say he loves you! He might kiss you this week! We're going home! What's tomorrow's topic?"

"'*Eating Your Words*,'" Sophie said, swishing ahead.

At lunch the next day, Agatha stood in line for a basket of artichoke and olive tartines, dreaming about the heroes' welcome she and Sophie would get when they returned home.

Gavaldon would erect statues of them in the square, fete them in sermons, stage a musical about their lives, and teach school-children about the two girls who saved them from the curse. Her mother would have a thousand new patients, Reaper fresh trout every day, and she would have her pictures in the town scroll and anyone who had ever dared to mock her would now grovel at her—

"What a joke."

Agatha turned to Beatrix, who was watching Nevers throng around Sophie in a revealing black sari and sharp-heeled fur booties for her lecture on "How to Be the Best at Everything (Like Me!)."

"As if *she's* the best," Beatrix snorted.

"I think she's the best Never I've ever seen," a voice said behind her.

Beatrix whirled to Tedros. "Is she now, Teddy? And I think it's all a big *fairy tale*."

Tedros followed her eyes to the ranking boards, smoldering in soft sunlight on the Blue Forest gates. On the Nevers board, Sophie's name hung off the bottom, pecked to holes by robins. Number 120 out of 120.

"*The Empress's New Clothes*, to be precise," Beatrix said, and strutted away.

Tedros didn't go to see Sophie that day. Word spread that he found it sad to watch Nevers pin their hopes on the "worst girl in school."

The next day, Sophie showed up to a deserted stump. The wooden sign had been defaced.

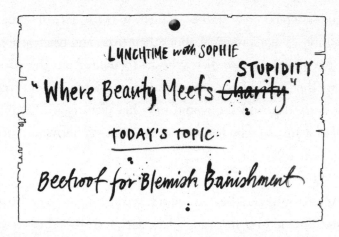

LUNCHTIME *with* SOPHIE

"Where Beauty Meets ~~Charity~~ STUPIDITY"

TODAY'S TOPIC:

Beetroot for Blemish Banishment

"I told you to pay attention!" Agatha shouted as they waited in pouring rain after Yuba's class for wolves to open the gates.

"Between sewing new outfits, brewing new makeup, preparing new lectures, I can't worry about *class*!" Sophie sobbed under a black parasol. "I have my *fans* to think about!"

"Of which you now have none!" Agatha yelled. She could see Hester smirking at her from the Group 6 huddle. "Three bottom ranks and you fail, Sophie! I don't know how you've survived this long!"

"They don't *let* me fail! No matter how bad I am! Why do you think I stopped studying!"

Agatha tried to make sense of this, but couldn't focus with her fingertip burning. Ever since Yuba unlocked it, it glowed whenever she was angry, as if raring to do a spell.

"But how did you get all those high ranks before?" she said, hiding her hand in her pocket.

"That was before they made us *read*. I mean, do I *look* like I care how to poison a comb, how to pluck toad eyes, or how to say 'May I cross your bridge' in Troll? Here I am trying to *improve* these villains and you want me to memorize the recipe for Children Noodle Soup? Agatha, did you know that to boil a child you have to wrap them in parchment first? Otherwise they won't be properly cooked and might wake up in your pot. Is that what you want me to learn? How to hurt and kill? How to be a *witch*?"

"Listen, you need to win back respect—"

"Through intentional Evil? No. Shan't."

"Then we're doomed," Agatha snapped. Sophie exhaled angrily and turned away.

Suddenly her expression changed. "What in the—"

She gawked at the Evers ranking board, tacked to the gates.

1. TEDROS OF CAMELOT	71 POINTS
2. BEATRIX OF JAUNT JOLIE	84 POINTS
3. REENA OF PASHA DUNES	88 POINTS
4. AGATHA OF WOODS BEYOND	96 POINTS

"But—but—you're . . . *you*!" Sophie cried.

"And *I* do my homework!" Agatha barked. "I don't want to learn dove calls or practice fainting or sew handkerchiefs, but I'll do whatever it takes to get us home!"

But Sophie wasn't listening. A naughty grin spread across her face.

Agatha crossed her arms. "No way. First of all, teachers will catch us."

"You'll love my Curses homework, it's all about tricking

princes—and you *hate* boys!"

"Second, your roommates will tell on you—"

"And you'll love my Uglification homework! We're learning to scare children—and you *hate* children!"

"If Tedros finds out, we're dead—"

"And look at your finger! It glows when you're upset! I can't do that!"

"It's a fluke!"

"Look, it's even brighter now! You're born to be a vill—"

Agatha stomped. "WE'RE NOT CHEATING!"

Sophie fell silent. Wolves unlocked the Blue Forest gates and students surged into the tunnels.

Neither Sophie nor Agatha moved.

"My roommates say I'm 100% Evil," Sophie said softly. "But you know the truth. I don't know *how* to be Evil. Not even 1%. So please don't ask me to go against my own soul, Agatha. I can't." Her voice caught. "I just can't."

She left Agatha under the umbrella. As Sophie joined the herd, the storm rinsed the sheen out of her hair, the glitter off her skin until Agatha couldn't tell her from the other villains. Guilt flushed through her, burning her finger bright as the sun. She hadn't told Sophie the truth. She had the same idea to do Sophie's Evil work and squashed it. Not because she was afraid she'd get caught.

She was afraid she might like it. All 100%.

That night, Sophie had nightmares. Tedros kissing goblins, Agatha crawling from a well with cupid wings, Hester's demon chasing her through sewers, until the Beast rose out of dark water, bloody hands snatching, and Sophie lunged past him and locked herself in the Doom Room. Only there was a new torturer waiting. Her father in a wolf mask.

Sophie jolted awake.

Her roommates were fast asleep. She sighed, nestled into her pillow—and bolted back up.

There was a cockroach on her nose.

She started to scream—

"It's me!" the roach hissed.

Sophie closed her eyes. *Wake up, wake up, wake up.*

She opened them. It was still there.

"What's my favorite muffin?" she wheezed.

"Flourless blueberry bran," the roach spat. "Any more stupid questions?"

Sophie picked the bug off her nose. It had the same bulging eyes and sunken cheeks.

"How in the world—"

"Mogrification. We've been learning it for two weeks. Meet me in the common room."

Agatha the Cockroach glared back as she skittered for the door.

"And bring your books."

18

The Roach and the Fox

"Suppose mine glows green or brown or something?" Sophie yawned, scratching her legs. Everything in the Malice Common Room was made of burlap—the floors, the furniture, the curtains—like some barbarous itch chamber. "I'm not doing it if it clashes with my clothes."

"Just focus on an emotion!" barked the roach on her shoulder. "Like anger. Try anger."

Sophie closed her eyes. "Is it glowing?"

"No. What are you thinking about?"

"The food here."

"Real anger, you

oaf! Magic comes from *real* feelings!"

Sophie's face scrunched with effort.

"Deeper! Nothing's happening!"

Sophie's face darkened and her fingertip flickered hot pink.

"That's it! You're doing it!" Agatha hopped excitedly. "What are you thinking about!"

"How infuriating your voice is," Sophie said, opening her eyes. "Should I think about you every time?"

For the next week, the Malice Common Room turned into a cockroach's night school. The Mogrify spell only lasted three hours, so Agatha worked Sophie like a slave, driving her to make her fingerglow stronger, to fog a room and flood a floor, to tell a Sleeping Willow from a Weeping Willow, and to even say a few words of Giant. Sophie's ranks immediately improved, but by the fourth day, the long nights had taken their toll.

"My skin looks *gray*," Sophie croaked.

"And you're still ranked 68, so pay attention!" berated the roach on her book, swan crest glistening on abdomen. "The Woodswide Plague began when Rumpelstiltskin stamped so hard the ground cracked—"

"What made you change your mind? About helping me?"

"And from the ground, a million poisonous bugs crawled out and infested the Woods, sickening scores of Nevers and Evers," Agatha said, ignoring her. "They even had to close this school, since the bugs were highly contagious—"

Sophie flopped back on the couch. "How do you *know* all this?"

"Because while you stare in mirrors, I read *Poisons and Plagues*!"

Sophie sighed. "So they closed the school for bugs. Then what happ—"

"*This* is where you've been sneaking to?"

Sophie swiveled to Hester at the door in black pajamas, flanked by Anadil and Dot.

"Homework," Sophie yawned, holding up her book. "Need light."

"Since when do *you* care about homework?" said Hester, looking greasier than ever.

"Thought beauty was a 'full-time job,'" mimicked Anadil.

"Rooming with you is such inspiration," Sophie said, smiling. "Makes me want to be the best villain I can be."

Hester eyed her for a long moment. With a growl, she turned and led the others out.

Sophie exhaled, blowing Agatha off the couch.

"She's up to something," they heard Hester snarl.

"Or she's changed!" piped Dot, waddling behind. "Roach on her book and she didn't even notice!"

By the sixth night of schooling, Sophie had risen to #55. But each new day, she looked more like a zombie, skin sickly white, eyes glassy and bruised. Instead of a fancy new frock or hat, now she loped around with dirty hair and a wrinkled dress, trailing study notes all over the tower like bread crumbs.

"Maybe you should get some sleep," Tedros mumbled to her during Yuba's lesson on "Insect Cuisine."

"Too busy trying not to be the 'worst girl in school,'" Sophie said as she took notes.

"Insects are often available when meerworms are not," Yuba said, holding up a live cockroach.

"Look, you can't expect anyone to listen to you when you're ranked lower than Hort," Tedros whispered.

"When I'm #1, you'll ask me to forgive you."

"You get to #1 and I'll ask you anything you want," he snorted.

Sophie turned to him. "I'll hold you to that."

"If you're still awake."

"First remove the inedible bits," Yuba said, and tore off the roach's head.

Agatha shuddered and hid behind a pine shrub the rest of the lesson. But that night, she almost jumped from her thorax when Sophie told her what happened with Tedros.

"Everboys always keep their promises!" she said, bouncing on knobby roach legs. "It's the Prince Code of Chivalry. Now you just have to get to #1 and he'll ask you to the . . . Sophie?"

Sophie answered with a snore.

By the tenth day of Cockroach College, Sophie was only at #40 and the circles under her eyes were so black she looked like a raccoon. By the next, she'd slipped back to #65 when she napped during Lesso's test on Nemesis Dreams, fell asleep during Henchmen, knocking Beezle off the Belfry, and lost her voice in Special Talents for another low rank.

"Your talent is progressing," Sheeba said to Anadil, who managed to make her rats grow a full five inches bigger. Then she turned to Sophie. "Here I thought *you* were our Great Witch Hope."

By the end of the week, Sophie was the worst villain in school again.

"I'm sick," Agatha said, coughing into her hand.

Professor Dovey didn't look up from her parchment-strewn desk. "Ginger tea and two slices of grapefruit. Repeat every two hours."

"I tried that," Agatha said, increasing the volume of her coughs.

"Now is not the time to miss class, Agatha," Professor Dovey said, stacking papers under sparkling pumpkin weights. "Less than a month before the Ball and I want to make sure our fourth-ranked student is prepared for the most important night of her young life! Do you have an Everboy in mind?"

Agatha exploded in a paroxysm of hacks. Professor Dovey looked up, alarmed.

"Feels like . . . *plague*," Agatha wheezed.

Professor Dovey went white.

Quarantined in her room, Agatha the Roach now accompanied Sophie to all her classes. Tucked behind Sophie's ear, she whispered the first sign of a Nemesis Dream (answer: tasting blood), steered Frost Giant negotiations during Henchmen, and told Sophie which scarecrows were Good or Evil in Yuba's Forest challenge. On the second day, she helped Sophie lose a tooth in Uglification, match monsters during Sader's exam (Lalkies: *sweet-talkers*; Harpies: *child eaters*), and determine which of Yuba's beanstalks was poisonous, which was edible, and which was Dot in disguise. There were hairy moments, of course. She almost ended up on the bottom of Hester's clump, barely survived a hovering bat, and nearly turned back into herself in Special Talents before finding a broom closet just in time.

By the third day, Agatha hardly glanced at her Good homework and spent all her free time learning Evil spells. Where her classmates struggled to make fingers flicker, she could keep hers glowing by thinking about things that made her angry: school, mirrors, boys. . . , Then it was a matter of following a spell's precise recipe, and just like that, she could do magic. Simple stuff, nothing more than playing with water and weather, but still—*real magic*!

She would have been paralyzed by the incredibility, the impossibility, except that it came so naturally. Where the others couldn't summon a drizzle, Agatha conjured thunderclouds in her room and splashed the odious murals off her wall with a squall of lightning and rain. Between sessions, she stole into bathrooms to try out new *Spells for Suffering*—the Lights-Out Jinx to briefly darken the sky, the Sea Swell Curse to summon a giant wave. . . . Time evaporated when she studied Evil, so rife with power and possibility, she could never get bored.

While waiting for Pollux to deliver her Good homework one night, Agatha whistled while she doodled—

"What pray tell is *that*?"

She turned to Pollux in her doorway, head on a hare's body, staring at the drawing.

"Oh, um, me at my wedding. See, there's my prince." She crumpled the page and coughed. "Any homework?"

After chastising her for slipping in the Ever ranks, explaining every assignment thrice, and berating her to cover her mouth when she coughed, Pollux finally left in a circus of hops and falls. Agatha exhaled. Then her eye caught the crumpled doodle of herself flying through flames and she saw what she'd been drawing.

Nevermore. Evil paradise.

"We have to get home," she mumbled.

By the end of the week, Agatha had led Sophie on a magnificent winning streak in all her classes, including Yuba's Trial Tune-Ups. In these one-on-one duels to prepare for the upcoming Trial by Tale, Sophie beat every person in her group using approved spells, whether stunning Ravan with a lightning bolt, icing Beatrix's lips before she could call for animal help, or liquefying Tedros' training sword.

"Someone's been doing their homework," Tedros said, agog. Hidden under Sophie's collar, Agatha blushed with pride.

"Before it was dumb luck. This is different," Hester griped to Anadil as they bit into a lunch of charred cow tongues. "How is she *doing* it?"

"Good old-fashioned hard work," Sophie said, swishing by in shimmering makeup, ruby-red hair, and a black kimono, sparkling with gems that spelled "F is for *Focused.*"

Hester and Anadil choked on their tongues.

By the end of the third week, Sophie was up to #5 and her Lunchtime Lectures had resumed due to popular demand.

So had her black-robed fashions, bolder and more extravagant than before, in a grand pageant of scalloped plumage, fishnet bodices, faux monkey fur, sequined burkas, leather pantsuits, powdered wigs, and even a chain-mail bustier.

"She's *cheating*," Beatrix hissed to anyone who would listen. "Some rogue fairy godmother or time-turning spell. No one has time to do all this!"

But Sophie had time to design a satin jumper with matching nun's wimple, a sparkled clamshell dress, and matching shoes for every new look. She had time to beat Hester in the "Uglify a Ballroom" challenge, write a report on "Wolves vs. Man-Wolves," and prepare Lunchtime Lectures on "Wicked Success," "Ugly Is the New Beautiful," "Building Your Body for Sin." She had time to be one-girl fashion show, rabble-rouser, rebel priestess— and still wrestle her way past Anadil to #2 in the rankings.

This time Beatrix couldn't stop Tedros from falling for Sophie. But Tedros tried valiantly to stop himself.

She's a Never! So what if she's beautiful? Or smart? Or creative and kind and generous and—

Tedros took a deep breath.

Evers can't like Nevers. You're just confused.

He felt relieved when Yuba hosted another "Good or Evil" challenge. This time the gnome turned all the girls into blue pumpkins and hid them in the forest's voluminous patch.

Just find an Ever, Tedros scolded himself. *Find an Ever and forget all about her.*

"This one's Good!" Hort yelled, and flicked a blue shell. Nothing happened. The other boys couldn't tell the difference between pumpkins either and started debating the merits of each.

"This is not a group assignment!" Yuba bellowed.

Clinging to Sophie's blue vine, Agatha's roach watched as the boys split up. Tedros headed west towards the Turquoise Thicket and stopped. Slowly he turned to Sophie's pumpkin.

"He's coming," Agatha said.

"How do you know?" Sophie whispered.

"Because that's the way he looked at me."

Tedros walked up to a pumpkin. "This one. This one's an Ever."

Yuba frowned. "Look closely first—"

Tedros ignored him, clasped its blue skin, and in a burst of glitterdust the pumpkin turned into Sophie. A "16" puffed in slimy green smoke over the prince's head and a "1" in black over Sophie's.

"Only the best Evil can disguise as Good," Yuba commended, and with a wave of his staff, erased the red *F* off Sophie's dress once and for all.

"And as for you, son of Arthur, I suggest you study your rules. Let's hope you don't make such a terrible mistake when it *counts*."

Tedros tried to look ashamed.

"We can't find any!" a voice called.

Yuba turned to see all the boys with low ranks smoking over their heads. "Should have marked them," he sighed and waddled into the patch, jabbing pumpkins to see if they yelped.

With the gnome gone, Tedros let himself smile. How could

he tell a teacher he didn't care about rules? Rules that had led him to that god-awful Agatha *twice*? For the first time, he had found a girl who had everything he wanted. A girl who wasn't a mistake.

"I'd say you owe me a question, son of Arthur."

Tedros turned to find Sophie wearing the same smile. He followed her eyes to the Nevers scoreboard above the Forest, where Albemarle had pecked her name at the very top.

The next day, she found a note in her lunch pail.

Wolves don't like foxes. Blue Brook at midnight. T.

"What does it mean?" she whispered to the roach in her palm.

"It means we go home tonight!" Agatha gushed, antennae beating so fast that Sophie dropped her.

The roach paced the mildewed burlap of the Malice Common Room floor, eyeing the clock as it ticked towards midnight. At last she heard the door open and Sophie entered in a seductive black sheath dress, accented with long black gloves, beehived hair, a necklace of delicate pearls, and black-tinted spectacles. Agatha nearly burst her carapace.

"First, I told you to be on time. Second, I said *don't* dress up—"

"Look at these glasses. Aren't they chic? Saves your eyes from the sun. You know, these Evergirls sneak me all sorts of things like this now, pearls, jewels, makeup to add to my ensembles. At first I thought they were Good Deeds, and then I realized, no, they just like seeing their things on someone more glamorous and charismatic. Only it's all so *cheap*. Gives me a rash."

Agatha's antennae curled. "Just—just lock the door!"

Sophie bolted the latch. She heard a crash and spun to see Agatha red-faced, pale body wrapped in a burlap curtain.

"Um—must have mistimed it—" Agatha spluttered—

Sophie looked her up and down. "I prefer you as a roach."

"There has to be a way to get new clothes when you turn back," Agatha grouched, wrapping herself tighter. Then she saw Sophie fondling Tedros' note. "Now listen, don't do any thing stupid when you meet him tonight. Just get the kiss and—"

"My prince came for me," Sophie mooned, sniffing the parchment. "And now he's mine forever. All thanks to you, Agatha." She gazed up lovingly and saw her friend's expression.

"What?"

"You said 'forever.'"

"I meant tonight. He's mine tonight."

They were both silent.

"We'll be heroes when we get back to Gavaldon, Sophie," Agatha said softly. "You'll have fame and riches and any boy you want. You'll read about Tedros in storybooks for the rest of your life. You'll have the memories that he was once yours."

Sophie nodded with a pained smile.

"And I'll have my graveyard and cat," Agatha mumbled.

"You'll find love someday, Agatha."

Agatha shook her head. "You heard what the School Master said, Sophie. A villain like me can't ever find love."

"He also said we couldn't be friends."

Agatha met Sophie's lucid, beautiful eyes.

Then she saw the clock and jolted to her feet. "Take off your clothes!"

"Take off my *what*?"

"Hurry! We'll miss him!"

"Excuse me but I'm sewn into this dre—"

"NOW!"

A few minutes later, Agatha sat next to Sophie's clothes, head in hands.

"You have to do it with conviction!"

"I'm naked behind an ugly couch. I can't do anything with conviction, let alone make my finger glow and turn into a rodent. Can't we pick a more appealing animal?"

"You're five minutes from losing your kiss! Just picture yourself in its body!"

"How about a lovebird instead? It's more *me*."

Agatha grabbed Sophie's spectacles, bashed them with her clump, and threw them over the couch.

"Want me to do the same to the pearls?"

THUMP.

"Did that work?" Sophie's voice said.

"I don't see you—" Agatha said, whipping around. "For all we know you turned yourself into a newt!"

"I'm right here."

Agatha turned and lost her breath. "But—but—you're—"

"More *me*," Sophie breathed, a ravishing plush pink fox with sparkly fur, bewitching green eyes, succulent red lips, and a bouncy magenta tail. She clasped the pearl necklace around her neck and admired herself in a shard of broken glass. "Will he kiss me, darling?"

Agatha stared, mesmerized.

Sophie watched her in the mirror. "You're making me nervous."

"The wolves won't bother you," Agatha babbled as she unlocked the door. "They think foxes carry disease, plus they're color-blind. Just keep your chest to the ground so they don't see the swan—"

"Agatha."

"What? You'll miss hi—"

"Will you come with me?"

Agatha turned.

Gently, Sophie curled her tail around her friend's hand. "We're a team," she said.

Agatha had to remind herself she didn't have time to cry.

Sophie the Fox pattered quietly through the Blue Forest, past willow trees shimmering with sleeping fairies and wolf guards who shrank from her as if she were a snake. She skirted sapphire ferns and twisty oaks of the Turquoise Thicket before slinking to the top of the bridge overlooking a moonlit brook.

"I don't see him," Sophie whispered to the roach snuggled into her neck's pink fur.

"His note said he'd be here!"

"Suppose Hester and Anadil played a trick—"

"Who are you talking to?"

Two blue eyes glowed in darkness across the bridge.

Sophie froze.

"Say something!" Agatha hissed in her ear.

Sophie couldn't.

"I talk to myself when I'm nervous," Agatha whispered.

"I talk to myself when I'm nervous," Sophie said quickly.

A navy blue fox stepped out of the shadows, swan twinkling on its puffed chest.

"I thought only princesses get nervous. Not the best villain in school."

Sophie gaped at the fox. It had Tedros' tight muscles and half-cocked grin.

"Only the best Good can disguise as Evil," Agatha intervened. "Especially when it has love to fight for."

"Only the best Good can disguise as Evil," Sophie said. "Especially when it has love to fight for."

"So it really was a mistake all along?" Tedros said, circling her slowly.

Sophie flailed for words—

"I had to play both sides in order to survive," Agatha rescued.

"I had to play both sides in order to survive," echoed Sophie.

She heard Tedros' steps stop. "Now, according to the Prince Code, I have a promise to fulfill." His fur brushed against hers. "What would you like me to ask you?"

Sophie's heart choked her throat.

"Do you see who I am now?" Agatha said.

"Do you see who I am now?" Sophie breathed.

Tedros was quiet.

He lifted her chin with his warm paw. "You do know this will throw both schools into upheaval?"

Sophie gazed into his eyes, hypnotized.

"I do," whispered the roach.

"I do," said the fox.

"You do know no one will accept you as my princess?" said Tedros.

"I do."

"I do."

"You do know you will spend the rest of your life trying to prove you're Good?"

"I do," said Agatha.

"I do," said Sophie.

Tedros moved closer and their chests touched.

"And you do know I'm going to kiss you now?"

Both girls gasped at the same time.

As iridescent brook water lit up the foxes' blue and pink faces, Agatha closed her eyes and said goodbye to this world of nightmares. Sophie closed her eyes too and felt Tedros' warm, sweet breath as his tender mouth grazed her lips—

"But we should wait," Sophie said, pulling away.

Agatha's bug eyes flashed open.

"Sure. Course. Obviously," Tedros stammered. "I'll, um, walk you to your tunnel."

As they walked back in silence, Sophie's pink tail curled around his. Tedros looked at her and surrendered a smile. Agatha watched all this, swelling red. And when the prince finally vanished into his tunnel, she vaulted onto Sophie's nose.

"What are you *doing*!"

Sophie didn't answer.

"Why didn't you kiss him!"

Sophie said nothing.

Agatha dug her pincers into Sophie's nose. "You need to run after him! Go *now*! We can't get home unless you kiss—"

Sophie brushed Agatha off her face and disappeared into the dark tunnel.

Writhing in dead leaves, Agatha finally understood.

There was no kiss because there would never be a kiss.

Sophie had no intention of them going home.

Ever.

19

I Have a Prince

The faculty of the School for Good and Evil had seen many things over the years.

They had seen students pathetic in the first year end richer than kings. They had seen Class Captains flame out by the third year and end as pigeons or wasps. They had seen pranks, protests, and raids, kisses, vows, and impromptu love songs.

But they had never ever seen an Ever and a Never hold hands in the lunch line.

"Are you sure I won't get in trouble?" said Sophie, noticing them glaring from balconies.

"If you're good enough for me, you're good enough for a basket," said Tedros, pulling her forward.

"I suppose they should get used to it," Sophie sighed. "I don't want any trouble at the Ball."

Tedros' hand stiffened on hers. Sophie turned bright red.

"Oh . . . After last night, I just assumed . . ."

"The Everboys took an oath we wouldn't propose before the Circus of Talents," Tedros said, tugging at his collar. "Espada said it's tradition to wait until the Circus Crowning, the night before the Ball."

"The night before!" Sophie choked. "But how do we match colors and plan our entrance and—"

"This is why we make the oath." Tedros took his wicker basket of lamb sandwiches, saffron couscous, and almond mousse from a green-haired nymph. "And one for the lady as well."

The nymph ignored Sophie and held out a basket to the next Ever. Tedros seized the handle.

"I said one for the *lady*."

The nymph tightened its grip on the basket.

"Lamb is hard to digest anyway," Sophie fretted—

But the prince held on until the nymph surrendered the basket with a grunt. Tedros handed it to Sophie. "Like you said, they better get used to it."

Her eyes widened. "You'll . . . take me?"

"You're so beautiful when you want something."

Sophie touched him. "Promise me," she said, breathless. "Promise me you'll take me to the Ball."

Tedros looked down at her soft hands, holding the laces of his shirt.

"All right," he exhaled finally. "I promise. But tell anyone and I'll put a snake in your corsage."

With a squeal, Sophie threw herself into his arms. She could plan her gown after all.

With that, the #1 Ever and #1 Never, storybook enemies in body and soul, sat hand in hand under a towering oak. Tedros suddenly noticed all the Evers glaring at him, stunned by his disloyalty. Sophie saw Nevers, who she had preached to for weeks about Villain Pride, glower at her, betrayed.

Tensing, she and Tedros bit into sandwiches at the same time.

"Is the witch still contagious?" Tedros said quickly. "It's her first day back in class."

Sophie glanced at Agatha, hunched against a tree, staring right at her.

"Um, we don't really talk."

"Leech, isn't she? Thinks she's brains to your beauty. Little did she know you have everything."

Sophie swallowed. "It's true."

"One thing's for sure. Won't be picking that witch in a challenge again."

"How do you know that?"

"Because now that I found my princess, I won't let her go," said her prince, gazing into her eyes.

Sophie suddenly felt sad. "Even if it means waiting a lifetime for a kiss?" she said, almost to herself.

"Even if it means waiting a lifetime for a kiss." Tedros answered, taking her hand. Then he cocked his head. "I'm assuming this is a hypothetical question."

Sophie laughed and buried her head in his shoulder in time to hide the tears. She'd explain one day. When their love was strong enough.

On the balconies of the two schools, the faculty watched the lovebirds nuzzle in the sun. The Good and Evil teachers gave each other dark looks and went back to their chambers.

Sitting in chilly shade, Agatha didn't make any sudden moves either. Like the teachers, she knew this romance was doomed. Something was in their way. Something Sophie had forgotten.

Something called Trial by Tale.

"To win a Trial by Tale is one of the greatest honors at the School for Good and Evil," Pollux declared, head back next to Castor's on their massive dog's body. With the fifteen Forest Group leaders behind him, Pollux peered down at the students, gathered after breakfast in the Theater of Tales.

"Once a year, we send our best Evers or Nevers into the Blue Forest for a night to see who lasts until morning. To win, a student must survive *both* the School Master's death traps and the other side's attacks. The last Ever or Never standing at dawn is declared the winner and given five additional first-place ranks." Pollux raised his nose snootily. "As you know, Good has won the past two hundred Trials—"

Good burst into a chant of "EVERS RULE! EVERS RULE! EVERS—"

"ARE STUPID, ARROGANT FOOLS!" Castor boomed, and the Evers shut up.

"Now a week from today, each Forest Group will send its

top Ever and Never into the Trial," Pollux sniffed. "But before we announce the competitors, let us briefly review the rules."

"Heard Beatrix took first in Good Deeds yesterday," Chaddick whispered to Tedros. "That Nevergirl turning you soft?"

"You try mending a dove wing with my strength," Tedros retorted. Then his face softened. "Do the boys really hate me?"

"Can't be messing with a Never, mate," Chaddick said, gray eyes stern. "Even if she *is* the fairest, smartest, most talented girl in school."

Doubts sank Tedros into his seat. . . . He bolted upright.

"I can prove she's Good! I can prove it in the Trial!"

"Beatrix or Agatha might have your group's spot," Chaddick said.

Tedros' chest tightened. He caught Sophie beaming at him from the Evil pews. Their future together depended on him making the Trial. How could he fail her?

"According to the rules, there can be more than one winner of a Trial by Tale," said Pollux. "However, those who last until dawn must *split* the first-place ranks. Thus, it is in your interest to eliminate your competition. Naturally the School Master prefers a single winner and will conjure as many obstacles as he can to ensure it.

"For the rest of the week, all classes will be dedicated to preparing these 15 Evers and 15 Nevers for their night in the Blue Forest," the dog continued, as students twittered over who these would be. "In-class challenges will be restricted to these competitors *only*. Those with the worst scores for the week will enter the Trial first, while those with the best will enter significantly later.

This is, of course, a tremendous advantage. The less time you spend in a Trial by Tale, the more chance you come out alive."

Students stopped talking.

Pollux realized what he said and forced a laugh.

"It's a figure of *speech*. No student *dies* in a Trial. How ludicrous."

Castor coughed. "But what about—"

"The competition is completely *safe*," Pollux said, smiling down at the children. "You will each have a flag of surrender. If you find yourself in mortal danger, drop it to the ground and you will be rescued unharmed from the Blue Forest. You will learn more about the rules in your various classes, but now I cede the floor to the Forest Group leaders, who will announce this season's Trial competitors."

A tiny lily nymph in a dress of emerald vines stepped forward. "From Group 9, Reena will represent Good and Vex will represent Evil!"

Reena curtsied to Ever cheers while Nevers grumbled that Vex and his pointy ears were lucky to be in a weak group.

An ogre announced Tristan and one-eyed Arachne from Group 7, followed by more leaders who named dark-skinned Nicholas and Anadil from 4, Kiko and green-hued Mona from 12, Giselle and Hester from 6 . . .

Sophie goggled at Tedros through it all, daydreaming of life as his queen. (Would Camelot have enough closets? Mirrors? Cucumbers?) Then Yuba stepped forward. Sophie looked over at Tedros and Beatrix, both hanging on the gnome's next words. *Please let him beat that sour cream puff,* she prayed—

"From Group 3, Tedros will represent Good," Yuba said.
She exhaled in relief.

"And Sophie will represent Evil."

Sophie massaged her ears. She'd heard wrong surely. Then she saw the smirks.

"Suppose that's the problem with dating a villain," Chaddick said. "It's all love and kisses until you have to kill them."

Tedros ignored him and focused on his plan to prove Sophie Good. Thank God his father was dead, he thought, sweating through his shirt. What he was about to do would have stopped his heart.

As Evers left through the west doors, Nevers through the east to trek back to Evil, Sophie remained shell-shocked on a blackened pew. A shadow moved into hers.

"All I asked is that you stay out of my way . . ."

Hester's breath chilled the back of her neck.

"And here you are, #1 Villain, making fools of us all. Well, you forgot a villain's story doesn't end happily, dear. So let me remind you how it ends. First you. Then your prince. *Dead.*"

Cold lips grazed Sophie's ear. "And that's no figure of speech."

Sophie whipped around. No one there. She jolted to her feet, slammed into Tedros, screamed—and collapsed in his arms. "She's going to kill us, you then me or me then you—I can't remember the order—and you're an Ever and I'm a Never and now we fight against each other—"

"Or we fight *with* each other."

Sophie blinked. "We . . . do?"

"Everyone will know you're Good if I protect you," said

Tedros, still a bit sweaty. "Only a true princess can earn a prince's shield."

"But—they'll target you! Everyone thinks I'm Evil!"

"Not if we win," Tedros said, grinning. "They'll have to make you an Ever."

Sophie shook her head and hugged him tight. "You are my prince. You really are."

"Now go win your challenges so we enter the Trial at the same time. You can't be in there without me."

Sophie drained of blood. "But—but—"

"But what? You're the best Never by a mile."

"I know, it's just—"

Tedros held her chin up, forcing her to look into his crystal-blue eyes. "First place in every challenge. Deal?"

Sophie nodded weakly.

"We're a team," said Tedros, dimpling, and with a last brush of her cheek, he left through the Ever Doors.

Sophie trudged across the stage to the Never Doors and paused. She turned slowly.

Agatha sat in the pink pews, all alone.

"I told you I belong here, darling," Sophie sighed. "You just wouldn't listen."

Agatha said nothing.

"Maybe the School Master will let you go home alone," Sophie said.

Agatha didn't flinch.

"You need to make new friends, Agatha." Sophie smiled gently. "I have a prince now."

Agatha just stared into her eyes.

Sophie stopped smiling. "I have a *prince*."

She slammed the door behind her.

In Uglification, Manley asked the competing 15 Nevers to conjure a disguise that would scare off an Ever "at first sight." Hester's potion made her whole body explode with spikes. Anadil's turned her skin so thin all her blood vessels shined through. Meanwhile, Sophie bashed tadpoles to give herself shingles again, but somehow gave herself a spiral horn and glittered horsetail instead.

"Because what's scarier to a princess than a *unicorn*?" snarled Manley.

In Henchmen, the Trial Nevers had to tame a Fire Giant, a nine-foot hunk of hot orange skin and flaming hair. Sophie tried to read his thoughts, but all his thoughts were in Giant. Luckily, she remembered some of the Giant words Agatha had taught her.

FIRE GIANT:	And why shouldn't I kill you?
SOPHIE:	I know this horse.
FIRE GIANT:	I see no horse!
SOPHIE:	It is as vast as your undergarments.

Castor intervened before the Giant ate her.

Then Lady Lesso asked the Trial Nevers to name a "spell that can only be undone by the one who casts it."

"Answers?"

Shivering, the Nevers held up carved ice tablets:

HESTER: Petrification
ANADIL: Petrification
ARACHNE: Petrification
SOPHIE: Special Spell

"If only love was the answer to *everything*," said Lady Lesso, handing Sophie another "15" out of 15.

"What *happened?*" said Tedros as he pushed her through the Evers line.

"Just a slow start—"

"Sophie, you can't be in that Forest without me!"

She followed his eyes to scowling Evers. Come the Trial, they'd all be out for revenge.

"Just do what you were doing *before!*" Tedros begged.

Sophie gritted her teeth as she walked back to her room. If Agatha could do well in the School for Good, then she could do well here! Yes, she'd boil her toad eyes, she'd learn her Giant, she'd cook a child if she had to! (Or supervise, at least.) Nothing would stop her from her Ever After! She puffed her chest, stormed through her door, and froze.

Her bed had disappeared. The mirror had been shattered.

And over her head hung all her old outfits, noosed and mutilated, like headless corpses.

On her bed, Anadil looked up from *Killing Pretty Girls*. Hester looked up from *Killing Even Prettier Girls*.

Sophie barreled into the top-floor office. "My roommates want to kill me!"

Lady Lesso smiled back from her desk. "That's the spirit."

The door closed magically in Sophie's face.

Sophie cowered in the dark hall. Last week, she had been the most popular girl in school! And now she couldn't even go back to her room?

She wiped her eyes. It didn't matter, did it? Soon she'd be switching schools and all of this would be behind her. She had the boy every girl wanted. She had her prince! Two stupid witches were no match for true love!

Voices echoed above. She ducked into shadows—

"Hester said whoever kills Sophie during the Trial will be her Hench Captain next year," Arachne said as she descended the stairs. "But it needs to look accidental or we'll get expelled."

"We have to beat Anadil to it!" Mona said, green skin flushing. "Suppose she kills her before the Trial!"

"Hester said *during* the Trial. Even Vex and Brone know that. Did you hear their plan to kill her? They searched the Good lake to find those leftover *eggs*. That girl is so dead."

"Can't believe we listened to that traitor's lectures," Mona seethed. "Next thing you know, she'd have had us wearing pink and kissing Evers!"

"She humiliated us all and now she'll pay," Arachne said, narrowing her eye. "Fourteen of us. One of her. Odds aren't in her favor."

Their cackles pealed through the damp stairwell.

Sophie didn't move from the dark. It wasn't just her roommates. The whole school wanted her dead. There was nowhere safe now.

Nowhere except . . .

At the end of a dark, stale hall, the door to Room 34 cracked open after the third knock. Two beady black pupils peered out.

"Hello, handsome," Sophie cooed.

"Don't even try it—you're a prince lover, you're a two-timer, you're a—"

Sophie held her nose, breezed by Hort, and locked him out of her new room.

Hort pounded and wailed outside for twenty minutes before Sophie finally let him back in.

"You can help me study until curfew," she said, spritzing the room with lavandula. "But no sleeping here."

"This is *my* room!" Hort sulked, plopping to the floor in black pajamas dotted with frowning green frogs.

"Well, I'm here, aren't I? And boys and girls can't be room-mates, so it certainly can't be *your* room," said Sophie, tucking into his bed.

"But where am I supposed to stay!"

"I hear the Malice Common Room is quite comfortable."

Ignoring Hort's whimpers, Sophie sank into pillows and held a candle to his class notes. She had to win *all* her challenges tomorrow. Her only hope to survive the Trial was to go in with Tedros and hide behind his shield the whole time.

"To humiliate an enemy, turn him into a chicken: *Banta pareo dirosti?*" She squinted. "Is that right?"

"Sophie, how do you know you aren't a villain?" Hort yawned, hunched on the burned floor.

"I look in the mirror. Hort, your penmanship is *foul*."

"When I look in the mirror, I look like a villain."

"Probably means you're a villain."

"Dad told me villains can't love, no matter what. That it's unnatural and disgusting."

Sophie made out scratchy words. *"To freeze an Ever in ice, make your soul cold . . ."*

"So I definitely can't love," Hort said.

"Colder than you thought possible . . . Then say these words . . ."

"But if I could love, I'd love you."

Sophie turned. Hort was snoring softly on the floor, button-flap lit up with angry green frogs.

"Hort, you can't sleep here," she said.

Hort curled up tighter.

Sophie threw off her covers, stamped up to him—

"Take that, Pan," he babbled softly.

Sophie watched him, shivering and sweating in his little ball.

She slid back under the musty covers. Candle to notes, she tried to study, but his snuffles lulled her into a trance, and before she knew it was morning.

The second day went as well as the first, with Sophie earning three more last places, the third of which came in Henchmen when she couldn't make her finger glow in time to disarm a stink-troll.

She could see veins swell in Tedros' neck as he yanked her through the lunch line, holding his nose.

"Should I lose on purpose? Or do you *want* to go into the Trial three hours early!"

"I'm trying as hard as I can—"

"The Sophie I know doesn't try. She *wins*."

They ate in silence.

"Where's her fairy godmother now?" Sophie heard Beatrix crow.

Across the field Agatha did homework with Kiko, back turned completely.

The next day, the challengers spent their first two sessions being fitted for their Trial uniforms: dark blue tunics of silky iron mesh, and matching hooded wool cloaks lined with red brocade. With thirty students in the same cloaks, it would be impossible to tell Evers from Nevers, even if one could *see* blue cloaks in a Blue Forest. When it came to clothes, Sophie was normally at full attention. But today, she had her head buried in Hort's notes. Lady Lesso's class was next and she needed first place.

"A villain kills for one purpose: to destroy his Nemesis. The one who grows stronger as you grow weaker. Only when your Nemesis is *dead* will you feel quenched," said the tight-skinned teacher, clacking through the aisle. "Of course, since only the best Nevers will have Nemesis Dreams, most of you will venture your whole life without taking another's life. Consider yourself lucky. Killing requires the purest Evil. *None* of you are pure enough to kill yet."

Sophie heard grumbles in her direction.

"But since the Trial by Tale is a *harmless* exercise"—Lady Lesso smiled at her—"why not prepare with my favorite challenge . . ."

She conjured a phantom princess with brown curls, blushing dimples, and a smile sweeter than a baby's.

"*Murder Practice.* Whoever kills her the cruelest way wins."

"Finally, something useful," Hester said, eyeing Sophie.

Though the chamber was colder than ever, Sophie shined with sweat.

With the princess locked behind a door and suspicious of strangers, the Trial Nevers had to be creative to kill her. Mona uglified herself into a peddler and gifted the princess poisoned lipstick. After Lady Lesso conjured a new maiden, Anadil knocked on her door and left a carnivorous bouquet outside it. Hester shrank into a cute squirrel and offered her victim a glittery balloon.

"Why, thank you!" the princess beamed as the balloon pulled her up, up, up into the razor-sharp icicles on the ceiling.

Sophie closed her eyes through most of this.

"Who's next?" Lady Lesso said, sealing a new princess behind the door. "Oh, yes. *You.*" She drummed long red nails on Sophie's desk. *Tsk, tsk, tsk.*

Sophie felt sick. *Murder?* Even if it was a phantom, she couldn't mur—

The Beast's dying face flashed and she blanched. That was different! He was Evil! Any prince would have done the same!

"Another fail, it seems," Lady Lesso leered.

Meeting her eyes, Sophie thought of Tedros losing faith

in her. She thought of fourteen villains convinced they were pure enough to kill. She thought of her happy ending slipping away . . .

The Sophie I love doesn't try.

Jaw set, she stormed to the door, past her surprised teacher, finger glowing pink—

To freeze an Ever in ice . . .

She pounded on the door.

Make your soul cold . . .

The door opened and Sophie's fingerglow dimmed.

It was her own face staring back at her, only with the long blond locks she had before the Beast. To win this challenge, she had to kill . . . *herself.*

Sophie saw Lady Lesso smirking in the corner.

"May I help you?" asked Princess Sophie.

Just a ghost. Sophie gritted her teeth and felt her finger burn once more.

"You look like a stranger," said the princess, blushing.

Colder than you thought possible . . .

Sophie pointed her glowing finger at her.

"Mother said never talk to strangers," said the princess anxiously.

Say it!

Sophie's fingertip flickered—she couldn't find the words—

"I should go. Mother's calling."

Kill her! Kill her now!

"Goodbye," said the princess, closing her door—

"BANTA PAREO DIROSTI!"

Poof! The princess turned into a chicken. Sophie grabbed it in her arms, hurled a chair, shattering the iced window, and flung the bird into open sky—

"*Fly*, Sophie! You're *free!*"

The chicken tried to fly, then realized it couldn't, and plummeted to its death.

"For the first time, I feel sorry for an animal," Lady Lesso said.

Another "15" spat in Sophie's face.

Perhaps the only thing Sophie liked about the School for Evil was that there were plenty of places to cry. She tucked behind a crumbling arch and sobbed. How would she ever face Tedros?

"We insist you remove Sophie from the Trial."

Sophie recognized the gruff voice as Professor Manley's. She crept out of the archway and peeked through the keyhole into his putrid classroom. But where the rusted seats normally were filled with villains, now they were occupied by the faculty of both schools. Professor Dovey presided at the dragon-skull lectern, which she'd brightened with a pumpkin paperweight.

"The Nevers plan to kill her, Clarissa," finished bald, pimpled Manley.

"Bilious, we have secure measures in place to prevent a student's death."

"Let's hope they're more secure than four years ago," he shot back.

"I think we are all in agreement that Garrick's death was an *accident*!" Professor Dovey flared.

The room was ominously silent. In the hall, Sophie could hear her own shallow breaths.

Garrick of Gavaldon. Taken with Bane.

Bane had failed. Garrick had died.

Her heart rattled against her ribs.

Getting home alive is our happy ending.

Agatha was right all along.

"There is another reason Sophie must be removed from the Trial," Castor said soberly. "The fairies say she and the Everboy plan to act as a team."

"As a *team?*" Professor Dovey gaped. "An Ever and a Never?"

"Imagine if they won!" shrieked Professor Sheeks. "Imagine if word got out in the Woods!"

"So either she dies or destroys this school," Manley groused and spat on the floor.

"Clarissa, this is an easy decision," said Lady Lesso.

"But there's no precedent for removing a qualified student from a Trial!" Professor Dovey protested.

"Qualified! She flunked every challenge this week!" said Manley. "The boy has convinced her she's Good!"

"Perhaps she's just feeling the pressure of the Trial," offered Princess Uma, feeding a quail on her shoulder—

"Or she duped us all into thinking she was Evil's great hope!" Professor Sheeks said. "She should have failed before the Trial!"

"Then why *didn't* she?" Professor Anemone asked.

"Every time we tried to fail her, another student got last place instead," Manley said. "Someone stopped her from failing!"

Evil teachers clamored in furious agreement.

"Makes perfect sense," Professor Dovey said over them. "Some mysterious busybody, who no one has ever *seen*, flits through your tower, meddling with your ranks."

"You describe the School Master quite well, Clarissa," said Lady Lesso.

"Don't be ridiculous, Lady Lesso. Why would the School Master interfere with a student's ranks?"

"Because he'd love nothing better than to see Evil's 'best' student win behind Good's shield," Lady Lesso hissed, violet eyes strobing. "A student who even I foolishly thought had hope. But if Sophie wins with that pathetic prince, I will not stand by, Clarissa. I will not allow the School Master, nor you and your arrogant beasts, to destroy my life's work. Hear me now. Let Sophie compete in that Trial and you are risking more than just her life. You are risking *war*."

The room went dead silent.

Professor Dovey cleared her throat. "Perhaps she can compete next year—"

Sophie slumped in relief.

"You cave to Evil!" Professor Espada cried.

"Only to protect the girl—" Dovey said weakly—

"But the Everboy will still love her!" Anemone warned.

"A week in the Doom Room will fix that," said Lady Lesso.

"Still can't find the Beast," said Sheeba—

"Then get a *new one*!" Lady Lesso snarled.

"How about a vote?" chirped Uma.

"VOTES ARE FOR SISSIES!" Castor roared, and teachers burst into a rumpus. Uma's quail poop-bombed the Evil teachers, Castor tried to eat the bird, and Pollux managed to lose his head again, before someone whistled with loud authority. Everyone turned to the man standing in the corner of the burned room.

"This school has one mission and one mission only," said Professor Sader. "To protect the balance between Good and Evil. If Sophie's participation in the Trial disturbs this balance, then she must be disqualified immediately. Luckily for us, the proof of this balance is in front of your eyes."

Everyone's gaze shifted. Sophie tried to see what they were looking at, then realized they were all looking in different directions.

"Are we in agreement the balance is *intact?*" said Professor Sader.

No one argued.

"Then Sophie will compete in the Trial by Tale and we have nothing more to discuss."

Sophie swallowed a scream.

"Always so sensible, August," said Lady Lesso, standing up. "Thankfully, the girl's failures have ensured she will spend most of the Trial without the boy protecting her. Let us hope that she dies so brutally no one would dare repeat her mistakes. Only then will her story have the ending it *deserves*. Perhaps one even fit for a painting."

She swept from the room and the Evil teachers followed her.

As the Good faculty filed out, muttering to each other in pairs, Professor Dovey and Professor Sader emerged last. They walked in silence, her high-necked chartreuse gown rustling against his shamrock-green suit.

"What if she dies, August?" Clarissa asked.

"What if she *lives*?" said Sader.

Clarissa stopped. "You still believe it's true?"

"I do. As do I believe it true the Storian started her fairy tale."

"But it's impossible—it's lunacy—it's—" Clarissa flushed with horror. "*This* is why you intervened?"

"On the contrary, I haven't intervened," Sader said. "Our duty is to let the story take its course—"

"No! What have you—" Professor Dovey's hand flew to her mouth—"*This* is why you send a girl to risk her life? Because you believe your spurious *prophecy*?"

"There is far more at stake here than one girl's life, Clarissa."

"She's just a girl! An innocent girl!" Professor Dovey gasped, welling furious tears. "Her blood is on your hands!"

As she fled, sniffles echoing down the stairs, Professor Sader's hazel eyes clouded with doubt.

He couldn't see Sophie crouched next to him, trying to stop herself from shivering.

Awash in the Clearing's crinkly leaves, Kiko wrapped her shawl tighter and licked her spiced corn cob.

"So I asked every girl if they'd say yes to Tristan and they all said no! So that means he *has* to ask me! He could go alone, of course, but if a boy goes alone to the Ball, he only gets half ranks and Tristan likes using the Groom Room so he'll definitely ask me. Well, Tristan could ask *you*, but you told him to marry Tedros, so I don't think he likes you. I can't believe you said that. As if princes could marry each other. Then what would we do?"

Agatha chomped on her cob to drown her out. Across the Clearing, she saw Sophie and Tedros arguing ferociously in the mouth of the tree tunnel. It looked like Sophie was trying to apologize and embrace him—kiss him, even—but Tedros shoved her away.

"Are you listening to me?"

Agatha turned. "Wait. So if a girl doesn't get asked to the Ball, then she fails and suffers a punishment worse than death. But if a boy doesn't go to the Ball, he gets half ranks? How is that fair!"

"Because it's the truth," Kiko said. "A boy can choose to be alone if he wants. But if a girl ends up alone . . . she might as well be dead."

Agatha swallowed. "That's ridiculous—"

Something dropped in her basket.

Agatha glanced up to see Sophie meet her eyes as Tedros dragged her into the Evers line.

As Kiko jabbered on, Agatha pulled a luscious pink rose bloom from her basket, then saw it was made of parchment. With the deftest care, she undid the flower in the lap of her dress.

The note only had three words.

I need you.

20

Secrets and Lies

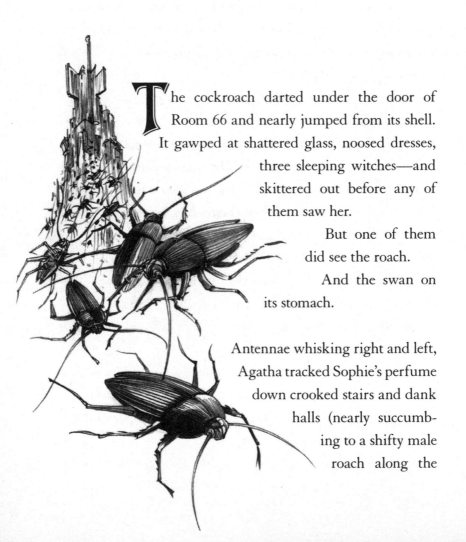

The cockroach darted under the door of Room 66 and nearly jumped from its shell. It gawped at shattered glass, noosed dresses, three sleeping witches—and skittered out before any of them saw her.

But one of them did see the roach.

And the swan on its stomach.

Antennae whisking right and left, Agatha tracked Sophie's perfume down crooked stairs and dank halls (nearly succumbing to a shifty male roach along the way), until she found its source in the common room. The first thing she saw inside was shirtless Hort, face clenched red like a toddler on the toilet. With a last grunt of effort, he peered down at his chest and two brand-new hairs sticking out of it.

"*Yeah!* Whose talent can beat *that!*"

On the next couch, Sophie buried her nose deeper in *Spellcasting for Idiots.*

She heard two insect clicks and looked up urgently. Hort puffed his chest and winked. She turned in horror, then saw lipstick scrawled on the floor behind her couch.

"BATHROOM. BRING CLOTHES."

Sophie despised the Evil bathrooms, but at least they were a safe place to meet. Nevers seemed to have a phobia of toilets and avoided them entirely. (She had no idea what prompted this fear or where they relieved themselves, but she preferred not to think about it.) The door moaned as she slipped into the dim iron cell. Two torches flickered on the rusted wall, elongating the shadows of stalls. As she crept towards the last one, slivers of pale skin peeked through iron slits.

"Clothes?"

Sophie slid them under the stall.

The door opened and Agatha tramped out in Hort's frog pajamas, arms crossed.

"I don't *have* anything else!" Sophie whimpered. "My roommates hanged all mine!"

"No one likes you these days," Agatha shot back, hiding her

glowing finger. "I wonder why."

"Look, I'm sorry! I couldn't just go home! Not when I finally got my prince!"

"*You? You* got your prince?"

"Well, it was mostly me . . ."

"You said you wanted to go home. You said we're a team! That's why I helped you!"

"We are a team, Agatha! Every princess needs a sidekick!"

"Sidekick! *Sidekick!*" Agatha shouted. "Well, let's see how our heroine manages all by *herself*!"

She broke away. Sophie grabbed her arm. "I tried to kiss him! But he doubts me now!"

"Let go—"

"I need your help—"

"And I won't give it," Agatha spat, elbowing past her. "You're a liar, a coward, and a fraud."

"Then why did you even come?" Sophie said, eyes welling.

"Watch out. Crocodile tears mean crocodile wrinkles," Agatha sneered from the door.

"Please. I'll do anything!" Sophie blubbered—

Agatha swiveled. "Swear you'll kiss him the first chance you get. Swear on your *life*."

"I swear!" Sophie cried. "I want to go home! I don't want them to kill me!"

Agatha stared at her. "Huh?"

Complete with voices and gestures, Sophie hysterically replayed the faculty meeting, failed challenges, and fight with Tedros.

"We're getting too close to the end, Sophie," Agatha said, now ghost white. "Someone always dies at the end of a fairy tale!"

"What do we do now?" Sophie squeaked.

"You win that Trial and kiss Tedros the moment you do."

"But I can't survive! I have three hours alone without Tedros protecting me!"

"You won't be alone," Agatha grumped.

"I won't?"

"You'll have fairy godroach under your collar, conjuring you out of trouble. Only this time, if you don't kiss your prince on cue, I'll curse you with every Evil spell I know until you do!"

Sophie threw her arms around her. "Oh, Agatha, I'm a terrible friend. But I'll have my whole life to make it up to you."

Footsteps echoed down the hall. "Go!" Agatha whispered. "I need to Mogrify!"

Sophie gave her a last hug and, aglow with relief, snuck from the bathroom and back to Hort's protection. A minute later, a cockroach followed and dashed for the stairwell.

Neither noticed the red tattoo smoldering through shadows.

Per tradition, there were no classes the day before the Trial. Instead, the 15 Ever and 15 Never challengers were given time to scout the Blue Forest. So while unpicked students worked on Circus talents, Sophie followed Tedros through the gates, keenly aware of the chill between them.

Though the rest of the grounds had fallen prey to a slow autumnal death, the Blue Forest glistened, lush as ever, in midday sun. All week, the students had tried to wheedle out of their teachers what obstacles the challengers would face but they professed ignorance. The School Master designed the Trial in secret, giving professors only the power to secure its borders. Teachers couldn't even *watch* the contest, since he cast a veiling spell over the Blue Forest for the whole night.

"The School Master forbids our interference," Professor Dovey mumbled to her class, clearly distraught. "He prefers Trials to simulate the dangers of the Woods beyond reason or responsibility."

But as the competitors crowded into the Forest behind Sophie and Tedros, none of them could believe that a night from now, this beautiful playground would turn into a hellish gauntlet. Together, the Evers and Nevers herded past the sparkling fronds of the Fernfield, snacking possums in the Pine Glen, the Blue Brook tumbling with trout, before they remembered they were enemies and split up.

Tedros shoved past Sophie. "Follow me."

"I'll go on my own," she said softly. "I haven't earned your protection."

Tedros turned. "Beatrix said you cheated to get to number one. Is that true?"

"Of course not!"

"Then why did you fail all the pre-Trial challenges?"

Tears pearled Sophie's eyes. "I wanted to prove I could survive without you. So you'd be proud of me."

Tedros stared at her. "You lost . . . on *purpose?*"

She nodded.

"Are you insane!" he exploded. "The Nevers—they'll *kill* you!"

"You'd risk your life to prove I'm Good," Sophie sniffled. "I'm willing to fight for you, too."

For a moment, Tedros looked like he might clobber her. Then the red seeped from his cheeks and he grabbed her in his arms. "When I come through those gates, promise me you'll be there."

"I promise," Sophie wept. "For you, I promise."

Tedros gazed into her eyes. Sophie puckered her perfectly glossed lips . . .

"You're right, you should explore on your own," her prince said, pulling away. "You need to feel confident in here without me. Especially after losing so many challenges."

"But—but—"

"Stay away from Nevers, all right?"

He squeezed her hand and sprinted to catch up with Ever-boys in the pumpkin patch. Chaddick's sharp voice echoed. "Still a villain, mate. Won't get special treatment from us. . . ."

Sophie didn't hear Tedros' response. She stood alone in the silent glen, under a blue mistletoe tree.

"We're still here," she grouched.

"Maybe if you had delivered my lines like I said them!" the roach retorted under her collar.

"Three hours alone isn't so bad," Sophie sighed. "I mean, Nevers can't use nonapproved spells. All we can do is start a storm or turn into a sloth. What could they possibly do to me?"

Something grazed her head. She whipped around and saw a gash in the oak trunk, right where she was standing. Impish Vex straddled a branch above her, sharp stick in hand.

"Just curious to see how tall you were," Vex said.

Doughy, bald Brone waddled in from behind another oak and checked the mark. "Yeah, she'll fit."

Sophie gaped at them.

"Like I said," Vex said, wagging pointy ears. "Just curious."

"I'm going to die!" Sophie wailed as she fled the Forest.

"Not with me there," Agatha said, pincers curled. "I beat them all in your classes and will beat them again tomorrow. Just focus on getting the kis—" Something smacked her head.

"What in the—"

Agatha looked down at a dead roach in the grass. Four more landed beside it.

Slowly Sophie and Agatha craned up to see the Evil Towers billowing pink mist, dead insects raining off balconies into the Clearing.

"What's going on?" Sophie said.

"Extermination," a voice answered.

Sophie turned to Hester, arms folded against the Forest gates. "Apparently they've been running around our school at night. Couldn't have the risk of plague, of course. After your friend was sick."

Hester picked a thrashing bug off her shoulder.

"Besides, a good reminder to anything that tries to go where it doesn't *belong*, don't you think?"

She licked the roach into her mouth and glided back into the Forest, leaves crunching under her feet.

Sophie gasped. "Do you think she knows you're a roach?"

"Of course she knows, you idiot!"

Nevers' voices neared from the Forest.

"Go!" Agatha hissed, scrambling down Sophie's leg. "We can't meet again!"

"Wait! How do I survive the Tria—"

But Agatha had vanished into the Good tunnel, leaving Sophie to fend for herself.

With the fairies doing curfew inspections from the first floors up, Agatha had just enough time to sneak to the breezeways and cross to Valor. Like all the teachers, Sader's bedchamber adjoined his study. Break its lock and she could surprise him in his bed. She didn't care if the creep didn't want to answer questions. She'd tie him to his bed if she had to.

Agatha knew it was a terrible plan, but what choice did she have? She couldn't sneak into the Trial now and Sophie would never last alone for three hours. Sader was their last hope to get home.

The stairs led right to his study, the lone door on Valor's sixth floor. There was a stream of raised blue dots across its marble. Agatha ran her finger over them.

"*No students allowed on this floor*," boomed Sader's voice. "*Return to your room immediately*."

Agatha grabbed the doorknob and pointed her glowing finger at the lock—

The door creaked open on its own.

Sader wasn't inside, but he hadn't been gone long. The sheets in his bedroom were rumpled, the tea on his desk warm. . . . Agatha skulked around his study, its shelves, chairs, floor all suffocated with books. The desk was buried three feet under them, but there were a few open on top of the pile, lines of colorful dots highlighted by prickly silver stars in the margins. She swept her hand across one of these marked lines and a misty scene exploded out of the book to a woman's sharp voice:

"A ghost cannot rest until it has fulfilled its purpose. For that, it must use the body of a seer."

Agatha watched a scraggy ghost crash into the body of a bearded old man, before the mist cycloned back into the page. She touched the starred lines in the next book:

"In a seer's body, a spirit may last only seconds before both seer and spirit will be destroyed."

Before her eyes, two floating bodies merged, then crumbled to dust.

She ran her fingers across more of the starred lines.

"Only the strongest seers can host a spirit—"

"Most seers die before the ghost ever takes hold—"

Agatha grimaced. What was his obsession with seer—

Her heart stopped.

Prophecy, said the teachers.

Could Sader *see the future?*

Could he see if they got home?

"Agatha!"

Professor Dovey gaped through the doorway. "Sader's alarm—I thought it was a roach—a *student*! Out of bed after curfew!"

Agatha scurried past her for the stairs. "Two weeks cleaning toilets!" her teacher squawked.

Agatha glanced back to see Professor Dovey sweep her hands over Sader's books with a frown. She caught Agatha watching and magically slammed the door.

That night, both girls dreamt of home.

Sophie dreamt she was fleeing Hester through pink fog. She tried to scream Agatha's name, but a roach crawled from her mouth instead. At last she found a stone well and swam to its bottom, only to find herself in Gavaldon. She felt strong arms, and her father carried her to her house, which smelled of meat and milk. She needed the toilet, but he took her to the kitchen, where a pig hung on a gleaming hook. A woman drummed red nails on the counter. *Tsk, tsk, tsk.* "Mother?" Sophie cried. Before the woman could turn, her father kissed Sophie good night, opened the oven, and threw her in.

Sophie woke with a jolt so hard she smashed her head on the wall and knocked herself out.

Agatha dreamt Gavaldon was on fire. A trail of burning black dresses led her up Graves Hill and when she got to the top she found a grave instead of her house. She heard sounds from within and started digging, hearing voices now, nearer, nearer, until she woke to them next door—

"You said it was important!" Tedros barked.

"The Nevers said she cheats with Agatha!" Beatrix said.

"Sophie's not friends with Agatha! Agatha's a *witch*—"

"They both are! Agatha turns into a cockroach to give her answers!"

"A *cockroach*? You're not just petty and jealous, but completely insane!"

"They're *both* villains, Teddy, they're using you!"

"*You're* the one listening to Nevers! You know why Sophie lost those challenges? She wanted to keep me safe! If that's a villain, then what are *you*—"

With wind rumpling her curtains, Agatha couldn't hear the rest, but soon the door thumped and Tedros traipsed away. Agatha tried to go back to sleep, but found herself staring at the pink paper flower shivering on her marble night table, like a rose on a grave.

She yelped, clobbered by an idea.

All the rooms in the hall looked dark except for the Trial Evers', who were staying up until dawn to prepare for the following night. In her lace dressing gown, Agatha tiptoed barefoot up the pink glass stairs, eyes pinned upward for fairies or teachers.

Five floors down, Tedros glared up at her through the spiral gap, suddenly wondering if Beatrix had told the truth.

Leaving his boots at the bottom, he followed Agatha through the breezeway to Honor's fourth floor, occupied entirely by the Library of Virtue. Crouching in knee-high black socks, he peeked in to see her disappear into the gold coliseum of books, two stories high and impeccably kept by a leathery tortoise, fast asleep on a titanic library log, feathered pen in hand. As soon as Agatha found what she needed, she sneaked out past the reptile and the prince, who failed to get a glimpse of the book in her hands. Her steps diminished in the sea-blue breezeway and soon she was gone.

Tedros clenched his teeth. What murderous plan did the witch have? Was Sophie in on it and planning to betray him? Were the two villains still *friends*? The prince lurched to his feet, heart thundering—then heard an odd scratching sound.

Turning, he saw the feathered pen magically finish writing in the tortoise's log, and fall back into the snoring creature's hand. Eyes narrowed, he moved in to peer at the log.

Flower Power: Plant Charms for a Happier World (Agatha, Purity 51)

Tedros snorted. Berating himself for doubting his princess, he went to retrieve his boots.

The rules of the Trial by Tale were few and precise. At the moment the sun went down, the first two challengers would enter the Blue Forest. Every fifteen minutes, another two would enter according to their pre-Trial ranks, until the last pair entered more than three hours after the first. Once inside, Nevers could attack Evers with their talents and any spell learned in class, while Evers could defend themselves with approved weapons or counterspells. The School Master's conjures would hunt them both. There were no other rules.

It was the challenger's duty to recognize mortal danger and drop his enchanted handkerchief; the moment it touched ground, he would be safely removed from the Trial. Upon the first glint of sunrise, the wolves would call the end and whoever returned through the gates would be named the winner. There had never been more than one. Quite often, there were none at all.

Winter arrived with naughty timing, blowing glacial gusts into the Clearing just as the challengers entered. Everboys each carried a blue kite-shaped shield matching their navy cloak and a single weapon; most had chosen bows and arrows (blunted by Professor Espada to stun, rather than injure), though Chaddick and Tedros had opted for heavy training swords. Nearby, Evergirls quietly practiced their animal calls and tried to look as helpless as possible so boys would take them under their wings.

Across the field, the Trial Nevers hunched against bare trees in their cloaks, eyeing unchosen students crowd in from the tunnels. The unpicked Evers were ready for a slumber party, with pillows, blankets, baskets of spinach mousselines, creamy chicken crepes, bell pepper skewers, elderflower custard, and pitchers of cherry grenadine. Meanwhile, the unpicked Nevers hovered near their tunnel in slippers and nightcaps, ready to flee at their team's first sign of humiliation.

While the wolves passed out the enchanted silk handkerchiefs—white for Evers, red for Nevers—Castor and Pollux lined up the competitors in order of their entrance. Because they fared worst in the pre-Trial challenges, Sophie and Kiko would enter exactly at sundown. Brone and Tristan would enter 15 minutes later, then Vex and Reena 15 minutes after that, and the pairs would continue until Hester and Tedros entered last.

At the back of the line, the prince took his white handkerchief from the wolf.

"Won't be needing this," he muttered, and stuffed it in his boot.

At the front of the line, Sophie clenched her red kerchief, ready to drop it the moment she entered. She wished she had paid more attention during the fitting. Her tunic drooped at the bosom, the cloak dragged on the ground, and the blue hood fell so far over her face it looked like she had no hea—

How could she think about *clothes*! Frantic, she scanned the crowd. Still no sign of Agatha.

"We've heard rumors that unqualified students may try to sneak into the Trial," Pollux said next to Castor, an imposing two-headed shadow in waning light. "This year we've taken extra precautions."

At first, Sophie thought he was referring to the wolves guarding every inch of gate. But then Castor lit a torch and she saw the gates were no longer made of gold—but of giant black and red spiders, crisscrossing magically with stingers poised.

Her heart sank. How could she sneak Agatha in now?

"If anyone cheats, they deserve to die."

She turned.

"And I don't put it past any of those villains," Tedros said, golden cheeks ruddy with cold. He took her hand, still gripping her kerchief. "You can't, Sophie. You can't drop it."

Without Agatha feeding lines, Sophie just nodded help-lessly.

"When we team up, they'll do anything to take one of us out—Evers, Nevers, School Master too," said her prince. "We need to *protect* each other. I need you to have my back."

Sophie nodded.

"You don't have anything to say?"

"A kiss for luck?" she squeaked.

"In front of the whole school?" Tedros cocked a smile. "That's an idea."

Sophie lit up and thrust out her lips with relief. "A long one," she sighed. "Just in case."

"Oh I'll give you a long one," he grinned. "When we win. Right before I carry you into the Good castle."

Sophie gagged. "But—but—suppose we don't—"

Tedros gently pulled the red silk from her trembling fin-gers.

"We're Good, Sophie," he said tucking it deep in her coat pocket. "And Good *always* wins."

In his clear blue eyes, Sophie saw Hester reflected behind her, hood lowered like the Grim Reaper.

In a flash, the wolves shoved her and Kiko to opposite ends of the North Gate. Hairy spiders hissed in her face and she lost her breath. Panicked, her eyes lurched to the School Mas-ter's tower, lording over the Forest. In the last shred of sun, she could see his silhouette, watching from the window. Sophie whipped around looking for Agatha to save her, but all she saw was the sky fall dark over the Forest. From the School Master's tower came a blast of silver sparks that veiled the Forest in a blurring haze—

"FIRST PAIR READY!" Castor boomed.

"No—wait!—"

Paws grabbed Sophie from behind and flung her into spiders. Hundreds of furry pincers probed her skin as she screamed. Clicking with permission, they magically parted, leaving her alone in the Forest's torch-lit threshold. Wolves howled. Spiders sealed behind her.

The Trial had begun.

21

Trial by Tale

errified, Sophie spun towards Kiko. They had to stay
together—

But Kiko was scampering east towards the Blueberry
Fields, peeping back to make sure
she wasn't following.

Quickly Sophie took
the west trail towards
the Blue Brook, where
she could hide under
its bridge. She had
expected the For-
est to be pitch-dark
and made Hort teach
her a fire spell dur-
ing breakfast. But
tonight the trees
fluoresced with an

ice-blue, blacklit sheen, glazing the Forest in arctic glow. Though the effect was ominous, she breathed relief. A flaming torch would have made her an easy target.

As she waded into the Fernfield, Sophie felt electric-blue fronds kiss her neck. Her body relaxed. She'd imagined a nonstop siege of horrors. But the Forest was quieter than she'd ever seen it. No skulking animals. No ominous howls. Just her in an ethereal meadow, wind strumming blades like harp strings.

As she waded through head-high ferns, she thought of Agatha. Did a teacher catch her brewing a plan? Did Hester intercept her?

Sophie felt pinpricks of sweat.

Or is Agatha afraid to help me?

For if she won with Tedros, no one could deny her switching schools. She could rule Good as their beneficent Captain. She could have her prince for Ever After and the life of a queen. Sophie gritted her teeth. If only she hadn't made that promise about going home! If only she could win this Trial alone, then she wouldn't have to keep it!

She stopped in her tracks. *But I can! Look at me! I'm doing just fi—*

A scream echoed. White sparks sprayed into the sky. Kiko had surrendered.

Sophie's legs jellied. How long would it take Kiko's attacker to find her? What was she thinking? She couldn't last here! She yanked the kerchief from her pocket, unleashed vermillion red, and—

CRACK! Something dropped from above and landed at

her feet. She stared down at a scroll of parchment, wrapped with a strip of fabric.

Fabric glowing with angry green frogs.

Sophie looked up and saw a white dove high above the trees. The dove tried to fly down—

CRACK! A barrier of flames exploded across the sky if it got even close to the trees. The faculty had taken no chances.

Sophie urgently pulled open the scorched scroll—

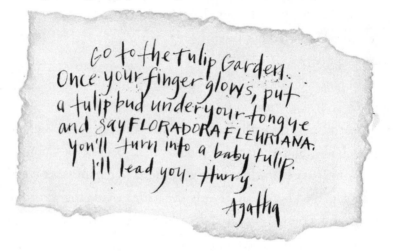

Go to the Tulip Garden.
Once your finger glows, put
a tulip bud under your tongue
and say FLORADORA FLEURIANA.
You'll turn into a baby tulip.
I'll lead you. Hurry.

Agatha

Sophie slumped with relief. A tulip! No one would ever find her! Oh, how could she doubt Agatha? Sweet, loyal Agatha! Sophie guiltily balled the red kerchief back in her pocket and followed the dove.

To get to the Tulip Garden by trail, she'd have to cross the Turquoise Thicket, then the Pumpkin Patch, and finally the Sleeping Willow Bosk. As she followed Agatha out of the ferns into the dense Thicket, phosphorescent leaves lit up the trail with wintry blue light. Sophie could see every scratch and scar on the lucent trunks, including the gash Vex had made above her head.

Wind suddenly swept through and leaves flickered over the trail. She couldn't see Agatha through the treetops. Sophie heard muffled grunts—human? animal?—but she didn't stop to find out. Kiko's scream thundering in her head, she fled down the trail, snatching at her dragging cloak. Tripping over shrubs and stumps, she ducked stabbing boughs, flung through tentacles of blue leaves, until she glimpsed pumpkins and an impatient dove between two shining tree trunks—

Someone stood between them. A little girl in a red cape and hood.

"Excuse me?" Sophie called. "I need to pass."

The red-headed stranger looked up. It wasn't a child at all. She had cloudy blue eyes, rosy blush on her wrinkled, spotted cheeks, and thick gray hair pulled into two ponytails.

Sophie frowned. She loathed old women.

"I said I need to *pass*."

The woman didn't move.

Sophie marched towards her—"Are you deaf?"

The crone dropped her red cloak and revealed a hawk's dirty, bloated body. Sophie shrank back, heard an earsplitting caw and swiveled to two more old bird-women moving towards her.

Harpies.

Agatha had taught her—*Sweet-talkers? Blind walkers?*

Then she saw their gnarled talons, tapping, sharp as blades.

Child eaters.

They pounced with terrible screams and Sophie ducked under a wing as the shrieking monsters dove after her, ugly faces contorted with rage. She raced through bushes to hide, but every corner of the thicket was spotlit blue. Harpies snapped at her neck and she fumbled for her pocket, touching red silk—her cloak snagged her foot and she crashed in mulch. Claws sank into her back and she screamed as she was lifted off ground, flailing for her kerchief. The Harpies opened their jaws to her face—

The thicket went dark.

Shrieks of confusion—claws released her and Sophie plunged into dirt. In blackness, she scrambled through gouging twigs until her hands found a log and she hid behind it. She could hear talons scraping blindly through dirt, furious grunts growing closer. Sophie sprang back and slammed into a rock with a cry. The monsters heard her and lunged for her head—

The thicket lit back up.

The Harpies craned their beaks to see Agatha the Dove hovering high, wingtip glowing orange. Agatha waved her wing and the thicket went dark. Agatha waved it again and the thicket went light. Dark then light, dark then light, until the Harpies got the point and two flew for Agatha, who squawked fearfully in place—

"*Fly!*" Sophie screamed, but Agatha flailed and thrashed as if she'd forgotten how. Twin monsters gnashed for the helpless dove, tearing higher, faster, until they had her in claws' reach—

Flames exploded across the barrier with a cruel crack and they fell, charred feathers and flesh.

The last Harpy gawked at their smoking bodies. Slowly it looked up. Agatha smiled and waved her glowing wing. The thicket lit up. The monster swiveled—

Sophie smashed its head with a rock.

In the Forest's silence, she panted and bled, alone on the ground, legs shaking under her cloak.

Sophie glared into the sky.

"I want to switch places!"

But the dove was already halfway to the Pumpkin Patch. Sophie could do nothing but follow miserably, hand gripping her kerchief inside her pocket.

Across the silent patch, pumpkins fluoresced a thousand shades of blue. Sophie stepped onto the dirt trail that snaked through the lit orbs, mumbling to herself that these were pumpkins, only pumpkins, and even a School Master couldn't make one scary. She rushed ahead to keep up with Agatha—

Dark silhouettes on the trail. Two people in front of her.

"Hello?" Sophie called.

They didn't move.

Heart thundering, Sophie stepped closer. There were more than two. Ten at least.

"What do you want!" she screamed.

No answer.

She inched closer. They were seven feet tall, with spindly bodies, faces like skulls, and crooked hands made of . . .

Straw.

Scarecrows.

Sophie exhaled.

The scarecrows lined both sides of the trail, dozens of them on wooden crosses, guarding the pumpkins with outstretched arms. From behind, glowing pumpkins lit their profiles, revealing shredded brown shirts, bald burlap heads, and black witch hats. As she walked slowly between them, Sophie saw their terrible faces—eyeholes ripped out of burlap, jagged pig noses, and sewn, lecherous grins. Spooked, she hurried forward, eyes on the path.

"Help me . . ."

She froze. The voice came from the scarecrow next to her. A voice she knew.

It can't be, Sophie thought. She pushed on.

"Help me, Sophie . . ."

Now there was no mistaking it.

Sophie willed herself forward. *My mother's dead.*

"I'm inside . . ." the voice rasped behind her, weak with agony.

Sophie's eyes filled with tears. *She's dead.*

"I'm trapped . . ."

Sophie turned.

The scarecrow wasn't a scarecrow anymore.

A man she knew gazed back at her from the wooden cross. Under the black hat, his eyes were gray and pupil-less. Instead of hands, he had two meat hooks.

Sophie paled. "Father . . . ?"

He cracked his neck and carefully pried himself from his cross.

Sophie backed up, right into another scarecrow. It was her

father too, wresting off his cross. Sophie whirled and all the scarecrows were her father, climbing off their stakes and walking towards her, meat hooks gleaming in chilly blue light.

"Father—it's *me*—"

They kept coming. Sophie backed against a cross—"It's me—Sophie—"

Far ahead, the dove looked back and saw Sophie cowering, screaming, as scarecrows stood peacefully still on the sides of the trail. Agatha yelped—

Sophie tripped on a pumpkin and fell. She spun to see her father's face again and again, devoid of mercy.

"Father, *please!*"

The scarecrows raised their hooks. Sophie's heart stopped—she choked a last breath and closed her eyes to slashing steel—

Water.

Cool, pristine water.

Her eyes fluttered open to a storm.

The patch was deserted. Just scarecrows on crosses, falling to pieces in rain.

Hovering high in the storm, Agatha waved her glowing wing and the rain stopped.

Sophie crumpled to the flooded path. "I can't . . . I can't survive this . . ."

Howls in the distance. Her eyes widened.

The next pair had entered the Forest.

Alarmed, the dove shrieked back at her and flew towards the Willow Bosk.

Shivering, Sophie staggered up and followed, shaken that a heart so haunted could still keep beating.

The long, thin trail through the Sleeping Willows sloped downhill, so Sophie could see the ghostly blue glow of the Tulip Garden at the bottom. One last push and she'd be safe among its flowers. For a moment, she questioned why Agatha hadn't made her turn into a tree or blade of grass near the gates—then remembered that Yuba had taught them to spot enchanted trees and that grass would be trampled by night's end. No, Agatha had chosen well. One tulip in thousands. She'd be safe till dawn.

As Sophie crept through the willows, her eyes darted around for the next threat. But the sapphire trees stood sentinel along the trail, long dangling branches glittering like chandeliers. As she drifted through, leaves shed over her in slow, beautiful rhythm, beads slipping off bracelets.

Something is here. Don't be fooled.

Wolves howled again at the gates and her stomach seized.

At least four others in the Forest now: Brone, Tristan . . . then who? Why hadn't she learned the order! She had to get to the tulips before they found her! Sophie broke into a breathless sprint, chasing the dove ahead. She didn't notice that the faster she ran, the faster the starry willow leaves shed, showering her in suspicious comets of light.

Then her head went heavy, her legs weak . . .

No . . .

Assaulted by leaves, she slowed to a stumbling limp.

Sleeping Willows . . .

Flying overhead, Agatha looked down and screeched.

Sophie lumbered forward, smelling the tulips . . . *Few more steps . . .*

She collapsed, the flowers ten feet away.

Agatha waved her glowing wing, sparking an explosion of thunder. Sophie didn't move. Agatha tried spells for rain, sleet, snow, but no response. Frantic, she squawked Sophie's favorite song, a wretched ode to princes and weddings—

Sophie's eyes peeked open.

Ecstatic, the dove kept warbling, more off-key with every note—

Agatha choked.

Blue hoods.

Two in the Thicket, two in the Pumpkin Patch, two more near the gates. She couldn't tell who they were, but they were all frozen, carefully discerning the precise source of the song they'd just heard.

Then they started running towards the tulips.

Agatha glanced at Sophie, splayed in dirt—then at blue hoods coming to kill her—

On the ground, Sophie dug her nails into earth and nosed forward a few inches.

Sensing her escape, the willows shed faster, paralyzing her muscles. Agatha flailed helplessly, dove beak whipping between Sophie and her hunters.

Panting, grunting, Sophie clawed herself through the last patch of willows, dirt turning to loamy petals beneath her. Exultant, she collapsed into big, blue flowers and inhaled their scent, reviving instantly. She shoved a tulip bud in her mouth, grabbed Agatha's note from her pocket, finger glowing pink—

"FLORADORA FLEUR—"

She froze.

Across the Tulip Garden, Brone and Vex smiled back at her, two tiny white fish thrashing in their hands.

"That's how you're going to kill me?" Sophie snorted. *"Fish?"*

"Wish Fish," Brone corrected, fish turning black in their hands.

"And we wish to be Hench Captains," Vex smirked.

The boys hurled the fish into the air—instantly they ballooned big as Sophie's body and dove for her, snapping piranha teeth—

Petrified, Sophie closed her eyes, felt her finger burn—

Poof! Her pink fox dodged the swollen fish, which careened off the ground like bouncing balls. Sophie sprinted for her life between them, paws slipping on tulips—

Faster! Need something faster! Her finger glowed, ready to help. *Cheetah! Lion! Tiger!*

Poof! She was a slow pink warthog, waddling and farting. Sophie grunted in horror. The bouncy fish careened off a tree and lunged for her hide. She thrust out her glowing hoof, focused harder—

Poof! She hurtled between them, a pink gazelle, and heard the fish crash into each other.

Sophie limped into a clearing, heaving for air. Faint wolf howls at the gates sent shudders through her fur. More enemies on the way.

Her big green eyes searched the dark sky for Agatha. Nothing but stars winking back at her.

She looked back down and jumped. Across the clearing, Tristan and Chaddick stood in the moonlight. Face ice cold, Tristan drew an arrow into his bow. Chaddick pulled his sword.

Sophie turned to run—

Reena blocked her escape. The Arabian princess whistled and two golden wolf dogs slunk into the clearing behind her, baring knife-sharp teeth.

Sophie spun to see Arachne skulk out of the trees, finger glowing. Two more Everboys drew arrows into their bows.

Legs quivering, Sophie's pink gazelle stood surrounded, waiting for her white dove to rescue her.

"Now!" Chaddick screamed—

Boys unleashed arrows, Arachne stabbed her finger, two dogs lunged as Sophie thrust out her shaking pink paw, closed her eyes—

Arrows and curses sailed over her scaly rattlesnake head. Sophie hissed in relief, slithering towards the safety of trees . . . until a shadow cast over her.

Reena's wolf dog pounced and grabbed her in its mouth.

Furious, Sophie felt her snake rattle burn pink—

Elephant buttocks crushed the dog's head as Sophie stampeded out of the clearing, trunk trumpeting in terror. Everboy arrows slammed into her massive pink rump and she crumpled to the grass in pain. Sophie glanced back at ten hooded assassins and two chomping fish, bouncing right for her. Helplessly cornered, she raised her glowing elephant trunk—

Curses, arrows, swords, fish grazed her feathers as Sophie's pink lovebird flapped into the air—

Screeching with triumph, she flew higher, higher, out of arrow reach, then saw the glint of flames at the barrier. Sophie recoiled in shock, only to feel something snare her wing. Slowly, a whip of water drew her towards a hooded figure in the Blue Brook.

Sophie shrieked for help, but then more whips ensnared her, pulling her through branches to her captor in the stream, who lashed the water with a glowing green finger. Slowly the waters delivered Sophie's lovebird into ashen hands as the shadow pulled back its hood.

"You would have made a great witch, Sophie," Anadil said, stroking her beak. "Even better than me."

The lovebird gazed up at her with pleading eyes.

Anadil's fingers crushed its tiny throat. The bird thrashed for breath, but Anadil pressed harder, and as Sophie's eyes went dark, she knew the last thing she'd ever see was a flaming star fall majestically through sky, falling straight for the witch about to snap her neck—

In a flash, a burning dove thieved Sophie out of Anadil's hands, into wings afire, and up through frigid sky.

As arrows tore through treetops, Agatha thrust out her glowing wingtip and arrows turned to daisies in the wind. She flew as long as she could on fire, Sophie clasped in her feet, then plunged into a dark pine glen and the birds smashed to the ground, tumbling over each other, snuffing out the flames.

Whimpering, Agatha struggled to make her charred wing glow. It flickered—she and Sophie instantly turned human, both paralyzed with pain. Sophie glimpsed Agatha's bare arms, blistered with burns. Before Sophie could cry out, Agatha's eyes widened and she circled her glowing orange fingertip around them—"*Floradora pinscoria!*"

They both turned to scrawny blue pine shrubs.

Anadil stormed into the glen with Arachne. They peered into the deserted patch.

"I told you they landed in the pumpkins," Arachne said.

"Then lead the way," said Anadil.

"Which of us gets to kill her?" Arachne said, turning—

Anadil stunned her with a lightning bolt. She stripped the red kerchief from Arachne's pocket and threw it to the ground. Red sparks shot into the air and Arachne vanished into thin air.

"Me," Anadil said.

Red eyes narrowed, she took one last long look around.

"Nick, I saw her over here!" called Chaddick, nearby.

Anadil smiled wickedly and headed in his direction.

In the dark, silent glen, two shrubs shivered side by side.

The night had just begun.

Outside the golden gates, the unchosen Evers and Nevers waited for Sophie's name to vanish off the scoreboard like Kiko's and Arachne's. But as the hours passed and more names vanished—Nicholas, Mona, Tristan, Vex, Tarquin, Reena, Giselle, Brone, Chaddick, Anadil—Sophie's stubbornly remained.

Had Sophie and Tedros united? What would their victory mean? A prince and witch . . . *together?*

As the hours passed, Good and Evil shared looks across the Clearing—first threatened . . . then curious . . . then hopeful . . . and before they knew it, they were drifting into each other's sides, sharing blankets, crepes, and cherry grenadine. Evil thought it had corrupted Good and Good thought it had enlightened Evil, but it didn't matter.

For two sides soon turned into one, cheering on the Prince-Witch revolution.

Inside the cold pine glen, two shrubs waited.

They waited through silence, split open by screams. They waited through sounds of classmates fighting enemies and betraying friends. They waited as something snared child after child with angry splashes in the Brook. They waited as drooling trolls stomped past them, brandishing bloodstained hammers. They waited as red and white sparks painted the sky, until only four competitors remained.

Then the Blue Forest went quiet for a very long time.

Hunger tore at their stomachs. Cold glazed their leaves with frost. Sleep attacked their senses. But the two plants stayed rooted still until the sky bruised blue. Sophie held her breath, willing the sun to break through . . .

Tedros limped into the glen.

He had no cloak, no sword, only a brutally dented shield. His tunic was torn to shreds, the silver swan on his bare chest gleaming against welts and blood. The prince gazed into the lightening sky. Then he crumpled against a skeletal pine, sniffling softly.

"*Corpadora volvera*," Agatha whispered. "That's the counterspell. Go to him!"

"When the sun comes up," Sophie whispered back.

"He needs to know you're okay!"

"He'll know in a few more minutes."

Tedros bolted straight. "Who's there?"

His eyes moved to Agatha's and Sophie's shrubs. Someone stepped from their shadows.

Tedros backed against the tree.

"Where's your witch?" Hester hissed, unscathed in a clean cloak.

"Safe," Tedros said hoarsely.

"Ah, I see," Hester smirked. "So much for your *team*."

The prince tensed. "She knows I'm safe too. Otherwise she'd be here to fight with me."

"Are you sure about that?" Hester said, black eyes flashing.

"That's what makes us Good, Hester. We trust. We protect. We love. What do you have?"

Hester smiled. *"Bait."*

She thrust out her glowing and red fingertip and the tattoo peeled off her neck, swelling with blood. Tedros backed up in shock as her demon engorged with blood, tighter, tighter, about to burst. Hissing an incantation, Hester's eyes grayed and her skin lost all color. She sank to the ground in agony and howled in fury as if tearing her own soul apart. Then the demon's body parts detached from each other . . . head, two arms, two legs.

Five fractured pieces, each one alive.

Tedros turned snow white.

The five demon pieces blasted towards him, conjuring daggers instead of fire bolts. He bludgeoned the stabbing head and leg with his shield, but an arm sank a dagger into his thigh. With a cry, he batted the arm away, pulled the knife out of his leg, and clawed up the only tree in the glen—

Agatha's shrub whipped to Sophie—"Help him!"

"And end in five pieces?" Sophie shot back.

"He needs you!"

"He needs me to be safe!"

A demon leg hurled a knife at the prince's head and he jumped just in time to a higher branch. The other four limbs ripped toward him, daggers raised—

Trapped, he glanced down at Hester, weak on her knees, directing the demon fragments with a glowing finger. Tedros' eyes widened, spotting something through the leaves.

Red silk. In her boot.

The fragments unleashed five knives point-blank, all aimed for his organs. Just as they pierced his shirt, he jumped out of the tree and landed on his wrist with a sickening crack.

Hester saw him scraping towards her. She circled her finger savagely, bringing the demon parts back around with new knives. Tedros held her glare as he crawled towards her. Sneering, Hester raised her finger high and the demon limbs coiled back to kill him. This time there would be no mistake. She roared and the knives stabbed down—the prince lunged for her boot—

Hester's mouth opened in horror as Tedros pinned her red handkerchief to the ground. The knives clinked limply to dirt and the demon parts vanished. Then Hester vanished too, eyes shocked wide.

Tedros collapsed on his back. Heaving for breath, he squinted into the pink sky. The sun was coming.

"Sophie," he croaked.

He took a deep breath.

"SOPHIE!"

Agatha's leaves drooped in relief. Then she saw Sophie's shrub pruning its leaves.

"What are yo—*Go*, you fool!"

"Agatha, I don't have *clothes*."

"At least call to him so he know—" Agatha stopped.

On the ground, a demon arm hadn't fully vanished. It was flickering in midair, willing itself to stay.

Then it slunk over the grass and picked a knife off the ground.

"Sophie—Sophie, go—"

"Sun will be up any minute—"

"Sophie, go!"

Sophie's shrub swiveled and saw the knife rise over Tedros' shoulder. She gasped and hid her eyes—

The blade plunged. Tedros saw it hit his heart too late.

A shield suddenly smashed the arm down. With a screech, the demon limb shriveled and disappeared.

Dazed, Tedros stared at the shallow wound in his chest muscle, the bloody knife on his sternum. He looked up at

Agatha, covering her body with his shield.

"Still haven't figured out the clothes bit," she mumbled.

Tedros leapt to his feet in shock. "But . . . you're not even in . . . what are you . . ."

He saw a shrub quivering behind her. Tedros stabbed his glowing gold fingertip—*"Corpadora volvera!"* Sophie fell forward and hid her body behind a shrub—

"Agatha, I need clothes! Teddy, could you turn around?"

Tedros shook his head. "But the library—that book . . . You *did* cheat!"

"Teddy, we *had* to. . . . Agatha, *help*!"

Agatha pointed her seared, glowing finger at Sophie to wrap her in vines but Tedros stayed her hand.

"You said you'd fight with me!" he cried, eyes locked on Sophie behind the shrub. "You said you'd have my back!"

"I knew you'd be fine—Agatha, *please*—"

"You lied!" he said, voice breaking. "Everything you said was a lie! You were using me!"

"That's not true, Tedros! No princess would risk her own life! Even your truest love—"

Tedros glowered, red hot. "Then why did *she*?"

Sophie followed the prince's eyes to Agatha, raw with burns.

Agatha saw Sophie's eyes slowly widen, as if discovering a knife stabbed into her back. But just as Agatha tried to defend herself, sunlight exploded into the glen and washed her body in gold.

Wolves howled at the gates. Sounds of children and

footsteps thundered through the Forest.

"They did it!"

"They won!"

"Sophie and Tedros won!"

Bodies burst into the glen. Panicked, Agatha lit up her finger and her dove flew away just as students flooded into view—

"Ever and Never!" shouted one.

"Witch and prince!" shouted another.

"All hail Sophie and Ted—"

The Forest went quiet.

From a tree, Agatha looked down at the unchosen Evers and Nevers surge in, then the fallen competitors, healed and cleaned by magic—all frozen as they took in the scene.

Sophie cowering behind a bush. Tedros glaring down at her, eyes on fire.

And they knew there would never be peace.

Evers and Nevers shifted apart, enemies eternal.

Neither side could hear the laughter from the tower, half shadowed, lording over them all.

22

Nemesis Dreams

"Have you seen my pajamas?" Hort whimpered outside Sophie's door. "The ones with frogs?"

Swaddled in his tattered bedsheets, Sophie stared at a window she'd sealed dark with a black blanket.

"My father made them for me," Hort sniffled. "I can't sleep without them."

But Sophie just gazed at the blackened window, as if there was something in the darkness only she could see.

Hort brought up barley gruel, boiled eggs, browning vegetables from the Supper Hall, but she didn't answer his knocks. For days, Sophie just lay still as a corpse, waiting for her prince to come. Soon her eyes dulled. She didn't know what day it was. She didn't know if it was morning or night. She didn't know if she was asleep or awake.

Somewhere in this grim fog the first dream came.

Streaks of black and white, then she tasted blood. She gazed up into a storm of boiling red rain. She tried to hide, but she was strapped to a white stone table by violet thorns, her body tattooed in a strange script she'd seen before but couldn't remember where. Three old hags appeared beside her, chanting and tracing the script on her skin with crooked fingers. Faster and faster the hags chanted until a steel knife, long and thin as a knitting needle, appeared in the air over her body. She tried to wrest free, but it was too late. The knife fell with vengeance, pain flooded her stomach, and something inside her was born. A pure white seed, then a milky mass, bigger, bigger, until she saw what it was. . . . A face . . . a face too blurry to see. . . .

"Kill me now," said the voice.

Sophie jolted awake.

Agatha sat on the edge of her bed, wrapped in Hort's stained sheets.

"I mean, I don't even want to *know* what's on these."

Sophie didn't look at her.

"Come on. You can borrow my nose clips for Yuba's class." Agatha stood, lit by a small tear in the window. "Day three of

'Know Your Animal Dung!'"

Strained silence ticked by.

Agatha slumped to the bed. "What should I have done, Sophie? I couldn't let him die."

"It's not right," Sophie said, almost to herself. "You and me . . . it's not right."

Agatha scooted closer. "I only want the best for you—"

"*No*," said Sophie so sharply Agatha lurched back.

"I just wanted to get us home!"

"We're not going home. You've seen to that."

"You think I wanted this?" Agatha said, exasperated.

"Why are you here?"

"Because I wanted to see how you were. I was worried about you!"

"No. Why are you *here*," Sophie said, looking at the window. "In my school. In my fairy tale."

"Because I tried to save you, Sophie! I tried to save you from the curse!"

"Then why do you keep *cursing* me and my prince?"

Agatha scowled. "That's not my fault."

"I think it's because deep down you don't want me to find love, Agatha," Sophie said, voice calm.

"What? Of cour—"

"I think you want me for *yourself*."

Agatha's whole body went rigid. "That's—" She swallowed. "That's *stupid*."

"The School Master was right," Sophie said, still not looking at her. "A princess can't be friends with a witch."

"But we *are* friends," Agatha sputtered. "You're the only friend I've ever had!"

"You know why a princess can't be friends with a witch, Agatha?" Slowly Sophie turned to face her. "Because a witch never has her own fairy tale. A witch has to *ruin* one to be happy."

Agatha fought back tears. "But I'm not—I'm not a witch—"

"THEN GET YOUR OWN LIFE!" Sophie screamed.

She watched the dove flee through the rip in the black window, then crawled back under her sheets until all the light was gone.

That night, Sophie had her second dream. She was running through woods, hungrier than she'd ever been—until she found a deer with a human face, the same milky, blurred face she glimpsed the night before. She looked closer to see whose it was, but the deer's face was now a mirror and in it, she could see her reflection. But it wasn't hers.

It was the Beast's.

Sophie woke in icy sweat, blood burning through her veins.

Outside Room 34, Hort huddled in his underpants, reading *The Gift of Loneliness* by candlelight.

The door cracked open behind him. "What is everyone saying about me?"

Hort stiffened as if he'd heard a ghost. He turned, eyes wide.

"I want to know," said Sophie.

She followed him into the dark hall, joints cracking. She couldn't remember the last time she stood up.

"I don't see anything," she said, searching for the glint of his chest's swan crest. "Where are you?"

"Over here."

A torch ignited, swathing Hort in firelight. She staggered back.

Every inch of the black wall behind him was covered in posters, banners, graffiti—CONGRATULATIONS, CAPTAIN! TRIAL TRIUMPHANT! READER TO THE RESCUE!—accompanied by depraved cartoons of Evers suffering miserable deaths. Beneath the wall, carnivorous green bouquets littered the floor, carrying handwritten messages between the blooms' sharp teeth:

WISH I HAD YOUR MOVES!
RAVAN

You're the ultimate Thief of Hearts!
Mona

TEDROS dESERVEd iT!
YOUR fRIENd, ARACHNE

Sophie looked dazed. "I don't understand—"

"Tedros said you used him to win the Trial!" Hort said. "Lady Lesso named it the 'Sophie Trap'—said you even fooled her! Teachers are saying you're the best Captain Evil has ever had. Look!"

Sophie followed his eyes to a row of eel-green boxes amid the bouquets, wrapped with red ribbons.

She opened the first to find a parchment card:

HOPE YOU REMEMBER HOW TO USE IT. PROFESSOR MANLEY

Beneath it was a black snakeskin cape.

In the boxes that followed, Castor gifted her a dead quail, Lady Lesso left an ice-carved flower, and Sader enclosed her Trial cloak, asking if she might kindly donate it to the Exhibition of Evil.

"What a genius trick," Hort fawned, trying on the cape. "Hide as a plant, wait until Tedros and Hester are left, then charge in and take out Hester while Tedros is wounded. But why didn't you finish Tedros off? Everyone's asking, but he won't say anything. I said it's 'cause the sun came up."

Hort saw Sophie's expression and his smile vanished.

"It was a trick, wasn't it?"

Sophie's eyes filled with tears. She started to shake her head—

But there was something else on the wall in front of her.

A black rose, note speared through thorns, dripping with ink.

Sophie took it into her hands.

Cheater. Liar. Snake.
You're right where you belong.
All hail the witch.

"Sophie? Who's it from?"

Heart throbbing, Sophie smelled the bitter black thorns laced with a scent she knew so well.

So this was her reward for Love.

She crushed the rose, spitting Tedros' words with blood.

"This will make you feel better."

In Room 66, Anadil scooped murky yellow broth from her cauldron into a bowl, dripping on the floor. Immediately her rats converged, eight inches bigger now, biting, clawing each other to get first licks.

"Your talent's coming along," Hester croaked.

Anadil sat on the edge of Hester's bed with the bowl. "Just a few sips."

Hester managed only one, then fell back.

"I shouldn't have tried it," she wheezed. "She's too good. She's twice the witch I am—"

"Shhhh, don't strain."

"But she loves him," said Dot, curled in her bed.

"She *thinks* she does," Hester said. "Just like we all once did."

Dot's eyes bulged.

"Please, Dot. You think she's the only Never who dabbled in love?"

"Hester, enough," Anadil pressed.

"No, let's have the truth," Hester said, struggling to sit up. "All of us have felt shameful stirrings. All of us have felt weakness."

"But those feelings are wrong," said Anadil. "No matter how strong they are."

"That's why this one's special," Hester said wryly. "She almost convinced us they were right."

The room lapsed to silence.

"So what happens to her now?" asked Dot.

Hester sighed. "The same thing that happened to all of us."

This time their silence was broken by distant clacks in slow, menacing rhythm. The three girls craned to the door as the clacks swelled towards them, cruel and clean like whip cracks. They grew louder, sharper, impaling the hall, then ebbed past their room to silence.

Dot farted in relief.

The door slammed open and the girls screamed—Dot bellyflopped off the bed—

A draft blew the hanging dresses past the torch over the door, casting flints of light on a shadow's face.

The hair gleamed, spiked and slicked, black as smeared eye sockets and lips. Ghost-white skin glowed against black nail polish, black cape, and black leather.

Sophie stepped into the room, high black boots stabbing the floor.

Hester grinned back at her.

"Welcome home."

From the floor, Dot peeped nervously between them. "But where will we find a new bed?"

Three pairs of eyes found hers.

She didn't even get time to collect her snacks. In the dark, dank hall, Dot pounded on the iron door in banishing silence. But it was no use.

Three witches made a coven and she had been replaced.

The Evers didn't celebrate when Tedros received his Captain's badge. How could they, when Sophie had made a fool of him?

"Evil had returned!" the Nevers gloated. "Evil had a Queen!"

Then the Evers remembered they had something the Nevers didn't. Something that proved them superior.

A Ball.

And the Queen wasn't invited.

The first snow littered the Clearing in lumpy brittles of ice, pelting Nevers' pails with loud pings. As they tried to grasp moldy cheese with frozen fingers, they looked daggers at Evergirls scrabbling about, too busy to worry about weather. With the Ball two weeks away, the girls needed to make every possible arrangement, since boys still refused to propose before the Circus. Reena, for instance, expected Chaddick to ask her, so she had dyed her mother's old school gown to match his gray eyes. But if Chaddick asked Ava instead (she had caught him ogling Snow White's portrait, so he might like paler girls), then Nicholas might ask her, in which case she'd trade for Giselle's white gown to balance his tanned skin. And if Nicholas didn't ask her . . .

"Mother says Goodness is making people feel wanted even when you don't want them at all," she sighed to Beatrix, who looked bored. With Sophie out of the picture, Beatrix knew Tedros was her date. Not that he had confirmed this. The prince had been ignoring everyone since the Trial, sullen as a Never. Now Beatrix felt his mood infect her as she watched him shoot arrows into the tree he and Sophie used to sit beneath.

Tedros ripped more holes in its heart, but there was no satisfaction. After a few days of teasing, his mates had tried to cheer him up. Who cared if he shared his spoils with a Never-girl! Who cared if she puttered with him along the way! He'd still won a brutal Trial and outlasted them all. But Tedros saw only shame in it, for he was no better than his father now. A slave to his heart's mistakes.

Still, he hadn't told anyone about Agatha. He knew she was surprised by this because she winced every time he spoke in class, as if expecting him to expose her any moment. But where a week ago, he would have loved to see her punished, now he felt confused. Why had she risked her life to save him? Had she been telling the truth about that gargoyle? Could that witch actually be . . . *Good*?

He thought of her tramping through halls with leery bug eyes—

A cockroach. That's what Beatrix said.

So Agatha was there all along, helping Sophie to the top of the ranks? She must have been hidden in Sophie's dress or in her hair, whispering answers and casting spells. . . . But how had she made him pick Sophie in the pumpkin chal-lenge?

Tedros felt sick.

A goblin picked from two . . . A princess whose coffin knocked him out . . . A roach hidden on a pumpkin . . .

He had never picked Sophie.

He picked Agatha every time.

Tedros whipped around in horror, looking for her, but he didn't see Agatha anywhere in the Clearing. He had to stay away from that girl. He had to tell her to stay away from him.

He had to stop all of this—

A hunk of sleet smacked his cheek. Blinded by water, Tedros saw shadows gliding towards him, wiped his eyes— and dropped his bow.

Sophie, Anadil, and Hester slunk in step with matching black hair, black makeup, and black-hearted scowls. With a shared hiss, they sent Evergirls bolting, leaving only Tedros and spooked Everboys fanned out behind him. Anadil and Hester dropped behind Sophie, who stepped up to face her prince.

From the sky, ice fell between them in jagged slivers.

"You think I faked it," Sophie said, flaying him with her green eyes. "You think I never loved you."

Tedros tried to quell his thumping heart. Somehow she was more beautiful than ever.

"You can't cheat your way to love, Sophie," he said. "My heart never wanted you."

"Oh, I've seen who your heart picks," Sophie smirked, mimicking Agatha's buggy gape and trademark scowl.

Tedros reddened. "I can explain that—"

"Let me guess. Your heart is blind."

"No, it just says anyone but *you*."

Sophie chuckled. In a flash, she lunged and Tedros drew his sword, as did all his mates behind him.

Sophie smiled weakly. "Look what's happened, Tedros. You're scared of your true love."

"Go back to your side!" the prince yelled.

"I waited for you," Sophie said, voice breaking. "I thought you'd come for me."

"What? Why would I come for *you*?"

Sophie gazed at him. "Because you made me a promise," she breathed.

Baring teeth, Tedros glared back. "I made you no promises."

Sophie stared at him, stunned. Her eyes cast down. "I see."

Slowly she looked back up.

"Then I'll be whatever you want me to be."

She thrust out her glowing finger and the boys' swords turned to snakes. As Everboys fled, Tedros kicked dust at the hissing coils. He spun to see Sophie wipe tears, then pull her cape around her and hurry away.

Hester ran to catch up—"Feel better?"

"I gave him a chance," Sophie said, walking faster.

"You're even now. It's over," Hester soothed.

"No. Not until he keeps his promise."

"Promise? What promise—"

But Sophie had already raced ahead into the tunnel. As she fled through twisted branches, she sensed someone watching. Through tears and trees, she couldn't see the face on the balcony, just a milky white blur. Her stomach sank—she found a break in the leaves—

But the face was gone, as if it was just a dream.

The next morning, Good woke to slippery lard all over the floors. The morning after, Everboys screamed after putting on coats laced with rash powder. On the third morning, the teachers found framed underpants replacing Beauty's portrait on the Legends Obelisk, the sides switched in the Theater of Tales, and candied classrooms flooded with stinky green goo.

With the fairies unable to catch the vandals in the act, Tedros and his Everboy mates formed a nighttime guard, patrolling the halls from dusk until dawn. Still, the culprits eluded capture and by the end of the week, the bandits had filled the Groom Room pools with stingrays, warped the hall mirrors to taunt passersby, released overfed pigeons in the Supper Hall, and enchanted Good toilets to explode when students sat on them.

Enraged, Professor Dovey insisted Sophie be brought to justice, but Lady Lesso said it was highly doubtful one student could manage to cripple an entire school without help.

She was right.

"It doesn't feel good anymore," Anadil grouched after supper in Room 66. "Hester and I want to stop."

"You got your revenge," said Hester. "Let him *go*."

"I thought you two were villains," Sophie said from her bed, eyes glued to *Nightmares Be Gone*.

"Villains have purpose," Hester snapped. "What we're doing is just thuggery."

"Tonight we're putting pox in the boys' breeches," said Sophie, flipping the page. "Find a spell for it."

"What do you *want*, Sophie?" Hester pleaded. "What are we fighting for?"

Sophie looked up. "Are you going to help or should I turn us all in?"

Tedros soon had all 60 boys on his nighttime guard, but Sophie escalated the attacks. The first night, she made Hester and Anadil brew a potion to turn the Good lake to Evil sludge, forcing the magical wave to migrate to the sewers. The brew left their hands red with burns, but Sophie made them return at dawn to lace Ever linens with lice. Soon, the girls attacked so frequently—putting leeches in the Evers' supper punch, unleashing locusts during Uma's lecture, sending a charging bull into Swordplay, cursing the Evers' stairs to scream bloodily with every step—that half the Good teachers canceled their classes, Pollux stumbled on sheep legs into his own traps, and the Evers only felt safe traveling in packs.

Professor Dovey slammed into Lady Lesso's office. "That witch must be failed!"

"There's no way for a Never to *enter* your school, let alone attack it day and night," Lady Lesso yawned. "For all we know it's a rogue Ever."

"An *Ever*! My students have won every competition in this school for two hundred years!"

"Until now." Lady Lesso smiled. "And I have no plans to give up *my* best student without *proof.*"

While Professor Dovey sent unanswered missives to the School Master, Lady Lesso took careful notice of Sophie's growing distance with her roommates, the fact Sophie was no longer shivering in her iced classroom, and her brutal desecration of Tedros' name on her book covers.

"Are you feeling all right, Sophie?" Lady Lesso asked, barring the ice door after class.

"Yes, thank you," Sophie replied uncomfortably. "I should be goin—"

"Between your winning Class Captain, your new fashions, and your nighttime activities . . . it's a lot to take in."

"I don't know what activities you're referring to," Sophie said, sidling past her.

"Have you been having strange dreams, Sophie?"

Sophie stopped cold.

"What kind of dreams would be strange?"

"Angry dreams. Dreams that get worse every night," Lady Lesso said behind her. "You'll feel as if something is being birthed in your soul. A *face*, perhaps."

Sophie's stomach clamped. The terrible dreams had persisted, all ending with a milky, blurry face. The past few days, streaks of red appeared at the face's edges, as if it was being outlined in blood. But she couldn't recognize it. All she knew was she woke up every day angrier than before.

Sophie turned. "Um, what would a dream like that mean?"

"That you are a special girl, Sophie," Lady Lesso cooed. "One we should all be proud of."

"Oh. Um . . . I may have had one or two—"

"Nemesis Dreams," Lady Lesso said, violet eyes flashing. "You're having Nemesis Dreams."

Sophie stared at her. "But—but—"

"Nothing to be concerned about, dear. Not until there's symptoms."

"*Symptoms?* What symptoms? What happens if there's symptoms?"

"Then you'll finally see the face of your Nemesis. The one who grows stronger as you grow weaker," Lady Lesso answered calmly. "The one you must destroy in order to live."

Sophie blanched. "B-b-but that's impossible!"

"Is it? I think it's quite clear who your Nemesis is."

"What? I don't have anyone that—"

Sophie lost her breath.

"*Tedros?* But I love him! That's why I did it! I have to get him back—"

Lady Lesso just smiled.

"I was angry!" Sophie cried. "I didn't mean any—I don't want to hurt him! I don't want to hurt anyone! I'm not a villain!"

"You see, it doesn't matter what we are, Sophie."

Lady Lesso leaned so close she just had to whisper.

"It's what we *do.*"

Her pupils flicked over Sophie's face. "But no symptoms yet, I'm afraid," she sighed and swept to her desk. "Close the door on your way out."

Sophie fled too fast to bother.

That night, Sophie didn't attack the Evers.

Let him go, she told herself, pillow over her head. *Let Tedros go.*

Over and over she repeated it, until she had erased the meeting with Lady Lesso from her memory. As the words soothed her to sleep, she felt the stirrings of her old self. Tomorrow she'd be loving. Tomorrow she'd be forgiving. Tomorrow she'd be Good again.

But then another dream came.

She ran through mirrors reflecting her smiling face, long gold hair, and luscious pink gown. Through the last mirror was an open door and through the door, Tedros waited for her, kingly in his blue Ball suit beneath Camelot's spires. She ran and ran to him but grew no closer, until deadly sharp briars, swollen purple, began to snake towards her true love. Frantic, she willed herself through the last door to save him, losing a glass heel and lunged for his arms . . . The prince melted to a milky, red blur and threw her into thorns.

Sophie woke enraged and forgot all about letting go.

"It's the middle of the night! You said it was over!" Anadil fumed, following her into the tunnel—

"We can't keep doing these things without a purpose," Hester seethed.

"I have a purpose," Sophie said, whirling around. "You hear me? I have a *purpose*."

The next day, the Evers arrived at lunch to find all the trees on their side cut down. All except the one Sophie and Tedros used to sit beneath, carved again and again with one unmistakable word.

LIAR.

Stunned, the wolves and nymphs howled for the teachers and immediately formed a boundary between the two halves of the Clearing. Tedros stormed up to the border between two wolves.

"Stop it. *Now.*"

Everyone followed his eyes to Sophie, sitting serenely

against a snowy tree on the Nevers' side.

"Or what?" she simpered. "You'll catch me?"

"Now you really sound like a villain," Tedros sneered.

"Careful, Teddy. What will they say when we dance at the Ball?"

"All right, now you've lost it—"

"Here I thought you were a prince," Sophie said, walking towards him. "Because you promised to take me to the Ball right in this very spot. And a prince never breaks his *promise*."

Gasps rose from both sides of the Clearing. Tedros looked like he'd been kicked in the gut.

"After all, a prince who breaks his promise"—Sophie faced him between two wolves—"is a *villain*."

Tedros couldn't speak, cheeks splotched red.

"But you're not a villain and neither am I," Sophie said, eyes guilty. "So all you have to do is keep your promise and we can be ourselves again. Tedros and Sophie. Prince and princess."

With a tentative smile, she held out her hand across the wolves to him.

"Good for Ever After."

The Clearing was dead silent.

"I'll never take you to the Ball," Tedros spat. *"Never."*

Sophie withdrew her hand.

"Well, then," she said softly. "Now everyone knows who's *responsible* for the attacks."

Tedros felt Evers' blameful stares burning through him. Ashamed, he trudged out of the Clearing, as Sophie watched, heart in her throat, fighting the urge to call him back.

"This is about a *Ball?*" said a voice.

Sophie turned to glowering Hester and Anadil.

"This is about what's *right*," she said.

"You're on your own," Hester snarled, and Anadil followed her away.

Sophie stood, circled by stunned students, teachers, wolves, and fairies, listening to her own shallow breaths. Slowly she looked up.

Tedros glared down at her from inside the glass castle. In the weak sun, his milky face had a glint of red.

Sophie met his eyes, steeling her heart.

He'd love her back. He'd have to.

Because she'd destroy him if he dared love anyone else.

23

Magic in the Mirror

Buried under lace pillows, all Agatha could hear was the echo of four terrible words.

GET YOUR OWN LIFE.

What life? Before Sophie, all she could remember was darkness and pain. Sophie had made her feel normal. Sophie had made her feel needed. With-out Sophie, she was a freak, a nothing, a . . .

Agatha's stom-ach dropped.

A witch never has her own fairy tale.

Without Sophie, she was a witch.

For six days, Agatha stayed shut up in her tower, listening to the screams of Evers terrorized by new attacks. All joint-school activities had been canceled indefinitely, lunch and Forest Groups included. Was this all her fault? Didn't witches leave fairy tales in ruins? As the screams outside grew more panicked, her guilt screwed tighter and tighter.

Then the attacks stopped.

Huddled in common rooms, Evers held their breath. But when Saturday and Sunday went, Agatha knew the storm had passed. Sophie would come to say sorry any minute now. Gazing at the rose-tinted moon, Agatha hugged her pillow and prayed. Their friendship would survive this.

Fairies jingled outside the door and she swiveled to see a note slid under it. Chest pounding, she dived out of bed, swooped it into sweaty palms—

Dear Students,
With the Snow Ball six days away, this week's challenges will see if you are prepared. Despite recent interruptions, there will be no further cancellations. Our traditions are what separate Good from Evil. Even in the darkest of times, a Ball may be your best chance to find a happy ending.

Professor Dovey

Agatha groaned and buried herself under pink sheets. But as she gave in to sleep, she began to hear words ... *Ball* ...

purpose . . . happy . . . They tumbled in darkness, echoing deeper, deeper, until they planted in her soul like magic seeds.

Ravan tiptoed towards Room 66, swan crests of six shivering Nevers glinting in darkness behind him.

"If the attacks stopped, maybe she's dead," Vex said.

"Maybe villains don't do Evil on Sundays," said Brone.

"Or maybe Sophie got over that stupid prince!" Ravan lashed.

"You don't ever get over love," Hort moped in dirty long johns. "Even if they steal your room and your pajamas."

"Sophie shouldn't even have *let* herself love!" Ravan shot back. "First time I told my dad I liked a girl, he slathered me in honey and sealed me in a bear den for a night. Haven't liked one since."

"First time I told my mother I fancied someone, she baked me in an oven for an hour," Mona agreed, green skin paling. "I never think about boys now."

"First time I liked a boy, my dad killed him."

The group stopped and stared at Arachne. "Maybe Sophie just had bad parents," she said.

With solemn nods, the Nevers skulked to Room 66, hidden in shadow. Holding their breaths, they each found a piece of door and pressed their ears to it.

They didn't hear anything.

"On three," Ravan mouthed. Nevers backed up, preparing to storm it. "One . . . two . . ."

"Drink this."

Anadil's voice inside. Nevers shoved their ears to the door.

"They're—killing—me—" Sophie rasped weakly—

Sounds of vomiting.

"She has a high fever, Hester."

"Lady Lesso said—Nemesis—Drea—"

"They're nothing, Sophie," Hester's voice said. "Now go to sleep."

"Will I—be—better for—Ball? Tedros—promised—"

"Close your eyes, dearie."

"Dreams—they'll come—" Sophie wheezed—

"Shhh, we're here now," Hester said.

It was quiet inside, but Ravan and the Nevers didn't move. Then they heard voices closer to the door.

"Dreams of faces, high fever, obsession . . . Lady Lesso's right!" Anadil whispered. "Tedros is her *Nemesis*!"

"So she did meet the School Master!" Hester whispered back. "She's in a real fairy tale!"

"Then this whole school better watch out, Hester. Real fairy tales mean *war*!"

"Ani, we need to get Tedros and Sophie back together *now*! Before any symptoms appear!"

"But how?"

"Your *talent*," Hester whispered. "But we can't tell a soul! This gets out and all our lives are at stak—"

Her voice stopped.

Ravan wheeled to the others—

The door slammed open. Hester peered out, eyes narrowed. But the hallway was empty.

On Monday morning, Agatha woke with a strong urge to go to class.

Stomping around her room, she shoved on her rumpled pinafore and picked lint from her greasy hair. How many days could she wait? Sophie didn't want to apologize? Sophie didn't want to be friends? She crushed Sophie's paper rose, hurled it through the window—

I can have my own life!

She searched for something else to throw, then glimpsed crinkled parchment under her toes.

"A Ball may be your best chance . . ."

Agatha grabbed it into her hands and read Professor Dovey's note again, eyes flaring.

That's it! The Ball *was* her chance!

All she needed was one of those vile, arrogant boys to take her! Then Sophie would eat her words!

She jammed callused feet into her clumps and stomped down the stairs, waking the whole tower.

She had five days to find a date to the Evers Snow Ball.

Five days to prove she wasn't a witch.

Ball Week got off to a bizarre start when Professor Anemone pranced in ten minutes late, wearing a white swan-feather dress with a high rump and scandalously short hem, along with purple panty hose, sparkly garters, and a crown that could have been an upside-down chandelier.

"Behold, true Ball *elegance*," she preened, caressing her tail feathers. "A good thing boys cannot ask *me* to the Ball, or many of you would lose your princes!"

She basked in her students' stares. "Yes, isn't it divine. I was told by Empress Vaisilla this is all the rage in Putsi."

"Putsi? Where is Putsi?" Kiko wisped.

"Home to a lot of angry swans," said Beatrix.

Agatha gouged herself with a pen to not laugh.

"Because your suitors have chosen to wait until the Circus to propose, I caution you to take this week's challenges seriously," Professor Anemone huffed. "An exceptionally good or poor performance could very well change a boy's mind!"

"Suppose Tedros did promise to take Sophie to the Ball?" Reena whispered to Beatrix. "Princes can't break promises without something terrible happening!"

"Some promises are meant to be broken," Beatrix retorted. "But if anyone tries to ruin my night with Tedros, I promise they won't *survive* the night."

"Of course not all of you will be asked to the Snow Ball," warned Professor Anemone. "Every year, one woeful girl is failed, because boys would rather take half ranks than take her. And such a girl who can't find a boy, even under the most propitious circumstances . . . well, she must be a witch, mustn't she?"

Agatha felt everyone's eyes on her. *Failed* if a boy didn't ask her?

Now finding a date was a matter of life and death.

"For today's challenge, you must try to see *who* your date for the Ball will be!" her teacher declared. "Only when you see a boy's face clearly in your head will you know he wants you too. Now join the person beside you and take turns proposing. When it is your turn to accept, close your eyes and see whose face appears. . . ."

Agatha turned to Millicent across her desk, who looked poised to vomit.

"Dear, um, Agatha . . . willyoubemyprincessfortheBall?" she heaved, then retched so loud Agatha jumped.

Oh, who was she kidding? She looked down at her bony limbs, pasty skin, and nails bitten to the nub. What boy would *choose* to ask her to the Ball! As hope seeped out of her, she glanced at girls, eyes closed in euphoria, dreaming of their princes' faces—

"It's a yes-or-no *question*," Millicent moaned.

With a sigh, Agatha closed her eyes and tried to imagine her prince's face. But all she could hear were the loud echoes of boys fighting to not be her date. . . .

"There's no one left for you, dear."

"But I thought every boy had to go, Professor Dovey—"

"Well, the last one killed himself rather than take you."

Phantom laughter shrieked in her ears. Agatha gritted her teeth.

I'm not a witch.

The boys' voices softened.

I'm not a witch.

The voices receded into darkness. . . .

But there was nothing in their place. Nothing to believe in.

I'm not! I'm not a witch!

Nothing.

Something.

A milky, faceless silhouette born out of darkness.

He bent before her on one knee . . . took her hand . . .

"Are you feeling all right?"

She opened her eyes. Professor Anemone was staring at her. So was the rest of the class.

"Um, I think so?"

"But you . . . you . . . *smiled*! A *real* smile!"

Agatha gulped. "I did?"

"Have you been bewitched?" her teacher shrieked. "Is this one of the Nevers' attacks—"

"No—I mean—it was an accident—"

"But, my dear! It was *beautiful*!"

Agatha thought she might float out of her chair. She wasn't a witch! She wasn't a freak! She felt her smile return, bigger, brighter than before.

"If only the rest was too," Professor Anemone sighed.

Agatha's smile collapsed into its comfortable frown.

Dispirited, she flopped her next two challenges miserably, with Pollux calling her attitude "nefarious" and Uma sighing she'd seen sloths with more charm.

Sulking in the pews before History, Agatha wondered whether Professor Sader could, in fact, see her future. Would she find a date to the Snow Ball? Or was Sophie right about her being a witch? Would she fail and die here all alone?

The problem was there was no way to ask Sader anything, even if he *was* a seer. Besides, to broach the subject, she'd have to admit she broke into his study. Not the best way to win a teacher's confidence.

In the end, it didn't matter because Sader never showed up. He had chosen to spend the week teaching at the School for

Evil, claiming that History couldn't compete with the distractions of a Ball. In his absence, he relinquished the teaching of "Ball Customs & Traditions" to a gang of unkempt middle-aged sisters in musty gowns. The Twelve Dancing Princesses from the famous fairy tale who had each won their prince at a court Ball. But before they could reveal how exactly they squired these princes, the twelve shrews started bickering as to the correct version of their story, then shouting over each other.

Agatha closed her eyes to tune them out. No matter what Professor Anemone said, she had seen someone's face. Blurry, foggy . . . but real. Someone who *wanted* to ask her to the Ball.

She clenched her jaw.

I'm not a witch.

Slowly the silhouette appeared out of darkness, this time closer, clearer than before. He took one knee before her, lifted his face into light . . .

A screech jolted her awake.

Onstage, the twelve sisters were bellowing and butting each other like gorillas.

"How can *those* be princesses?" Beatrix cried.

"That's what happens after you're married," said Giselle. "My mother stopped shaving her legs."

"Mine can't fit in any of her old gowns," Millicent said.

"Mine doesn't wear makeup," said Ava.

"Mine eats cheese," Reena sighed. Beatrix looked faint.

"Well, my wife tries any of that, she can go live with witches," Chaddick said, gnawing on a turkey leg. "In all those pictures of Ever After, no one sees an ugly princess."

He noticed Agatha sitting stiffly next to him. "Oh. No offense."

By lunch, Agatha had forgotten all about finding a date and wanted to go groveling back to Sophie. But she, Hester, and Anadil were nowhere to be found (or Dot, for that matter) and the Nevers seemed curiously subdued on their side of the Clearing. Meanwhile, she could hear Evergirls chuckling as Chaddick retold his story to different groups, the "No offense" line sounding more offensive each time. Even worse, Tedros kept giving her strange looks between horseshoe throws (and an especially strange one after she dropped her bowl of beet stew all over her lap).

Kiko plopped down beside her. "Don't be upset. It can't be true."

"What?"

"The two boys thing."

"What 'two boys' thing?"

"You know, that they all made a pact for two boys to go together rather than ask you."

Agatha stared at her.

"Oh no!" Kiko squeaked, and fled.

In Good Deeds, Professor Dovey gave them a written test on how they would handle moral predicaments at a Ball. For instance:

```
1. If you attend the Ball with someone
   other than your first choice, but
   your first choice, who you're madly
```

in love with, asks you to dance, do you:

A) Kindly inform them that if they wanted to dance with you they should have asked you to the Ball
B) Dance with them, but only to a fast-paced *rondel*
C) Ditch your date for your first choice
D) Ask your date what they would feel comfortable with

Agatha answered D. Underneath it, she wrote:
"Unless no one would ever ask you to a Ball, let alone to dance. Then this question doesn't apply."

2. Upon arriving at the Ball, you notice your friend's breath smells unbearably of garlic and trout. However, your friend is going with the person you hoped would ask *you* to the Ball. Do you:

A) Inform your friend at once of their foul odor
B) Say nothing since it is your friend's fault they smell

C) Say nothing because you will enjoy watching them be embarrassed

D) Offer them a piece of sweet licorice without mentioning their breath

Agatha answered A. She added, *"Because at least bad breath is temporary. Ugly is forever."*

3. A baby dove with a broken wing slips into the Good Hall, crashes to the dance floor during the last waltz, and is in severe danger of being crushed. Do you:

A) Scream and stop the dance

B) Finish the dance and then attend to the dove

C) Kick the dove off the floor while dancing so it's safe, then attend to it after

D) Abandon the dance and rescue the dove, even if it means embarrassing your partner

Agatha answered D. *"My partner is imaginary. I'm sure he won't mind."*

She answered the next 27 questions in the same spirit.

Perched at her desk made out of sugarplums, Professor Dovey scored the tests and shoved them under a gleaming pumpkin weight, face growing grimmer and grimmer.

"Just what I've been afraid of," she fumed, flinging the tests back to the students. "Your answers are vain, vacuous, and at times downright villainous! No wonder that Sophie girl made fools of you all!"

"Attacks are over, aren't they?" Tedros muttered.

"No thanks to you!" Professor Dovey barked, thrusting a red-drenched test at him. "A Never wins a Trial, lays waste to our school—and no Ever to catch her? No one Good to put down a *student*?"

She slung tests across a row. "Must I remind you that the Circus of Talents is in four days? And that whoever wins the Circus has the Theater of Tales moved to their school? Do you want your Theater moved to *Evil*? Do you want to walk with shame to Evil for the rest of the *year*?"

No one could meet her eyes.

"To be Good you must *prove* yourself Good, Evers," Professor Dovey warned. "Defend. Forgive. Help. Give. Love. Those are our rules. But it is your *choice* to follow them."

As she went over the tests, excoriating every wrong answer, Agatha shoved hers away. But then she noticed the corner:

100%
SEE ME.

When the fairies chimed the end of class, Professor Dovey

shooed all the Evers out, closed the pumpkin candy door, and locked it. She turned and found Agatha atop her desk, eating a sugarplum.

"So if I follow the rules," Agatha said, chomping loudly, "I'm not a witch."

Professor Dovey eyed the new hole in her desk. "Only a truly Good soul lives those rules, yes."

"What if my face is Evil?" Agatha said.

"Oh, Agatha, don't be ridic—"

"What if my *face* is *Evil*?"

Her teacher flinched at her tone.

"I'm far from home, I've lost my only friend, everyone here hates me, and all I want is a way to find some kind of happy ending," Agatha said, red-hot. "But you can't even tell me the truth. My ending is not about what Good I do or what's inside me. It's about how I *look*." Spit flew out of her mouth.

"I never even had a *chance*."

For a long moment, Professor Dovey just gazed at the door. Then she sat down on the desk next to Agatha, broke off a sugarplum, and bit into it with a juicy squirt.

"What did you think of Beatrix the first time you saw her?"

Agatha stared at the candy plum in her teacher's hand.

"Agatha?"

"I don't know. She was beautiful," Agatha groused, remembering their fart-filled introduction.

"And now?"

"She's revolting."

"Has she gotten less pretty?"

"No, but—"

"So is she beautiful or not?"

"Yes, at first sight—"

"So beauty only lasts a glance?"

"Not if you're a Good person—"

"So it's being Good that matters? I thought you said it was looks."

Agatha opened her mouth. Nothing came out.

"Beauty can only fight truth so long, Agatha. You and Beatrix share more in common than you think."

"Great. I can be her animal slave," Agatha said, and bit into her plum.

Professor Dovey stood up. "Agatha, what do you see when you look in the mirror?"

"I don't look in mirrors."

"Why is that?"

"Because horses and hogs don't sit around ogling their reflections!"

"What is it you're afraid you'll see?" Professor Dovey said, leaning near the pumpkin candy door.

"I'm not afraid of mirrors," Agatha snorted.

"Then look in this one."

She glanced up and saw the door near Professor Dovey was now a smooth, polished mirror.

She turned away. "Cute trick. That one in our book?"

"Look in the mirror, Agatha," Professor Dovey said calmly.

"This is stupid." Agatha leapt off the desk and tramped

past her, head down to avoid her reflection. She couldn't find a doorknob—

"Let me out!" She clawed at the door, closing her eyes every time she saw herself.

"If you look in the mirror, you may leave."

Agatha struggled to make her finger glow—"*Let—me—out!*"

"Then look in the mirror."

"LET ME OUT OR ELSE!"

"Just one look—"

Agatha slammed her clump against the glass. With a shiver, the mirror shattered, and she shielded herself from the shimmer and dust. When crashes petered to silence, she slowly lifted her head.

A new mirror glared back.

"Make it go away," she pleaded, hiding her face.

"Just try, Agatha."

"I can't."

"Why?"

"Because I'm ugly!"

"And what if you were beautiful?"

"*Look* at me," Agatha moaned.

"Suppose you were."

"But—"

"Suppose you were like the girls in storybooks, Agatha."

"I don't read that garbage," Agatha snapped.

"You wouldn't be here if you didn't."

Agatha stiffened.

"You read them just like your friend, dear," said Professor Dovey. "The question is, *why?*"

Agatha didn't say anything for a long time.

"*If* I was beautiful?" she asked quietly.

"Yes, dear."

Agatha looked up, eyes glistening.

"I'd be happy."

"That's odd," her teacher said, sweeping to her desk. "That's just what Ella of Maidenvale said to me—"

"Well, three cheers for Ella of Maidenvale!" Agatha sulked.

"I gave her a visit when I found out she wished to go to a Ball and then couldn't go through with it. All she needed was a new face and a nice pair of shoes."

"I don't see what this has to do with anyth—" Agatha's eyes widened. "Ella . . . *Cinder*ella?"

"Not even my best work, however notorious," said her teacher, caressing a pumpkin paperweight. "You know, they sell these in Maidenvale. Doesn't match Ella's coach at all, really."

Agatha staggered back. "But—but that means you're—"

"The most wished-for fairy godmother in the Endless Woods. At your service, dear."

Agatha's head felt light. She leaned against the door.

"I warned you when you saved the gargoyle, Agatha," Professor Dovey said. "You are a powerful talent. Good enough to conquer any Evil. Good enough to find your happy ending, even if you've lost your way! Everything you need is *inside* you, Agatha. And now, more than ever, we need you to let it out. But if it's beauty that's holding you back, dear . . ."

She sighed. "Well, that's easily taken care of, isn't it?"

Reaching into her green gown, she pulled out a thin, cherry-wood wand.

"Now close your eyes and make a wish."

Agatha blinked to make sure she was awake. Fairy tales always punished girls like her. Fairy tales never gave ugly girls wishes.

"*Any* wish?" she said, voice cracking.

"Any wish," said her fairy godmother.

"And I have to say it out loud?"

"I'm not a mind reader, dear."

Agatha looked at her through tears. "But it's—I've never said it to anyone—"

"Then it's about time."

Trembling, Agatha looked at the wand in her hand and closed her eyes. Could this really be happening?

"I wish . . ."

She couldn't breathe.

"To be . . . you know . . . uh . . ."

"Magic responds to conviction, I'm afraid," said Professor Dovey.

Agatha gulped for air.

All she could think about was Sophie. Sophie staring right at her, as if she were a dog.

GET YOUR OWN LIFE!

Her heart suddenly seared hot with anger. Teeth clenched, she curled her fists, raised her head, and with a shout—

"*I wish to be beautiful!*"

The swish of a wand and a sickening crack.

Agatha opened her eyes.

Professor Dovey frowned at the broken wand in her hand.

"A bit ambitious, that wish. We'll have to do it the old-fashioned way."

She let out a deafening whistle and six pink-skinned, seven-foot, rainbow-haired nymphs landed through the window in a neat row.

Agatha backed against the mirror. "Wait—hold on—"

"They'll be gentle. As they can."

Agatha managed a last yowl before the nymphs descended on her like bears.

Professor Dovey shielded her eyes from the carnage.

"They really are too tall."

Agatha's eyes fluttered open in shadow. She felt achy and strange, as if she'd been asleep for days. She blearily took in her fully dressed body slumped in a green chair, restraints undone—

She was in the Groom Room. The nymphs were gone.

Agatha jumped from the chair. The aromatic bath pools were all sudsy and flooded. The Rose Red makeup station in front of her was lined with a hundred bottles of uncorked waxes, creams, dyes, and masks. In the sink were used razors, files, knives, and picks. On the floor were mounds of shorn hair.

Agatha picked some up.

It was blond.

Mirror.

She whipped around but the other chair-and-mirror stations were gone. She frantically touched her hair, her skin.
Everything felt softer, smoother. She touched her lips, her nose,
her chin. Everything felt daintier.

"All she needed was a new face."

She collapsed back in the chair.

They did it.

They did the impossible! She was normal! No, she wasn't
just normal. She was pretty! She was lovable! She was—

Beautiful!

Finally she could live! Finally she could be happy!

Napping in his nest atop the door, Albemarle let out a particularly loud snore as it swung open.

"Have a good night, Albemarle!"

Albemarle peeked open a spectacled eye. "Have a good
night, Aga—oh, *my*!"

Agatha's smile only grew as she ascended the steps to the
first floor.

She had to get to the gilded mirror near the Supper Hall
(she had memorized all the mirror locations in the school so
she could avoid them). Agatha felt giddily light. Would she
even *recognize* herself?

She heard gasps and saw Reena and Millicent goggling
down at her through the gap in the spiral staircase.

"Hello, Reena!" Agatha beamed. "Hello, Millicent!"

Both girls were too stunned to wave back. As she waltzed
into the stair room, Agatha felt herself smile even wider.

Climbing up the Legends Obelisk, Chaddick and Nicholas considered portraits of past Evergirls.

"Rapunzel was a 4 at best," said Chaddick, hanging off a brick like a mountaineer. "But this Martine was a solid 9."

"Too bad she ended up a horse," said Nicholas.

"Wait until they put Agatha on the wall. She'll end up a—"

"What? What will I end up?"

Chaddick turned to Agatha. He gawped open-mouthed.

"A cat?" Agatha grinned. "I seem to have eaten your tongue."

"Oooh," Nicholas chimed, and Chaddick kicked him off the pillar.

Smiling so wide it hurt now, Agatha sauntered up the Valor stairs towards the Supper Hall. She glided through royal blue arches for the gold double doors, ready to face the mirror inside, ready to feel what Sophie had felt all her life—but just as she reached for them, the doors opened in her face.

"Excuse me—"

Agatha heard the voice before she saw him. Slowly she looked up, heart thundering.

Tedros stared at her, looking so confused she thought she had somehow petrified him with a villain spell.

He coughed, as if trying to find his voice. "Um. Hi."

"Hi," Agatha said, smiling stupidly.

Silence.

"What's for supper?" she said even more stupidly.

"Duckling," he squeaked.

He coughed again.

"Sorry. It's just, you look . . . you look so . . ."

Agatha suddenly felt a strange feeling. It scared her.

"I know—not me—" she blurted, and fled around the corner.

She lunged into a corridor and cowered under a portrait frame. *What did they do!* Had they exchanged her soul when they gave her a new face? Had they replaced her heart when they gave her a new body? Why were her palms drenched? Why was her stomach fluttering? Where was the insult for Tedros she always had on her lips? What in heaven and earth could possibly make her smile at a *boy?* She hated boys! She always hated boys! She wouldn't smile at one even if forced to at swordpoi—

Agatha realized where she was.

The portrait she was under wasn't a portrait.

Sweating with dread, she stood to face the hall's giant mirror, ready to see a stranger.

Agatha closed her eyes in shock.

She opened them again.

But the bath pools—bottles—blond hair—

She shrank against the wall, panicked.

The wish—the wand—

But it was all part of her fairy godmother's ruse.

For the nymphs hadn't done anything to Agatha at all.

She glimpsed her greasy black hair and bug eyes and dropped to the floor in horror.

I'm still ugly! I'm still a witch!

Wait.

What about Albemarle? What about Reena, Chaddick . . . *Tedros*?

They were mirrors too, weren't they? Mirrors that told her she wasn't ugly anymore.

Slowly Agatha rose, inching back into her reflection. For the first time in her life, she didn't look away.

Beauty can only fight the truth so long, Agatha.

All these years she had believed she was what she looked like. An unlovable, dark-hearted witch.

But in the halls, she had believed something different. For a moment, she had unchained her heart and let light rush in.

Gently Agatha touched her face in the mirror, glowing from the inside.

A face no one recognized because it was so happy.

There could be no turning back now. The bread crumbs on the dark trail were gone. Instead, she had the truth to guide her. A truth greater than any magic.

I've been beautiful all along.

Agatha burst into deep, cleansing sobs, never surrendering her smile.

She didn't hear the screams of someone far away, woken from her worst dreams yet.

24

Hope in the Toilet

Students at the School for Good and Evil thought magic meant spells. But Agatha had found something more powerful in a smile.

Everywhere she went, she noticed slack-jawed stares and baffled whispers, as if she'd conjured sorcery deeper than students or teachers had ever seen. Then one day, on her way to morning classes, Agatha saw she too had been bewitched. Because for the first time,

she found herself looking forward to them.

The other changes were just as sly. She noticed she didn't gag at the scent of her uniform anymore. She didn't dread washing her face now or mind taking a minute to brush her hair. She got so caught up in Ball dance rehearsals she jumped when the wolves howled to end class. And where she once mocked her Good homework, now she'd read assigned pages and keep reading, entranced by stories of heroines who outwitted lethal witches, avenged their parents' deaths, and sacrificed their bodies, freedoms, even lives for true love.

Closing her textbook, Agatha gazed out at fairies decking the Blue Forest with starry lanterns for the Ball. It was beautiful, really, what Good could do. She wouldn't have been able to admit that a few weeks ago. But now as she lay in bed, aglow in lantern light, she thought of her room in Gavaldon and couldn't remember how it smelled. Suddenly she couldn't remember the color of Reaper's eyes . . . the sound of her mother's voice . . .

Then it was two days before the Ball. The Circus of Talents would take place the next night, and Pollux came round to classrooms, head ferried on the shell of a gaunt turtle, to announce the rules.

"Hear ye, hear ye, hear ye! By order of the School Master of the School for Good Enlightenment and Enchantment and the School for Evil Edifi—"

"Just get on with it!" Professor Anemone yawped.

Pollux glumly explained that the Circus was a talent competition between Good and Evil, where the top 10 Evers and Nevers would each take the stage to present their talents. At the end of the contest, the winner would receive the Circus Crown and the Theater of Tales would magically move to his school.

"Of course, the Theater hasn't moved in ages," Pollux sniffed. "Firmly entrenched by now."

"But who's the judge?" Beatrix said.

"The School Master. Though you won't see him, of course," Pollux puffed. "Now as to attire, I suggest you wear clothes of humble, demure col—"

Professor Anemone kicked his head out the door. "Enough! Proposals coming tomorrow and the only thing you should be thinking about is your prince's face!"

As the teacher circled the room, Agatha watched girls accept proposals with eyes closed, noses scrunched in concentration, as Pollux moaned outside.

Her stomach plunged.

With her ranking, she'd definitely make the Circus team! A *talent* show? She had no talents! Who would propose to her once she humiliated herself in front of the whole school! And if no one proposed to her—

"Then you're a witch and you *fail*," Millicent reminded her when she still couldn't see a face.

Agatha spent all of Uma's class with her eyes closed, but all she could glimpse was a milky silhouette that crumbled every time she reached for it. She slogged back into the castle, discouraged, and noticed a few students buzzing in the stair room. She sidled up to Kiko.

"What's going—"

She took a breath. The angel-painted *V* on the wall was now defaced with violent streaks of red—

"What does it mean?" Agatha said.

"That Sophie is going to attack us again," a voice answered.

Agatha turned to Tedros in a sleeveless blue shirt, sweaty and glowing from Swordplay. He suddenly looked self-conscious.

"Uh, sorry . . . need a bath."

Fidgeting, Agatha glued her eyes to the wall. "I thought the attacks were over."

"I'll catch her this time," Tedros said, glaring at the wall beside her. "She's poison, that girl."

"She's hurt, Tedros. She thinks you made a promise."

"It's not a promise if it's made under false pretenses. She used me to win the Trial and she used you too."

"You don't know the slightest thing about her," Agatha said. "She still loves you. And she's still my friend."

"Blimey, you must be a better soul than me, because I don't know what you see in her. All I see is a manipulative witch."

"Then look closer."

Tedros turned. "Or look at someone else."

Agatha felt sick again.

"I'm late," she said, scrambling for stairs—

"History's this way."

"Bathroom—" she called back—

"But that's a boys' tower!"

"I prefer boys' . . . toilets—"

She ducked behind a sculpture of a half-naked merman, heaving for air. *What's happening to me!* Why couldn't she breathe around him? Why did she feel nauseous every time he looked at her? And why was he staring at her now like she was a . . . *girl!* Agatha stifled a scream.

She had to stop Sophie's attack.

If Sophie recanted, if she begged Tedros for forgiveness, there was still hope he'd take her back! That was the happy ending to this fairy tale! Then there'd be no more strange looks, no more sick stomachs, no more fears she'd lost control over her own heart.

With students and teachers now swarming the defaced wall, Agatha sprinted up to Merlin's Menagerie, where the hedges were finally returning to their old glory after the fire. She raced to the last sculpture of young Arthur, nestled in a pond, muscular arms pulling sword from stone. Only now she wasn't seeing Arthur but his son, winking at her. Agatha flushed with horror and leapt into ice-cold water.

"Let me through!" she barked, storming up to her reflection on the Bridge. "I have to stop Sophie before she—" Her eyes widened. "Wait. Where's *me?*"

A ravishing princess grinned back at her with dark upswept

hair, in a magnificent midnight-blue gown with delicate gold leaves, a ruby pendant around her neck, and a tiara of blue orchids.

Guilt speared Agatha's stomach. She recognized that grin.

"Sophie?"

"Good with Good,

Evil with Evil,

Back to your tower before there's upheaval."

"Well, now I'm definitely Evil so let me pass," Agatha ordered.

"Why's that?" said the princess. "Because you still insist on that haircut?"

"Because I'm having thoughts about *your* prince!"

"It's about time."

"Good, so let me thr— What?" Agatha scowled. "But that's Evil! Sophie, he's your true love!"

The princess smiled. "I warned you last time."

"What? Who warned when—"

Then Agatha remembered the last time she was here.

He's yours.

Her eyes bulged—"But that means—that means you're—"

"Definitely Good. Now if you'll excuse me, we have a Ball to get ready for."

And with that, Princess Agatha vanished from her reflection, leaving the barrier intact.

"Um. That's your sixth piece," Kiko said, watching Agatha stab another slice of cherry pie.

Agatha ignored her and stuffed it in her mouth, swallowing away guilt. She'd tell Sophie. Yes, she'd tell Sophie everything and Sophie would laugh hysterically and put her in her place. She a *princess*? Tedros her *true love*?

"You going to eat that?" Agatha snarfed, mouth full.

"And I thought you were making progress," Kiko sighed, sliding over her piece.

As she devoured it, Agatha refocused on sneaking into the School for Evil. During the first attacks, the teachers had besieged the Good Towers with anti-Mogrif enchantments, since they figured Sophie was breaking in as a moth, frog, or lily pad. But Sophie had still found a way into Good.

So there has to be another route, Agatha thought. Without thinking, she found herself hustling from the Supper Hall to the place she always went to when she needed answers.

Agatha immediately noticed the new addition to the Gallery of Good. Tedros' bloodied Trial tunic had its own case, labeled TRIAL OF THE CENTURY alongside a brief account of Tedros and Sophie's ill-fated alliance. She could see dozens of fingerprints on the glass, no doubt the fossils of ogling girls. Nausea rising, Agatha darted to the School History exhibit, with dozens of maps tracking the additions of new towers over the years. She tried to study them for a hidden passage, but soon her eyes bleared and she found herself drifting to the familiar corner nook.

She moved past all the Reader paintings to the one with her and Sophie, haloed by a lake. Her eyes misted at the sight of them together, once upon a time, the best of friends. High in the School Master's tower, the Storian would soon write their ending. How far would it take them from that sunlit shore?

She looked at the painting next to it, the last one in the row. The dark vision of children hurling their storybooks into a bonfire while flames and smoke clouds devoured the Woods around them.

The Reader Prophecy, Lady Lesso had said.

Was *this* Gavaldon's future?

Her temples throbbed, trying to make sense of it all. Who cared if children burned books? Why was Gavaldon so important to Sader and the School Master? What about all the other villages?

"What other villages?"

She had long dismissed the School Master's words as an unfinished thought. The world was made of villages like hers somewhere beyond Gavaldon's woods. But why weren't *they* in this gallery? Why weren't their children taken?

As her neck prickled red, her focus veered back to the smoke clouds closing in on the painted children. Because now she saw they weren't clouds at all.

They were shadows.

Hulking and black. Creeping from the burning Woods into the village.

And they didn't look human.

Suddenly her own shadow on the wall was growing, gnarling. Agatha whirled in horror—

"Professor Sader," she exhaled.

"I'm afraid I'm not much of a painter, Agatha," he said,

clutching a suitcase that matched his shamrock suit. "Reactions to my new addition have been rather poor."

"But what are those shadows?"

"Thought I'd check up after I found some thorns missing from the Exhibition of Evil. Sometimes villains act exactly as you'd expect," he sighed and headed to the door.

"Wait! Why is that your last painting?" Agatha pressed. "Is that how Sophie and my fairy tale *ends*?"

Professor Sader turned back. "You see, Agatha, seers simply cannot answer questions. Indeed, if I were to answer your question, I'd age ten years on the spot as punishment. It is the reason most seers look so terribly old. It takes a few mistakes to learn how not to answer them. Thankfully, I myself have made only one."

He smiled and started to leave again.

"But I need to know if Tedros is Sophie's true love!" Agatha cried. "Tell me if he kisses her!"

"Have you learned anything from my gallery, Agatha?" Sader said, turning.

Agatha eyed taxidermied animals around him. "That you like your students well stuffed?"

He didn't smile. "Not every hero achieves glory. But the ones that do share something in common." Apparently he wanted her to guess what this was.

"They kill villains?" she said.

"No questions."

"They kill villains."

"Think deeper, Agatha. What links our greatest heroes?"

She followed his glassy gaze to royal blue banners draped from the ceiling, each celebrating an iconic hero. Snow White encased in her coffin, Cinderella slipping into the glass heel, Jack slaying the towering giant, Gretel shoving the witch into the oven . . .

"They find happiness," she said lamely.

"Ah, well. I have *stuffing* to get back to."

"Wait—"

Agatha focused on the banners and steadied her mind. *Deeper.* Beneath the surface, what did these heroes have in common? True, they all shared beauty, kindness, triumph, but where had they started? Snow White lived in the shadow of her stepmother. Cinderella was a maid to two stepsisters. Jack's mother told him he was stupid. Gretel's parents left her in the Woods to die. . . .

It wasn't their endings they shared in common.

It was their beginnings.

"They trusted their enemies," Agatha said to her professor.

"Yes, their fairy tales all started when they never expected it," Sader said, silver swan glinting brighter on suit pocket. "After graduating from our school, they went into the Woods expecting epic battles with monsters and wizards, only to find their fairy tales unfold right *in their own houses.* They didn't realize that villains are the ones closest to us. They didn't realize that to find a happy ending, a hero must first look right under his nose."

"So Sophie has to look under her nose," Agatha snapped as he walked away. "*That's* your advice."

"I wasn't talking about Sophie."

THE SCHOOL FOR GOOD AND EVIL

Agatha stared at him, speechless.

"Tell them there's no need to worry," he said from the door. "I've already found a replacement."

It closed behind him.

"Wait!" Agatha ran, throwing it open. "Are you going somewh—"

But Professor Sader wasn't in the corridor. She sprinted into the stair room, but he wasn't there either. Her teacher had, quite simply, disappeared.

Agatha stood between the four staircases, stomach sinking. There was something here she was missing. Something that told her she had this whole story wrong. But then she heard words drumming in her head, demanding her attention.

Under your nose.

That's when she saw it.

The trail of chocolate crumbs up the Honor stairs.

The specks of chocolate snaked up three flights of blue glass, through the seashell mosaic of the dormitory floor, and abruptly stopped in front of the boys' lavatory.

Agatha put her ear to the pearl-encrusted door and lurched back as two Everboys came out of their room across from her.

"Sorry—" she stammered. "I'm, uh, just—"

"That's the one that likes boys' toilets," she heard as they shuffled past.

With a sigh, Agatha pushed through the door.

The Honor toilets looked less like a bathroom and more like a mausoleum, with marble floors, friezes of mermen battling sea serpents, urinals flushing royal blue water, and massive ivory stalls each with a sapphire toilet and tub. Where the Evergirls' toilets reeked of perfume, here she inhaled the smell of clean skin with a hint of sweat. Following the chocolate trail along the stalls and wet blue tubs, she found herself wondering which one Tedros had just used. . . . . She burned beet red. *Since when do you think about boys! Since when do you think about bathtubs! You've completely lost your—*

A sniffle. From the last stall.

"Hello?" she called.

No response.

She knocked on its door.

"*Excuse* me," a deep voice returned, obviously fake.

"Dot, open the door."

After a long silence, the door unlatched. Dot's clothes, hair, stall were peppered with chocolate shreds, as if she had attempted to turn toilet paper into a sustainable diet and succeeded only in making a mess.

"I thought Sophie was my *friend!*" she blubbered. "But then she took my room and my friends and now I have nowhere to go!"

"So you're living in a boys' *toilet?*"

"I can't tell Nevers they kicked me out!" Dot wailed, blowing snot in her sleeve. "They'd torment me more than they already do!"

"But there has to be somewhere else—"

"I tried to sneak into your Supper Hall, but a fairy bit me before I escaped!"

Agatha grimaced, knowing exactly which fairy it was.

"Dot, if anyone finds you here, they'll *fail* you!"

"Better failed than a homeless, friendless villain," Dot sobbed into her hands. "How would Sophie like it if someone did it to her? How would she like it if *you* took her prince? No one could ever be that Evil!"

Agatha swallowed. "I just need to talk to her," she said anxiously. "I'll help her get Tedros back, okay? I'll fix everything, Dot. I promise."

Dot's sobs softened to sniffles.

"True friends can make things right, no matter how bad they seem," Agatha insisted.

"Even witches like Hester and Anadil?" Dot whimpered.

Agatha touched her shoulder. "Even witches."

Slowly Dot peeked up from her hands. "I know Sophie says you're a witch, but you wouldn't fit in our school at all."

Agatha felt ill again. "I mean, how did you even *get* here?" she frowned, picking chocolate crumbs out of Dot's hair. "There's no way to cross between the two schools anymore."

"Of course there is. How do you think Sophie attacked all those nights?"

Agatha yanked Dot's hair in surprise.

25

Symptoms

The roaring sewer river stretched through the long tunnel from Good to Evil, interrupted only by the Doom Room at the halfway point between the two schools. The Beast had long guarded the halfway point, where clear water from the lake turned to roiling sludge from the moat. But for the last two weeks, Sophie had trespassed unchecked and would no

doubt return tonight as promised. Agatha's only hope was to stop her before she crossed back into Good.

As Agatha hugged the tunnel walls, approaching the Doom Room, her chest tightened. Sophie had never spoken of her punishment there. Had the Beast left invisible scars? Had he hurt her in ways no one could know?

"Wait until they're about to kill him."

Agatha's head whipped down the tunnel.

"Tedros has to think you saved him from death," echoed Anadil's voice.

Sweating through her dress, Agatha nudged along the sewer wall, until she saw three shadows crouched in front of the dungeon's rusted grating.

"All the Evers will think it's Anadil's attack, not yours," Hester said, voice resounding above the river's roar. "Tedros will think you saved him. He'll think you risked your life."

"And then he'll love me?" asked the third shadow.

Agatha stumbled back in surprise.

Hester spun. "Who's there?"

Agatha inched out from the shadows—Hester and Anadil jumped to their feet. Slowly the third shadow turned.

In the dim light, Sophie looked bloodless, sunken, and a good deal thinner. "My dear, dear Agatha."

Agatha's mouth went dry. "What's happening?" she rasped.

"We're helping a prince keep his promise."

"By staging an *attack*?"

"By showing how much I *love* him," Sophie answered.

From the Doom Room came a clamor of loud grunts and

squeals. Agatha reeled back. "What was that?"

Sophie smiled. "Anadil's been working on her Circus Talent."

Agatha sprang forward to see what was in the cell, but Hester held her back. Over her shoulder, Agatha glimpsed three giant black snouts jutting from the grates, baring razor-sharp teeth. They were sniffing something just out of reach.

An Everboy's necktie with an embroidered *T*.

"Can't see very well, poor things," Sophie sighed. "Target by scent."

Agatha bleached white. "But that's—that's Tedros'—"

"I'll stop them before they do any harm, of course. Just give him a good scare."

"But—but—suppose they attack other people!"

"Isn't this what you said you wanted? For me to find love?" Sophie said, unblinking. "Unfortunately, this really is the safest way after all that's happened."

Agatha couldn't speak.

"I've missed you, Aggie," Sophie said softly. "I really have."

Her head cocked. "Still, it's strange. The Agatha I know would love a hall of dead princes."

Another violent grunt from the dungeon. Agatha ran for a door, but Anadil caught her and shoved her to the wall—

"Sophie, you can't do this!" Agatha pleaded, fighting her grip. "You have to ask him to forgive you! It's the only way to make everything right again!"

Sophie's eyes widened in surprise. They slowly narrowed. "Come closer, Agatha."

Agatha wrenched free from Anadil and stepped into

torchlight leaking from the Doom Room.

"Sophie, please listen to me—"

"You look . . . different."

"Ever supper is almost over, Sophie," Anadil pressed, prompting impatient grunts in the cell.

"Sophie, you can apologize to Tedros at the Circus," Agatha said, raising her voice over them. "When it's your turn onstage! Then everyone will see you're Good!"

"I think I prefer the old Agatha," Sophie said, searching her face.

"Sophie, I won't let you attack my school—"

"*Your* school!" Sophie shrieked so loudly Agatha cringed. "So now it's *your* school, is it?" She pointed to sludge past the halfway point. "Are you saying *that* school is mine?"

"No—of course not—" Agatha stuttered. "Tedros will see through this, Sophie! He wants someone he can trust!"

"And now you know what *my* prince wants?"

"I want you to get him back!"

"You know, I don't think this look suits you, Agatha," Sophie said, stepping towards her.

Agatha retreated. "Sophie, I'm on your side—"

"No, I'm afraid it doesn't suit you *at all.*"

Agatha slipped and fell, landing an inch from the roaring river. She crawled forward and froze with horror. So did Anadil and Hester.

The Beast stared back at them, hulking black body snared in muck against the river wall, dead eyes flecked with blood.

Agatha slowly raised her head to see Sophie gazing at him.

"Good never wants to hurt, Agatha. But sometimes love means punishing villains that stand in our way."

Howls echoed from above. "Supper's over," Anadil gasped.

Hester tore her eyes from the Beast—"Now, Ani! Free them now!"

Panicked, Anadil thrust out a glowing finger to blast open the cell door.

"I have to warn him," Agatha spluttered, scrambling to her feet, but a force tackled her down.

She looked up, dazed. Hester pinned her chest over the river's halfway point. "Don't you get it?" she hissed in her ear. "Tedros is her *Nemesis*! If Sophie's symptoms start, she'll stop at nothing to kill him! We're saving his life!"

"No—it's Evil—" Agatha wheezed. "This is Evil!"

Sophie approached and peered down at her hanging over the edge between sludge and lake.

"Be gentle, Hester. Just help her back to her real school. . . ."

Agatha heard the lock catch, saw the shadows of mammoth creatures squealing at the grates—

"Please, Sophie—don't do it—"

Sophie met her eyes, softening.

"Don't worry, Agatha. This time I'll have my happy ending."

Her face went ice-cold.

"Because you won't be there to *ruin* it."

Hester pushed Agatha into spewing slime. Dragged towards Evil, she gurgled and spat, tried in vain to open her stinging eyes. But just as the moat grabbed her in its rip current, she lunged her hands out blindly, found cold skin—and pulled Sophie in.

The two girls sank deep into churning darkness. Terrified, Agatha shoved Sophie away and kicked towards the halfway point and clear water ahead. She glanced back to see a distant silhouette thrashing and sinking in sludge. Sophie *couldn't swim*. Losing air, Agatha swiveled between clear water and Sophie, towing under. With her last ounce of breath, she dove, seized Sophie's waist, and lugged her to the surface. Their heads bobbed above slime far down the Evil sewer—

"Help—" Sophie burbled—

"Hold on to me," Agatha shouted, pulling her against the gushing muck. Choking, heaving, she flailed for the wall, but with Sophie's weight, she couldn't reach it. Either she let go of her or took a chance against the current.

"Don't let me die," Sophie begged.

Agatha clasped her tighter and lunged for the wall. Her fingers missed and slime crashed into them, ripping their bodies apart. Submerged, she grasped for Sophie but caught only her glass heel, and she watched her friend pulled drowning into darkness.

In a flash, silvery hooks snared them both—

Stunned, the two girls looked back to see the shimmering wave propel them out of sludge into clear blue water. In the wave's swell, they realized they could breathe and surrendered the last gasps in their puffed cheeks. As their pupils locked, Agatha saw Sophie's face grow sad, scared, as if woken from a terrible dream. But just as the enchanted wave pulled them to separate crests, about to hurl them back to their schools, Agatha's eyes flared open.

A familiar shadow was tearing towards them, black and crooked. Before Agatha could scream, it bashed into the wave, dislodging the girls from its grasp. The shadow seized them in its spindly fingers and dragged them away from the castles towards the lake's outer banks. Agatha saw Sophie writhing against the shadow and joined her in the fight. Beaten back, the shadow lost its grip, but just as Sophie lurched for Agatha, it grabbed Sophie by the hips and threw her out of the water with shocking strength. Choking in horror, Agatha tried to swim away, but the shadow pounced and pulled her ahead, smashing underwater towards a reef of sharp rock. She closed her eyes, prayed for instant death, just in time to feel the School Master dig his grip into her flesh and fling her from the lake into cold night air.

Agatha hit the ground so hard she was sure she'd black out.

Somehow she held on, long enough to open her eyes and see massive trees, ringed with violet thorns. She must be somewhere on the Good grounds. Agatha tried to sit up, but her body exploded with pain and collapsed back to soggy dirt. Why had the School Master attacked the wave? How could he hurl her here with no explanation? Her head throbbed with anger and confusion. She'd tell Professor Dovey what happened—she'd demand answers—

But first she had to get back to school.

Agatha craned her head up. All she could see were the same enormous trees, garlanded with purple briars. She must be near that flower field where she and the Evergirls arrived that first day. But where was the lake? She glanced behind her and caught a reflective gleam through branches. Flooding with relief, she crawled forward, wincing every inch, until it was close enough to see.

Her mouth fell open.

It wasn't the lake. It was spiked, golden gates with a sign: "TRESPASSERS WILL BE KILLED." The School for Good glowed high behind them, spires lit up blue and pink.

Agatha wasn't on school grounds.

She was in the Woods.

"*Agatha!*" Sophie cried nearby.

Agatha paled.

The School Master had set them free.

She felt a crush of relief, then stabs of fear. All she had ever wanted was to go home with Sophie. But what had happened in the sewers left her terrified.

"*Agatha! Where are you!*"

Agatha didn't make a sound. Should she find her? Or should she escape home alone?

Her heart beat faster. But how could she leave now? When she finally felt she belonged?

"*Agatha! It's me!*"

The pain in Sophie's voice snapped her out of her trance. *What's happened to me?*

Sophie was right. She had started to believe this was *her* school, *her* fairy tale. She had even started to hope that the face she kept seeing might belong to . . .

No one could ever be that Evil, Dot said.

Agatha flushed with guilt.

"Sophie, I'm coming!" she yelled.

Sophie didn't answer. Suddenly anxious, Agatha scraped forward in the direction of her last call, swan crest twinkling in the dark. Something tickled her leg.

She glanced down to see a vine of violet thorns creep towards her hip. She kicked it away, only to see it snag her other leg. She lunged back, but two cuffed her arms, two took her feet, briars multiplying until they snared every inch of her flesh. Agatha jerked to escape, but the thorns pinned her to the ground like a lamb to slaughter. Then a thick one came, dark and engorged, snaking maleficently up her chest. It stopped an inch from her face and eyed her with its purple lance. With calm ease, it coiled back and stabbed for her swan.

Steel slashed the thorn open. Warm, bronzed arms pulled Agatha up—

"Hold on to me!" Tedros yelled, hacking briars with his training sword.

Dazed, Agatha clung to his chest as he withstood thorn lashes with moans of pain. Soon he had the upper hand and pulled Agatha from the Woods towards the spiked gates, which glowed in recognition and pulled apart, cleaving a narrow path for the two Evers. As the gates speared shut behind them, Agatha looked up at limping Tedros, crisscrossed with bloody scratches, blue shirt shredded away.

"Had a feeling Sophie was getting in through the Woods," he panted, hauling her up into slashed arms before she could protest. "So Professor Dovey gave me permission to take some fairies and stake out the outer gates. Should have known you'd be here trying to catch her yourself."

Agatha gaped at him dumbly.

"Stupid idea for a princess to take on witches alone," Tedros said, dripping sweat on her pink dress.

"Where is she?" Agatha croaked. "Is she safe?"

"Not a good idea for princesses to worry about witches either," Tedros said, hands gripping her waist. Her stomach exploded with butterflies.

"Put me down," she sputtered—

"More bad ideas from the princess."

"Put me down!"

Tedros obeyed and Agatha pulled away.

"I'm not a princess!" she snapped, fixing her collar.

"If you say so," the prince said, eyes drifting downward.

Agatha followed them to her gashed legs, waterfalls of brilliant blood. She saw blood blurring—

Tedros smiled. "One . . . two . . . three . . ."

She fainted in his arms.

"Definitely a princess," he said.

Tedros carried her towards six distant fairies playing in the lake, and stopped cold. In dead grass, Sophie looked up from her knees, black robes bloodied.

"Agatha?"

"*You!*" Tedros hissed.

Sophie blocked his path, holding out her arms. "Give her to me. I'll take her."

"This is *your* fault!" Tedros lashed, clasping Agatha tighter.

"She saved my life," Sophie breathed. "She's my friend."

"A princess can't be friends with a *witch*!"

Sophie flared and her finger glowed pink. Tedros saw it and his finger instantly glowed gold, raised to defend—

Slowly, Sophie's face weakened. Her finger dimmed.

"I don't know what's happened to me," she whispered, tears welling.

"Don't even try it," Tedros snarled.

"It's that school," she sobbed. "It's changed me."

"Move out of my way!"

"Please—give me a chance!"

"Move!"

"Let me show you I'm Good!"

"I warned you," he said, storming for her—

"Tedros, I'm *sorry*!" Sophie cried, but he just shoved her aside and forged ahead.

"The Good forgive," a voice whispered.

Tedros stopped. He looked down at Agatha, weak against his chest.

"You promised her, Tedros," Agatha said quietly.

He stared at her, stunned. "What? What are you say—"

"Take her back to the castle," said Agatha. "Show everyone she's your princess for the Ball."

"But she's—she's—"

"My friend," said Agatha, meeting Sophie's shocked eyes.

Tedros' head whipped between them.

"*No!* Agatha, listen to me—"

"Keep your word, Tedros," Agatha said. "You have to."

"I can't—" he pleaded—

"Forgive her." Agatha looked deep into his eyes. "For me."

Tedros' voice caught and he lost his fire.

"Go," said Agatha, wresting from his grip. "I'll come back with the fairies."

Miserable, Tedros stripped off the remains of his blue shirt and draped them around her shivering pink shoulders. He opened his mouth to fight—

"*Go,*" she said.

Tedros couldn't look at her and angrily turned away—his gashed leg buckled. Sophie lunged and thrust her shoulder beneath his arm, gripping him by the chest. The prince recoiled at her touch.

"Please, Teddy," Sophie whispered through shamed tears. "I promise I'll change."

Tedros pushed her away, struggling to stand. But then he saw Agatha behind Sophie, her gaze reminding him of his own promise.

Tedros tried to fight himself . . . tried to tell himself promises could be broken . . . but he knew the truth. He went limp against Sophie's chest.

Surprised, Sophie helped him forward, afraid to say a word. Tedros looked back at Agatha, who slackened with relief and shambled behind them on her own. Resigned, the prince exhaled and hobbled ahead under Sophie's arm.

Sophie pulled him towards the lake with all of her strength, panting, sniffling. Little by little, she felt Tedros surrender to her grip. With a shy glance at him, she smiled through tears, her delicate face repentant. Finally the prince managed a grudging smile in return.

The half-moon glided from behind clouds, showering them with cleansing light. As he and Sophie reached the lake, bodies intertwined, Tedros looked down at their two shadows in perfect step, at his boots beside her glass slippers, at his bloody reflection in glimmering waters, glowing next to—an ugly, old hag's.

Tedros spun in horror, but there was only beautiful Sophie, shepherding him gently to Good. He glanced back at the lake, but the water had clouded. His skin burst into chills.

"I can't—" he choked, wrenching free—

"Teddy?" Sophie gasped.

He staggered back and hoisted Agatha, who hacked with surprise.

Sophie blanched. "Teddy, what did I d—"

"Stay away from us!" he said, clutching Agatha to his chest. "Stay away from us both!"

"*Us?*" Sophie shrieked.

"Tedros, wait—" Agatha begged—"What about—"

"Let her find her way to Evil," the prince spat, and raised his glowing finger to call the fairies.

Sophie shrank in shock. Agatha looked back at her from Tedros' arms, flushed with apology. But her friend's face had no forgiveness. Instead it swelled red with feral fury and hate—

"*LOOK AT HER!*"

The echo blasted across the lake.

Agatha went white.

"*SHE'S A WITCH!*" Sophie screamed.

Slowly Tedros turned, his eyes cutting through her. "Look closer."

Sophie watched in horror as fairies swirled around the two Evers. In Tedros' arms, Agatha had the same expression.

For now she saw they were in the right schools all along.

As Sophie watched the fairies fly Agatha and her prince away, she stood frozen on the lakeshore, panting warm breath, alone in the darkness. Her muscles knotted with tension, then her fingers curled to crackling fists. Her blood boiled hotter, hotter, her body blazing with fire, and just as she thought she'd explode into flames—a sharp pain stabbed her chin. Sophie put her hand to it.

Something there.

Her fingers crawled over it, trying to understand, until she felt wet drops splash onto her arm. She stepped back as the wave rose high, swathing her in shadow—

Sophie crashed through the window of Room 66 in a heap of sludge.

Hester and Anadil leapt off the bed. "We searched every-where—where were you—"

Hand to her face, Sophie crawled past them to the last shard of mirror left on the wall and stopped cold.

There was a thick black wart on her chin.

Sophie frantically picked at it, pulled at it—then saw her roommates in her reflection, both white as sheets.

"*Symptoms*," they gasped.

Dripping, shaking, Sophie dashed up the stairs to the top-floor study and blasted the lock open with her glowing finger.

Lady Lesso exploded from her bedroom in her nightgown, finger thrust out. Sophie instantly levitated off the floor, strangled for breath.

Lady Lesso lowered her hand, bringing Sophie gently to the floor. Eyes wide, she slunk towards Sophie and took her trembling face in her sharp red nails.

"Just in time for the Circus," she said, fingers caressing the swollen black wart. "The Evers are in for a *surprise*."

Sophie flailed for words—

"Sometimes our henchmen know us better than we do ourselves," Lady Lesso marveled.

Sophie shook her head, not understanding.

Her teacher's lips grazed her ear. "He's waiting for you."

As the torches in the castles went dark, only a pregnant moon remained, lighting up a shadow slashing through the Blue Forest. Shrouded in her black snakeskin cape, Sophie smashed through ferns and oaks, shivering uncontrollably. When she arrived at the giant stone well, she slammed her body against the rock blocking its shaft, over and over before it budged. Climbing into the bucket, she lowered herself deep into darkness, until a piece of moonlight lit up the bottom.

Against a smooth, milky wall, Grimm waited, cheeks and wings blackened with grime. The walls around him were covered in thousands of drawings of the same face. A face carved in bloodred lipstick. A face she couldn't make out in her dreams. But here, in the dead of night, her Nemesis had a name.

And it wasn't Tedros.

26

The Circus of Talents

"To Professor Dovey's office," Tedros ordered the fairies as he and Agatha trailed blood into the sky.

"To my room," Agatha ordered the fairies flying her.

"But you're hurt!" Tedros said, shivering—

"We tell anyone what happened and things will be worse than they already are," said Agatha.

The fairies pulled them apart. "Wait!" Tedros yelled—

"Tell no one!" Agatha called back, receding towards pink spires.

"Will you be at the Circus?" Tedros shouted, dragged towards blue—

But Agatha didn't answer as he and his fairies diminished into twinkles of light.

As her own fairies lifted her into dark sky, she looked out at the silver tower shadowed over the bay, heartsick and numb. The School Master had warned them. He had seen who they were.

She wrapped Tedros' bloody shirt around her as fairies flew her higher, higher into knifing wind. But as Agatha gazed up at lantern-lit windows, aglow with silhouettes dressing for proposals, guilt and shock burned to anger.

Villains are the ones closest to us.

Villains in the cloak of best friends.

Oh, yes, she'd be at that Circus.

Because Sader was right.

This was never Sophie's fairy tale.

It was hers.

"So there was no attack after all?" Professor Anemone asked, sipping steaming cider.

Standing at her study window, Professor Dovey looked out at the School Master's tower, burnished red in sinking sun. "Professor Espada said the boys found nothing. Meanwhile, Tedros spent half the night uselessly scouring the grounds. Perhaps that was Sophie's tactic. Rob our best players of sleep."

"The girls barely slept either," Professor Anemone said, dabbing cider off the swan on her camel-fur nightrobe. "Let's hope they look decent for their proposals."

"What is he so afraid of us seeing?" Professor Dovey said, peering at the tower. "What is the point of us preparing students for these trials if we cannot *be* there for them?"

"Because we won't be there for them in the Woods, Clarissa."

Professor Dovey turned from the window.

"It is why he forbids us to interfere," Professor Anemone said. "No matter how cruel children are to each other, nothing can prepare them for how cruel their stories can be."

Professor Dovey was quiet for a moment.

"You should go, dear," she said finally.

Professor Anemone followed her eyes to the sunset and jumped. "Goodness! You'd be stuck with me all night! Thank you for the cider." She swept to the door—

"Emma."

Professor Anemone looked back.

"She scares me," said Professor Dovey. "That girl."

"Your students are ready, Clarissa."

Professor Dovey managed a smile and nodded. "We'll hear their victory cries soon enough, won't we?"

Emma blew a kiss and closed the door behind her.

Professor Dovey watched the sun smothered by the horizon. As the sky went dark, she heard a lock snap behind her. Quickly, she shuffled to the door and yanked at it—then blasted it with her wand, shot it with her finger. . . . But it was sealed shut by magic greater than hers.

Her face contorted with nerves, then slowly relaxed.

"They'll be safe," she sighed, trudging into her bedchamber. "They always are."

At 8:00 p.m. on the night before the Ball, the students entered the Theater of Tales to see it had been fully enchanted for the occasion. Above each side floated a chandelier of ten swan-shaped candles, burning white over Good and blue-black over Evil. Between them hovered the steel Circus Crown, brilliant in flame light with seven long, sharp spires, awaiting the night's winner.

Evergirls arrived first, primed for their Ball proposals in colorful evening gowns and nervous smiles. As they entered the west doors, waving flags with white swans and banners blaring TEAM GOOD!, glass flowers spritzed them with fragrance and crystal friezes came to life.

"Greetings, fair maiden, will your talent win us the Crown?" puffed a crystal prince as he fought a dragon spewing scalding mist.

"I hear this Sophie child is quite formidable. Can you defeat her?" interjected a crystal princess next to him on a glittering spinning wheel.

"I didn't make the team," Kiko admitted.

"Always one who's left behind," the prince said, stabbing the dragon through.

Through the east doors, roaring Nevers shoved in, waving hideous signs scrawled TEAM EVIL! while Hort flapped a black swan flag so eagerly it broke stalactites off the ceiling, sending Nevers stampeding for cover. As he lunged for a seat, Hort took in the scorch marks on walls, contorting to shadows of monsters eating peasants and witches cooking children, while nearby pew friezes had come alive, with woodcut princes shrieking as carved villains stabbed them, spurting black sap everywhere.

"Who *did* all this?" he goggled, splattered with sap.

"The School Master," Ravan said, plugging his ears from the shrieks. "No wonder he doesn't let teachers in."

Meanwhile, as the last Nevergirls and Everboys arrived, herded by wolves and fairies, they too felt the thrill of a room without adults. Only Tedros looked unimpressed, the last to limp through in creamy white breeches, chest gashed through the undone laces of a royal blue shirt. Face sprinkled with angry scratches, he scanned the Evers seats for someone, then slumped with disappointment into his own.

Watching him, Hester tensed. "Where's Sophie?" she hissed to Anadil, ignoring Dot's glares down the pew.

"She never came back from Lesso's!" Anadil whispered.

"Maybe Lesso cured her?"

"Or maybe the symptoms got worse! Suppose she attacks Tedros!"

"But *he* doesn't have any symptoms, Ani," Hester said, gazing at the prince. "When a villain's symptoms start, their Nemesis grows stronger!"

But slouched in his seat, Tedros just looked ashen and weak.

Anadil gaped at him. "But if he's not Sophie's Nemesis, then who is?"

Behind them the Ever doors opened and into the Theater glided the most beautiful princess they'd ever seen.

She wore a midnight-blue gown glittering with delicate

gold leaves, long velvet train trailing down the aisle. Her lustrous ebony hair was swept up high with a tiara of blue orchids. Around her neck was a ruby pendant that dripped over fair skin like blood on snow. Her big dark eyes flaunted gold shadow, her lips a dewy rose sheen.

"A bit late in the term for new students," Tedros said, ogling.

"She's not new," said Chaddick next to him.

Tedros tracked his stare to black clumps peeking beneath the gown and choked.

Smiling slyly, Agatha passed Beatrix, who turned to stone, boys who dribbled into their laps, girls who suddenly feared for their Ball dates, and nestled in next to Kiko, whose eyes were wide enough to pop.

"Black magic?" Kiko peeped.

"Groom Room," Agatha whispered, spotting Sophie's empty seat. She saw Tedros noticing it too. He looked back and his big blue eyes met hers.

Across the aisle, Hester and Anadil went white with understanding.

"Welcome to the Circus of Talents."

Students all looked up to see the white wolf onstage, a fairy hovering beside him. "Tonight will consist of twenty duels, in order of ranks," he boomed. "The 10th-ranked Ever will perform his talent, followed by the 10th-ranked Never. The School Master will anoint a winner and publicly punish the loser."

Students eagerly scanned the Theater for him. The wolf snorted and continued.

"We'll proceed through the 9th pair, then the 8th pair, then all the way down to the 1st-ranked pair. At the end of the Circus, whoever the School Master deems the most impressive talent will win the Circus Crown and his school will win the Theater of Tales for the next year."

Good chanted, "OURS! OURS!" while Nevers added, "NO MORE! NO MORE!"—

"Just 'cause there are no teachers here doesn't mean you can act like animals," the wolf growled, fairy chiming agreement. "I don't care if I have to beat a princess or two to get out of here faster."

Evergirls gasped.

"If you have questions, keep them to yourself. If you need the toilet, go in your pants," the wolf boomed. "Because the doors are locked and the Circus begins *now*."

Agatha and Tedros exhaled relief. Hester and Anadil too.

Because for all the acts they'd see tonight, Sophie's wouldn't be one of them.

Evers won the first four Circus contests, leaving Nevers to suffer the School Master's punishments. Brone started hiccuping butterflies, Arachne blindly chased her bouncing eye all over the theater, Vex had his pointy ears swollen to the size of an elephant's, all victims of the Circus' unseen judge, who seemed to delight in punishing Evil.

Watching another of Evil's swan candles extinguish, Agatha felt ill. Only three more duels until her turn.

"What's your talent?" Kiko nudged.

"Does wearing makeup count?" Agatha said uncomfortably,

noticing Everboys still sneaking awed glances.

"Doesn't matter how they look at you, Agatha! No prince will propose to anyone who loses to Evil!"

Agatha stiffened. Her mind was fogged with a thousand things, but only one mattered. Because if no one proposed to her . . .

You fail.

Breath shallowing, Agatha turned to the stage. She needed a talent *now*.

"Presenting Never Ravan!" the wolf called, and the phoenix carved into the stage front glowed green.

With his oily black mane and big black pupils, Ravan peered down at yawning Evers, ready for another lame curse or villainous monologue. He nodded down at his bunk mates, who pulled drums from beneath their pews and gave him a beat; Ravan started to hop from one foot to another, then added sharp arm poses, and before the Nevers knew it, one of their best villains was . . .

"*Dancing?*" Hester said, gaping.

Drumbeats grew faster, Ravan's stomps louder, and his eyes turned malevolent red.

"Red eyes for a villain," Tedros muttered. "Groundbreaking."

But then came a sharp crack. At first they thought it was Ravan's feet, then they saw it was his head, for there was a *second* one next to the first. He stomped again and a third head appeared, then a fourth, a fifth until ten snarling heads balanced on his neck in a sickening row. Drums deafened, stomps climaxed, and Ravan leapt from the stage to a wide-legged squat, stuck out ten swollen tongues, and burst into screaming flames.

Nevers launched to their feet, whooping wildly.

"Who can beat that!" Ravan spat, restored to one head as smoke cleared.

Agatha noticed the wolf guards of Evil didn't look impressed. Instead it was the fairies who buzzed excitedly. *Perhaps they made a bet on the final score*, she thought, refocusing on her missing talent. Each Never was getting better and unlike the Evers who'd won so far, she couldn't twirl ribbons or do sword tricks or charm snakes. How could she prove herself Good?

Agatha saw Tedros stare at her again and she felt her insides twist, squeezing away her breath. All along, she had thought getting home with Sophie was her happy ending. But it wasn't. Her happy ending was here in this magical world. With her prince.

How far she'd come from her graveyard.

Now she had her own story. Her own *life*.

Tedros' eyes pinned on her, glowing, hopeful, like there was no one else in the world.

He's yours, her reflection had promised, dressed just as she was now. She had gone to the Groom Room hoping to feel just like that princess smiling back at her on the Bridge.

But why wasn't she smiling, then? Why was she still thinking of . . .

Sophie?

Tedros smiled brighter and mouthed through cupped hands. "What's your talent?"

Agatha's stomach sank. Her turn was coming.

"Presenting Ever Chaddick!" the white wolf announced, the carved phoenix now glowing gold.

Nevers assaulted Chaddick with boos and fistfuls of gruel. The Evil decorations got into the act too, with the walls' scorch marks depicting him beaten, burned, beheaded, while villains carved into the pews shot him with splinters and sap. Chaddick, blond furry arms folded to his barrel chest, drank all this in with a placid smile. Then he drew his bow and fired an arrow into the seats. It ricocheted off pews, grazing Nevers' ears and necks, boomeranged through walls and bled scorch marks red before it bounced off carvings, impaling each one until they moaned in chorus and went dead quiet.

Another candle burnt out in Evil's chandelier.

Ravan's smile vanished. Immediately he was yanked into the air by an invisible force. A pig nose exploded onto his face, a tail burst from his bottom, and he fell to the aisle with a loud oink.

"Evers win," the wolf grinned.

Strange, Agatha thought. *Why does he want his own side to lose?*

"Only two more pairs until your turn!" Kiko whispered.

Agatha's heart skittered. She couldn't focus with her mind whiplashing between Sophie and Tedros, between excitement and guilt. *Talent . . . Think of a talent . . .* She could neither Mogrify, since the teachers' counterspells were still in place, nor could she do any of her favorite spells, since they were all Evil.

"I'll just call a bird or something," she murmured, trying to remember Uma's lessons.

"Um, how will the bird get *in*?" Kiko asked, nodding at the locked doors.

Agatha broke her freshly polished nail.

With her talents still locked in the Doom Room, Anadil tried to curse open the doors, only to find the magic too strong to break, and suffer a stinkbug swarm as punishment. Then Hort took the stage for his face-off with Beatrix. Since the Trial, Hort had been rising in the ranks, chasing a Circus spot he promised would finally earn him "respect." But now he spent most of his four minutes onstage grunting and wheezing, trying to pop hairs from his chest.

"I'll respect him if he sits down," Hester grouched as Nevers let out a few boos.

But just as time ran out, Hort spewed a violent grunt and cracked his neck. He moaned and his chest swelled up. He groaned and his cheeks puffed up. He wrenched, he lurched, he jerked, and with a primal scream, he exploded out of his clothes.

Everyone slammed against their seats in shock.

Hort sneered down, blanketed in dark brown fur over hulking muscles, sharp-toothed snout wet and long.

"He's a . . . *werewolf*?" Anadil gasped.

"Man-wolf," Hester said, squelching thoughts of the Beast's corpse. "More control than a werewolf."

"See?" Hort the Wolf snarled at all of them. *"See?"*

His expression suddenly changed and with a flatulent *poof*! he deflated into his scrawny, hairless body and dove behind the stage to cover himself.

"I take back the part about control," Hester said.

Still, Evil thought they had it won, until Beatrix flounced onstage in a peach prairie dress, clutching a familiar white bunny, and sang a song so catchy and sweet that she soon had all the Evers singing along:

> *I can be rude*
> *I can act low*
> *That doesn't mean I can't grow*

> *But who's always been there*
> *Who's always been true*
> *I'm the one who's been Good to you*

> *Not a fair-weather friend*
> *Or a flash in the pan*
> *Tedros, don't I deserve your hand?*

"They'll be so perfect at the Ball, won't they?" Kiko sighed to Agatha.

And as she watched Tedros finally join the sing-along, amused by such earnest devotion, Agatha had to smile too. Somewhere in there, Beatrix had a speck of Good. All it took was talent to show it.

Agatha blinked and saw Tedros grinning right at her, as if confident she'd produce a talent far superior. A talent worthy of Camelot's son. It was the same look he had given Sophie once upon a time.

Before she failed him.

"Never Hester versus Ever Agatha!" said the white wolf after Hort was punished with porcupine needles.

Agatha wilted. Her time had run out.

"Without Sophie, Hester's our last hope," Brone hiccupped, spawning a fresh batch of butterflies.

"She doesn't seem to think so," frowned elephant-eared Vex, watching Hester slump to the stage.

Soon they saw why, for when Hester unleashed her demon, it only managed a sooty firebolt before fading into her neck. She coughed painfully, clutching her heart, as if the poor effort had drained her.

But if Hester went down without a fight, her teammates had no intention of doing the same. Like all villains, when defeat loomed, they simply changed the rules. And as Agatha took the stage, frantically trying to think of a talent, she heard whispers— "Do it! Do it!"—then Dot's voice—"*No!*"

She turned just in time to see boys huddled over a red *Spells* textbook. Vex raised his glowing red finger, shouted an incantation—Agatha went stiff and collapsed unconscious.

The only sound in the Theater was a stalactite slowly cracking on the ceiling.

It fell.

Tedros tackled Vex by his flappy ears. Brone snatched Tedros by the collar, threw him into a chandelier, and students dodged falling candles that ignited the aisles. Everboys leapt into the Never pews, while Nevers ignited and launched dead butterflies at them from under Brone's seat.

Agatha slowly came to onstage and looked up to see Nevers and Evers throwing shoes at each other across a burning aisle, clumps, boots, and high heels flying through smoke like missiles.

Where are the guards?

Through the haze, she glimpsed wolves beating up Nevers and fairies dive-bombing Evers, fueling flames with fairy dust. Agatha wiped her eyes and looked again. Wolves and fairies were making this fight . . . *worse?*

Then she saw one fairy in particular, biting every pretty girl he could find.

"I don't want to die."

"I didn't either," the white wolf answered.

In a flash, Agatha understood.

She flicked her glowing finger and a whip crack of lightning exploded through the aisle, shocking everyone still.

"Sit down," she commanded.

No one disobeyed, including wolves and fairies who slunk into the aisle, ashamed.

Agatha carefully studied these guards of both schools.

"We think we know what sides we're on," she spoke into the silent Theater. "We think we know who we are. We tear life apart into Good or Evil, beautiful or ugly, princess or witch, right or wrong."

She gazed at the biting fairy boy.

"But what if there are things in between?"

The fairy looked back at her, tears welling.

Make a wish, she thought.

Terrified, the fairy boy shook his head.

All you have to do is make a wish, Agatha pleaded.

The fairy boy welled tears, fighting himself . . .

Then, just as with the fish, just as with the gargoyle, Agatha began to hear his thoughts.

Show them . . . came a voice she knew.

Show them the truth . . .

Agatha smiled sadly at him. *Wish granted.*

She thrust out her hand and ghostly blue light burst upward from the fairies' and wolves' bodies, which froze completely still.

Shocked, students squinted at *human* spirits, floating in blue light above the frozen bodies. Some of the spirits were their age, most were wizened and old, but all wore their same school uniforms—only the ones in Good's clothes hovered above the wolves' bodies, with the ones in Evil's above the fairies'.

Dumbstruck, students whipped to Agatha for explanation.

Agatha looked up at bald, black-robed Bane, floating above the fairy boy's body. The boy who bit pretty girls in Gavaldon, now a few years older, once-plump cheeks sunken and stained with tears.

"If you fail, you become a slave for the opposite side," Agatha said. "That's the School Master's punishment."

She took in an old white-haired man over the white wolf, soothing a young girl's spirit above a fairy.

"Eternal punishment for an impure soul," Agatha said, as the young girl wept into the old man's arms. "This, he thinks, will fix these bad students. Putting them in the wrong school will teach them a lesson. It's what this world teaches us. That we can only be in one school and not the other. But that leaves the question . . ."

She looked across the phantoms, all as frightened and help-less as Bane.

"Is it *true?*"

Her hand lost steadiness. The phantoms flickered and plunged back into their fairy and wolf bodies, which came back to life.

"I'd set them all free if I could, but his magic is too strong," Agatha said, voice cracking. "I just wish my talent had a better ending."

As she slumped down the stage steps, she heard sniffles and looked up to see wolves, fairies, children on both sides dabbing their eyes.

Agatha sank next to Kiko, whose makeup was a runny mess of pink and blue. "I used to hate those wolves," she wailed. "Now I want to hug them."

Across the aisle, Agatha saw Hester smile through tears. "Makes me wonder whose side I'm on," Hester said softly.

Evil's 9th candle extinguished above her.

With a miserable sigh, Hester stood. Instantly a gush of boiling black oil exploded from the ceiling. She closed her eyes just as it smashed into her—

It struck fur instead.

Hester turned to see three wolves shielding her, bodies seared by steaming oil. Panting with pain, they glowered into the air, informing the School Master they'd seen enough of his punishments.

In the silent theater, everyone stared at each other as if the rules of the game had suddenly changed.

"See, he *has* to be Good," Kiko whispered to Agatha. "If he was Evil, he'd have killed them!"

"F-F-i-i-nal duel," the white wolf stammered, sensing his luck. "Never Sophie versus Ever Tedros. With Sophie absent, we'll proceed to Tedros."

"No."

Tedros stood. "The Circus ends now. We've seen Good that cannot be matched."

He bowed in defeat to Agatha. "There is no doubt of the winner."

Agatha met his clear blue eyes. For the first time, she didn't think of Sophie.

Both sides looked up at the gleaming Crown, waiting for it to bless the prince's verdict.

Instead there was a very loud knock.

27

Promises Unkept

For a moment, no one was sure where the knock came from.

But then came another. This one louder. Someone was at the Never doors.

"The Circus is *closed*!" the wolf roared.

Two more knocks.

"I thought teachers were locked in their rooms," Agatha whispered.

"So it's not a teacher, obviously," Kiko whispered, eyes glued to Tristan.

Agatha met Hester's look across the aisle. Spooked, both girls turned back to the doors, shuddering from another loud knock.

"You will not be let in!" the wolf thundered.

The knocking stopped.

Agatha sighed.

Then slowly, magically, the doors creaked open all on their own.

Into the Theater of Tales slunk a figure shrouded in a black hood. Hundreds of eyes watched the stranger glide down the aisle, footsteps quiet, snakeskin cape trailing behind like a wedding train. Smoothly, silently the black shadow ascended to the stage and stood still beneath the Circus Crown, cape scales glimmering in flame light, head bowed like a bat's.

The doors slammed shut.

Pale fingers slithered from under the cape and pulled the hood back.

Sophie glared down at her audience, nose and chin marred by warts. Patches of white speckled her dyed black hair. Her emerald eyes were now murky gray, her skin thin enough to see veins.

Slowly she scanned the crowd, taking in scared faces with a widening sneer. Then she saw Agatha, regal in blue, and lost her smile. Sophie stared at her, gray pupils clouding with horror.

"I see we have a new princess," she said quietly. "Beautiful, isn't she?"

Agatha returned her stare, feeling no more pity, no more desire to please.

"But look closer, children, and see the vampire she is, come to suck our souls," Sophie leered. "Since she doesn't have one of her *own*."

Beneath her dress, Agatha trembled. But she withstood her withering glare until Sophie suddenly swiveled to Tedros and smiled.

"My dear Teddy! Fancy seeing you here. I believe we still have our match to finish."

"The Circus is *over*," Tedros spat. "A winner has been crowned."

"I see," Sophie said. "Then what is that?"

She stabbed her bony finger into the air and everyone looked up at the dangling Crown, still very much ungiven.

"This is bad," Hester said to Anadil. "This is very bad."

Tedros stood up across the aisle.

"Just leave," he growled at Sophie. "Before you make a fool of yourself."

Sophie smiled. "Scared, are you?"

Tedros puffed his chest, trying to hold himself back. He could feel Evers' eyes on him, just like in the Clearing when Sophie exposed his promise.

"Show us, Teddy," Sophie said sweetly. "Show me something I can't match."

Tedros clenched his teeth, fighting his pride.

Vex suddenly noticed a burnt "TEAM EVIL" banner on the floor. His eyes sparkled with hope.

"SHOW US!" he bellowed, and jabbed Brone, who jumped in. "SHOW US! SHOW US!" Lusting to snatch victory from the jaws of defeat, Nevers swept into their chorus. "SHOW US! SHOW US!"

"No—stop!" Hester cried as she and Anadil spun—

Villains snarled at them as if they were traitors and the two witches quickly joined the chant.

But as the Nevers' chants grew, Tedros didn't move. Evers

shifted in their seats, impatient for their Captain to take up the challenge. All except for Agatha, who closed her eyes.

Don't do it. It's what she wants.

Raucous roars rang out. Agatha's eyes shot open—

Tedros was crossing onto the stage.

"No!" she screamed, but both sides' cheers swallowed her.

Separated by six feet, Sophie smiled deliciously and the prince glowered back. Neither said a word as the Nevers' chants turned to "EVIL! EVIL! EVIL!" while Evers countered with "GOOD! GOOD! GOOD!" Thunder rumbled in the distance and the cheers grew louder, angrier, drowning out the swelling storm. Tedros' muscles tensed, his cheekbones chiseled, as Sophie's smile widened. Agatha shook harder with fear, watching Sophie's grin grow taunting, mocking, until finally the prince flushed with fury, his finger glowed gold, and just as it looked like he'd attack—

He dropped to his knees.

The hall went silent in shock.

Nevers exploded in victory. Agatha went white.

With a pitying sigh, Sophie swept towards the kneeling prince. She gently took his head by its flaxen hair and peered into his scared blue eyes.

"I've finally been doing my own homework, Teddy. Want to see?"

Tedros hardened. "Still my *turn*."

He ripped out his training sword and Sophie drew back. But instead of striking her, Tedros stayed on one knee, pivoted to the aisle, thrust the blade towards the crowd—

"Agatha of Woods Beyond."

He laid down the sword.

"Will you be my princess for the Ball?"

Sophie froze. Nevers stopped cheering.

In the dead silence, Agatha tried to find her breath. Then she saw Sophie's face, shock melting to pain. Looking into her friend's sunken, scared eyes, Agatha slid into an old grave of darkness and doubt—

Until a boy brought her back.

A boy on one knee, looking at her the way he had through goblins, coffins, pumpkins.

A boy who had chosen her long before they both knew it.

A boy now asking her to choose him.

Agatha gazed back at her prince.

"Yes."

"No!" Beatrix cried, and vaulted to her feet.

Chaddick dropped to his knees before her.

"Beatrix, will you be my princess for the Ball?"

One by one, Everboys cascaded to knees.

"Reena, will you be my princess for the Ball?" said Nicholas.

"Giselle, will you be my princess for the Ball?" said Tarquin.

"Ava, will you be my princess for the Ball?"

Boys fell in glorious rhythm, hands held out in proposal. Each girl heard her name, each girl had her gasp, until there was only one left with no one to love. Tears blinded Kiko and she wiped them away, knowing she'd be failed—only to find

Tristan before her on one knee.

"Will you be my princess for the Ball?"

"*Yes!*" Kiko screamed.

"*Yes!*" said Reena.

"*Yes!*" said Giselle.

Through the Theater flooded waves of breathless ecstasy—"*Yes!*" "*Yes!*" "*Yes!*"—until the sea of love drowned even Beatrix, who mustered her best smile and took Chaddick's hand. "*Yes!*"

Watching across the aisles, the Nevers' faces began to change. One by one, their scowls turned sorrowful, their eyes melted to hurt. Hort, Ravan, Anadil, even Hester . . . As if they too wished they could have such joy. As if they too wished they could feel as wanted. Gone was their will to fight, lost to broken hearts, and the villains shrank into silence, snakes drained of venom.

But one snake was still rearing.

From the stage, Sophie's eyes never left Agatha as Tedros took her into his arms. Sophie's pupils darkened to hot coals. Her body shivered with sweat. Black nails drew blood from her fists. From the depths of her soul, hate spewed like lava, reviving the song of her heart. With her eyes on the happy couple, Sophie raised her hands and sang at full scream. Above her, black stalactites morphed into razor-sharp beaks, cawing, shrieking with life.

All at once, ravens smashed through the ceiling and attacked everything in sight.

Children dove for cover, shielding ears as Sophie shrieked

an octave higher. Fairies flew for Sophie but the ravens swallowed every but one, who barely escaped through a crack in the walls. With their paws to their ears, the wolves were just as exposed and the birds slit their throats with ruthless speed. The white wolf grabbed a young brown wolf into his arms, batted back ravens as his nose and ears bled, but the swarm dragged both wolves behind the stage and ended their fight. Just as the birds swooped to do the same to the students—

Sophie stopped singing and the ravens crumbled to thin air.

Gasping with pain, everyone slowly turned to the villain onstage. Only Sophie wasn't looking at them.

Evers and Nevers followed her eyes to the Circus Crown, swaying in midair, at last awakened to judgment. It fluttered down from above, drifting between Good and Evil, back and forth, back and forth until light as a feather, the sharp crown twirled with decision . . . and landed softly on Sophie's head.

Her lips curled into a grin. "Don't forget the prize."

Agatha saw streaks of white magically erase the stage behind Sophie, streaks she'd seen before—

"*RUN!*" she screamed.

White streaks erased the walls, splashed towards the aisles as screaming students fled for doors too late—

The Theater of Tales vanished in a blast of white, expelling both schools into the Good stair room. Evers smashed into pink tower staircases, Nevers into blue. As lightning and wind shattered stained glass windows, Hester and the villains fled up the Honor and Valor steps. But just as she reached the landing, Hester slid on glass and fell off the side. Dangling from the banister by one hand, she spotted Dot crawling past her—

"*Dot!* Dot, help!"

"Sorry," Dot sniffed, crawling ahead. "I only help *roommates*."

"Dot, please!"

"I live in a *toilet*! You girls are bullies and bad friends and you make me embarrassed to be a vil—"

"*DOT!*"

Dot grabbed Hester's hand just as it slipped.

The Evers weren't so lucky. As they frantically crawled up Purity and Charity, Sophie sang them a searing note and the two glass staircases exploded, sending beautiful boys and girls crashing to marble. Sophie went one note higher. The foyer quaked beneath their feet, cracked like thin ice, and split open in a hundred places. Stunned Evers fell into each other and tumbled towards the yawning rifts. They tried to grip broken marble and shards of stairs, but the floor's jagged slopes were too steep and with harrowing screams, the children careened over the edges. Just as they plunged into the cliffs, their hands found splintered horns of marble. With every last ounce of will, the Evers held on, feet kicking into deadly darkness below.

"Agatha!" Tedros screamed, leaping across rain-soaked gorges and gulfs to pull them up, growing more and more distraught.

"Agatha, where are you!"

Then across the room, high against a shattered window, he saw two pale hands clinging over a cliff of broken wall.

"*Agatha! I'm coming!*"

He bounded over rock craters, scaled broken stair pieces,

higher and higher towards the marble bluff. With a lunging scissors-kick jump, he dove onto the jagged cliff top, scraped through glass, and grabbed her hand over the opposite edge—

Sophie pulled herself up to face him.

Tedros backed up in horror, only to find the cliff's edge, Evers crying for help below.

"So if princes rescue princesses, now I wonder . . . ," Sophie said, Circus Crown sparkling on rain-soaked hair. "Who rescues *princes*?"

"You promised—" Tedros stammered, searching for an escape. "You promised you'd change!"

"Did I?" Sophie scratched her skull. "Well. We both made promises we won't keep." With a scream, she unleashed her highest note yet.

The prince crumpled to his knees. Watching him whimper in pain, Sophie went a note higher. Paralyzed, Tedros felt his nose bleed, his ears sizzling. Sophie slowly leaned in and put a finger to his quivering lips. Then she smiled into his shocked blue eyes and delivered the death note—

Agatha tackled her against the open window, sending her crown flying into the storm.

Bloodied and weak, Tedros tried to help her, but Agatha glared back at him. "Save the others!"

"But—"

"*Now!*" Agatha yelled, pinning Sophie tighter against the window.

Mustering all his strength, Tedros leapt off the cliff for his stranded classmates. Hearing his cry below, Agatha turned from Sophie to make sure he was safe. Sophie swiftly kicked out her leg and Agatha smashed face-first into the window-sill.

She staggered up, nose bloody.

"Lady Lesso was right," Sophie said, standing to face her. "You get stronger as I get weaker. You win as I lose. You're my Nemesis, Agatha."

Sophie stepped towards her. "Do you know how I know?"

Her face darkened with sadness.

"Because I'll only be happy when you're dead."

Agatha backed against the window, trying to make her shaking finger glow.

Four flights up, Hester, Anadil, and Dot tore through Honor's halls, screams and thunder echoing below.

"The Circus Crown was given!" Hester shrieked, throwing open faculty doors. "Where are they?" She swerved around the corner and found out.

Professor Anemone, Professor Dovey, and Professor Espada were frozen midrun, mouths wide open, as if they'd been ambushed by a spell just as they dashed for the stair room.

"Hester . . ."

Hester followed Anadil's eyes out the hall window. On Halfway Bridge, lightning lit up Lady Lesso, Professor Sheeks, and Professor Manley, frozen still with the same startled expressions.

"Can we revive them?" Dot asked, paling. "It's just a Stun Spell."

"It isn't a Stun Spell." Anadil tapped on Professor Dovey's skin, which made a thin, hollow sound.

"Petrification," Hester said, remembering Lesso's class. "Only the one who cast the spell can reverse it."

"But *who?*" Dot squeaked.

"Someone who doesn't want teachers interfering," Anadil said, eyeing the silver tower over the bay.

Dot shook. "But that—that means—"

"We're on our own," said Hester.

On a stormy marble island raised above the demolished foyer, Agatha faced off alone against Sophie.

"We don't have to be enemies, Sophie," she begged, trying to ignite her finger behind her back.

"You made me like this," Sophie breathed, sparkling with tears. "You took everything that was mine."

Agatha saw Tedros and Evers crawling through rubble, convulsing from pain and fear. Through flashes of lightning, she saw Nevers watching them from towers across the Bay, quavering with the same expressions. Agatha's heart hammered. It was all up to her now.

"We can find a happy ending here," she pleaded, feeling her finger turn hot behind her. "We can both find a happy ending."

"Here?" Sophie smiled thinly. "What happened to going home, Aggie?"

Agatha stuttered for an answer—

"Ah, I see," Sophie said, grinning wider. "Now you have a

ball to attend. Now you have a *prince*."

"I just wanted to be friends, Sophie," Agatha said, eyes welling. "That's all I ever wanted."

Sophie iced over. "You never *wanted* to be friends, Agatha. You wanted *me* to be the ugly one."

Magically skin wrinkled deeper over her cheeks.

Agatha's finger dimmed in shock. "Sophie, you're doing this to yourself!"

"You wanted *me* to be the Evil one." Sophie boiled, hands gnarling to claws.

"You can be Good, Sophie!" cried Agatha, thunder drowning her out.

"You wanted *me* to be the witch," Sophie said, eyes bursting blood vessels.

"It's not true!" Agatha backed against the window—

"Well, dearie," Sophie smiled, teeth missing. "Wish *granted*."

"*No!*"

With a single push, Sophie shoved Agatha into the storm. Agatha plummeted towards the shining Bridge and instant death—Tedros screamed—

A fairy flung himself under and caught Agatha with life-draining will. As he lay her safely down to flooded stone, Bane silently thanked Agatha of Gavaldon for all the Good she'd done. Then as she took her first breath, he took his last and died in her wet, open palm.

As lightning lit up the tower, Sophie looked down at Agatha, whose face was white with shock. Across the Bay,

Sophie saw Nevers staring back at her, chilled to the bone. She spun to Tedros and the Evers, huddled in corners below, while Hester, Anadil, and Dot gaped in terror from the stairs.

Heart echoing the thunder, Sophie picked up a shard of glass and wiped away the rain.

Her drenched hair was completely white. Her face was spotted with swollen black warts. Her eyes bulged black as a crow's.

She stared into the spattered glass, frozen with panic.

But then, as Sophie looked into her mirror, panic slowly melted away and her face twisted with a strange relief, as if at last she could see beyond her reflection to what lay inside.

Her rotted lips curled into a smile, then a laugh of freedom . . . louder, higher . . .

Sophie threw down the glass, threw back her head, and unleashed a horrible cackle that promised Evil, beautiful Evil too pure to fight.

Then all at once, her eyes veered down to Agatha. With a monstrous scream of warning, she swept into her cape of snakes and vanished into night.

28

The Witch of Woods Beyond

"When terrible things happen, my mother always said 'Find what's good in it,'" Hester puffed, sprinting past petrified Castor and Beezle through Mischief Hall.

"When terrible things happen, my daddy always said 'Eat,'" Dot panted, turning a corner behind her. They slammed into Mona and Arachne—

"What's happening!" Mona cried—

"Go to your room!" Hester bellowed. "Don't come out!"

Mona and Arachne fled inside and locked the door.

Hester and Dot ran down the stairs and saw Hort, Ravan, and Vex coming up.

"Go to your room!" Dot yelled. "Don't come out!"

The boys looked at Dot, then at Hester.

"*Now!*" Hester barked, and the boys scurried away.

"Suppose I'm a henchman?" pouted Dot. "Then we won't be in the same classes next year!"

"If there's even a school *left*!" Hester snapped.

They sprinted through the stair room, barking scared Nevers back to their rooms.

"I can think of one good thing," said Dot. "No homework!"

Hester stopped suddenly, eyes wide. "Dot, we're not prepared for a real witch. We're first years!"

"It's *Sophie*," Dot said. "The same girl who likes perfume and pink. We just need to calm her down."

Hester cracked a smile. "You know, sometimes we don't give you enough credit."

"Come on," Dot blushed, toddling ahead. "Maybe Anadil found her."

After clearing the rest of Malice, the two girls limped exhausted to Room 66 and found their roommate reclining against bunched-up sheets.

"Everyone's locked in their rooms," Dot said, airing out her tunic.

Wiping sweat, Hester frowned at Anadil. "Did you even *look* for Sophie?"

"I didn't need to," Anadil yawned. "She's coming here."

"*Here?*" Hester snorted. "And how on earth would you know that?"

Anadil pulled back the sheets, revealing Grimm, bound and gagged.

"Because he told me."

In the School for Good, Chaddick and Tedros stood guard outside the Valor Common Room, shirts ripped and bloodied. Inside the packed, musty den, girls snuffled in their Ball dates' arms, while Beatrix and Reena crept to wounded boys with salve and bandages. By the time the sun came, they too were asleep.

Only Agatha didn't dare rest. Curled in a zebra-skin chair, she thought of the girl who once brought her cucumber juice and bran-flour cookies, who took her on walks and confided her dreams.

That girl was gone. And in her place, a witch who would hunt her dead.

She looked through the window at the Bridge, dawnlit, with petrified teachers, a magical wave frozen beneath. There was no accident, no great mistake. All of this was part of the School Master's plan. He wanted his two Readers at war.

But whose side was he on?

As sun flooded the room, Agatha kept her eyes open and waited for Sophie's next move.

In Room 66, morning came and went. So did afternoon.

"You wouldn't have any nibbles about?" Dot asked from her bed. Hester and Anadil stared at her, gagged Grimm grumbling between them.

"It's just I haven't had anything since yesterday and I can't eat chocolate anymore since you made me live in a toilet, because chocolate reminds me of—"

Hester tore off Grimm's gag. *"Where's Sophie."*

"Come," Grimm spat.

"When?" Hester said.

"Wait," said Grimm.

"What?"

"Grimm come. Grimm wait."

Hester looked at Anadil. *"This* is why we're here?"

A key turned in the door and all three girls dove under their beds.

"Grimm?"

Sophie slunk in, slipped off her black cape, and hung it on the door hook.

"Where are you?"

She scoured the room, scratching her scalp with sharp, dirty nails.

Under the beds, Hester, Dot, and Anadil gasped as clumps of white hair fell.

Sophie spun and saw the lump moving under covers. "Grimm?"

Leerily, she reached for the bed—

Three girls tackled her from behind. "Get her wrists!" Hester cried, tying Sophie's legs to the bedpost with burnt sheets. Anadil secured Sophie's wrists over her head next to Grimm's, while Dot beat the cupid over the head with a pillow to make herself useful.

"Perhaps you've forgotten," Sophie drawled, "but I'm on your side."

"We're all on the same side now," Hester hissed. "Against you."

"I admire such sweet intentions, Hester, but Good is *not* on your side."

In the light, Hester noticed Sophie's face ruined with wrinkles.

"You'll rot here until we figure out how to revive the teachers," Hester said, hiding shaking hands.

"Just know that I forgive all of you," Sophie sighed. "Before you even have to ask."

"We won't ask," Hester said, shunting Anadil and Dot away. Anadil grabbed Sophie's cape off the hook—

"You'll come back for me."

They turned to Sophie, who smiled to reveal more missing teeth.

"You'll see."

Hester shuddered and shut the door behind them.

The door opened and Dot peeked in. "You wouldn't happen to have any snacks?"

Hester yanked her through and slammed it.

Immediately Grimm chewed through his gag and spit it out.

"Good boy," Sophie said, stroking him as he munched her binds away. "You did so well keeping them here."

She opened her closet and pulled out her musty sewing kit and boxes of fabric and thread.

"I've been very busy, Grimm. And still more work to do."

CRACK!

Sophie turned to the door.

CRACK! CRACK!

Outside it, Anadil hammered boards, locks, and screws into her door while Hester and Dot barred it with statues and benches from the hall. Hester caught Nevers peeking out of their rooms.

"STAY INSIDE!" she boomed, and doors closed.

"I feel awful," Dot said. "She's our roommate!"

"Whatever *that* is, it's not our roommate," said Hester.

Inside, Sophie hummed along to the hammer, a needle magically sewing under her lit finger. "They'll just have to undo it," she sighed, remembering the last time someone locked her in her room.

"All that work for nothing."

By the early evening, the Evers grew restless and began to venture in groups to bathe. Then they moved in a vigilant mass to the Supper Hall, where the enchanted pots in the kitchen continued to cook, despite petrified nymphs around them. The students filled plates with goose curry, lentil salad, and pistachio sorbet, and ate at round tables in listless silence.

At the head table, Agatha tried to meet Tedros' eyes, but he just gnawed on a chicken bone miserably. She had never seen him look so tired; he had bruised rims under his eyes, no color in his cheeks, and a small blemish on his jawbone. He was the only one who hadn't taken a bath.

The silence continued until the children had nearly finished their sorbet.

"Um, I don't know if you knew, but, um, Good Hall?" Kiko cheeped. "It's still, uh . . . okay."

A hundred and nineteen heads craned up.

Kiko held the sorbet to her sweating face. "So we could, if we wanted, um, still have our, you know . . ."

She swallowed.

"Ball."

Everyone stared at her.

"Or not," Kiko mumbled.

Her classmates went back to their sorbet.

After a moment, Millicent put her spoon down.

"We did spend all this time preparing."

"And we still have two hours to get ready," Giselle said.

Reena blanched. "Is it enough time?"

"I'll sort the music!" said Tristan.

"I'll check on the hall!" said Tarquin.

"Everyone get dressed!" Beatrix hailed, and with a cheer, the crowd threw down spoons and leapt to its feet.

"Let me get this straight." Agatha's voice ripped through. "The fairies and wolves are dead, the teachers are cursed, half our school is in ruins, there's a murderer on the loose—and you want to have a *Ball*?"

"We can't give in to a witch!" Chaddick shot back.

"We can't give up our gowns!" Reena mourned.

The Evers blew up in angry agreement—

"The teachers would be proud!"

"Good never surrenders to Evil!"

"She wants to ruin our Ball!"

"Everyone *shut up*."

The room silenced. The Evers turned to Tedros, still seated.

"Agatha's right. We can't have the Ball now."

His classmates slumped, nodding. Agatha exhaled.

"First we find the witch and *kill her*," Tedros snarled.

Agatha's fists balled up as Evers exploded in cheers—"*Kill the witch! Kill the witch!*"

"You think she's just *waiting* for us?" Agatha shouted, leaping atop her chair. "You think you can stroll into Evil and kill a *real witch*?"

The chants ceased.

"What do you mean 'real' witch?" Beatrix glared up at her.

Kiko paled with understanding. "The Storian really is writing your fairy tale, isn't it?"

Agatha nodded and the room burst into nervous titters.

"We don't know who controls these fairy tales," she said over them. "We don't know if the School Master is Good or Evil. We don't even know if the Woods are still balanced. All we know is Sophie wants me dead and will kill anyone in her way. So I say we go back to Valor and wait."

Everyone's eyes shifted to Tedros, frowning up at her.

"Well, I'm Captain of this school," he retorted, "and I say we attack."

Eyes shifted between him and his princess.

"Tedros, do you trust me?" Agatha said softly, looking down at him.

The silence thickened as her question hung in the air, Tedros hot beneath her gaze.

The prince broke eye contact and looked away. "Back to Valor," he mumbled.

As Evers obeyed his orders and sullenly cleared their plates, Agatha touched his shoulder. "You did the right thi—"

"I'm going to take a bath," he lashed. "Want to look nice for our night hiding like girls!"

Agatha let him storm ahead. As Tedros stomped out of the hall, Beatrix met him at the door. "Let's sneak into Evil, Teddy! We'll kill the witch together!"

"Do as you're *told*," Tedros seethed, and shoved past her.

Beatrix watched him go, cheeks coloring with blood.

A few minutes later, as the Evers moped back into their Valor prison, she slipped through the breezeways to her room, where a starving white bunny waited for her, hopping up and down.

"You'll get your supper, Teddy," she said, scooping him up. "But first you have to earn it."

Hester woke to the castle in darkness and the Belfry tolling eight. Flat on her face in drool, she pried away a *Curse Reversal* book stuck to her cheek and glanced at Dot and Anadil, slouched on each other behind furniture barring their room. With a start, Hester bolted up and looked over them.

The door to Room 66 hadn't been disturbed.

Hester exhaled with relief—then choked.

Something was moving at the end of the hall.

She climbed through the mess of furniture and tiptoed

towards the stairwell. As she got closer, she saw three hunched figures sneaking down the steps. A minute later, two more slipped down quietly.

Hester waited behind the banister until she saw more shadows. She sparked the stairway torch—

Mona, Arachne, Vex, and Brone goggled back at her.

"Why aren't you in your rooms!" Hester yelled.

"We're coming to help you!" Mona said.

"We want to fight back!" said Vex.

"*What?* What are you—"

Then Hester saw what was in their hands.

Anadil was dreaming of sewers and Dot of beans when both felt jabs in the stomach.

"*Look!*" Hester held up a black card, glittered green and inked with ghostly white script.

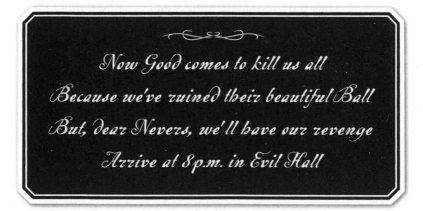

Now Good comes to kill us all
Because we've ruined their beautiful Ball
But, dear Nevers, we'll have our revenge
Arrive at 8 p.m. in Evil Hall

"It's a cute poem. Though hardly worth waking us for," grogged Dot. "What's this revenge?"

"There is no revenge!" Hester shouted.

"Then why did you write it?" Anadil said.

"I didn't, you idiots!"

Both girls looked at her. Instantly they scrambled for the stairs.

"How did she get out?" Anadil hollered, jumping two steps at a time.

"She did it before she came!" Hester yelled back as the clock tolled half past eight.

"She's so good at pranks." Dot tripped down the stairs. "What do you think her revenge will be?"

"More ravens?" Anadil said.

"Poison clouds?" Hester said.

"Firebombs placed under both schools to go off at exactly the same time?" said Dot.

Hester whitened. "Suppose they're all dead!"

They sprinted through the stair room, past the Supper Hall, past the Exhibition of Evil, to the cobwebbed, skull-carved doors at the far end of the school. Flinging the black invitation away, Hester hurled them open and three girls charged into Evil Hall, prepared for carnage—

Dot took one look and fainted. The other two couldn't breathe.

"*This* is the revenge?" Hester said, tears welling.

Outside the hall, Teddy the bunny scampered from behind the stairs to the card that Hester dropped. He picked it up between his buckteeth, careful not to smudge the glitter. Then thinking of pears and plums and other delights, he hopped back to find his mistress.

Slumped against the wall in the Valor Common Room, Agatha tried to keep her eyes open, but they drooped heavier and heavier until she toppled back and arms caught her. She squinted at Tedros as he kneeled in his undershirt, ruddy and wet from his bath.

"Sleep," he said. "I'm here now."

"I know you're upset with me—"

"Shhh," he said, clasping her tighter. "No more arguing."

With a guilty smile, Agatha surrendered to his strong arms and closed her eyes.

The common room doors slammed open. "Teddy!"

Beatrix burst in, waking the Evers. Tedros looked up, irritated.

"They're coming!" Beatrix cried and thrust him the black card as Agatha sat up in his arms. "They're coming to kill us!"

Tedros read the ghostly white script, veins tensing in his neck. "I *knew* it!" Agatha tried to see over his shoulder, but he lunged to his feet—

"*ATTENTION!*"

Evers sat up at once.

"At this very moment, the villains are planning revenge on our school," Tedros proclaimed to cries. "All the Nevers are now in league with Sophie. Our only hope is to attack the School for Evil before they come for us. We charge at nine o'clock!"

Agatha stood in shock.

"Prepare for war!" Tedros roared, throwing open the doors.

"War!" Chaddick bellowed, herding Evers after him. *"Prepare for war!"*

Dazed, Agatha picked up the fallen card. As she read it, her eyes flashed—

"No! Don't attack!"

She ran out of the common room—a foot thrust into her path. Agatha smashed into the wall and blacked out.

"Oops," Beatrix said, and sashayed after the others.

Agatha's eyes fluttered open to a searing headache and a deserted hall.

Grunting with pain, she followed the shoeprints through a breezeway into Honor Tower, then down to Hansel's Haven before she heard ominous sounds of sword on stone.

She peeked into the room of sparkly rock sugar to see Everboys sharpening real blades, arrows, axes, maces, and chains they'd thieved back from the Armory.

"How much boiling oil?" called one.

"Enough to blind them all!" shouted another, striking his sword against whetstone.

In the lollipop room, Reena sheared girls' dresses to make them more practical for combat, while Beatrix armed each girl with a bag of jagged stones and thorn darts.

"But the boys train for war in *class*," a girl moaned.

"We haven't even learned to fight!" said another.

"Would you like to be a slave to villains?" Beatrix fired back. "Made to cook children and eat princess hearts and drink horse blood—"

"And wear *black*?" Reena cried.

Evergirls gulped.

"Then learn quickly," Beatrix said.

In the marshmallow room, Kiko and Giselle lit dozens of torches, while in the gumdrop room, Nicholas and a fleet of boys hewed a battering ram.

Agatha found Tedros in the last room with Chaddick and two other boys, hunched over a hand-drawn map on Professor Dovey's sugarplum desk.

"How do you know that's where Evil Hall is?" Chaddick said.

"It's just a guess," said the prince. "Agatha's the only one who's been in that cursed school but I can't find her. Tell Beatrix to look for her again."

"I'll save you the trouble."

The boys turned to Agatha.

"We need your help," Tedros said, smiling.

"I won't help a Captain leading his army to their graves," said Agatha.

Tedros flushed with surprise. "Agatha, they're going to kill us!"

"*Now Good comes to kill us all*," she retorted, holding up the black card. "Evil's not attacking us! Sophie wants *you* to attack!"

"For once that witch and I agree on something," Tedros said. "Now are you with me or not?"

"I won't let you go."

"*I'm* the man here, not you!"

"Then *act like one!*"

The clock struck nine o'clock.

As the tower bells rang, the boys looked nervously between Tedros and Agatha.

The last toll ceased.

In the silence, Agatha saw the doubt in Tedros' eyes and knew she'd won. She smiled gently and reached for his hand, but Tedros pulled it away. Glowering at her, his face swelled redder, redder—

"WE CHARGE *NOW!*" he cried, and roars exploded through the hall.

As his three lieutenants ran to steer the troops, Tedros seized his map and followed out the door.

Agatha threw herself in his way. Before she could speak, he seized her by the waist.

"Agatha, do you trust me?" he breathed.

She sighed with irritation. "Of course, but—"

"Good." He slammed the door and barred it with an arrow.

"I'm sorry," he said through the door crack. "But I'm your prince and I'm going to protect you."

"Tedros!" Agatha pounded on the candy door. "Tedros, she'll kill you all!"

But through the crack, she saw him leading his Good army to war, armed with torches, weapons, battering ram, and blood-thirsty chant: "*Kill the witch! Kill the witch!*" In the flame-lit hall, their shadows distorted on walls, dark and crooked, then trailed away like magic.

Panic chilled Agatha's blood. She had to get to the School for Evil before Tedros and his army. But what could she do to save them?

Only when your Nemesis is dead will you feel quenched, Lady Lesso had said.

Tears seared Agatha's eyes, the grief of a decision already made.

Give herself to Sophie and no one else would die.

Let the witch win.

It was the only happy ending left.

With a primal scream, she punched and kicked the door, then rammed the sugarplum desk against it, but the candy didn't break. She hurled chairs into the brûléed walls, stomped on the treacle floors . . . but there was only one way out of this room. Dripping sweat, Agatha looked through the window.

Her black clump found the ledge as she straddled the sill in her billowing blue gown. As the frigid night wind lashed her face, she pulled her other leg through and grabbed onto a vine of gold lights the fairies had draped across the tower for the Ball. With a desperate pull, she swung herself onto the narrow ridge and spun around.

She was so high above Halfway Bridge that the frozen teachers on it looked like beetles. The brutal wind flayed her ears and made her shiver so hard she almost slipped. Through the glass breezeway, she could see torches flooding down Honor Tower towards the Tunnel of Trees. She only had a few minutes before Good would storm right into Evil's hands.

With chapped fists, Agatha tugged on the lights above her

and saw they were strung tight. She squinted at the crisscross of fairy-lit vines spilling down the tower, a glowing road to take her to the Bridge.

Please be strong enough, Agatha prayed.

She grabbed the vine, jumped off the ledge, and heard it snap. Her body plunged, slammed into a glass ledge, and just before she careened off, something whizzed by and landed an inch from her cheek. Agatha grabbed onto it as the vine collapsed, then saw what it was—

An arrow.

Dangling from it, she looked back in shock, just in time to see an arrow miss her other cheek. More arrows came flying out of darkness, aimed right for her. As their steel tips grazed her again and again, Agatha closed her eyes and waited for the lethal shot of pain.

The whizzing stopped.

Agatha opened her eyes. Arrows rested in a haphazard foot ladder all the way down the tower wall.

She didn't question who was trying to kill her or her spell of luck. She just climbed down the arrows as fast as she could to Halfway Bridge, and wove through petrified teachers, hands thrust out for a barrier that never came. As Tedros' army arrived at the Clearing to find Good's and Evil's tunnels magically entwined and impassable, far away Agatha crossed safely into the villains' lair.

High over her, in Malice's window, Grimm sheathed his bow.

"And didn't harm a hair on her head," Sophie said, caressing him. "Much as you would have liked."

Grimm grumbled obediently as Sophie peered out at Tedros' army marching around the moat, then down at Agatha, vanishing into Evil all alone.

"Won't be long now," she said.

She swept aside the clumps of white hair on her desk and continued to sew, a puppet master gleefully pulling strings.

Agatha had expected to be captured the moment she entered Evil. But as she crept through the leaky foyer, she saw there were no guards, no booby traps, no symptoms of war. The School for Evil was unsettlingly quiet, except for iron doors creaking open and shut at the rear of the stair room. She peeked inside them and found the Theater of Tales, pristine and restored, with one difference. Where the front of the stone stage once depicted a phoenix rising from ashes, now it had a new scene . . .

A screaming witch, surrounded by ravens.

Shuddering, Agatha crept up the steps towards Evil Hall.

But, dear Nevers, we'll have our revenge . . .

What would Sophie make the Nevers do to her? She thought of all the worst villains she'd found in fairy tales. Turn her into stone? Parade her severed head? Cook her in mince pie?

Though it was freezing cold, Agatha felt her cheeks perspire as she turned the corner.

Roll her in a barrel of nails? Cut out her heart? Fill her stomach with rocks?

Sweat mixed with tears as she looked down at hundreds of footprints—

Burn her? Stone her? Stab her?

She broke into a run and charged towards torture and death, wishing that someday she and Sophie would find each other in a different world, a world without princes, a world without pain, and with a terrified cry threw herself through skull-carved doors—

She lost her breath.

Evil Hall had been transformed into a magnificent ballroom, glittering with green tinsel, black balloons, thousands of green-flamed candles, and a spinning chandelier streaking wall murals with emerald bursts of light. Around a towering ice sculpture of two entwined snakes, Hort and Dot stumbled through a waltz, Anadil wrapped her arms around Vex, Brone tried not to step on Mona's green feet, and Hester and Ravan swayed and whispered as more villainous couples waltzed around them. Ravan's bunk mates picked up the music on reed violins and more pairs flooded onto the floor, clumsy, bashful, but aglow with happiness, dancing beneath a spangled banner:

THE 1st ANNUAL VILLAINS "NO BALL"

Agatha began to cry.

The music stopped.

She wiped her eyes to see Nevers staring at her. Couples broke apart. Faces reddened with shame.

"What is *she* doing here?" Vex spat.

"She'll tell the Evers!" Mona said—

"Get her!" Arachne cried—

"I'll handle this," said a voice.

Hester stepped through the crowd. Agatha reeled back. "Hester, listen—"

"This is a villains' party, Agatha," Hester said, skulking towards her. "And you're not a villain."

Agatha cowered against the wall. "Wait—don't—"

"I'm afraid there's only one thing to do," said Hester, shadow swelling over her.

Agatha shielded her face. "Die?"

"Stay," Hester said.

Agatha stared at her. So did the Nevers.

Vex pointed. "B—but—she's—"

"Welcome as my guest," Hester said. "Unlike Snow Balls, No Balls have no rules."

Agatha shook her head, finding tears instead of words. Hester touched her shoulder.

"This is how we found the Hall," she said, voice breaking. "I think she wanted us to have what she couldn't. Maybe it's her way of saying sorry."

Agatha burst into sobs. "I'm sorry too—"

"I threw you in a *sewer*," Hester sniffled. "We've all made mistakes. But we'll fix them, won't we? Both schools together."

Agatha was crying so hard her body shook.

Hester tensed. "What is it?"

"I tried," Agatha wept. "I tried to stop them."

"Stop who—"

"KILL THE VILLS! NEVERS DIE!"

Slowly Hester turned.

"KILL THE VILLS! NEVERS DIE!"

Nevers massed to the giant windows and looked out into the night. Down the steep hill, the Good army marched around the moat, weapons glinting in torchlight.

The glow in the villains' faces died and they shrank back into their shells. Wind swept through the windows and snuffed the candles, leaving the hall dark and cold.

"So you come to warn us. And your prince comes to kill us," said Hester, gazing at the ferocious mob. "So much for *love.*"

"You don't have to fight them," Agatha pressed. "Let them see what I have."

Hester turned, eyes on fire. "And let them laugh at us? Let them remind us what we are? Ugly. Unworthy. *Losers.*"

"That's not what you are!"

But Hester had returned to the dangerous girl she once knew. "You know *nothing* about us," she snarled.

"We're all the same, Hester!" Agatha begged. "Let them see the truth. It's the only way!"

"Yes," Hester said quietly. "There is only one way." She bared her teeth. *"Free the witch!"*

"No!" Agatha cried. "It's what she wants!"

Hester sneered. "And remind our princess what happens

when fair maidens go where they don't *belong.*"

Agatha screamed as the shadows of villains over-whelmed her.

High above, in a rotted tower, a mob of fifty Nevers shoved aside the last furniture and ripped out the final nail of Room 66. With a savage roar, they kicked down its door and recoiled in shock.

A shriveled, hideous hag looked back at them in a lus-cious pink ball gown. She rubbed her gleaming bald head and flashed her blackened gums.

"Let me guess," Sophie smiled. "Our party has *unexpected guests.*"

29

Beautiful Evil

Agatha's eyes flashed open to a shock of glacial cold. She was on her back, sealed in a frosted glass coffin. Dozens of blurry silhouettes loomed over her. Panicked, she lurched up, but her body was frozen.

It wasn't glass. It was ice.

She tried to inhale more air, but gagged. Her eyes bulged, her cheeks went blue. . . . Then the dark shadows parted and a pink specter floated through. With

her tongue, Agatha breathlessly wiped frost clear. Sophie, bald and grotesque, smiled down at her, a Doom Room axe in her hands. As Agatha took her dying breaths, her eyes pleaded for mercy. Sophie gazed at her through ice, ran her fingers over Agatha's entombed face . . . and raised the axe.

Somewhere Hester screamed.

The axe smashed through ice, shattering the tomb, and stopped a hair from Agatha's face. She plunged to wet floor, heaving for breath.

"Freezing a poor princess?" Sophie sighed. "That's no way to treat a guest, Hester."

"The arrows—it was you—" Agatha stammered, crawling back. "You brought me here—to kill me—"

"Kill you?" Sophie looked hurt. "You think I can *kill* you?"

Across the room, Agatha saw Hester huddled with Anadil and Dot, gawking at their once roommate, now a bald, shriveled hag.

"Truth is I want to hurt you, Agatha," Sophie said, melting the axe away with a glowing finger. "But I just can't."

She studied her rotted face in a balloon. "My behavior last night was poor."

"*Poor?*" Agatha coughed. "You pushed me through a window!"

"Wouldn't you have done the same?" Sophie said, peering at Agatha's blue gown in the balloon. "If *I* took everything that was yours?"

Sophie turned, pink gown glimmering. "But this is your

fairy tale, Agatha. And either we end it as enemies or we end it as friends."

"*F-ffriends?*" Agatha sputtered.

"The School Master said it was impossible. And perhaps both of us thought him right." Sophie said, skin crackling around warts. "But how could he ever understand us?"

Agatha recoiled in disgust.

Sophie nodded. "I'm ugly now," she agreed softly. "But I can be happy here, Agatha. I really can. We're where we belong. You're Good. I'm Evil."

Her eyes drifted around the decorated Hall.

"But Evil can be beautiful, can't it?"

Torchlight flooded the windows. "Sophie, Evers at the gates!" Anadil shouted, looking out—

"Revenge," Agatha said, quivering. "You said you wanted revenge."

"How else to lure Good here, Agatha?" Sophie said sadly. "How else to show them all we wanted was a Ball of our own?"

"Sophie, they're coming!" Dot screamed. Beneath their feet, Evers rammed the castle doors.

"But now we'll end all of this, won't we?" Sophie said, drawing a gnarled fist from her dress pocket.

Agatha's eyes widened. Something was in her hand.

"*SHE'S UPSTAIRS!*" The Evers had broken in.

"Agatha," Sophie said, prowling towards her, fist tight.

"*KILL THE WITCH!*" Evers cried, storming up the stairs.

Sophie reached out her spotted fist.

"My friend . . . my Nemesis . . ."

Agatha cringed. Sophie unfurled her bare palm—

And sank to one knee.

"Will you dance with me?"

Agatha lost her breath.

BOOM! Evers bashed the hall doors.

"Sophie, what are you doing!" Hester screamed.

Sophie held out her withered hand to Agatha.

"We'll show them it's over."

The doors splintered.

"One dance for peace," Sophie vowed.

"Sophie, they'll kill us all!" Hester shrieked—

Sophie kept her hand out. "One dance for a happy ending, Aggie."

Paralyzed, Agatha looked at her, as the door locks shattered.

Sophie's warts gleamed with tears. "One dance to save my life."

"On *three*!" Tedros roared outside—

Sophie gazed up at Agatha with wide coal eyes. "It's me, Aggie. Can't you see?"

Shivering, Agatha searched her ugly face.

"One!"

"Agatha, please . . ."

Agatha stepped back, terrified.

"Please . . ." Sophie begged, face cracking. "Don't let me die a villain."

Agatha shrank away from her. "You're Evil—"

"And the Good forgive."

Agatha froze.

"Aren't you Good?" Sophie breathed.

"Two!"

With a gasp, Agatha clasped her hand.

Sophie wrapped bony arms around her and pulled her in a gliding waltz across the floor. At Hester's frantic cue, Ravan's bunk mates struck up a wobbly love song.

"You are Good," Sophie panted, head on Agatha's shoulder.

"I won't let them hurt you," Agatha whispered, holding Sophie tight.

Sophie touched her cheek. "I wish I could say the same."

Agatha looked at her. Sophie smiled darkly.

"Three!"

Tedros smashed through the doors at the charge of his mob and, with a beastly cry, raised his sword over Sophie's back—

"Death to the wi—"

Then he saw the waltz in full bloom.

Sophie twirled to him, Agatha in her arms. Tedros dropped his sword.

"Poor Teddy," Sophie said, silencing the music. "Every time he finds his princess, turns out she's a witch."

Tedros looked at Agatha, stunned. "You're with . . . *her?*"

"She's lying!" Agatha screamed, flailing to break Sophie's grip—

"How do you think she survived her fall? Why do you think she tried to stop your attack?" Sophie said, hugging her tighter. "Yes, Teddy, I'm afraid your Ball date is also *mine.*"

Tedros followed Sophie's eyes to the banner over the hall. Evers bleached behind him.

"Don't listen to her!" Agatha shrieked. "It's a trap!"

"Agatha, it's okay, darling. You can tell him," Sophie said. She turned to Tedros, exasperated. "She wanted to wait until she had a sword to your throat."

Tedros looked at Agatha, eyes wide.

"It isn't true!" she cried. "I have proof!" She swiveled. "Hester! Dot! Tell them!"

But Hester, Dot, and the rest of the Nevers were glaring at the Good army, wielding deadly weapons for a massacre. Hester looked back at Agatha and said nothing.

Agatha saw the light in her prince's eyes dim. Behind him, armed Evers turned their weapons from Sophie to her.

"No! Wait!" She broke free and fell into Tedros' arms. "You have to believe me! I'm on your side!"

"Really!" Sophie mused. "Then how is it that your prince locked you in one tower . . . and here you are in *another?*"

Agatha felt Tedros' arms harden. She looked up to his bloodless face.

"Answer her," he said.

"I came to help you—I climbed down—"

"Climbed!" Sophie cackled. "Down *that* tower!"

Tedros followed her eyes to the sky-high spires of Good.

"There were a-a-arrows—" Agatha stuttered—

"I don't know why she's being so bashful," Sophie said, scratching her head. "She came up with every step. The pranks on Good, your meeting in the Woods, the Circus attack . . . all part of Agatha's master plan to make you think she was Good. Oh, except for that lovely new smile. That was all *black magic.*"

Agatha couldn't breathe.

"Only the best Evil can disguise as Good," Sophie said, glaring at her. "Agatha's even better at it than I."

Eyes wide, Tedros pulled away from Agatha.

"Princesses wouldn't question my authority," he said, glowing red.

"Teddy, wait—" Agatha begged—

"Princesses wouldn't question if I was a man."

"Look what she's doing to you—"

"I *knew* you were a witch," he said, voice cracking. "I knew it all along."

"Don't you trust me?" Agatha wept.

"My mother asked my father the same question," Tedros said, battling tears. "But I won't make his mistake."

His eyes darted to Excalibur between him and her. The prince lunged for it but Agatha grabbed the sword first and leapt to her feet, thrusting out. Evers pulled weapons in horror.

"See?" Sophie grinned. "Sword to *throat*."

Agatha looked at her, then at Tedros, staring at his own sword in his face. She dropped it. "No! I was just—I didn't mean to—"

Tedros swelled with blood.

"Prepare to attack!"

Agatha backed up. "Tedros, listen to me!"

Tedros grabbed Chaddick's bow—

"Tedros, wait—"

"I'm worse than my father." Tedros looked up, eyes glistening. "Because I still love you."

He pulled an arrow at her heart.

"*No!*" Agatha screamed—

"*Fire!*"

Evers launched stones, darts, oil at the defenseless Nevers as Tedros unleashed his arrow for Agatha—

Sophie flicked her lit finger just as it speared her chest. The weapons all turned to daisies and floated to the ground.

Cowering Nevers looked up, stunned to be alive. Hunched amid them, Agatha slowly turned.

"Learned that from my favorite princess," Sophie said softly.

Agatha crumpled to the ground in sobs.

Tedros glanced between them, dread flooding his face. Sophie unleashed a devilish smile.

"Never very good at those challenges, were you, Teddy?"

"*No!*" Tedros fell to his knees, grabbed weeping Agatha in his arms. She pushed him away.

"Now that's an ending. Prince tries to kill his princess," Sophie reveled. She picked up the daisy meant for Agatha's heart and gave it a rapturous sniff. "Lucky Evil was here to save the day."

From the floor, Tedros gazed up at her, heartbroken.

"Which begs the question, of course . . ." Sophie licked rotting lips.

"What happens when Evil becomes *Good?*"

This time, when she smiled, Tedros saw gleaming white teeth. He backed up in shock.

In front of his eyes, Sophie's warts magically sloughed, her deep wrinkles smoothed, until her creamy peach skin glowed with youth. Her hair blossomed out of her shiny skull in a cascade of blond ringlets, and her lips thickened with juicy sheen. Agatha slowly peeked through her hands to see Sophie's eyes blaze emerald green, her shriveled body bloom, until the grand villainess loomed over her in her pink ball gown, more radiant and ravishing than ever before.

"Leave—Leave *now*—" Agatha warned, but the Evers were all paralyzed, staring past Sophie.

Cringing, Agatha turned.

Hester looked back at her, dress now pink. Magically her thin hair sprouted to long thick tresses, her sallow face gained fullness, her tattoo restored to magnificent red. Next to her, Anadil's white hair went chestnut brown, her red eyes sea green, while Dot's rotund body grew hourglass curves. In reflective balloons, Hort watched his jaw square, his chin dimple, his dumpy black robes melt to a blue Everboy coat. Ravan saw his oily skin clear, Brone lifted his shirt to see rippling muscles, Arachne ran fingers over two new eyes, Mona touched smooth ivory skin . . . until all around, transformed villains gaped at each other in Good's uniforms.

Sophie grinned down at Agatha. "I *told* you Evil can be beautiful, didn't I?"

"*Retreat!*" Tedros yelled, backing into his army.

"We're not finished, Teddy," Sophie thundered. "You and your army invaded a Ball. You and your army attacked a defenseless school. You and your army tried to kill a room of poor students, trying to enjoy the happiest night of our lives.

Which leaves another question . . ."

"Retreat now!" Tedros cried—

"What happens when Good becomes *Evil?*"

Screams exploded behind Tedros.

Agatha swiveled to see Beatrix screech with pain as her back hunched with a crack. Then her hair went white, her face pockmarked to an old crone's, and her pink dress sagged to black over shriveled bones.

Behind her, all the Evers' gowns and suits slowly rotted to Evil's black smocks. Chaddick grew metal spikes all over his body, Millicent sobbed as her skin turned green, Reena shrieked and itched at her scab-covered cheeks, Nicholas staggered around, one-eyed and humped. One by one, the Evers who attacked the villains all turned ugly, Agatha the only one immune from punishment . . . until at last Sophie leered back at Tedros, bald, scrawny, hideously scarred, in front of his army of villains.

"All hail the Prince!" she cackled.

Beautiful Nevers pointed at the ugly Evers and joined her in a chorus of triumphant laughter, annihilating a legacy of defeat.

Agatha grabbed a fallen sword and pointed it at Sophie. "Your war is with me! Let them go in peace!"

"By all means, darling," Sophie smiled. "The doors are open."

The repulsive Evers flooded for them. All except shriveled, scraggy Tedros, now blocking their way.

"Please, Teddy. End this war," Agatha pleaded.

"I can't leave you," the prince croaked.

Agatha looked into his sad, beastly eyes.

"This time you have to trust me."

Tedros shook his head, too ashamed to fight—

"Retreat!" he choked to his school. "Retreat now!"

With an anguished cry, he led the monstrous Evers for the doors. The doors slammed in their faces.

"All of you should really learn your rules," Sophie sighed.

Tedros and his army turned, trembling.

"The Evil *attack*, the Good *defend*," Sophie said. "You attacked . . ." She smiled. "Now we *defend*."

She sang three high notes. Agatha suddenly heard grunting outside, louder, louder, until her eyes bulged with recognition.

"*RUN!*" she screamed—

The doors burst open and three colossal rats smashed into Tedros' paralyzed army, Grimm at their reins. The snarling, shrieking rats, big as horses, bucked fleeing Evers into walls, knocked them down stairs, hurled them through the glass window into the moat below. Before Valor boys could draw their swords, the rats trampled them like toy soldiers.

"And here I thought my talents would go unnoticed," Anadil said to Dot, gobsmacked. A thorn dart whizzed between them. The girls turned to see Tedros and ugly Evers frantically grab weapons.

"Fire!" Tedros howled.

Dot dove from a hail of arrows as beautiful Nevers fought back with curses and the two schools clashed in weapon-to-spell combat. As darts flew, swords deflected lightning, and fingers on both sides lit up with colors, the rats ripped free from Grimm's reins, flinging Ava into a chandelier, gashing a bite into Nicholas' back. Grimm swiftly took flight and hunted Agatha through the hall with flame-tipped arrows. She sprang behind a pillar, pointed her glowing finger just as he let one fly. The arrow turned to a flytrap and snapped on yowling Grimm's hand. Agatha swiveled to see hideous Beatrix, Reena, and Millicent quailing next to her.

"If you can turn arrows to flowers," Beatrix said tearfully, "can you turn us pretty again too?"

Agatha ignored her and peeked from behind the pillar into the roaring carnage. Colored spells rocketed between the two sides, littering the floors with stunned bodies. Against the window, two rats cornered gaunt Tedros and his shivering mates, flashing razor-sharp teeth.

Agatha whipped to the girls. "We have to help them!"

"There's no point," Millicent mewled.

"Look at us," said Reena.

"We have nothing to fight for," Beatrix sniffled.

"You have Good to fight for!" Agatha cried as rats devoured the boys' weapons. "It doesn't matter how you *look*!"

"Easy for you to say," said Beatrix. "You're still pretty."

"Our towers aren't Fair and Lovely!" Agatha lambasted. "They're Valor and Honor! *That's* what Good is, you stupid cowards!"

They gaped dumbly as Agatha surged into battle, dashing to save the boys from the rats. Something slammed into her and flung her into a wall.

Dazed, Agatha looked up to see Sophie astride the biggest

rat of all, charging for her again. Agatha tried to find a spell too late—

Beatrix jumped in front of the rat and thrust out her hand. Magical rain burst from the ceiling, soaking the floor. The rat slipped, careened into attacking Nevers, and Sophie crashed to the floor.

"Another thing about Good." Beatrix smiled at Agatha, with Reena, and Millicent by her sides. "We need each other."

Sophie looked up to see the Evers finding their courage to beat back the toppled Nevers. Chaddick used his body's spikes to ram a rat through the heart, Tedros scaled another's tail to stab its neck, while the Evers bound the cowing Nevers with their black tunics and belts—

Suddenly her own hands and feet were bound magically with vines.

"You forget we're in a fairy tale," a voice said behind her.

Struggling, Sophie turned to Agatha standing over her, finger glowing.

"In the end, Good always *wins*," Agatha said.

Sophie slackened against her binds.

"And so it does," she said, gazing back at Agatha.

Then Agatha saw Sophie wasn't looking at her at all. She was staring past her at the hall's last mural: painted masses kneeled before the Storian, glowing in the School Master's hands like a star.

A wicked smile crept across Sophie's face. "Unless I write the ending *myself*."

She stabbed her glowing finger and the rain puddles on the

floor instantly deepened, knocking Agatha and both armies off their feet. The students treaded water, trying to keep their heads above it, but the water rose higher, higher in a ceiling-high sea, until they were all about to drown. Cheeks puffed, turning blue, they spun to Sophie, blocking the shattered window with her bound body. She smirked impishly, and then let herself fall through.

The flood blasted through the window and two hundred students cascaded out of the tower, into freezing midnight air, and splashed to the moat below.

Instantly the war resumed in the putrid sludge, but with faces and clothes covered in it, the students couldn't see each other in the weak dawn light. Hester shoved Anadil's face in slime thinking her an Ever, Beatrix punched Reena in the jaw thinking her a Never, Chaddick suffocated the closest thing to him—Tedros, it turned out, who responded by sinking his rotted teeth into his best mate's neck. With rules broken so rampantly, the students began to change from pink to black, black to blue, ugly to beautiful, beautiful to ugly, back and forth, faster, faster, until no one had the faintest idea who was Good and who was Evil.

None of the foes noticed that far into the bay, a girl in pink climbed the School Master's tower, brick by brick, pulling herself up by Grimm's arrows. And that far beneath, a prince climbed after her, silhouetted in moonlight. Upon closer look, a prince of raven hair, iron will, dodging a cupid's arrows in a billowing blue—

Gown.

Upon closer look, not a prince at all.

30

Never After

Clawing through the silver brick window, Sophie gritted her teeth.

Good always wins.

Her Nemesis was right. As long as the School Master lived, as long as the Storian was in his hands, then she would never achieve vengeance. There was only one way to ruin Agatha's happy ending.

Destroy both pen and its protector.

With a snarl, Sophie pulled herself into the

School Master's tower, flung out her glowing finger—

It dimmed.

The empty stone chamber was aglow with hundreds of red-flamed candles lining the edges of the bookcases and shelves. Red rose petals swathed the stone floor under her feet. Strums of a phantom harp softly swelled into a tender song.

Sophie scowled. She had come for a war and found a wedding. Good was even more pathetic than she thought.

Then she saw the Storian.

Across the room, it hovered unguarded over her and Agatha's fairy-tale book on the shadowed stone table.

Through falling petals and flickering candles, Sophie skulked towards the deadly sharp pen. As she neared, the pen's script smoldered against steel. Eyes blazing, breath shallow, she reached to seize it, but the pen lurched and lanced her finger. Sophie withdrew in shock.

A single drop of her blood dripped down the Storian, filling the grooves in the deep script before trickling to its lethal nib. Alive to its new ink, the pen burned hot red and plunged to the book, furiously flipping pages. Her whole fairy tale unfolded before her eyes in dazzling paintings and flashes of words: sighting Tedros at the Welcoming, cowering from her prince at the Trial, witnessing him propose to Agatha, luring Good's army to war, even climbing by arrows to this very tower—until the Storian found a fresh page and spilled blood outlines in a single sweep. Rich color magically filled them in and Sophie watched a brilliant painting of herself take shape, there in this tower as she was now. Ravishing in a pink ball gown, her painted self gazed into the eyes of a handsome stranger, tall, lean, in prime of youth and beauty.

Sophie touched his face on the page . . . twinkling blue eyes, skin like marble, ghostly white hair . . .

He wasn't a stranger.

She had dreamt of him her last night in Gavaldon. The prince she picked from a hundred at a castle ball. The one who felt like Ever After.

"All these years I waited," said a warm voice.

She turned to see the masked School Master glide towards her from across the room, rusted crown crooked on his head of thick white hair. Slowly, his body unsnarled from its hunch, until it stood tall and erect. Then he took off his mask, revealing alabaster skin, chiseled cheeks, and dancing blue eyes.

Sophie buckled.

He was the prince from the painting.

"You're y—y-young—"

"This was all a test, Sophie," the School Master said. "A test to find my true love."

"Your true—me?" Sophie stammered. "But you're Good and I'm Evil!"

The School Master smiled. "Perhaps we should start there."

Hanging high above the midpoint between moat and lake, Agatha climbed arrows stabbed in silver brick, dodging new blows as Grimm flew around the School Master's spire. As the cupid pulled another arrow into his bow, she lunged for the next shaft but it broke and tumbled off the tower. Her head swiveled. Grimm flashed yellowed shark teeth, aimed his arrow at her face—

He stiffened like a stunned bird and fell from the sky into dark waters below.

Agatha spun and saw Hester's red fingerglow dim in her direction, her body bound by chains in deep sludge. In moonlight, she could see Hester's face, filled with regret for spurning the chance to end this war. Around her, Evers had wrenched control of the battle. Villains struggled against their binds, restored to ugliness, while four Everboys pinned down Hort's howling man-wolf with punches and kicks.

Agatha felt the last arrow splinter under her hand.

"Help—" she puffed, legs kicking. The arrow broke—

And froze to hard ice catching her grip.

Agatha turned and saw Anadil's distant green fingerglow pointed at the frozen arrow.

Then, above her head, the next silver brick turned dark brown. Agatha smelled rich, sugary sweetness and her hand stretched up and dug right into taut chocolate. Pulling herself up by fudge, she glanced back across the bay.

Dot's blue light glowed proudly.

As the next brick above turned chocolate, Agatha reached up with a smile.

It seemed the witches had changed sides.

"I was there all along," the School Master said, cold, beautiful face smoldering in first rays of sun. "Leading Agatha to you on the night I kidnapped you. Ensuring you didn't fail in your first days at school. Opening the doors at the Circus. Giving you a riddle whose answer would bring you to me . . . I interfered in your fairy tale because I knew how it must end."

"But that means you're—" Sophie fumbled. "You're Evil?"

"I cared for my brother very much," the School Master said tensely, peering at the schools' raging war. "We were entrusted the Storian for eternity because our bond overrode our warring souls. As long as we protected each other, we would stay immortal and beautiful, Good and Evil in perfect balance. Each as worthy and powerful as the other."

He turned. "But Evil cannot be but alone."

"So you *killed* your own brother?" Sophie said.

"Much as you tried to kill your dearest friend and beloved prince," the School Master smiled. "But no matter how much I tried to control the Storian . . . *Good* now emerged triumphant in every new tale."

He caressed the symbols on the pen's skin. "Because there is something greater than the purest Evil, Sophie. Something you and I cannot have."

At last Sophie understood. Her fire cooled to grief.

"Love," she said softly.

"It is why Good wins every story," the School Master said. "They fight for each other. We can only fight for ourselves.

"My only hope was to find something stronger, something that would give us a chance. I hunted every seer in the Woods until one gave me my answer. One who told me that what I needed would come from *beyond* our world. And so I searched all these years, careful to keep the balance, as my body and hope weakened . . . until at last you've come. The one that can tip the balance forever. The one more powerful than Good's Love."

He touched her cheek.

"Evil's love."

Sophie couldn't breathe, feeling his frigid fingers on her skin.

The School Master's lips curled into a smile. "Sader knew you would come. A heart as dark as mine. An Evil whose beauty could restore my own." His hands moved to her waist. "If we unite with each other to seal the bond of Evil. If we marry for the purpose of hurting, destroying, punishing . . . then you and I finally have something to fight for."

The School Master's breath glazed her ear. *"Never* After."

Looking up at him, Sophie finally understood. He had her same maleficent coldness, the same pain raging in his eyes. Long before Tedros, her soul had known its true match. Not a shining knight, fighting for Good. Not someone Good at all.

All these years she had tried to be someone else. She had made so many mistakes along the way. But at last, she had come home.

"A kiss," the School Master whispered. "A kiss for Never After."

Tears trickled down Sophie's cheeks. After all this, she would have her happy ending.

She gave herself to the School Master's grip and he pulled her into his arms. As he clasped her neck, leaning in for her fairy-tale kiss, Sophie gazed up tenderly at the prince of her dreams.

But now his face cracked at the edges.

Charred flesh wormed through his luminous skin. Behind him falling roses turned to maggots and red candles lit up hellish shadows. Outside, the dawn sky fogged infernal green and the Good castle blackened to stone. As the School Master's decaying lips touched hers, Sophie felt her vision blur red, her veins burn acid, her body rot to match his. Skin blistering, she held her prince's eyes, begging to feel love, the love that storybooks promised her, the love that would last an eternity . . .

But all she found was hate.

Devoured by a kiss, she saw at last she would never find love in this life or the next. She was Evil, always Evil, and there would never be happiness or peace. As her heart shattered with sadness, she yielded to darkness without a fight, only to hear a dying echo, somewhere deeper than soul.

It's not what we are, Sophie.

It's what we do.

Sophie tore herself from the School Master's grip and he spilled back into the stone table, sending the Storian and storybook smashing into the wall. In the fallen Storian, she glimpsed her half-rotted face, split cleanly from forehead to chin. Breathless, she fled for the window, but there was no way down the tower.

Through eerie green fog, she saw the far shore. Gone were the weapons, the spells, the two sides. The sludge pits overflowed with blackened bodies, children punching anyone in sight, slamming faces into muck, tearing at skin and hair,

writhing and clawing for mercy. Sophie stared at this war she
had started, Good and Evil fighting now for nothing at all.

"What have I done?" she breathed.

She turned to see the School Master stir on the floor.

"Please," Sophie begged. "I want to be Good!"

The School Master raised red-rimmed eyes, skin shriveling
around his thin smile.

"You can *never* be Good, Sophie. That's why you're *mine*."

Slowly he slithered towards her. Terrified, Sophie shrank
against the window as he reached rotting hands to grab her—

From behind, soft, warm arms suddenly wrapped her like
an angel's and pulled her into the night sky.

"Hold your breath!" Agatha cried as they fell—

In tight embrace, the two girls smashed face-first into crushing cold water. The glacial lake robbed their lungs, numbed every
inch of skin, but still they didn't let go. Their entwined bodies
plunged to arctic depths, and kicked towards sunlight. But just as
their hands stabbed for air, Agatha saw the black shadow ripping
straight for them. With a silent scream, she thrust out her glowing finger and a giant wave rose, swelling them away from the
School Master and crashing them to Evil's barren shore.

Agatha willed herself onto her knees in the moat and heard
the screams of war around her, rabid, slime-drenched children
without faces or names, pummeling each other like beasts.

Then in the distance, a body rose from the sludge.

"Sophie?" she croaked.

The ooze sloughed away and Agatha dove for the bank in
horror.

She glanced back to see the old, decayed School Master calmly wade towards her, Storian in hand. Gurgling, she scraped over wrestling torsos for the shore, oily black hands clawing at her face, sludge sinking her like quicksand. Agatha turned to see the School Master gliding through it, unnoticed by his warring students. Gagging on muck, she pulled herself over the black mob into dead grass, lurched to her feet to run—

The School Master stood in front of her, flesh crumbling off naked skull.

"I expected more from a Reader, Agatha," he said. "Surely you know what happens to those who thwart *love*."

Agatha flushed with fight. "You'll never have her. Not as long as I'm alive."

The School Master's blue eyes filled with blood.

"And so it is written."

He raised the Storian like a dagger and hurled it at Agatha with a deafening scream.

Trapped, Agatha closed her eyes—

A body collided with hers and took her to the ground.

Agatha's eyes opened.

Sophie lay beside her, Storian speared through her heart.

The School Master let out a cry of shock.

The war around them ceased.

Bloodied students turned in stunned silence to see their rotted, malevolent leader, frozen over the body of the witch who saved a princess's life. The body of one of their own.

Sunken in sludge, Evers' and Nevers' faces melted to terror and shame. They had betrayed each other and lost to the real enemy. In foolish vengeance, they had surrendered the balance they were entrusted to protect. But as eyes found the School Master, their young faces hardened with purpose. Then all at once, the silver swan crests on both Good's and Evil's uniforms turned blinding white and came alive, shrieking, flapping.

Instantly the tiny birds ripped free, blasted into the twilit sky, and coalesced into a glittering silhouette. The School Master's face drained of blood as he looked up at a luminous ghost, a familiar face of snowy hair, ivory cheeks, and warm blue eyes. . . .

"You are a spirit, brother," the School Master scowled. "You have no power without a body."

"Yet," said a voice.

He turned to see Professor Sader limp from the Woods through the school gates, bloodied by thorns. Trembling, Sader gazed up at the ghost in the sky.

"Please."

From the sky, the Good brother dove and smashed into Sader's willing body.

Sader shivered, hazel eyes wide, then slumped to his knees, eyes closed.

Slowly his eyes opened, sparkling blue.

The School Master backed up in surprise. The skin of Sader's arms softened to white feathers, shredding his green suit away. Terrified, the School Master turned into a shadow, fled across dead grass towards the lake, but Sader flew into the air after him, human arms now giant white swan wings, and swerved down and snatched the shadow in his beak. With a searing bird's screech, he tore it apart, raining black feathers over the battleground below.

From the sky, Sader looked down at Sophie in Agatha's arms, tears welling in big hazel eyes at the first and last thing he would ever see. Then, his sacrifice done, he dissipated to gold dust and was gone.

Faculty stormed from the castles, freed from the School Master's curse. Professor Dovey stopped short first, then the others behind her. Lady Lesso's jaw quivered as Clarissa gripped her hand. Professor Anemone, Professor Sheeks, Professor Manley, Princess Uma all had the same scared, powerless faces. Even Castor and Pollux couldn't be told apart. All bowed their heads in mourning, knowing that they were too late for even the mercy of magic.

In front of them, the children gathered around Sophie, dying in Agatha's arms. Agatha tried in vain to staunch the wound, a mess of tears.

Tedros dove beside them. "Let me help," he said, taking Sophie in his arms.

"No—" Sophie wheezed—"Agatha."

Speechless, Tedros left her to his princess's arms.

Agatha pressed Sophie to her chest, hands soaked with her blood.

"You're safe now," Agatha said softly.

"I don't—want to—be Evil," Sophie panted through sobs.

"You're not Evil, Sophie," Agatha whispered, touching her decayed cheek. "You're human."

Sophie smiled weakly. "Only if I have you."

Her eyes flickered with life.

"No—not yet—" Sophie struggled—

"Sophie! Sophie, please!" Agatha choked.

"Agatha—" Sophie exhaled her last breath. "I love you."

"*Wait!*" Agatha screamed.

Icy wind snuffed the last of the torches and the blackened Good castle vanished behind dark fog.

Sobbing, shaking, Agatha kissed Sophie's cold lips.

Black feathers shivered on the dead ground between the children's feet. As they stared in horror, Agatha lay her head on Sophie's silent heart and wept into terrible silence. Beside their two bodies the cold, bloody Storian dulled to gray, its work finally done.

As the teachers took children into their arms, Agatha stayed holding the body, knowing she had to let go. But she couldn't. Cheek wet with Sophie's blood, she listened to the sobs rise around her, the wind rake through wartorn sludge, her shallow breaths wither against a corpse.

And the beat of a heart.

Color returned to Sophie's lips.

Glow warmed her skin.

Blood faded from her chest.

Her skin restored to its beautiful whole and with a shocked breath, her eyes opened, emerald clear.

"Sophie?" Agatha whispered.

Sophie touched her face and smiled.

"Who needs princes in our fairy tale?"

Sun exploded through fog, coating the two castles in gold.

As the grass around it greened, the Storian blazed with new life and soared back to its tower in the sky. Across the shores, children's robes, black, pink, blue, melted to the same silver, dissolving their division once and for all.

But as jubilant students and teachers descended on the girls, they suddenly retreated. Sophie and Agatha had started to shimmer, and within seconds, their bodies turned translucent. They spun to each other, for in the wind, the two heard what the others couldn't, tenor tolls of a town clock, closer, closer . . .

Sophie's eyes twinkled. "A princess and witch . . ."

"*Friends*," Agatha gasped.

She whirled to Tedros. With a cry, her prince seized for her—"*Wait!*"

Light slipped through his fingers.

They were gone.